I0762058

ANNA SPARROWS

Littles & Lace: The Complete Collection

Volume 1

First edition

This book was professionally typeset on Reedsy.
Find out more at reedsy.com

Also by Anna Sparrows 438

Asher's Answer - Preface

While this is a low-angst, sweet & cute romance, this book contains mentions of homophobia, domestic abuse, gun violence, anxiety and panic attacks. It is still a work of fiction, though, so some suspension of disbelief may also be necessary with regards to the trajectory of Charlie's career. Apologies in advance if my cursory research into policing appears informed by pop-culture more than real situations.

Also, please bear in mind that this book is an MM Age Play/Age Regression romance between consenting adults and **does** include ABDL and wetting. I am a firm believer in not yucking someone else's yum, so if this kink squicks you, don't read it. Life's too short to read something you don't enjoy.

Chapter One – Asher

What's more humiliating than being kicked out of home by your already homophobic father because he opened your private delivery to discover the adult-sized diapers, onesies, and pacifier you'd bought yourself on a drunken whim? Turning up to your boyfriend's place with your rolling suitcase filled with the only possessions you could gather in ten minutes, only to find him balls deep in someone else.

Someone with breasts and a vagina.

"So, Ash," Cooper says, rubbing the back of his neck awkwardly, as though I didn't just drop my bags and loudly interrupt him midcoitus. "This…thing…between you and me? Kind of more experimental than anything, y'know?"

No. No, I didn't know. But I sure as shit do now.

I open my mouth to tell him that bisexuality and pansexuality are each valid parts of the spectrum, but close it when I realize that, even so, I just caught the asshole cheating on me.

How'd I miss the signs?

"I…" I have no idea what I actually want to say. His new lover chooses this moment to saunter across the hallway behind him, from the bedroom into the bathroom. Buck naked. Objectively, I can see she's hot, even if I'm not interested in women. All blonde hair to her waist and hourglass curves.

Feminine in all the ways I'm masculine. I sigh and give up whatever fight was left in me. "Okay. Yeah. Whatever."

That's me, Asher Scanlon: pacifist, submissive, and complete, utter coward.

Coop's gray-blue eyes fill with relief.

Should it hurt more that we're over? It probably should. Honestly, though, I'm more upset that he was my last option for a place to stay. Being an unemployed student with zero social life (because I've let Cooper dominate all aspects of my life for the last year) has left me without a backup plan. Somehow, I don't think any of his buddies —who he's spent months trying to convince me are totally my friends too, even though they barely acknowledge my existence— are going to let me couch surf at their places, either.

"You're the best, Ash." Cooper slugs me in the shoulder all bro-style.

That's what the last year has been reduced to. Ugh.

Then he looks down at the suitcase and duffel I'd dropped when I'd walked in on him and...what was her name? Bethany? Bianca? He kind of introduced her during the awkward 'What is going on?' portion of the evening. And yeah, alright, her name doesn't matter. I'm just trying to distract myself from the inevitable.

Cooper's reddish-brown eyebrows furrow as he looks at my meager possessions. "The hell?" He looks back up at me. "What's with the bags?"

An hour ago, I would have fallen into his arms and sobbed out the whole sorry story, screw my embarrassment over my secret interests. But he's not my person anymore, and even though my throat is tight with emotion, I manage to hold back my breakdown. "Dad kicked me out," I tell him with a shrug. "I was planning to crash here, but—"

"Coop, are you going to fuck me properly or not?"

I can't help snorting at the classy interruption. "For obvious reasons, I think that's a bad idea." I finish, gesturing toward the bathroom.

Cooper, at least, has the decency to appear apologetic. "Shit. Asher, I'm sorry." He hesitates, then offers, "You can take the couch?"

"Honestly?" I bend down and pick up my bags, shaking my head. "I'd rather cut off my dick with a rusty spoon at this point." With what little dignity I have left after my hellish afternoon, I straighten my shoulders and jut my chin toward the bathroom. "Good luck with that."

Then I leave his place, haul my bags back into the trunk of my beaten-up old sedan, and rest my head on my steering wheel.

"What the actual fuck do I do now?"

* * *

I wind up parking my car in one of the parking structures on the college campus. I've got two weeks left on my monthly parking permit, though I know Campus Security does frequent sweeps and if I'm caught living in my car that'll only end badly. Instead, I grab the backpack I keep in the back seat and fill it with a few necessities from my hastily packed luggage, including my laptop and its charger, and make my way toward the library, recalling that it's open twenty-four hours to cater to students' random schedules.

It's not the best plan in the world, but it's the only one I've come up with. I can pretend to have fallen asleep studying if I get caught sleeping on one of the inviting giant beanbags in a reading nook. The stress of the day has my Little side simmering just beneath the surface and I employ every trick in the book to keep Little Ash from making an appearance.

I've been able to keep this side of me well hidden —indulging in Little play and regressing only when I've been completely alone— and I have no intention of slipping publicly. Hell, not even Cooper knows about my interest in the BDSM lifestyle, and I'm more relieved about that now than ever. Sometimes I worry that he suspects some of my kinks. I might have slipped and called him Daddy in the bedroom a time or two. But he's never said anything. He might be a cheater, and incredibly selfish, but he isn't a horrible person.

Or maybe I'm just that starved for affection.

Either way, it's been too long since the last time I allowed myself to enter my Little headspace and I'm terrified that, with the additional stress of suddenly being homeless and without any support, I'm going to snap and drop into it without meaning or wanting to. As much as I enjoy giving up control, I want to be able to manage when I do. It has to be on my terms. Unfortunately, when I'm particularly anxious, that's not always possible.

"Suck it up, Scanlon," I mutter to myself as I trudge toward the library's reading nook, hoping that hearing the words out loud might trick me into believing they're coming from a Daddy or a Dom. "Gotta be a big boy right now."

It's late in the evening and there's nobody else around to hear my deranged murmurings, which is a good thing because I don't know that I could fight off the embarrassment of anyone hearing that. Of them potentially working out my secret.

As I finally sink into the welcoming embrace of cotton-covered polystyrene balls with my laptop perched on my thighs, I begin to relax. I've got a laundry list of things I need to work out. I need to find a place to live, which means finding a job, which probably means dropping out of college. I can't afford school now anyway — Dad made that crystal clear when he told me I was out on my ass and cut off completely.

A sob threatens to tear its way from the back of my throat, but I bite down on my clenched fist and hold it back through sheer willpower. I refuse to cry over anything that man said to me.

Dropping out isn't the worst thing that could happen, I tell myself after taking deep, meditative breaths. *I hate college anyway.*

I was only doing the damn business degree to shut my father up. So what if I've only got a semester left? It's not as though I was going to use the degree, is it?

At twenty-two, I should probably have a better idea of what I do want to do with my life, but I'm spiraling right now, so thinking beyond getting myself through the next few days isn't possible.

I spend the next couple of hours applying for jobs online —everything from simple cashier positions to administrative support— and then start scrolling real estate listings for anyone in search of a roommate within my extremely limited budget. My eyes grow heavy as I read listing after listing, and soon enough I'm drifting into oblivion.

Chapter Two – Charlie

"So then I told the punk to beat it before I went full Dom on his ass and… You're not even listening, are you?"

I shake my head and turn to my younger brother, an apology already on the tip of my tongue. His dark-brown eyes narrow at me and he lobs a fry from his plate across the table in our dingy station lunchroom. It hits me in the chest and I scowl, trying to brush off the tiny dot of grease it left on the light-blue material. "Asshole." I huff. "Was that necessary?"

"Charlie, you weren't listening to me," he whines.

I roll my eyes. "Yeah, you're *really* selling the Dom vibes, Josh."

Josh scoffs, but a smile is tugging at his lips. He's as far from a Dom as anyone can get, and we both know it. Still, to look at him you wouldn't guess he's actually a pretty adorable sub.

We're both cops, with him fairly new to the force, having graduated from the Academy last year, and we both like our gym time. At six foot three, I eclipse his height by about two inches, but he's broader across the chest than I am. His eyes are dark where mine are blue, but we both sport the same dark hair and stubble across our matching jawlines.

But that's where the similarities end. Even though there's eight years of age between us, we have a close enough relationship that we're aware of each other's kinks. In fact, he can thank me for introducing him to the world of age play where we've both found our niche.

"Speaking of," he asks, "you gonna check out The Grove with me tonight?"

We're both rostered off for the next couple of days, and it's been a long time since either of us saw any action. He's predominantly a scene Little, while I'm a mostly lifestyle Daddy.

After my last breakup, I've been questioning whether the right boy is out there for me. I'm looking for someone whose Little side is more fluid, who doesn't mind that my job is unpredictable and that the hours mean that a rigid schedule is impossible for me to uphold. I need someone who connects with me, not only as a Daddy when they're Little but also as a partner and a lover when they're Big. An equal, I guess. I don't mind being a caregiver, but I don't want it to be a twenty-four-seven thing. But I don't just want scheduled scene play, either. I'm fussy like that.

It all feels a bit like a pipe dream at this point. Maybe hitting up The Grove —a club which caters to all aspects of the BDSM community, located on the fringe of the city— isn't a bad idea. If nothing else, spoiling a boy rotten for a night will be more relaxing than heading home to jerk off to porn.

"You meeting someone specific there?" I ask Josh, smirking because he's a bit of a brat and has chased off the last couple of Daddies he's played with. I've never tried to fill that role for my baby brother because it just feels weird, since I usually equate the lifestyle with my sexual relationships. But I've still got a setup at my place with all the kiddie comforts he could need for emergency Little time just in case. He's never had to use it, but the unspoken offer is there. He's currently living with our parents, so there's no chance for him to indulge at home.

He rolls his eyes. "Nah. After Declan, I'm taking a break. But it's been a while and" —he rolls his neck and shoulders— "I'm getting antsy to let go, y'know?"

"I get it," I assure him gently. Because, yeah, I do. The last few months without a boy in my life have been difficult. I genuinely like having someone to care for, even without the sex. (But, Christ, I miss the sex, too.) Checking my watch, I offer, "My shift's over at five. Should we meet there around eight?" It gives me time to shower, change, and have dinner.

"Sounds good." Josh stands and balls up the remains of his take-out meal. He checks his own watch and exhales. "I've gotta get back to it. I'll see you there." My partner, Max, nods at him as they cross paths on Josh's way out of the break room.

Even though we work in the same precinct, Josh and I are on different teams. It's not often we get the chance to meet for lunch, but it's been a slow week. The city's not exactly a criminal hotspot, not any worse than other cities in the country, but we still have to deal with our share of break-ins, assaults, and domestic violence.

With Josh still green, he's got an easy beat to walk over by the college campus downtown. Max and I cover the shadier areas in the city proper. Our arrests generally happen after dark, though some of the local dealers have been brazenly conducting their business in daylight lately. More often than not, we respond to calls and do footwork for the detectives in the precinct. It works for me.

"Josh looks good," Max observes with a grin as I toss my own shit into a waiting trash can. He's a handful of years older than me and has been my partner for the past three years. He knows just how anxious I was about my kid brother joining the force.

I nudge his shoulder with my own. "Yeah, turns out he's a natural." As far as I'm aware, Max doesn't know anything about our kinkier lives, but I've previously confessed my concerns that Josh's naturally more submissive nature had me worried at his choice of career. But it turns out it helps with talking to people; getting witness statements and talking people down from volatile situations are kind of his forte.

"He looks up to you, Charlie." Max bobs his head, a lock of blond hair falling across his eyes. He blows it back. "It's cute."

I can't help laughing. "Don't ever call him cute to his face. You'll live to regret it."

Then we're out of the building, climbing into our patrol car, and our conversation turns to other things.

Chapter Three – Asher

I stare with wide eyes at the cop in front of me, willing myself to not burst into tears. I've managed to get away with my plan of essentially living on campus for four days, but the Campus Security guy must have gotten suspicious after seeing me asleep in the same place three nights in a row. I've been showering in the on-campus gym and living off packets of instant ramen, rationing what little money I have because I still haven't found a job.

The tall, buff police officer who came to investigate Security's call has me wanting my blankie and binkie But *that* would only get me thrown into the psych ward at this point, so I try to paste on a winning smile and convince the guy —"Officer J. Walker" his name tag reads, and I do my best not to crack a jaywalking joke because I'm sure he's heard it before— that it's all a misunderstanding.

"P-please," I tell him, hating the shakiness of my voice. "I've just b-been researching late, a-and it's all totally aboveboard." My voice has pitched higher and my thumb has inched toward my mouth. I suck on it briefly, then catch myself and withhold a groan. Unable to completely remove it, I bite down on it and hope the cop thinks it's just an anxious tic. "I didn't mean to do a-anything wrong."

Because I'm a good boy. I swear it. I'm a very good boy. These words almost leave my lips and I bite down harder on the tip of my thumb to prevent it from happening.

Oh, God, no. Not now. I force my thumb back out of my mouth and clench my jaw tight. *I am an adult.*

"Hey, it's okay." The cop's tone is low and soothing, and he reaches out to steady me. His dark eyes are warm and with the way they flicker to my thumb, awkwardly hovering near my lips, they light with understanding. *Fuck.* "Asher, right?" I nod, and he continues. "Asher, breathe for me, buddy."

He leads me out of the library, shouldering my backpack and guiding me with a hand between my shoulder blades. "We're just gonna sit out here in the sunshine and have a chat, okay?"

I can't get arrested. I can't. I wasn't hurting anyone.

If I get arrested, who's going to want to hire me? Who'll let me rent a room?

"Nobody's arresting anyone," he assures me as he leads me over to a bench near the front gardens of the campus. I can feel the burn of a blush on my cheeks.

"I said that out loud, huh?"

The policeman's lips quirk. "You did. I'd say you're stressing out more than you realize." He drops my bag onto the seat between us and reaches for the zipper. "I'm guessing you've got a blanket or stuffie or something in here that'll help with that."

My lower lip wobbles because, yeah, I do, and fuck him for knowing that. I feel vulnerable and exposed and embarrassed. "I… I can't…" My gaze darts around, keenly aware that I'm drawing curious stares from passersby. Or maybe it's the attractive man in the uniform who is doing his level best to talk me down from an anxiety attack. Either way, I don't need people seeing. I certainly don't want people knowing.

"Is there anyone I can call for you?" He lowers his voice and tries to look me in the eye. "A Daddy or a Mommy?"

Damn it, he really does know. Is it that obvious?

"No…no one," I manage to get out before my voice breaks. I feel myself slip a little further. "No. No Daddy." Then I'm hyperventilating because, fuck, I wish I did have a Daddy. I wouldn't be in this mess if I did. I'd have someone to stay with. Someone to care for me. And I wouldn't have to hide this part of me. Not all the time. Maybe not ever. But that's just a dream, and it'll never happen.

I don't have the guts to go looking for a Daddy. I haven't even been brave enough to anonymously join an online group, and the idea of seeking out a local munch petrifies me.

As far as I'm concerned, I do have to hide this side of me, and I am alone, and I'm scared. I'm terrified, actually.

Why can't I be normal?

"Asher, breathe," the officer commands gently, and I try. I really do. But my hands are shaking, and the stress of the last few days is building, and the tears are coming...and I can't stop any of it.

"Okay, new plan," he decides, lifting my bag back to his shoulder as he stands and lightly pulls me up by my bicep. "We're going to go for a drive, okay? And, no, you're not under arrest. Don't panic."

Except then I'm being guided into the back of a freaking police car and he's murmuring with his partner, an older lady who keeps shooting me concerned looks through the rearview mirror. She reverses the car out onto the street while he pulls out his phone and calls someone, pitching his voice low as he talks; but he turns in his seat and keeps his dark-brown eyes on me.

I hang my head in shame and let the tears roll down my cheeks. At least I'm not sobbing.

I hadn't thought things could get more embarrassing than they were at the beginning of the week, but I'd been wrong.

* * *

I must have fallen asleep during the drive, because I'm gently being shaken awake by another cop. He looks a lot like Officer Jaywalker, but his eyes are a deep shade of blue and have a couple of laugh lines in their corners where Jaywalker does not. Also I can't help noticing that his scruff is thicker and darker, and I have the urge to rub my cheek across his jaw like a cat.

What the actual fuck is wrong with me?

"Hey, bud," this cop croons, smiling at me with what feels like genuine warmth. "You're safe, okay? And definitely not under arrest."

"Well, that's something," I say with a sigh, closing my eyes and shaking my head. I can see the original cop lurking behind this one on the other side of the open car door.

"So, my name's Charlie," this new cop tells me with the same warm tone that should not be sending happy vibes to my Little self. I try to push that headspace further away even as Charlie leans over me and unbuckles my belt for me in a classic Daddy move. "And I think we should go inside and have a chat, okay?"

I panic at the thought of having to go into a freaking police station, but as Charlie takes my hand and helps me out of the car, I frown in confusion at the house in front of me. "What... Where are we?" The original officer hands me my backpack and, despite myself, I cuddle it in front of me like a plush toy.

"My house," Charlie says calmly, as though it's perfectly normal for police officers to go rogue and bring young guys on the brink of a meltdown to their personal homes. He nods his head at the cop that looks like him and adds, "Thanks, Josh. I've got him from here."

Wait. Hold up. I'm being left here with this new guy all alone? Nope. This is how serial killer movies start.

The thought is such a valid one, in fact, that I stamp my foot and repeat it aloud.

Charlie chuckles and shakes his head, and Josh —who I've decided I will forever call Jaywalker out of spite— pats me on the shoulder and assures me, "It's okay, Ash. I promise. Charlie's going to look after you. He's good at that." Before I can read too deeply into the statement, Josh closes the rear car door and climbs back into the passenger seat gracefully. The window slides down and he says, "I'll see you later," before the car pulls away from the curb. It's then that I notice a second car —a sleek, black, later-model SUV— parked in the driveway.

"C'mon, Asher." Charlie coaxes me forward to the clapboard home.

It's two stories, painted gray with white accents, with a wraparound porch. It's got a cute cottage feel about it. Welcoming and homey.

Just the sort of façade a serial killer wants you to see.

"I'm not a serial killer." Charlie laughs, and once again I realize I've spoken my thoughts out loud. "And I know this is unorthodox, but Josh said you've been sleeping in the library on campus and that you panicked and lapsed into Little space when he got there to talk to you..." He turns and frowns at me, because the second he mentioned "Little space" I froze. "Shit." He bounds back down the three front stairs and takes my hand in his. This action feels better than it has a right to. "Come on, baby. Inside. We'll talk."

Baby.

Nobody's ever called me baby. Not even Cooper. It's a generic endearment, but it feels like fireworks have exploded inside me. My heart hammers and my head feels fuzzy, and Little Ash comes hurtling back to the surface.

"'Kay," I respond, allowing him to tug me up the front stairs of his picturesque house and into the little foyer.

Inside is just as pretty as outside. It's all polished timber floors and white walls with French provincial-style furnishings. Painted white surfaces, golden-hued wood, and gray linens. The whole thing is like something straight out of a magazine. It's almost incongruous with the very manly police officer who apparently lives here.

Maybe the decorating is his wife's doing?

I don't like that thought, and I don't want to analyze why very closely.

I'm still clutching my backpack, but soon enough Charlie's in front of me, easing it out of my tight grip.

"We're just gonna put this down here," he tells me, setting it on the floor inside the doorway before opening the zipper and digging around inside the bag. He pulls out my blankie —a faded green fleece decorated with bunnies— and my binkie, holding both out to me. I take them with shaking hands, my cheeks on fire.

Nobody else has ever seen these items, let alone touched them, but he's just handing them over as though this is totally normal.

"Juice?" he asks me while he gently guides me through the open-plan living and dining areas and into the kitchen at the back of the house. It's a U-shaped kitchen with gleaming appliances and a large central island with three high-backed stools set in front of it. So far, there's no sign of a wife. I'm not relieved. I'm not. "Or milk, or water?"

"Juice, please," I answer and bring my blankie up to my face. I stroke the corner against my cheek, trying to calm my racing heart as a sippy cup is carefully slid in front of me. I inhale sharply.

"It's okay," Charlie repeats in that deep, low voice that has *Daddy* written all over it. Even if I have had zero experience with Daddies to this point, I can't help but feel like I'm reading him correctly on this. Plus, you know, the sippy gives him away. He nudges the cup. "Go on, you can drink it."

I'm a little overwhelmed by how open and accepting this simple action is. Additionally, it's been so long since I allowed myself a chance to be Little that, when I pick the cup up, I smother another sob.

"Hey." Before I know it, I'm being held against an incredibly firm chest and a large, masculine hand is carding through the mop of curls on my head. "It's alright, baby. It's okay."

I'm not exactly a small guy. I'm five foot eleven, and I've worked hard to bulk up since my teens. But cradled by this man, I feel Little…and unexpectedly cared for. How is that possible when we've only just met? It's not a bad feeling, but it makes me instantly more vulnerable and a touch confused.

The last vestiges of my resolve break, and the tears I shed in the back of Josh's car are nothing in comparison to the meltdown I have now. But Charlie holds me through it all, through the snot and the tears and the heaving, body-wracking cries, soothing and rocking me until I've exhausted myself.

Then he helps me lift the cup to my lips, encouraging me to drink, and I do.

Chapter Four – Charlie

When Josh texted me near the end of my shift with his concerns about a kid who'd been caught living in the campus library, I wasn't quite sure what to expect. The follow-up phone call informed me that the kid had panicked, slipped into a Little headspace, and didn't seem to have anyone to support him; it also cinched my resolve to help, even if only for one night. If nothing else, I'd help my brother with his job. I had a particular set of skills and experiences that could help in this situation, after all.

Then he and his partner, Samara, had pulled up with the kid asleep in the back seat. I chatted briefly with them about the situation and Sam leveled me with a knowing look, even though I know Josh wouldn't have told her anything about my personal life. She's an observant cop and a smart woman. Having watched the kid in the backseat interact with Josh before he told her that I had a unique perspective that could help, she's surely put two and two together.

It doesn't bother me. I'm not ashamed of my preferences or my kinks, especially when my desire is to live the lifestyle and not just play temporary scenes. I've always known that, sooner or later, my personal and private lives were going to intersect. As long as it doesn't impact my ability to do my job, my colleagues shouldn't care.

The kid, though. God, he's adorable. He's got wide hazel eyes, a mop of chestnut-colored curls on his head, and an athletic build, with broad shoulders that taper down to slim hips and strong thighs. He's perfection, and from the moment I saw him, the desire to hold and protect and look after him fired along my synapses.

Don't rush this, I remind myself. *The poor kid will need you to go slow.* Josh said Asher was shaken and flighty, and apparently terrified of admitting he indulges in Little play for comfort.

Considering Josh's observations, Asher's breakdown in my kitchen should not have surprised me, but his cries twist something inside me. I'm a Daddy through and through. Holding him as he sobs is heart-wrenching, even though it feels so good to step back into this role. It will be difficult to hold back and pace myself with this boy, especially when I can see how desperately he needs someone to care for him.

He finally exhausts himself and I get him to drink from the cup that seems to have set this whole thing off. He sags against me, and I'm filled with so much warmth that it takes me a moment to get my bearings.

"Okay, baby," I murmur, and I just can't resist dusting my lips over the top of his head. The endearment comes naturally around him —he's so much softer and more fragile than a simple 'boy'— but he hasn't protested my use of the word the few times it has slipped out already. I need to rein my enthusiasm in, but rational thought is failing me.

Asher sighs and snuggles into my chest, and I'm officially a goner. Five fucking minutes alone with this kid, and I'm wrapped around his little finger. I can't even pretend that it's not happening. Josh will be insanely proud of himself when he checks in later: he would have taken one look at Ash and pegged him as my type. He knows me too well, and as I rub my hand over Ash's back, I can't bring myself to be bothered by that. In fact, I want to thank my brother. *God, I'm such a sap.*

"Come on." I tenderly urge the boy in my arms to stand. "Let's clean up your face and get comfy, okay?"

He's pliant now. I want to praise him for being so brave and for knowing that, usually, being led into a stranger's house can be unsafe...but now's not the time for that conversation. No, he's too far gone, too wrung out and lost in his head, and I'm going to care for him until he's Big again. Only then will we talk about the bigger issues at hand.

I lead him back through the living area and up the stairs that start near the foyer. Up here, there are three bedrooms as well as two bathrooms: the main bathroom and the ensuite, which is attached to the primary bedroom. At the top of the stairs, I head straight for the main bathroom and sit him gently on the edge of the tub. His gaze scans the space, and he blinks when he notices the basket of bath toys, but he doesn't say a word. I'm sure he's worked out by now that I'm a Daddy.

I pull a bright-blue washcloth from the cupboard beneath the sink and run the faucet until the water is warm. Then I wet the cloth, wring it out, and wipe over Asher's face, clearing it of the dried tears and snot.

"Thank you," he murmurs, so quietly that I almost miss it.

"My pleasure, baby," I tell him, then take his hand and head back out into the small living area that connects all the rooms. "I've gotta change my shirt," I explain, leading him toward the couch, "but I'll be right back."

There's a small TV up here, and I consider offering to put on some cartoons, but I am only going to be a minute or two at most, and he's not exactly in the right mindset to focus on anything. What he needs is a nap; I hesitate, wanting to ask him if he needs to be diapered beforehand, but I can tell that to ask as much would tip him over the edge again. If seeing a sippy cup was enough to break him, I'm certain a diaper would be too much to handle right now.

I make quick work of changing out of my uniform shirt in favor of a soft green T-shirt, and I return to the boy on my couch with haste.

"Okay, bud. Nap time."

He blinks up at me owlishly, as though trying to process the words.

"You're drained," I tell him, dropping to a crouch in front of him. "You've had a big day. A nap will help you feel better."

"Yeah..." he says with a slow nod. He's not quite in Little space, but he's certainly not with me as an adult, either.

"Do you need to potty first?"

The question snaps him to attention and his cheeks flush. "Uh...yeah."

"Do you need help?"

Asher shakes his head quickly, the blush in his cheeks deepening. "No." But there's *something* in his gaze that tells me this isn't a hard limit for him. Almost like embarrassment and curiosity melding together: a simmering enthusiasm he can't quite stifle in time.

Interesting.

"Okay," I say, not pushing the issue. I lead him back to the main bathroom. "Do your thing, wash your hands, and then I'll show you your room."

"My room?" he echoes, hovering in the doorway of the bathroom.

I nod and can't resist swatting at his cute little ass. "Potty first. Scoot." I barely remember to grab his blankie from his hand before he carries it in there with him.

Asher has the presence of mind to close the door, and it's not long before I hear the toilet flush and the faucet run. He opens the door, his eyes much sharper than they were before he headed into the bathroom. "You don't have to do this," he says. "And I'm sorry to have put you through" —he makes a vague hand gesture between us as his cheeks turn adorably pink again— "everything."

Cocking an eyebrow, I reach out and hold his chin between my thumb and index finger, tilting his head up to look at me. "I want to do this, Asher. And we're going to talk it all through. But I honestly think you should have a nap first." I keep my voice low but firm. "Would you be more comfortable talking now, or after a nap?"

His eyes dart from side to side as they look into mine, and I can tell he's gauging my resolve. There's spirit inside this kid, and I suspect that once he's comfortable he'll be a lot of fun. On a shaky inhale, he grudgingly admits, "After a nap."

"Good boy." I'm not oblivious to the shiver these words of praise send through him. Letting go of his chin, I press a kiss to his forehead, delighting in the renewed blush it causes, and take his hand in mine again. "Come on. Let's see your room."

I hand him back his blankie and take him to the bedroom on the far side of the stairs, the one just on the other side of the living space from the primary suite. When I open the door, I try to see the space from an outsider's perspective. It's big enough to house a queen-size bed with two bedside tables comfortably, but there's also a low-lying bookshelf which is covered in kids' books, a few plush toys, and a little set of Duplo bricks currently built into a castle shape. The bed's quilt cover has splashes of primary colors against a white backdrop, and the lamps on either side of the bed look like they've been built from Lego blocks.

"Oh," Asher breathes as he steps into the space, and I watch as his eyes go round and shiny. "Wow."

"You like it?" I know he does. It's warm and welcoming and perfect for a little boy, but I want to hear him say it.

He swallows roughly and nods. "It's amazing."

The walls are painted a pale blue with fluffy white clouds scattered abstractly. The carpet is a deep shade of blue and is lush and thick beneath our feet. In the built-in cupboard, I have a selection of onesies and pajamas which should fit him, as well as new pairs of training pants and some diapers…but they can all wait for another time.

And yeah, I'm honestly that hooked on this boy already. I don't care how insane that sounds. He's clearly uncertain and vulnerable, but if Josh is right and Asher doesn't have anyone? I want to be his someone. Well, I want to try. At the very least, I want to help him get back on his feet. I'm not letting this beautiful boy become another statistic.

"I'm glad you think so," I reply to his assessment, unable to hide my pride. "It's yours for as long as you want it."

He pins those wide hazel eyes on me in surprise. "*What*? You don't even know me. I—"

"Shh." Smoothing my hand through his curls, I shake my head. "We'll talk after your nap, I promise."

Asher makes a strangled sound at the back of his throat, his disbelief more than obvious. However, it doesn't stop him from cautiously inching toward the bed. I take the lead, pulling back the covers and gesturing for him to climb up; then I slide in beside him and pull him close, until his head is resting on my chest. I remember that I picked his pacifier up from the kitchen bench after his crying jag, and I pull it from my pocket and offer it to him. After a brief moment of hesitation, he takes it. He casts me another careful look from under his long lashes before he pops the pacifier into his mouth, and my heart squeezes.

Usually, I'd offer to read a book, but he's not entirely Little and I think just getting him used to my presence is enough for now.

Behind the rhythmic sucking sound, Asher's breathing evens out within fifteen minutes, and it takes a handful more for me to gently pull away. I help him out of his socks and shoes and watch him for a few more seconds before I force myself to walk out the door.

Chapter Five – Asher

It's dark when I wake up, and I blink as my eyes adjust to the dim light filtering through the window of the strange room.

It takes me longer than I'd like for the day's events to click into place in my brain; but when they do, I leap out of the sinfully comfortable bed and pause as my bare feet hit the carpet. My Binky drops from my mouth and hits the plush blue surface with a dull thud. I scoop it up and shove it into my hip pocket, wiggling my toes.

Charlie must have removed my shoes and socks while I napped.

He's such a Daddy, my brain helpfully supplies, and I fight the urge to groan. Despite my earlier meltdown at college, I don't need a Daddy. Adding additional complications to my life right now would not be a smart move. Especially when I've never explored this aspect of my life with anyone else. I'm not ready.

Except this entire afternoon did feel magical.

From being held and rocked, to the kisses on my forehead...hell, even the embarrassing potty talk. It's all I've ever dreamed about. Plus, he has toys and a huge bathtub and coloring books and kids' books to read and...it's all too good to be true. As if a man as insanely attractive and perfect as Charlie would want to be *my* Daddy. I'm too unpredictable. Too inexperienced with this kink. I've only read a little bit online, after all: just enough to experiment with being Little on my own. I'm too ashamed —too broken and anxious, even— to be a good Little for someone else.

I find my shoes and socks tucked neatly away in front of the door and pick them up, snag my blankie off the bed, then quietly pad across the small living area and down the stairs. I just make it to the front door and lift my backpack when Charlie's deep voice stops me. He speaks with firm finality, demanding attention. "*Asher*."

My shoulders drop in resignation, and I turn to face him, feeling guilty for attempting to flee without saying a word. He's got his arms folded and a frown on his face that tells me he knows exactly what I was trying to do.

Unable to meet his gaze, I try not to drool over his biceps because *hot damn* they're something else.

"I was just—"

"Running away?" His tone is dry, but there might be a tiny bit of amusement in it.

I nod. "I'm sorry. You've been…" I struggle to find the right words. "…unbelievably good about my whole…well, *me*." I hang my head. "But I can't stay here."

"I hate to tell you this, kiddo, but you can't live in the library on campus, either."

I startle at how close he sounds now and when I look up, he's directly in front of me. There's not even a foot of space between us. And, huh, did he smell this delicious earlier? Fuck. *Focus, Ash*.

I try to take a step backward, but I meet a wall of firm muscle and squeal.

"Easy there, bud." The front door is open and the police officer who didn't exactly arrest me but who did put me in the back of his patrol car is standing behind me, his hands up in the universal gesture of surrender. He shoots an amused look over the top of my head. "You still haven't gotten him inside? It's been hours, Charlie."

"Fuck you," Charlie shoots back with a smile. "He's just woken up from a nap. I've been cooking dinner." He looks at me and then the other cop. "Ash, you remember my brother, Josh."

Brothers. Well, that makes sense. They do look very alike, only I guess that Josh is closer to my age and Charlie's a little older than us. Maybe thirty? Not that it matters. I'm not planning on sticking around.

With my heart still beating madly from the surprise of backing into the younger of the two, I glance between them and attempt to charm my way out. "Well, as fun as it's been playing 'Hot Cop, Hotter Cop,' I'm just gonna go now."

"I hope I'm Hotter Cop," Josh says playfully, while Charlie groans and pulls me back via my backpack.

"You're an idiot," Charlie tells his brother, then gives me a gentle shove into the living room. "And you and I have a lot to talk about."

"Do we have to?" I ask, managing to keep the whine from my tone.

"Yes," he answers plainly. I'm guided to the couch, and he sits beside me, turning his body in to face mine until our knees bump.

"Josh, can you keep an eye on the spaghetti sauce?" He directs the question over my shoulder in his brother's direction, and we all hear the dismissal for what it is.

But Josh calls back his agreement, and his footsteps fade away as he heads further into the house.

Then Charlie's blue eyes are on mine again, and he takes my hands in his, as if he's afraid I'm going to run if he doesn't tether me down. To be fair, he's not far off the mark. I send a look of longing in the direction of the front door, but Charlie squeezes my hands, silently demanding my attention again.

"Let's start with the easy stuff first, okay?" he says, and I snort because there's nothing about my situation that's easy. His eyes narrow. "Why were you living in the library? And don't try and tell me that it's all a misunderstanding. Josh said Security has footage of you using the showers in the gym and going back to the library every night for the last week."

"It's only been three nights." I sigh, concluding that the jig is up. "And it's only been while I try to find a new place."

"What happened to your old place?"

I flinch. The wound is still raw, and humiliation thrums through my veins.

"Ash?"

When I look up, his eyes are full of compassion and concern, and that has me talking, even though I really don't want to. "My dad kicked me out. He…well, he opened a package of stuff that he really shouldn't have" —my cheeks burn— "and he flipped out. Called me…" The words aren't ones I want to repeat, burned deep into my psyche, making the shame and embarrassment I already felt ten times worse. "Well, he called me a bunch of names and told me I had ten minutes to pack my essentials and get out."

"Oh, baby." The words are soft, but Charlie's expression pulls into a scowl after he says them. I know the look is intended for my dad, but I pull back from him instinctively. The anger on his face is immediately schooled into sympathy; I don't know if that makes me feel much better. "I'm sorry. Your dad's a dick." He squeezes my hands. "Go on."

"So…I did. And then I went to…"

"To?" He prompts me to continue.

"To my ex's place." My face burns again. "He wasn't exactly my ex until I walked in on him with his new girlfriend. So, fuck me, right?" I feel so stupid all over again. How could I not have seen what Cooper was doing? "And, other than him, I don't have any friends. I'm… I'm not exactly an extrovert, and Cooper kind of dominated my life for the last year…" Likely a tactical move on his part. I'm rational enough to see that now. I don't know how I manage to keep my shit together when I finish by saying, "I didn't have anywhere else to go…"

I'm wrapped in strong arms and breathing in the spicy scent of Charlie's cologne before I know it. I can feel myself trembling, but unlike earlier, I don't fall apart. The nap and my earlier breakdowns have helped me get myself back under control.

"The stuff your dad found…" Charlie begins slowly, still holding me. He can probably feel my heart race as my embarrassment kicks in. "It was kinky stuff, right? *Little* things?"

I can only nod, shame turning my stomach into a lead weight.

Charlie pulls me in tighter and I wind up in his lap with my face pressed into the crook of his neck. It's not an unpleasant place to find myself. And, damn, he really does smell good.

"Sweetheart, there's nothing wrong with being Little, you know that, right?"

His words make my heart sing, but I still feel my face flame and I shake my head. "I'm a freak," I mutter, repeating one of my dad's less disturbing descriptions. I'd already been feeling abnormal, but his bellows of rage had cemented my worries.

"No, baby, you're not."

"Says the hot cop who doesn't wonder what it's like to wear a diaper." My stomach turns to lead again, the words having bypassed my filter entirely.

Jesus fucking Christ, who is in control of my mouth?

Charlie chuckles and rubs my back. "I don't want to wear one, no…but I like changing them."

Dead. I am officially dead. But, before I can say anything, his brother asks, "What about a hot cop that *is* into wearing them occasionally? Am I a freak?"

"*What?*" I squeak, pulling my bright red face away from Charlie long enough to stare across the room at Josh.

He's leaning against the archway that separates the living room from the dining area, casual as you please. He shrugs. "It's not a lifestyle thing for me, but I like to play occasionally." He gestures to Charlie with a jerk of his stubbled chin. "This one's *always* in Daddy mode, but you've probably realized that by now." He cocks his head, gaze flitting back to his brother. "Dinner's good to go, by the way."

Still in a state of shock, I allow Charlie to push me up and lead me to the kitchen with his hand on the small of my back. I glance back and forth between the brothers. Far be it from me to judge, but… "Do you two ever…?"

"No." Charlie's reply is quick and vehement. He helps me climb up and sit at the middle stool before I even notice, then walks around the kitchen island, gathering plates and cups for dinner. "Nope. He's my brother. That'd be weird because, for me, being a Daddy's always gone hand in hand with my sexual relationships. But," he adds, and I suspect it's more for Josh's benefit than mine, "if he ever needed me to, I'd be his caregiver in an emergency."

Josh smiles back at him softly. "It's appreciated, big brother." Then Josh leans in and nudges me with his shoulder. "So...am I a freak?"

"No!" I frown. "I wouldn't ever think that."

"Cool." He smirks. "So what's the difference? Why's it okay for me and not you?"

"I..." I stop. I don't have an answer to that.

A child-sized melamine bowl of spaghetti with a thick tomato sauce is slid in front of me, and I look across the counter to meet Charlie's sparkling eyes.

"Exactly," he says, then produces a sippy cup of milk. My stomach flip-flops, a strange surge of affection washing over me. His next words only make the feeling stronger. "So now you just have to work on reminding yourself that you're perfect as you are."

* * *

Josh gives me a hug after dinner, then hugs his brother and leaves after saying something about visiting a grove by himself. I don't really follow, but Charlie tells him to have fun and call if he needs to. I wipe my mouth on a napkin and insist on helping Charlie with the dishes, and he relents when he realizes that I'm not going to be swayed.

"So...you're a twenty-four-seven Daddy, then?" I ask when we're back in the living room.

I feel braver now. Josh talked all through dinner about his experiences as a Little, allowing me to ask questions —even ones I thought were silly— and the whole conversation made me feel normal. Or, at least, like maybe I'm in a place where I'm safe to indulge in my weird fantasies. I decide to latch on to this newfound confidence and freedom to talk about it while I can. Before my insecurities get the better of me again. Temptation simmers inside me when it comes to this man, so keeping conversation going seems like the safer option here. I mean, we only just met, and I know next to nothing about him.

Charlie shrugs. "Yeah… I guess? It's not something I can switch on and off. I mean, I don't expect to be in a relationship with someone who's Little for every waking moment. In fact, I don't want that at all. But even during adult time, I like to look after my partners, I guess."

My lips tug upward because, yeah, I can definitely see that in him. Still, I can't help but wonder whether my presence is going to throw a wrench in the works. "Will my being here interrupt something?"

"Interrupt something?" he asks, frowning. I resist the urge to smooth my thumb over the crease between his dark eyebrows.

I look at my lap, twiddling my fingers. "Like a preexisting relationship?" The words come out quiet and cautious, and I feel a pang of jealousy at the very thought. Which is ridiculous, because Charlie might have taken care of me today, but he's not mine to be jealous over.

He's silent for a minute. "Baby," he says, and once again he's tilting my chin up and forcing me to look at him. "There's nobody. But I'd like to explore our connection if you're up to it."

"Our…" I trail off, gesturing between the two of us. "As in…" I swallow. "You and me?"

My dick twitches at the suggestion. That simmering temptation threatens to boil over.

He cups my cheek and my heart thumps wildly. "Yes." His expression is almost painfully tender. "You and me."

"Y-you don't even know me," I protest, but I'm leaning into him anyway. It's magnetism.

Yes, I just got out of a relationship (one which my heart wasn't ever in, because otherwise Cooper's cheating would have actually hurt) and I've just met this man…but I can't stop myself from wanting him.

Is it too soon to feel this way? *Probably*. Is acknowledging that going to prevent me from wanting him? *Nope*.

"Which is why I said I'd like to explore the connection," Charlie answers, sounding amused. "We can go slow…but I already know your interests and mine are more than compatible." He hesitates. It almost seems strange to see the uncertainty on his face. "Unless you're not interested. That won't change the offer of a room and board, okay? I just…" He shrugs. "I'm interested in you, and I'm not gonna hide that."

I force back the urge to do a little happy dance. This seems too good to be true.

"But…I'm not sure how often I'll want to be Little."

"That's okay. Like I said, I'm not looking for someone who is always Little. I want a boyfriend to take on dates and hang out with, too."

The way he says it is guarded, and I wonder why. Is it possible his last Little didn't want that? I've read that some people want to be looked after constantly, but I grew up with a controlling father, so I can't imagine not having some semblance of independence. But I'm getting ahead of myself here.

My gut twists as another realization hits me: I can't offer Charlie *anything*.

"Well… I can't exactly bring any value to this relationship. I mean, I'm homeless and jobless and it'll look like I'm using you…"

I'm pulled into his lap midway through my rant. This is rapidly becoming a position I enjoy far too much. "Sweetheart," he assures me with soothing tones, "you're not homeless. You live here now. And you're actively looking for a job: one will turn up soon. Also, I know you're not using me. If anything, I worry that you'll feel obligated…"

"But I—"

I'm silenced with a kiss to my lips.

His kiss is everything and I'm lost to it within seconds. He kisses me chastely at first, but I open for him and our tongues twist together, finding a rhythm that feels as natural as breathing.

In his mouth, I can taste the sweetness of the cola he'd had with dinner, and I melt into him. He kisses me with intent, but it's not overwhelming. Fuck the fact that we've only just met; this feels too good to stop.

There's no pressure in Charlie's kiss, but there's obvious desire. With me straddling him on the couch, I can feel his erection pressing against mine and it's so much more intense than any other kiss I've had in my life.

Part of me wonders if that's because he knows my deepest, scariest secrets —the kinks I've been ashamed of for years— and that he accepts them... Hell, he even wants to partake in them. Or maybe it's the inherent power play. He's a Daddy and I'm... Well, I want to be his little boy.

"Oh *fuck,*" I curse, feeling my balls tightening. That last thought almost sent me right over the edge. I haven't come in my pants since my early teens.

Charlie groans into my mouth. The sound is insanely hot.

Deepening the kiss, I take my pleasure from his mouth and continue to grind against him.

This should feel weird.

I hardly know this guy, and I only broke up with Cooper a few days ago —not that we'd had sex recently, come to think of it— but the blood flow to my brain isn't working so well right now. Besides, Charlie is letting me set the pace here, and I get the feeling that he'd stop the moment I asked him to.

I have no intention of doing that. People have sex with others they've just met all the time, right? Isn't that what one-night stands are? Just because we didn't meet in a club or on a hookup app doesn't mean we're not both looking for the same thing...not that I want this to be a one-night hookup, mind you. I don't think Charlie does either. Anyway, even if that is the case, the only people who can judge us in this moment are ourselves, and I get the feeling Charlie wants this as much as I do.

If he doesn't think it's weird, neither do I.

"Baby..." He breathes the word against my lips, and the gravel in his voice almost does me in. He sounds as needy as I feel. It's empowering.

My breath quickens as I rut against his answering hardness, and I know I'm going to go over the edge. I don't want to come in my pants, but I don't want to stop, either. I buck my hips and hear myself fucking *mewl,* "I... I'm gonna..."

"It's okay." Charlie's big, rough hand is at my fly. He's popping the button and lowering the zipper, and the relief once he springs my dick from the constrictive material is immediate. "I've got you."

Those beautiful, reassuring words are heaven to my ears.

I open my mouth to say something, but the words leave me because that same hand is stroking me —skin on skin, my precum easing the way— and it takes all of three pumps of his fist before I'm shooting over his hand and his shirt, crying out my release as I come.

I feel boneless as he tucks me back into my underwear but leaves my jeans undone. He wipes his hand on his already filthy shirt, and I shake off the post-orgasmic haze and reach for his cock.

"Not tonight," he says, carefully holding my wrist, and I frown. He's hard as steel in his pants. I don't understand.

"Why not?"

Charlie leans forward and presses a soft kiss to the tip of my nose. "Tonight was about you."

If I had needed any further proof that he was genuine about not pressuring me, this would do it.

Chapter Six – Charlie

I'm moving too fast. I know I am. This poor boy has been through hell this week, he's still hesitant about indulging his Little side, and here am I just taking advantage of his vulnerability. Someone needs to take my Daddy card away because the shit that I just pulled? Not cool. Not in the least. I really don't want Ash thinking that I'm only offering him the room because I expect things from him.

"Come on," I tell him, swatting his firm, pert ass to scoot him off my lap. "How about we head upstairs, do some coloring then watch a movie, hmm?"

"Coloring?" he questions.

I shrug. "Part of the lifestyle is routine. I know you're not in your Little headspace right now, but…it might help to start up a routine to give yourself some Little time every night?"

Over dinner, he'd said that he tried to give himself Little time whenever he knew he'd have a few hours alone, and that it helped him manage his stress levels. When that time became harder to come by, he felt his ability to control his emotions and his Little headspace slipping. If Little space is his coping mechanism, it makes sense that it's going to be where his brain goes when he's overwhelmed.

"Of course," I add as he stares at me with blatant skepticism, "you're free to be Little here whenever you need. Some people flow in and out of their

Little headspaces in a more fluid state." I imagine this is how Ash will be as he gets more comfortable in his skin. Given my own desires, I hope he'll choose to share that lifestyle with me. I can't picture him being Little more often than not, but I can see us falling into a routine that works with my erratic work hours.

Maybe I'm projecting, but it almost feels like I've manifested the unicorn Little of my dreams.

But I'm getting ahead of myself again.

"Right." He blinks as we stand at the bottom of the stairs, giving a little shake of his head. "It's going to take a while to get used to all this, I guess. Having my urges normalized, I mean."

"They *are* normal," I insist. I'm going to repeat this mantra until it sinks in. "Sexuality is a spectrum. BDSM and kink is a spectrum within the spectrum. None of it is shameful."

His shoulders lift and droop in a helpless shrug.

"Would it help you to meet others like you? Like us?" I don't know why I'm doing this, why I'm pushing so hard when it's only his first day in my home, but I'm desperate for him to understand that he's got nothing to be embarrassed about. "Because I can take you to The Grove. It's a BDSM club, and they have a huge, dedicated space for age play. Josh was heading there tonight."

Those hazel eyes of his are round, and his mouth has formed an O of surprise. "Wow. Are there that many of us in the city?"

I nod. "Yes." And because I'm an asshole, I repeat slowly, "Because. It's. Normal."

He surprises me by laughing. It's a gorgeous laugh. Carefree and contagious. Another glimpse into the beautiful little boy I know he'll be. "Okay." The smile he offers me is warm. "It's normal to have kinks. I get it. But, Charlie, I don't want to go to a club tonight. Maybe another time? I just…" He turns bashful. "I'd like to do what you said and…y'know… explore this thing between us for now."

How can I deny him that when I want the exact same thing? I hold his cheeks in my hands and press my lips to his in a sweet kiss that I hope imparts everything I can't put into words. "I'd like that, too."

His grin turns cheeky. "So…do I have to call you Daddy?"

My dick, which had managed to calm down from not being allowed to come earlier, swells back up almost instantly. Swallowing roughly, I shake my head. "That's a title I have to earn, baby," I inform him, "and only when you're comfortable with using it. This whole thing" —I gesture wildly— "is all about comfort and consent and, ultimately, trust. We need to talk about rules and expectations and limits…"

We'd touched on some of it over dinner. Josh's perspective had been a godsend. But if Ash and I are going to give this whole thing a shot, we need to sit down and make sure we're both on the same page. No more impromptu hand jobs or making out, until we know where we stand.

"Maybe," I say slowly, my hand finding its place on the small of his back as I guide him up the stairs, "instead of coloring, tonight we can go over some of the information online about the lifestyle? Together? And we can start talking about those things. If that's what you want."

Ash's eyes soften and his expression is filled with gratitude. Even if I'm afraid I'm pushing him too fast and too soon, that look settles my concerns. So does his reply. "That sounds good."

So it's what we do. I change into a new T-shirt and boxers, and we settle in on the couch upstairs with our laptops balanced on our respective thighs. I let him Google and explore at his own pace, and he asks questions as he goes.

He cocks his head at me at one point, flicking his laptop screen for emphasis. "So…safe words are a thing even with regression stuff?"

"Hell yeah," I acknowledge. "Consent is the first rule of any kink play, and it has to be explicit. Even though we're not doing anything physically taxing for the most part, there's emotional and mental comfort to consider."

"Do—" He clears his throat. "Do you have a safe word?"

"I like the traffic light system." *The darling of the BDSM world.*

Those gorgeous eyes light up with excitement. "Oh, that's clever! Can I use that?"

I can't stop myself from leaning over and kissing him gently. "Of course."

He beams and then turns back to his laptop. While he's researching, I'm shopping. I'm buying him new clothes —Big and Little both— and toiletries and toys. I've ordered extra diapers and wipes and bottles, because his curiosity is rapidly turning to enthusiasm, and I want to be prepared for him. Additional groceries follow, because even if he's not officially my boy, he's living here now, and I'm going to care for and provide for him.

"So…the diaper thing," he queries softly, not long after I've placed the last of my orders.

I turn to him, trying to keep my expression neutral. It's not a surprise that he's gone there. It's one of the bigger concerns for most people new to exploring age regression. "Yeah?"

He squirms in his seat. "Is it… I mean, do people actually…"

"Wet them?"

Just the words send another delicious flush of embarrassment over Ash's skin, and I have the urge to cuddle him and never let him go. He's such a sweet boy.

He coughs. "Uh…yeah. That."

"They do, yeah." I say it as though it's not a big deal, because for me, it's not. "But that's not an immediate thing, or even expected. Some people are content to wear them purely for aesthetics or the feel of it. Others start that way and work their way up to being comfortable enough to lose themselves entirely in their Little headspace."

"*Entirely*?" he asks, then scrunches his nose. "Oh, no, sorry, *eww*. Poop is a hard limit." He gags exaggeratedly.

I can't help my burst of laughter at his horrified expression. "That's fair, baby. Totally fair." But then I can't help teasing a little, cocking an eyebrow at him. "But wetting's okay?"

"Charlie!" The blush which had faded comes back with a vengeance.

Still, he doesn't say no. I didn't expect him to. He's already admitted that he's curious about it, and my guess is he might one day genuinely enjoy the freedom that comes with letting go that way…once he trusts himself and his Daddy wholeheartedly. I smother a pang of yearning to be that Daddy. To earn that much trust from this skittish man.

Too fast, Charlie.

I blame my mother for how quickly my investment in this potential relationship has bloomed. She's notorious for her hyperactivity, too.

When Ash yawns, I glance at my watch and decide it's probably past the bedtime I would usually set for a little boy. But we've covered a lot of ground over the past couple of hours and have gotten to know each other better. After he shyly agreed that he's just as interested in an "us" as I am, we moved onto negotiations.

We've decided on some basic rules, honesty with each other being the most significant of them. He's agreed to watch his language and follow my instructions when he's Little, and we'll treat each other as equals and partners the whole way.

We went over the concept of consequences for breaking the rules, and I was clear that, in my world, spanking is a "funishment" and part of game play only. Actual consequences might range anywhere from being stood in a corner to writing lines to being grounded. He agreed with it all.

I send him off to use the bathroom and brush his teeth, and when he comes back out of the bathroom and into his bedroom, he blinks at the new pajamas I hold out to him, complete with a brand-new pair of training pants.

"Uh…" he says, looking from the clothing to me and back again.

"How long have you been cycling through the same pair of jeans with different shirts?" I ask delicately. "I'd like to throw them in the wash."

"Okay," he acknowledges after another moment's thought. Then he swallows. "Will you, um, help me get dressed?"

He's Big right now, but the step toward the relationship I so badly want to cultivate with him squeezes my heart. I can see his own longing reflected in his hazel eyes, and that convinces me that he's not just doing this because he knows I want it. He wants it, too. I'm proud of him for voicing the request. "I would love that, baby."

In his room, I help pull his plain gray T-shirt over his head, then push his jeans and underwear over his hips and down his legs. I learn that his blush travels down his neck and over his chest, and I want to kiss every spot it touches, but I don't push my luck. This is only day one. We have time.

We have forever, says a traitorously hopeful voice at the back of my head.

I ignore that voice in preference of pulling the training pants up his long legs, paying no attention to his semihard cock. I've already pushed those boundaries further than I'm comfortable with for one night. Ash scrunches his nose adorably and wriggles.

"They're tight," he complains lightly, glancing down at the spaceship print over his bulge. Then a small smile tugs at his lips. "But…I think I like them."

I'm sure my answering grin makes me look goofy as fuck, but I couldn't care less. "It makes me happy to hear that." I'm making an effort to talk to him like I would if he was Little. The routine is important for both of us and will make the transition easier for him.

I tap his left calf muscle, encouraging him to lift the leg to get his new pj's on next. These are loose cotton pants covered in paw prints. The matching shirt has a puppy on it. He steadies himself on my shoulders as I help him step into them.

When he's fully dressed, he's adorable and I tell him so.

"Thank you." He bites the corner of his lip, and my cock surges back to life again.

"We, uh, we haven't discussed sleeping arrangements," I tell him, adding, "but there's no expectation for you to sleep in my bed. Not now…and not ever if you're not comfortable with it."

"I mean, you've already jerked me off today," he teases, and the reminder of my lapse in control does nothing to ease my erection. "But…maybe for tonight, can I stay in here? Just to get my thoughts together?"

I never want him to feel uncomfortable or coerced in any way. This all has to be his choice. "Of course, sweetheart. But I'm going to leave my door open a crack, and if you need me at all during the night, call out or come get me, okay?"

Ash's expression turns soft and a little grateful. "I'd like that. Thanks, Charlie."

This beautiful boy is going to be the death of me.

Chapter Seven – Asher

I wasn't lying when I told Charlie that I liked his very Daddy-esque suggestion of keeping his door open. When I'm anxious, I'm prone to nightmares, so it's soothing to know that there's someone there just in case. *A Daddy*, my brain sing-songs helpfully.

I'm trying to ignore just how easily I'm accepting this entire change of circumstances. What are the chances that the perfect man for me is (a) single and (b) willing to move me into his home without ever having met me before? But there's absolutely no pressure coming from him to do anything that I'm not comfortable with, and he seems to genuinely want to look after me. *Me*. It's mind-boggling. Nobody has ever cared like this before. Like, *ever*.

That said, I've read enough about the Daddy mindset that I know it's not all that strange. He probably sees a Boy struggling and, because he's obviously a good man (the cop thing gives that away, not to mention how kind and caring he has been), he's driven to help. Besides that, there's a mutual attraction between us —if the impromptu hand job earlier is any indication— which doesn't hurt.

For the first time in ages, I allow myself to feel a flicker of hope that maybe I will have a chance to explore all the interests I thought I'd have to keep secret forever. This both thrills and terrifies me.

Charlie asks me my traffic light color when he goes to sit on the bed beside me. He's selected a kid's book from the shelf under the window and, even though it's late, he wants to read me to sleep.

"Green," I tell him without hesitation, ignoring the butterflies in my belly when he smiles widely.

It should feel strange to snuggle up next to this man I've known for all of a few hours, but there's something *right* about it. Maybe it's just the relief of having a roof over my head, of having a full tummy and no fear of being caught breaking rules. Whatever it is, there is nothing daunting about being tucked against his solid chest with one of those muscular arms wrapped around my shoulders, holding me in place. His large palm is smoothly stroking my side in a rhythmic up-and-down motion, and he's reading *The Poky Little Puppy* in a perfect Daddy voice, all low and lulling. I drift off into dreamland far sooner than I want to.

However, I wake up in the middle of the night with my heart pounding and a small cry of terror on my lips. The nightmare is already fading, but the fear has well and truly set in. It takes me a minute to get my bearings. There's a strip of light filtering in through the half-open doorway, and as my brain engages, I remember the day's events all over again.

I'm not quite Big, but I'm not Little either. I'm hovering in this strange mental space where I *want* to crawl out of bed and take Charlie up on his offer, but the adult in me thinks it'll be too much of an imposition. I don't need him to regret taking me in like the pathetic street urchin I've become. Clutching at my blankie, I fiddle with the fraying corner while I mull over my options and try to talk myself down from the nightmare-induced panic.

"Ash?" Charlie's voice is gravelly with sleep, and the strip of light from the living area widens as he opens my door fully. "Can I come in?"

I open my mouth to tell him I'll be fine, but the word "Please" tumbles out instead. I sound meek and vulnerable even to my own ears.

He steps inside the room, backlit from the living room light, and my breath catches. He's wearing the soft T-shirt from earlier over a pair of low-slung flannel pajama pants. His more-on-top hairstyle is all mussed from sleep, the longer strands sticking up at odd angles. He radiates raw masculinity beneath the sweet softness of his concerned-Daddy expression.

My stomach does somersaults as he steps closer.

"Bad dream?" His voice is schooled into what I'm coming to recognize as his usual low, soothing tone. It makes me want to leap from the bed and throw myself into his arms.

Picking at the fraying edges of my blankie, I nod.

"Scoot over," he urges softly, and I comply without a second thought.

A voice at the back of my head tells me I'm already getting too attached, that it's dangerous to rely on him for comfort so readily, but I do my best to ignore it as Charlie climbs onto the bed beside me. He extends his arm and I cuddle up beside him without hesitation, not ignorant of the way he sighs happily.

Something about that sound silences my doubts. He genuinely wants this, too. If we both want the same things, why should I fight it?

With his arm wrapped around me again, Charlie uses that hand to card through my hair and I lean into the touch, savoring it. "Wanna talk about it?" he asks gently.

"I can't remember the dream," I explain, my eyes already getting heavy again under his gentle ministrations. "I don't usually. Just the feeling."

His hand keeps moving, his large, thick fingers massaging my scalp. "Do you have nightmares a lot?"

"Mm-hmm," I answer. "It's worse when I'm stressed." The last few nights have been full of interrupted sleep. It's probably part of why I finally broke when I was faced with the cops. With Josh.

Charlie makes a sympathetic sound, but it doesn't feel like he's pitying me. I'm glad. I hate pity. "I'm here now," he murmurs, and those words help the lingering fear recede further. "I'm here, and you're safe."

Warmth spreads through my chest and I blink back tears of relief. As embarrassing as breaking down in front of Josh was, I'm starting to think that maybe it wasn't so bad that it happened after all. Especially not if this thing with Charlie works out.

* * *

A week later, I've officially settled into Charlie's place. He had those first couple of days off, which helped us get used to living together, and then he went back to work. At first it was weird being treated like a child whenever he got home from work, but now I look forward to it. Hell, after the first few days, I've started to need it.

Charlie was right about routine helping. And now, after a week, slipping into my Little headspace in the evenings is starting to feel natural. I drift into my own little world where the stresses of adult life can't touch me. I color or watch cartoons or play with toys, and I'm in a happy little bubble where I feel safe and cared for. The feeling is addictive, and I can understand why this becomes a twenty-four-seven lifestyle for people. To be honest, even though I can't see it being an all-the-time thing, I can see myself easily slipping in and out of my Little headspace without too much drama.

And that scares me a bit, because there's still a tiny voice at the back of my mind that says it's abnormal.

However, the more time I spend being Little, especially with Charlie's encouragement, the less that voice bothers me.

I'm genuinely happier than I can ever recall being. Even when I'm Big, I'm enjoying life. I've been applying for jobs and keeping the house clean and tidy while Charlie's at work.

I still pause to pinch myself every so often, because Charlie is everything I've ever hoped for in a partner. Despite there being almost a decade between us, we're on similar wavelengths. We share the same taste in movies, argue playfully over music, and even read similar books. Conversation is consistently effortless, which surprises me because it feels like I've known him for years.

Additionally, the chemistry between us, regardless of whether I'm Big or Little, is hot as fuck. We still haven't gone beyond hand jobs (he's determined not to rush our relationship, especially while I'm still learning how to be myself in all headspaces), but his cuddles and kisses are the stuff of dreams.

And his brother is a hoot.

Most evenings, Josh drops by for dinner and lets me ask him my newest round of questions about being Little. He's become my best friend next to Charlie, and I honestly can't imagine not having either of them in my life, even though a week ago they'd been complete strangers to me.

"Whatcha thinkin' about?" Josh prods from beside me.

We're both sitting on our stools at the kitchen island, each of us coloring in while Da— *Charlie* makes dinner. Tonight, Josh is more playful than usual, and I'm starting to realize through the haze of my own Little space that he's as Little as I've ever seen him.

I tear up a bit because this is my first ever playdate with another Little.

"Chaaaaaarlie," Josh calls, sounding horrified, "Ash is *crying*."

Da— *Charlie's* in front of me in a second, all warm blue eyes and concern. His big hand is rubbing circles on my back, and it feels so right and *so* satisfying: like a final puzzle piece clicking into place. "Baby, what's wrong?"

I beam back at him, hoping that he understands that these are happy tears. "Josh is Little," I explain, finding it hard to express myself in this headspace. "He's my friend and he's Little like me."

"Oh." A smile spreads across Charlie's face, and I clap my hands because, yeah, he gets it. Plus, I get a thrill from making him happy. "Yeah, he's Little today." He ruffles my hair. "You like having a friend to play with, huh?"

I nod excitedly. "Yup! My first playdate."

His expression turns all mushy, and words I'm definitely not prepared to say dance on the tip of my tongue. It's only been a week, but I'm pretty sure I am falling hard for this man. This flawless man, with his sexy-as-sin body, and the uniform that plays right into a whole different set of kinks for me, and his perfect *Daddy-ness*. How can I feel so much, so quickly?

The blogs I've read all say that BDSM relationships tend to speed ahead more quickly than traditional ones, but this feels like a bullet train. Charlie has given me everything I've ever dreamed of and then some, and it's only been a week. What more is there to come? Has everything peaked? Will things go downhill from here?

With how good this has been, I can't help but feel like I need to steel myself for the inevitable crash.

But while I'm in my Little space, those worries don't trouble me as much. All I know is I'm happy and carefree, and I have a Little friend and an *awesome* Daddy.

An awesome Daddy who is staring at me with wide, shining eyes.

My confusion at Charlie's stunned expression must show because Josh giggles and nudges me again. "You called him Daddy and broke him."

Oh. Oops.

I aim for my most cherubic smile. "Sorry, Daddy." *Damn it.* "I mean, Charlie."

Charlie laughs a watery laugh and wraps me in one of his soul-warming hugs. "I'm happy to be your Daddy, little lamb."

And oh. *Oh.* Little lamb. That's new. That's new and I love it. But I'm too Little to explain just how much.

"*Baa*," I blurt at him instead.

Josh dissolves into a new peal of giggles and I throw my orange crayon at him.

"Chaaaarlie!" Josh complains.

It's my turn to giggle.

Daddy tells us both to behave and we settle back into coloring, but I'm too busy floating on air to focus on what I'm doing.

* * *

"So," I say later that night, after Josh has left and I've come out of my Little headspace. We're lying side by side in Charlie's bed, even though I've been sleeping in my own. I haven't felt ready to move into his bed, but now I can't imagine going back to mine. There was a fundamental shift in our dynamic today, and we need to talk about it. "Little lamb, huh?"

Charlie grins and runs his hand through my curls. "It seemed like a suitable nickname."

He's been on cloud nine all night. I have my guesses as to why. Still, I can't help sounding shy and insecure when I ask, "And...you're okay that I called you...*y'know?*"

He arches an eyebrow. "Do I know?"

"*Daddy.*" I sigh, feeling the blush on my cheeks. I think I've blushed more in the last week than in my entire lifetime combined. *Damn pale skin.* "You're okay that I called you Daddy?"

I squeal as Charlie pulls me snug against him and rolls over me, grinding his obvious arousal against mine. "I've been hard since you said it," he confesses, then kisses me until I'm writhing and breathless.

"Does that mean you'll finally fuck me" —I smirk— "*Daddy?*"

I know I've hit my mark when his cock twitches against me, concealed as it is by the layers that separate us. I make a note to use this newfound information whenever and wherever I can.

"Language, little lamb," Charlie teases back. But the rule only applies when I'm Little, and I'm definitely not feeling Little right now, though we have fooled around during my Little time, too.

"Baa-*fucking*-aaa," I shoot back. He laughs and the sound goes straight to my cock. I arch my hips up against him. "But seriously, I'm dying here."

"We can't have that," he agrees before kissing me again. He spears his tongue into my mouth in a deliciously filthy kiss that feels like an imitation of what he'd like his dick to do to my ass. And I'm totally on board with that.

"Lube," I beg as he pulls back and pushes up my shirt. It's got *Looney Tunes* characters on it. He'd found it at Target in the men's section, and I love it. But right now, it's gotta go. His tongue and teeth tease my nipple and I cry out. "*Fuck.* Lube. Fingers. My ass. Now." My breathing hitches when he moves to the other nipple. "*Please, Daddy.*"

Ah, the magic words. They get him moving, leaning further over me to dig through his bedside table for lube and a condom. I use the advantage of this position to unbutton his jeans and pull the zipper down. His cock pushes the material of his boxer briefs out toward me, and I palm him through the cotton, teasing over the damp spot where he's dripping precum.

"Uh-uh," he says playfully, moving out of my reach now that he's got the supplies we need in hand. "Patience."

I want to complain, but I arch my hips up from the mattress as he makes short work of pulling down my pj's and the training pants he dressed me in earlier. I pull my shirt off and throw it in the same direction that he just tossed my pants. He sits back, resting his ass on his heels as he sweeps his heated gaze over my naked body.

Obviously he's seen me naked before, but this time feels different. There's no undercurrent of sweetness or of the cute, playful relationship between Daddy and his boy. This is all heat and longing. I take my hand to my cock and stroke it to tease him.

He groans and bats my hand away, replacing it with his. "This is mine, baby. You don't get to touch it unless I say so."

Fuck if that doesn't make me go hot all over. And with the way my dick jumps and leaks in his loose hold, there's no hiding how much I enjoy it.

"You'd better get fucking naked soon," I growl up at him, just before our mouths connect for another dirty, delicious kiss.

When he pulls away again, he smirks, still lazily stroking my cock. "Or what, Ash?"

"Or…" I try to think of a punishment I could throw his way, but his hand's far too distracting, and I'm not the dominant one in our relationship. I don't have any idea what sort of ultimatum I could give him. At least, not while I'm Big. If I were Little, I'd probably come up with something ridiculous that would have him laughing indulgently. "Or…*ugh*." I drop my head back onto the mattress with a chuckle that morphs into a needy whine. "I don't know. Just strip already." Propping myself on my elbows, I look back up at him and bat my lashes. "Please, Daddy? I've always wanted to watch a cop-themed striptease."

Charlie laughs and shakes his head, gesturing with his free hand to the soft cotton T-shirt and the tented boxer briefs he's wearing beneath his open jeans. "Does this look like a uniform to you?"

"I have a *very* vivid imagination."

He grins but releases my erection and shuffles backward off the bed.

Standing in front of me, he lifts the hem of his T-shirt and then whips the whole item over his head in a smooth move that has me questioning whether or not he actually has practice as a stripper. But then my gaze is drawn to his muscular chest, with its smattering of dark chest hair, and across to those insane biceps of his, then down the defined abs that put my lightly toned stomach to shame. He's all hard ridges, where I have a little softness to my belly. His opened jeans hang loose on his hips, and the prominent V shape of his form dips directly into the waistband of his boxer briefs like an arrow directing me to the promised land.

"Fuck me," I mutter, because this is the first time I've seen him shirtless. I've felt those abs beneath my fingers. I've even lifted his shirts before to lick at his skin. But putting the whole picture together is breathtaking. "You're the hottest man ever." My cock drips in agreement.

He preens for a moment, then hooks his fingers in the waistband of his underwear and pushes them and his jeans to the ground. His cock is glorious, as it has been the last couple of times I've glimpsed it. It's thick but not insanely long, veiny, and purpled at the head. A bead of pearly precum gathers at the tip as I eye it, and I lick my lips.

Charlie groans. "Baby, that's cruel."

"What's cruel is you still standing there instead of getting back over here and fucking me with that monster of yours."

I've jerked him off a couple of times now, but I haven't really gotten to take him in, and I can't stop looking. Can't stop imagining what he tastes like. What he's going to feel like inside me. He's definitely bigger than either of the two men I've been with before, and that's slightly daunting.

"Hey." Charlie crawls back over the bed until we're face-to-face again. Concern has his eyebrows pulling together. "Where'd you go just now?"

I want to laugh it off, but our first rule is honesty, so I reach for his cock and spread some of his precum over his length, slowly stroking him as I confess, "I've only been with two other guys…" I'm only twenty-two and not an extrovert, so I'm sure this doesn't come as a huge shock to him. He nods. "And you're, uh, bigger than either of them was."

Instead of grinning or laughing or acting like he's won some sort of competition, Charlie gives me a soft smile full of understanding. He scooches in closer, gently rocking his hips toward mine until our cocks brush against each other and *fuck,* that feels good. "If you're not comfortable, baby, we can stop any time, okay? We can just do this instead." He has the lube in his hand and pops the cap with his thumb, drizzling a little of the liquid down between us, and I catch it with my palm and spread it over our connecting erections.

Holy fuck.

How the hell does this feel so good?

I give in to the sensations for a moment, rocking up to meet him, squeezing both our shafts together, groaning as electricity seems to zap through my veins. Then I come back to the conversation. "I want..." I say, as though that's actually going to explain anything. But the pleasure is making it difficult for the words to come out. I try again. "I want you to fuck me. I really, really do." I swallow. "Can we just...take it slow?"

There's a part of me that wants to say 'screw that' and go fast, demanding that he take me hard and rough so I can feel him for days; but I'm smart enough to know that, at least for our first time, I'd regret it.

"Of course, baby." I get the feeling that he had no intention of doing otherwise anyway.

Charlie brings our mouths together in a sweet, sensual kiss, and before long I'm spreading my legs and guiding his fingers to my hole. Then there's lube, and he's teasing the rim slowly, pushing the pad of his finger in and out maddeningly, and I break the kiss both to praise and to complain, "Oh my God, Charlie..."

He turns prep, which has only ever been a perfunctory, mandatory thing in my previous relationships, into exquisite foreplay. There's a fuck-ton of lube used, but soon I'm writhing on three thick digits. I'm arching off the bed as he hooks his fingers and brushes my prostate again and again until I'm certain I'm going to come without even touching my cock. I'm babbling and begging, and I swear that he's edging me, until the crinkle of the foil condom wrapper has me sighing in bliss because —*fucking finally*— my Daddy is going to fuck me into the mattress.

He takes his time, rocking into me slowly, his lubed hand working my cock to distract me from the initial discomfort and burn of the intrusion. And yeah, he's bigger than I've had before, but after he bottoms out and I breathe for a moment, I love the full feeling of him inside me.

"Move," I say. I urge him by rocking my hips up, even though he's got me pretty much pinned to the mattress; he's supporting his weight now on his forearms, which are on either side of my head. I begged for this position, needing to see his face, to feel his warmth spread over me, and it's everything I hoped it would be.

"You're so perfect around me, baby," Charlie's voice is raspy and strained, "and it's been a while for me. I'm not gonna last."

That makes me feel even better. I'm the reason he's on the razor's edge. I'm the reason he's got that almost-pained, blissed-out look on his face. *Me*. It's a heady feeling.

"Me too," I admit as he starts the slow drag back out and then thrusts back in. With a swivel of his hips *just so*, he grazes my prostate again. "Fuck, *yes*. Right there."

He repeats the movement. My cock, pinned between our bodies, dribbles precum and we're pressed so close together that it's smearing between us. There's a slick-enough slide and friction there that I don't think either of us needs to wriggle a hand in to stroke it.

Again and again, Charlie repeats the movement that's making me whimper and groan, and I can feel a delicious pressure building inside me. The wave of my orgasm is cresting. I'm too fucking close but I don't want to stop it.

"You feel so good," Charlie insists, and he does the swivel–thrust thing again.

My balls tighten. White light sparks behind my eyes. The coil of tension inside me is perilously close to snapping.

"I… Charlie, *Daddy*, I… I'm…" His hips go again and I'm flying. "*Coming*!" I cry, pushed over the edge with that last thrust. Neither of us has actually touched my cock, and yet I'm spurting ropes of cum between us, and with his body pressed against mine and his movements picking up, it's spreading everywhere. It's filthy and amazing and my dick makes an effort to jerk again because this entire experience has been so intensely hot.

"Fuck." Charlie draws the word out as he follows me over the edge, his hips stilling and his cock jerking as he releases into the condom, still deep inside me.

I wince as he carefully pulls out. He kisses my stomach, heedless of the mess there, before he backs off the bed and goes to dispose of the trash. He returns with a couple of warm, damp cloths and cleans me up before he does himself.

I fall asleep snuggled up next to him, naked and sated.

Chapter Eight – Charlie

I've created a monster. In the two weeks since we first had sex, Ash has jumped me at every opportunity. I'm thirty-one and I don't consider myself old by any means, but I'd completely forgotten what the libido of a twenty-two-year-old was like. And let's not get started on his refractory period. That boy can come five times in a two-hour period. *Five.* That has to be a superpower. I consider myself lucky when I can get it up a second time within an hour.

Josh thinks it's hilarious. I mean, of course he would; he's twenty-three. He's got the same boundless energy as my boyfriend.

Boyfriend.

The word still makes me all warm and fuzzy inside. But not as much as "Daddy" does. It doesn't get old, hearing my little lamb call me by the title. Whether it's during sex or spoken in his higher-pitched, almost innocent Little Ash voice, it's music to my ears.

In the three weeks we've been together, I've watched him come out of his shell. He's no longer the anxious, confused mess he had been when I first set eyes on him. He's still got reservations about fully letting go and sinking deep into his Little headspace, but he goes further and further every time, and with each day we learn something new about Little Ash.

Josh has been beyond helpful with that process. When Ash admitted that having playdates made it easier to dip into his Little space, Josh was more than happy to join him. Most evenings, they color, play with blocks, or —as they did a couple of nights ago— create stories together using Ash's ever-growing pile of stuffed toys as a cast of characters in their imaginative play.

As much as I've enjoyed watching Ash begin to discover his Little side, it's been a revelation watching my brother indulge his own. He might argue that he's just a scene player, but I'm not so sure that's the case. I have my suspicions about his actual desires, but I'm not going to push him. If he wants to talk about it, he knows where to find me.

When I walk through the front door tonight, thankfully at a reasonable hour, I'm not surprised that Ash greets me at the front door. However, I am surprised that he's Big. Our usual routine sees him indulging in Little time before dinner and Big time before bed. After sex, he alternates depending on his mood.

"I got a job!" he cheers, and I beam at him because I know it's been eating away at him.

He deferred his studies, deciding that with only a semester left to go, it would be silly not to finish them one day. But he's continued to stress about not contributing to bills, even though it's not something I care about.

I wrap him in my arms as he throws himself at me, and I spin us around while he laughs. "Baby, that's fantastic news!" I'm unable to stop myself from cupping his jaw and kissing those ridiculously plump lips of his. "Which job?"

As we head into the dining room, he holds my hand and pushes me down into one of the chairs at the table, facing it sideways away from the table itself. Straddling my lap and looping his arms behind my neck, he says, "Administrative assistant at a law firm downtown."

"Oh" —I smirk— "*fancy*. Does that mean I get to see you in a suit?"

He nods, but the smile slips. "I don't have a suit. Or any corporate clothing."

"We can fix that," I assure him, but I know this is going to lead to one of the only things we ever argue about.

When he's Little, Ash is oblivious to my buying new things for him. But when he's Big, he's guilt ridden and doesn't understand how much I enjoy providing for him. Some part of me wonders whether his awful father made him feel like a burden and a leech, but it's not a topic I'm willing to bring up. I'd much rather just spoil him and make up for any shortfalls in his old life.

"I—" he starts, but I press my index finger to his lips.

"No arguments. I'm buying you what you need."

Ash pouts and then sucks my finger into his mouth, twirling his tongue around it.

Moaning in response, I lift my hips up, my hardening cock finding his. "You're a pest," I accuse, but it's without heat. "I have to make dinner."

"Or," he drags the word out, slipping off my lap and to his knees in front of me, "I could help you with *this* now." He palms my obvious erection.

We've both been tested recently, so after a talk we decided to ditch condoms, which means blow jobs are infinitely more enjoyable for both of us. "God, baby." I run my hand through his soft curls, musing absently that he's probably due a haircut. "You're going to be the death of me."

That's all the permission he needs. His nimble fingers undo my belt and the button above my fly, then he's unzipping my pants and tugging my cock out of my underwear through what little space he's created. He kisses the tip sweetly before licking the head as though it's a lollipop. He's teasing me and I love every second of it.

But he's got very little patience and it's not long before he's taking as much of my cock into his mouth as he can, wrapping his hand around the base because my cock doesn't quite fit without him gagging. His mouth is heaven, all warm, wet suction, and it's not going to take him long to get me off. Especially not when I hear his zipper go down, the snick of the cap of a bottle of lube, and then the wet sound of his hand shuttling up and down his own cock.

The idea that he's planned for this, to the point of having lube with him, is heady and arousing as fuck, and I tell him so.

He moans around me while he sucks and bobs his head, and the vibrations inch me closer to the edge of my orgasm. "Baby," I warn him, my voice tight and gruff, "I'm close."

He sucks harder, his hand works faster, and with a shout I lift off from the chair and come hard down his throat. He sucks and licks me clean until the hypersensitivity is too much, and I gently push his head away. I glance down just in time to watch him spurt over his hand and onto the polished timber between his spread knees.

"That's my good boy," I praise, and he grins up at me with the most lust-drunk expression I've seen on his face, his eyes half-lidded and dopey.

He's gorgeous, I think. *He's gorgeous, and he's all mine.*

* * *

Two weeks later, it's official: Asher loves his job. Suit shopping had been fun for us both, as had the intense orgasms we'd shared after we'd gotten home, both riled up from teasing each other during the shopping trip. He looks at ease in business pants and a crisp dress shirt, almost as natural as he does in training pants and a onesie. The two sides of him couldn't be more different, but the dichotomy captivates me.

It turns out I really do like having my cake and eating it, too.

I get to be Daddy, but I also get the partner that I've always wanted. We're equals as adults. We get to hang out, have a beer, see grown-up movies...but we also get to indulge our other needs, too. I get to play make-believe with him, or with race cars or blocks, read him books, bathe him and give him nightly snuggles...and neither of us feels like we're missing out on anything. Or, at least, that's my impression.

"So, are you ever going to introduce your boy to your friends, or will he be your little secret forever?" Josh asks me over lunch.

"He's not a secret," I snap back, feeling far more defensive than I should. I jab a carrot stick in his direction. I've been packing Asher's lunch and my own at the same time, and it's just easier to prep the same snacks for both of us. "We've only been together, like..." I tilt my head from side to side, as if I don't know that it's been exactly five weeks and three days. "...five weeks."

"Uh-huh." Josh gives me a look that says I'm not fooling anyone. "You're head over heels for him already, big brother. Does it matter how long it's been? And also, don't you think the guys are gonna start poking their noses in if you don't touch base?"

I shrug. My friends are all fairly easygoing, and they get that my work schedule is unpredictable. We can go months at a time without catching up, and I've been staying somewhat involved in the group chat, so they know I'm alive. "They'll meet him eventually."

The guys in question —Chance, Spencer and Ted— are Daddies like me. I met Ted at The Grove years back when I was getting involved with my first Little and needed some mentoring. Spencer and Chance came along in a similar fashion when our littles at the time were close and had playdates often. All four of us have been in and out of relationships with littles in recent years, and Spence is the only one of us currently in a long-term relationship, since he has his Little, Emma.

Well, he *was* the only one. Now that I have Asher, that makes two of us, I suppose. Ash and I may only have been together for a couple of months, but I can see us being together long-term. Maybe the guys really *should* meet him soon. Damn Josh for being right. *Again.*

Josh sometimes joins our circle of friends, but he's usually more comfortable when other subs are around. I understand that all the Daddy Dom attention can be overwhelming when you're the only sub, especially when you're a brat like my brother.

I've waited too long to respond, though, and Josh's impatience wins out. "Okay, look, I might have an ulterior motive," he admits when his initial line of questioning fails to get him the result he wants.

Arching an eyebrow, I lean back in my seat. "This should be interesting."

"I met a new Little at The Grove and I think he'd be good for Chance."

Huh. Not what I'd expected. "You know I'm not into matchmaking, J."

He holds up his hands in surrender. "I know, I know. But he's new to town and he's into all that gaming stuff like Chance is..." He shrugs. "Plus he's hot. A bit older than most boys, and a lot bulkier, but Chance has never gone for the young twink type."

I find it ironic that Josh is talking about not fitting the boy stereotype. With the way he's built, nobody could call him a twink, either.

"I don't matchmake," I reiterate with a sigh. "But if he's looking to make friends who understand the lifestyle, sure. I'll organize a get-together with the guys, and you should invite him along. If nothing else, he and Ash might hit it off." My boy would probably love some additional playdates with other littles.

And that's how, a week later, I wind up hosting a potluck at my house on my next weekend off.

I've got the grill fired up in the backyard with burgers cooking, and I'm keeping a cautious eye on Asher, who keeps glancing nervously at the clock. The guys are going to start arriving in the next fifteen minutes or so, and the closer we get to that point, the more anxious Ash seems.

"Josh," I say, and I sigh when another glance in Asher's direction is met with more fidgeting and lip biting. "Watch these patties for me."

He takes over without argument, and I make my way to my boyfriend. He's Big right now but squirming and clearly nervous. "Come on, babe." I usher him inside, into the living room where his blankie is draped over the couch. He clutches at it the second we sit. "Talk to me."

"I don't want to embarrass you in front of your friends," he admits, and there's a hint of Little Ash in the way he speaks. It's been a while since I've seen him quite so anxious, and I hate that I'm responsible for it. Even though Ash and I had talked about this meeting and his potential concerns the night Josh brought the idea up, I should have known he'd panic.

"Little lamb, you won't. I promise."

His lower lip wobbles.

"If you wanna be Little for today, nothing's stopping you."

Those hazel orbs go wide with abject horror. "In front of strangers? Fuck no."

"Language," I say to correct him, and he arches an eyebrow.

"The rule is only while I'm Little, Charlie."

"You're not entirely Big right now," I reason.

Ash moves to argue and then sighs. "No, you're right. I'm… God, I don't know what I am."

"Nervous," I say, keeping my tone soft and supportive. "And that's okay. But baby…Little or Big, they're gonna love you." I've already told him that the guys are all involved in the same kink circle, and that none of them would ever judge Asher or me. "If anything, I'm gonna have to keep my eye on Ted. He might try to steal you away."

Ted's in his midforties and is probably the person I'd call my best friend, aside from Josh. He talked me through all of my concerns when I took on my first Daddy role, and he's a calming influence in my life. Almost like a big brother, something I never had growing up, what with being the eldest of four. Josh is the third born; we have a sister, Maisy, in between us, and our youngest sibling is Axel, who is in his senior year of high school. I've already told Ash all of this, too. But I haven't told Ash that, yeah, Ted and I seem to share very similar tastes.

Telling him as much now has the desired effect. He laughs and shakes his head, relaxing in his seat. "He's got zero chance of that."

"I'm glad to hear it."

We talk through his concerns a little more until he's as relaxed as I'm going to get him. And when the doorbell rings and he doesn't freeze up, I count that as a win.

Chapter Nine – Asher

Charlie's friends are actually awesome. His best friend, Ted, hasn't arrived yet, but everyone else has, and so has Josh's new friend, Matteo. He asks to just be called Matt, and everyone's doing just that.

When Josh told me that Matt's a Little like us, I thought he was kidding. If anyone could look more like a Dom, it would be Matt. But, then again, Josh doesn't exactly fit the sub mold either. And, if I'm being really honest, I'm also not exactly a twink. Of the three of us, though, I'm definitely the closest fit to the stereotype.

Then there's Emma, Spencer's Little girlfriend. She's gorgeous. Today she's Big like the rest of us, but her hair's still in long, dark pigtails and her lips are painted bright pink. She's as bubbly as the brightly colored dress she's wearing, and I'm immediately comfortable talking to her.

The two Daddies, Chance and Spencer, aren't exactly intimidating, though. Chance looks like an ordinary guy in his midthirties. He's got a bit of a dad bod, a scruffy reddish beard, and his hair is cropped really short because, according to him, it's starting to thin. Spencer is tall and lanky, with glasses and wild dark hair. But he has a friendly smile, and the way he looks at Emma makes me feel all fizzy inside because it's a lot like the way Charlie looks at me.

We're all lounging around the big outdoor dining table nursing beers

—or wine coolers for Emma and me— when the doorbell rings. Charlie looks over his shoulder at me before he goes to answer it, and I smile widely at him. It means a lot to me that he's always checking in, even if only with a glance here and there.

I'm still grinning when he brings Ted through.

And then my stomach drops.

"Holy shit," I say under my breath, because *Ted* is Theodore Masters. The senior partner at the law firm I've just started working for. He might be dressed down in jeans and a dark Henley, but it's still the same man. My boss. My boss's boss, if I want to get technical. "Shit. Shit. Fuck."

"Hey." Josh is closest to me, and his hand moves to my back. It's not quite as good as Charlie's, but it's helping to stave off the anxiety attack of my boss discovering my secret life. And yeah, if I were thinking rationally, I'd realize that I've also just discovered his, but being outed as a Daddy is much less disturbing in my books. "Ash," he says softly, "breathe."

This doesn't really help because all it does is bring everyone's attention my way. Including Charlie's. How the hell could Charlie not have connected the dots that the law firm I work for is the same one where his best friend is senior partner? Or did he know and just not tell me?

"Baby." Charlie's hand has replaced Josh's and he's rubbing slow, soothing circles at my back. I can feel how red my face is, but I can't look up. Not at the people around the table. Not at Charlie. "Baby, talk to me."

I shake my head. I can't. I can't do words right now.

"I think I'm the issue," Ted's voice offers — a voice I've heard around the office and always thought of as paternal. He sounds chagrined and a little apologetic.

Beside me, Charlie sounds confused. "How?" The part of me that worried he'd kept the information from me relaxes a tiny bit.

"Asher's the firm's newest admin assistant," Ted answers easily, and I still can't look up. "And I imagine it's jarring to have the boss just saunter in on a gathering like this."

He doesn't spell it out. Doesn't have to. We all know what we are.

"Well. Fuck." I want to laugh at Charlie's assessment, but I can't. Instead,

I'm still paralyzed by anxiety.

I feel ridiculous because, honestly, the situation should be comedic. But the part of me that's terrified of people finding out that I'm *abnormal* can't be reasoned with.

Charlie continues and he's close enough that I can feel him shaking his head. "I didn't know. How the hell did I miss that?"

"The firm was bought out recently. It changed names a few months back. You probably didn't recognize it." Ted's voice is getting closer, and I squeeze my eyes shut because I don't want this. I don't want to have this conversation. Not with my boss's boss. Not in front of all of Charlie's friends.

But it's happening anyway, because on my other side, where Josh was sitting, the tall, imposing figure that is Theodore Masters crouches down. I catch the movement out of the corner of my eye. "It's alright," he says in a low, gentle voice. "Why don't you head inside with your...with Charlie and take a minute to process, okay?"

There are probably all sorts of meaningful glances being exchanged above my head. I'm flooded with embarrassment and hating that I can't just react to this situation like a normal person. Surely I should just be able to laugh it off and say "Ha, well that was awkward, let's never speak of this at work" and let that be the end of it. But I can't.

A couple of seats away, Emma's bright voice cuts into the tension. "Daddy, I have to go potty. Can you take me?"

I want to hug her, because it's obvious that she's trying to take the attention off me. She was Big; there was no other reason for her to ask the question. The sound of chairs scraping tells me people are moving around, and in that moment, I feel free to take advantage of the distraction. I launch from my seat and practically race into the house and up the stairs. I know that Charlie's on my heels, but I don't wait for him.

I practically fling myself into my kid's bed, even though I haven't slept in it in weeks. I try to burrow under the covers, but Charlie's slipping in beside me before I get the chance.

"I had no idea, Ash. I would have warned you if I did."

"I know," I answer. "And I know that it doesn't change anything, him knowing about me being..."

"Little?"

I think we both know I was going to say something derogatory. But I nod. "I just... I panicked and then I couldn't stop panicking and now I've humiliated myself and ruined your get-together with your friends—"

As usual, Charlie pulls me into his lap midway through my freak-out. He's rocking me gently and pressing kisses to the top of my head, and I'm struck by the thought that I'm not just falling for this man, I'm actually in love with him. What a great time to have that revelation.

Well done, Scanlon. Idiot.

"You haven't ruined a damn thing, little lamb." He's gentle and reassuring. "They all understand."

I shake my head. "You can do so much better than a broken Little who's prone to stupid panic attacks."

"Hey, stop it." The gentleness is gone from his tone. This is one hundred percent Daddy admonishment. He manhandles me in his lap, turning me and forcing my chin upward. "Look at me, Asher."

I do as he asks because I can't ignore that tone.

His blue eyes are soft and full of emotions that I'm too afraid to put a name to. "Baby, you're not broken. And panic attacks happen to everyone." When I scoff, he frowns. "Do you know how many cops have PTSD or other anxiety disorders? Or marines, or firefighters, or any other first responders or members of the armed forces?" I swallow and shake my head, and Charlie keeps talking. "Or any career, really. Anxiety isn't limited to any one kind of person, and it doesn't mean you're broken if you're struggling with it." He presses his forehead to mine. "But if you genuinely feel this way, I want to help you. I think... I think maybe you should talk to someone. A professional."

I want to argue that I don't need therapy, but when I open my mouth to do that, the words die on my tongue. With my panic receding, I consider the situation downstairs and conclude that there was no real reason to react like I did. My issues are in my head, and pushing them down or pretending they don't exist isn't going to make them go away.

"Okay," I agree quietly, much to Charlie's surprise. "I think you're right."

When he finally coaxes me back downstairs, I'm tense with embarrassment but nobody treats me any differently. I still apologize to the table for my freak-out, but everyone scrambles to shut the attempt down quickly. I eventually relax back into conversation, quietly thanking Emma for her diversion, and she shrugs and says she likes to dip into her Little headspace at random anyway. I can relate to that, and it helps me relax a bit more.

As the evening ends and people start leaving, I note that Ted's hanging around and resign myself to having to talk to him after all. I've avoided him for the afternoon, but I also know that he's my Daddy's best friend and not talking to him isn't going to help anything.

While Charlie talks to Spencer about arranging a playdate for me and Emma —who has slipped back into her Little headspace quite happily and is swinging Spencer's hand between them while sucking her thumb— Ted pulls me aside.

"I really am sorry for earlier, Ash," he says, and I blink at him.

Objectively, he's a handsome man. His brown hair is on its way to gray, and he fits the whole silver-fox vibe well, even if the 'silver' part is still developing. He's not as well built as Charlie or Josh, but he's still tall and broad shouldered, with a toned stomach and a butt that looks pretty damn good in those jeans of his. Not that I was looking, of course. His eyes are more amber than Josh's darker-brown orbs, and they're warm as he looks at me. It settles any of my remaining nerves.

"Why are you sorry? I'm the one who lost it and made a scene."

Ted shakes his head. "Without any warning, your boss wandered into a gathering where you were supposed to feel safe and relaxed. In your place, I'd have felt apprehensive as well." He reaches out and squeezes my shoulder. "But in some ways, this is a good thing. If you're ever in need of a safe space at work for any reason, come to my office. I can get you comfortable and call Charlie."

I can't help but well up with affection for him because it's such a thoughtful offer. I doubt I'll ever take him up on it, but just knowing that he'd do that for Charlie's sake tells me he's a good guy. "Thank you," I say, because there's not much else I can. "I appreciate that."

Then he hugs Charlie goodbye, and once Ted's gone, it's just the two of us left. I slip into my Little headspace a lot quicker than usual, and Daddy seems to understand.

"It's been a big day, huh, little lamb?" he asks, holding my hand as we climb the stairs.

"Yup," I agree, the stress and panic melting away the deeper I sink into my Little space.

"How does an early bath sound?"

I practically bounce on the balls of my feet. "Bath time!" I love bath time. There's something super relaxing about the combination of warm water and bubbles. Plus the splashing! Splashing makes everything better.

"Okay, bud, go potty and I'll get the water running."

I walk over to the toilet, not even blinking at the fact that Daddy's still in the bathroom, and then frown down at my jeans. Suddenly, the button and zipper seem like a lot of work. Biting my lip, I squirm.

"Ash, you okay?"

I don't even hesitate. "Help?"

In the back of my mind, I know this is another step forward for us. The toileting thing is not something either of us have discussed beyond my original questions. But after hearing Emma ask for help today, something's clicked and my curiosity's piqued. Worst case, this will feel too weird, and I won't ask again. But none of that's really at the forefront of my thoughts right now. Not with the running water going and the sudden desperate urge to pee.

"You sure?" Daddy asks, because he's obviously more cautious than I am. "Traffic light?"

"*Green.*" A little frustration bleeds into my voice. I'm wriggling now, trying to stave off an accident. "I need to go potty." The running bath water is all I can hear. "I need to go *bad*."

His hands quickly undo the button and zipper and tug down my constrictive training pants. The respite is instantaneous, but I'm not so

Little that I need him to help me aim right now. He chuckles and backs away at my sigh of relief as I evacuate my bladder.

That was too close.

A part of me feels far too curious about what might have happened if I had wet myself, but that's smothered quickly. Pushing that boundary is just a bit too far out of my comfort zone. Too close to my hard limits about humiliation, even while I'm Little. But it does kind of remind me of my curiosity about diapers…and *using* them.

After I wash my hands, Daddy helps pull my shoes and socks off, then my pants and underwear, and finally my shirt over my head. Then he guides me into the bath and laughs as I happily splash about. He's given me my favorite toy boat, and my duckie, and asks me questions about their adventures as they go plowing through the cascade of bubbles.

"Ready for me to wash you?"

The water's getting tepid, so I nod. I'm used to this now. He dunks a washcloth under the water, squeezes some body wash onto it, and glides it over my skin. Some nights this gets me hard, but I'm too Little to be distracted by the sensations tonight. Not even when he gets me to lift up so he can wash my dick and my bottom.

We washed my hair last night, so tonight there's no need to get my hair wet. Instead, after I'm rinsed off and Daddy declares me clean, he pulls the plug and helps me out, drying me thoroughly with the waiting fluffy towel.

When we get to my bedroom, he pulls out my pj's as usual; but instead of my training pants, he grabs a diaper.

My eyes go wide. Even though I'm Little, I'm still anxious about this. But, given that I came close to peeing all over the floor barely twenty minutes ago, I can see why this is the next logical step. Hell, my own thoughts drifted that way earlier, too.

"Traffic light?" Daddy says, watching my face very closely.

"Green…and a bit yellow?"

He smiles and pats the bed. "Up." I comply, my gaze drawn to the item still in his hand. "Wanna explain the yellow?"

Licking my lips, I force my Big thoughts forward. "It's…a big step," I manage to get out. "Like...am I going to feel silly?" But my cock is twitching, giving away my interest. There's no hiding that. "I... I don't have to use it, though, right?"

"No, not at all." Charlie's staring down at me with a huge smile. "But I'm so proud of you for being brave enough to try wearing it. And if you hate it, we'll take it off and add it to the hard limits list."

Somehow, I don't think I'm going to hate it, and we both seem to recognize that. But I still nod and settle back into my Little headspace. It only takes a few moments. "Okay, Daddy."

He beams back at me, then gently taps the side of my left thigh. "Bridge." Planting my feet on the mattress, I lift my hips up and hear the crinkle of the diaper as he gets it positioned under my butt. "Okay, down."

The padded surface beneath me is...curious. It's obviously thicker than my training pants, but not entirely unpleasant. Daddy's hands smooth a barrier cream over me in slow, sensual movements that, even Little, I really enjoy. I'm powdered next, and then Daddy brings the front of the diaper up between my legs and smooths it over my semihard cock, which *really* seems to like this new kind of stimulation. His lips quirk upward, but he doesn't mention it as he brings one adhesive tab across the side and front of the diaper, and then does the same on the other. He runs his fingers along the inseams, checking the fit and making sure the leak guards are secure. Not that I'm planning on testing them.

"How does that feel?" Daddy asks me.

I wriggle a little, testing out the odd weight of it. "Strange, but...soothing? Uh, reassuring, even?" As the assessment leaves my lips, it hits me. In an instant, I know that even though I'm not comfortable using a diaper right now, one day I will be.

That thought frightens me. It makes me feel weird and wrong: no grown-ass man should consider peeing in a diaper, right? Except it's an accepted part of the age-regression lifestyle, so it's a hang-up I have to get over...and despite the lingering concerns that it's abnormal, I really, really want to get past it.

"Okay, where'd you go? Those weren't Little thoughts."

Daddy's getting way too good at reading me nowadays.

With burning cheeks, I explain my thought process, and he reassures me that these feelings are normal, that there's no rush, but that he'll be more than happy to change me it when it happens.

When. Not *if*.

I add that to my mental list of "conversations I never thought I'd have with another man" and move on.

The pj's he's selected for me are actually a footie onesie with snaps along the inseams of my legs. I'm more than aware that they're there to make it easier for changing diapers, and that thought should not make my dick even harder, but it does. When I get up to model the ensemble for Daddy, I can feel myself waddling, unused to the shape and bulk of my newest Little accessory. It feels kind of ridiculous, but the besotted expression on Daddy's face is totally worth it.

Well, that and how much I secretly enjoy it, too.

Chapter Ten – Charlie

Ash in a diaper is easily the cutest thing I've ever seen. Ever. The fact that he wakes up hard as a rock the morning after I put the first one on him and tells me that he wants me to rub him to orgasm through the padding is hotter than it has any right being.

"You're not allowed to play with yourself when you wear one of these," I tell him, but my hand is over the hard bulge of his arousal anyway, and he's rocking up against it. "Not unless I say it's okay."

"Uh-huh," he answers, but I don't think he's actually listening to this new rule. "Daddy, it feels so good."

At least cleanup is going to be quick and easy, but I don't tell him that this is not how he should wet all his diapers. I know that's a line he's not ready to cross yet. I'm proud that he was able to voice that he's serious about trying one day, though. It's yet another big step forward for him.

"That's it, baby," I murmur, watching the rapture on his face. I give him a squeeze through the plastic and cotton, and he moans. Ash doesn't often wake up Little, or even Little adjacent, so I'm indulging the both of us right now. I'll rub one out in the shower after this. "Come for me, little lamb."

After a few more thrusts he does just that, crying out in pleasure before going limp and sated. I watch him, and a few moments later he crinkles his nose and squirms. It's adorable. "Ugh…"

"Need a change?"

He nods, and I walk him back into his room, laying out a towel before getting him to climb onto the bed. "We'll just get you into your big boy clothes after we take care of this, okay?"

"Training pants?"

"Always." Even under his suits, they've become his preference. They keep his Little urges content and remind him he has a Daddy who loves him enough to help him get dressed.

I don't make a big deal of stripping the diaper off or of wiping him down. By the time he's clean, he's Big and grinning at me. "I could get used to that being our new morning routine," he says playfully.

"Speak for yourself." I gesture at the tent in my boxers. "I need to do something about this before I can function."

Ash sits up, still naked, and scoots down the mattress until he's sitting on the edge of the bed and I'm standing between his spread legs. He grabs at my ass, pulling me closer, then mouths over the top of my erection through the cotton of my shorts. My hands card through his hair, more to steady myself than encourage him.

"How about I take care of Daddy now?"

It's not an offer I can refuse.

* * *

When we first retrieved Ash's car from the college parking structure, I'd had every intention of taking it to a mechanic for a proper evaluation. But he didn't use it for the first few weeks of living with me, and then when he got his job, it was too late. So it comes as no surprise to me when he calls me near the end of my shift one evening to complain that the thing won't start.

"It's probably just the battery," I tell him, even though I honestly know nothing about cars. "But I get off work in half an hour. Can you chill at the office until I can swing by to get you?"

"Yeah." He sighs heavily. "Stupid car. I wanted to get home early to cook you dinner. Switch things up a bit."

Awww. My boy's incredibly thoughtful.

"We can get takeout and crash on the couch," I reply. "And you can surprise me with your cooking skills another time."

From the driver's seat of our patrol car, Max makes kissy faces at me, teasing me like a good partner should. I give him the finger. Then a call comes in on the radio, and we're the closest to it. My heart sinks as I conclude that I'm not getting off work on time after all, and I have to relay the information to Ash.

"It's fine," he assures me, but there's a tension to his voice that I don't like. "I'll… I'll catch the bus home and there'll be something for you to heat up for dinner."

We say our goodbyes and I call Josh, asking him if he can go rescue my boyfriend from his broken-down piece-of-shit car. When Josh can't —because he's also stuck at work— I relent and call Ted, belatedly realizing that I should have just called him to start with.

I can hear the jangle of his keys as he agrees, and he keeps me on the line as we chat while he jogs down from the office to their allocated parking garage. "Okay," he eventually says, "I see him. I'll take him back to my place and you can pick him up on your way home, whenever that might be."

"You're a lifesaver, man," I say gratefully, then end the call. Max has an eyebrow raised, but we've just pulled up at the address we're supposed to be attending to and we need to focus on our jobs.

I'm just relieved to not have to worry about Ash.

* * *

By the time I make it to Ted's place, I'm exhausted. The call had been a domestic violence dispute that turned devastatingly ugly, and we had to take a billion witness statements, talk to paramedics, and alert child services because there was a kid involved. I'm beyond brittle by the time I ring Ted's doorbell.

When he answers the door and takes one look at me, he ushers me into his state-of-the-art kitchen and shoves a beer in my hand.

"Your boy is napping," he says, tilting his head toward his playroom. "Tuckered himself out with the train set."

I take a healthy swig from the bottle in my hand and hiss through my teeth as the liquid hits the back of my tongue. "I'm surprised he was comfortable enough to be Little around you," I say, then recall how deeply Little he was after the nearly disastrous get-together at my place. "Did he go to the bathroom before he crashed?"

"He did. And no, he didn't need my help."

It's a relief to have a friend who understands the lifestyle, and I feel a tiny bit guilty for being pleased that Ash is only comfortable enough to be that Little for me.

"Just a heads-up, though," Ted adds, and the tension is back in my shoulders. "He had a pretty shitty day at work. We've got auditors here, and they made a lot of demands on the admin staff."

All I want to do is storm into that playroom and wrap my boy in a hug. "Then his car wouldn't start, and I couldn't be there for him." Guilt eats away at me.

Ted's hand squeezes my shoulder. "None of that is your fault, and he knows it."

It still doesn't make me feel any better. "I'm his Daddy. I'm supposed to—"

"Charlie, you need to trust him as much as he trusts you. You're in a consenting adult relationship together. Remember that. Besides, Ash isn't a full-time Little, and it's pretty obvious that your job is also stressful right now."

Well. Damn. "I hate it when you're right."

"I'm always right."

I laugh, and more of the tension from today slips away. Then there are footfalls behind me and a sleepy "Charlie?"

"Hey, babe." I set down my beer and turn to face Ash. He's got a crease across his cheek from whatever he'd fallen asleep on, and his flop of curls is all mussed. Even though he's in his business pants and dress shirt, he's adorable. I open my arms, and he walks into my embrace, kissing my cheek.

"Long day?" he asks me, nuzzling into the short beard I've grown.

"Yeah. I hear yours was pretty crappy, too."

"Ugh, don't remind me." He pulls away to grin at Ted, and it makes me so happy to see them getting along. "Thanks for the rescue, by the way. And the nap. I needed both."

"I told you," Ted brushes him off, waving his own beer in the air between us, "any time. And if tomorrow's anything like today, head into my office and steal some Little time if you need to relax and regroup. I have a stash of coloring books and some blocks there."

What he doesn't divulge is that they're there because his last Little boyfriend used to visit him in the office, something Ted absolutely adored. I know he misses being someone's Daddy as much as I did, but it's not a topic I push him on. He'll move forward when he's ready.

"I appreciate that," Ash replies, and we all know that he's not going to take Ted up on the offer. But I'm happy to know that, in an emergency, my best friend is there for my boy.

"Should we get burgers on the way home?" Ash asks, and I take that as my cue to give Ted back his space.

"Burgers sound fantastic."

Chapter Eleven – Asher

Charlie and I have our first actual fight three months into our relationship. I don't even know what starts it. One second, I'm asking him for his opinion on buying a new car now that I've got some savings behind me, and the next we're yelling at each other.

And, okay, maybe I do know what started it.

Because he constantly wants to buy me things and I hate being a leech.

"You're not a leech, you're my boyfriend!" He's seething, and a part of me finds this amusing because instead of fighting with negativity, he's yelling nice things at me.

But apparently smirking at him only makes him angrier.

"What the fuck is funny about that?"

I try to explain, but I can't get the words out for laughing.

Then he's laughing too, and then we're kissing, and…fight? What fight?

"Watching you all angry is fucking hot," I tell him, my hands scrabbling at his belt as he pushes me up against the nearest wall. "You get all loud and shouty and dominating…"

That's also something to think about. Even a month ago, having him angry and shouting at me would have left me a sobbing, anxious wreck. But between therapy and the night at Ted's, something has changed.

We always agreed to be equals in our relationship, but after that night, Charlie started confiding in me a bit more when he was struggling. And that made me feel like I was supporting him just as much as he was supporting me.

"You like me all dominating," he acknowledges, his voice rough. Probably from all the shouting. Or because I've just wrapped my hand around his cock.

"I do," I tell him with a shit-eating grin. "But sometimes I like to be a bit dominating, too."

He chuckles and his voice turns indulgent. "Bossy, maybe."

"Yeah, okay, I'll take that."

Charlie grinds into me, trying to get my hand to pump him. Because I have zero self-restraint, I do. "You'll take my cock" is his retort.

"Mmm," I hum in agreement. Then I nibble at his earlobe, feeling Big and bold enough to whisper, "but maybe one day you'll take mine?"

I am not anticipating that he'll come in my hand over that, but he does, swearing all the way.

"Holy fuck, Charlie." I laugh, wiping my hand on his underwear because he's already come in them. "What the hell?"

I mean, sure, it's been a few days since the last time either of us came, but that was still unexpected.

Charlie's not usually one to blush, but there's a pink tinge to his cheeks. "You kind of hit on something I've been thinking about for a little while, and I really liked it."

My lips curve into a knowing grin. "You don't say…"

"Shut up." He laughs, shaking his head. "But yeah, the idea of you fucking me is" —he gestures down to his pants— "that much of a turn-on."

"I'll remember that." The promise is full of heat, and we seal it with a kiss that reminds me I'm still hard as steel.

"Let Daddy take care of that," Charlie says, dropping to his knees in front of me. And I do.

* * *

Playdates have become a consistent element of my life now. Josh is still my favorite companion, but I have to admit that I tend to go deeper into my Little headspace when I'm with Emma or, surprisingly, Matt. Part of me occasionally wonders just how ridiculous it would look to an outsider to watch a forty-something, tattooed, biker-looking dude and some preppy, college-aged guy crawling around on the floor wearing diapers and sucking on pacifiers. But in Charlie's house it feels natural, and he always seems fondly amused to watch us play.

Matteo doesn't have a Daddy, but Charlie told him he's happy to be his caregiver during these playdates, too, which means Matt can be comfortable letting go and falling into his Little space. That makes me so proud of my Daddy. Whether he's doing it for me, or just because he's a natural caregiver, it doesn't matter. It's still selfless, because he and Matt don't have the sort of bond that he and I do, but he still kisses Matt's boo-boos, cuts up his meals, and cuddles him on his other side during story time.

"Your Daddy's the best," Matt says as we stack blocks in the corner of the living room.

I look over and smile at Charlie, because I know he's listening, even if he's pretending to read a grown-up book. "Yeah, he is."

"You're lucky," Matt replies, only now he seems sad. His voice goes all tight and crackly. "I miss my Daddy."

Uh-oh. I'm not good with tears. Especially not when I'm Little. I pat Matt's big back and try to comfort him. "You'll find a new Daddy," I say. Then I add, in case it's not already clear, "But not mine."

Charlie snorts and I look up again to frown at him. He's got his nose back in that book.

Hmm.

Matt's studying the yellow block in his hand like it has all the answers to life's problems. "I know. But if I could have a Daddy, I'd want one as nice as yours."

"I'm very lucky," I agree. I'm not super deep in Little space today, and I'm glad because I feel like Matt needs someone to talk to. Where I'm at right now seems to be just right. "Have you gone looking for a new Daddy?"

Mine just fell into my lap (or, rather, I guess I fell into his) but I know there are groups online, or munches, and The Grove apparently holds 'adoption' nights for unattached littles and caregivers to meet and mingle and play.

"I tried." Matt sighs and topples the tower we were building. "The last Daddy I met said I was too big and too old to be Little." He looks at the rug, his voice sounding smaller and more vulnerable than I've ever heard it before. Hurt seems to radiate from him. "They all do."

"Assholes."

Daddy pipes up from the couch, "Language, Ash."

Whoops.

Still, I'm kind of incensed right now; so instead of heeding the warning, I turn back to Matt. In my rage, I've slipped further out of my Little space, though I'm still not Big. Not with Matt still Little, too. "No, seriously, fuck that guy. Fuck them all."

"Asher!" Daddy's standing up now with his arms folded and a stern look on his face.

I pout. "But, Daddy…"

"What are the rules?" He holds firm.

Matt's looking between us with wide eyes because not many people get to hear Daddy's cranky voice. And usually, I don't push my luck with him. The last time was over not eating my peas —because, *eww, peas*— and I'd had to stand in the corner for five minutes. But this time, I'm too frustrated over the pain some random douche-canoe has caused my friend.

Ignoring Daddy, I turn back to Matt. "All those guys are fuckheads, and they're *wrong*."

"You've been warned, bud." Daddy's pulling me to my feet and marching me to the naughty corner. "*Ten* minutes."

I had cried over the pea thing, sniffling in the corner because I'd been bratty and I knew it. But this? Nope. I'm in the right.

I'm fidgeting after five minutes, but I'm not even close to feeling sorry for swearing.

At the ten-minute mark, when Daddy comes to ask me if I've thought about what I've done, I nod. But instead of apologizing like he expects, I fold my arms across my chest and say, "I'm not taking it back. The guys who said that to Matt can kiss my ass."

I'm pretty sure he looks amused for a moment —even a little proud— but then he schools his expression and says, "You'll be writing lines if you're not careful, Ash."

I roll my eyes. That's not going to change anything, and we both know it.

"Asher." He sighs heavily, and now I start to wonder if maybe I shouldn't have been quite so bratty about it. "Whether I agree with your assessment or not, the rule is no swearing when you're Little."

Uh-oh. He's right.

"It's about behavior and limits. And I'm disappointed that you blatantly ignored me and continued to do the wrong thing. That sort of behavior isn't appropriate for little boys, and you shouldn't have said those words to Matteo while he was also Little, even if they weren't directed at him."

My brain is stuck on one word. *Disappointed? Oh no.*

Guilt begins to churn in my gut. He's never been disappointed in me. It hurts.

"Do you understand? I'm not happy with the way you chose to behave or the fact that you intentionally ignored me when I reminded you of the rules. You were deliberately naughty."

My sinuses sting with impending tears and my throat goes tight. I hate disappointing Daddy. Hate it. I want him to love me. I want him to be proud of me. My bottom lip quivers. I can't look him in the eye. The word "disappointed" is still echoing around my head.

"Oh, baby," he says softly, and then I lose it, flinging my arms around his neck and apologizing through heaving, messy sobs. It's been a long time since I last lost it like this.

When I tell him that I'm sorry for being a disappointment, he shakes his head next to mine. "That was a poor choice of words on my part, baby. *You* will never be a disappointment. The choices you made to break the rules and ignore me? Yeah. But *never* you." He holds me and rubs my back until I'm calm, and then surprises me by adding, "I'm sorry if I wasn't clear about why I was disciplining you, little lamb. And we'll talk about that properly when you're Big."

Communication is a big thing for Charlie. We ended up adding it as an afterthought to the honesty rule. It's important to him that we learn from any of these little struggles as we go, and I love how seriously he takes that — how seriously he takes *us*, whether I'm Little or big or somewhere in between.

* * *

Another addendum to the honesty rule? Lying by omission or deflection is still lying.

This isn't something we stumble upon through play. It's an issue that builds because I still find it difficult to voice the things I'm interested in trying. Like bottles. Charlie made it clear at the very beginning that he's waiting on me to set the pace for new experiences, and I appreciate that so much…but sometimes I just want him to make the decision for me.

We're wandering through Walmart the day after Matt's playdate. As we coast down the baby aisle Charlie asks, as he always does, if there's anything here I want. He watches me closely as my gaze flits to the bottles and then away.

I shrug. "I'm good."

He stops the cart and gives me *the look*. My dick stirs in my jeans because it's such a Daddy expression and it's fucking hot. When he pairs it with a low, warning-laden "Asher…" I need to shift my stance.

"I didn't ask if you were good," he adds, still not moving us further along the store. "I asked if there's anything you want."

My therapist, an awesome woman who has an intimate understanding of BDSM lifestyles, has been working with me to understand that there's nothing shameful in my kinks or interests. I'm a consenting adult with a supportive partner who wants all the same things I do. My fears and hang-ups, while totally normal, are just that: internal issues. Things I need to work through.

But I'm still struck by embarrassment as I stand here under the store's fluorescent lighting, even though there's nobody else in the aisle but Charlie and me.

Charlie's expression softens and he reaches for my hand, squeezing it. "You're my big, brave boy, remember. And I can't be the Daddy you need unless I know *what* you need."

His words help. This affirmation that he wants these things, too, but that he won't push for things that make me uncomfortable. As Ted says, it's a partnership. When I'm Little, I still have responsibilities in that role. Charlie's job is to take care of me, and mine is to let him know my needs. He's not a mind reader, even if sometimes I feel like that's what he's doing. I've just been good at giving him nonverbal cues.

"I…" I take a deep breath, then eye the bottles again. "Can we give bottles a try?"

Charlie's eyes light up, and he nods. "I have some at home," he informs me, and I'm not surprised. He squeezes my hand again. "What about a new toy?"

"You don't need to bribe me," I tease, but I reach for a set of bath paints that have grabbed my eye and he laughs, setting them in the cart and kissing the top of my head.

"It's a reward for being so brave."

I might roll my eyes, but the praise warms me from the inside. And later that afternoon, when I've been diapered and am snuggled up against Daddy on the couch, sucking milk through a bottle while he reads me a story before naptime, I feel like being brave is definitely worth it.

Chapter Twelve – Charlie

I can't stop thinking about Asher fucking me. We've spoken about it once —when I embarrassingly blew my load at the mere mention of it happening— but he hasn't brought it up again, and I don't want to push him.

Our sex life is definitely not lacking. We've been together almost four months now, and he's still like the freaking Energizer Bunny. But tonight, as we're rolling around the big king-size bed in the primary suite, playfully wrestling while we nip and tease with our mouths, I can't get the idea out of my head.

Our cocks slide against each other, drawing moans from each of us, and I give in and reach for the bedside table. It's another game we play: who's going to break and beg first. From where he's sucking a hickey into my clavicle, Ash chuckles.

"I knew it'd be you," he teases, then bites at my pec, knowing that it drives me wild when he gets a bit rough.

The thing about this game? Nobody ever loses.

I laugh and grind my erection into him, smearing precum over his belly. "You cheated—you've been sending me sexy messages and making me hard all day." Thankfully, Max is a good enough partner not to say anything.

"Sorry not sorry." Ash squeezes my ass.

That's as good a cue as any for me to blurt, "So are you ever going to live up to your promise and fuck me?"

He freezes for a moment, then reaches for my bearded jaw so he can look me in the eye, all traces of playfulness gone. He's entirely an adult in this moment, and even though I adore all sides of him, this sharp, heated stare is incredibly sexy. "Are you sure you want that?"

I realize now that I haven't been fair to him. I've been reminding him over and over that if there's something he needs, he has to tell me…but I haven't given him the same courtesy in response.

"Ash," I tell him, my heart hammering in my chest, "I love you." He inhales sharply. We've danced around those words and have never said them. "I've loved you since… God, I think since I met you." I can't pinpoint the moment, but I started falling hard from the second I locked eyes on his beautiful hazel pair. "There's nothing I want more right now than to give you all of me and have all of you in return."

"I love you, too," he whispers, blinking back tears. It's a huge deal for him —for us— and I wait for him to process this new development.

He peppers kisses over my beard and cheeks before softly connecting our lips, slowly moving our tongues together as he lifts his hips up and rocks into me. We're both still hard and leaking, and the kiss goes from languorous to hot and heavy before too long.

When we part for air, his hands are back on my ass. "I've never topped…" he confesses. "I won't last. Especially bare."

"It'll be perfect because it's you," I insist. "We don't need to set any world records tonight. Or ever."

"But I want it to be good for you and—"

"Baby, it will be." Then, for good measure I repeat, "Because. It's. You."

To get him out of his head, I kiss him again until the tension melts away from his shoulders. Then I roll us so I'm on my back and he's on top of me, and I press the bottle of lube I grabbed earlier into his hand. After sliding a pillow beneath my hips, Ash slicks his fingers and teases my hole with light, tentative touches at first, until I'm begging and bearing down on his finger.

It's not long before he's scissoring two inside me, and I have to breathe through the stretch and the burn. It's been a while —a long, long while—since I bottomed, but I need this. Need him. When the pain starts to ebb and give way to pleasure, my babbled begging starts up again and Ash smiles into the kiss he places on my lips.

"Can you take a third?"

"I'm gonna need to if you're going to fit," I answer, gasping as he crooks his fingers and brushes my prostate. "Jesus, Ash. Baby, more of that..."

He gives me exactly what I asked for, adds extra lube and then a third finger. By the time he deems me ready, I'm on the edge of coming. This might be his first time topping, but he clearly understands from experience what makes for enjoyable prep. Then he lubes his neglected cock up and strokes it a few times, putting on a show just for me, before notching the head at my entrance. He stares down at me with laser focus as he inches in. Once he's made it past the tight ring of muscles and I've breathed through the additional burn, he sinks inside me slowly with short, smooth thrusts of his hips.

"You're so fucking tight and hot," he says through gritted teeth. "Daddy... *fuck...*" He bottoms out and stills, breathing hard. "You're amazing." He leans down, with his hands planted on the mattress on either side of my shoulders, and kisses my chest, then asks, "You okay?"

"Uh-huh," I answer, feeling full and loved and a little overwhelmed. "I'm good. Just...move when you're ready." I want to demand that he start moving, but he's still my boy and I'm not forcing him if he needs more time.

Above me, Ash sets his jaw and starts rocking his hips languidly.

It feels so fucking good.

"Charlie..." He exhales after a few thrusts. "*Daddy*, I'm already so close..." He's still moving, though, and he shifts his angle experimentally and I see stars for a moment as he grazes that magical spot inside me.

"Do that again and I'll beat you there," I growl out, grabbing his hips and fucking up onto him, trying to find that angle again.

It takes a little maneuvering, but when he gets it I shout, opening my eyes again to catch him grinning at me.

Then he bends and we kiss sloppily.

"Fuck, I love this," he says against my mouth, our panting breaths mingling. "I love you. So much."

"Me too," I murmur, before he rests his weight on one elbow to reach between us and pump my cock in time with his movements. "Oh, Ash, baby, yes…"

He speeds up and we're both close, our breathing ragged, sweat slicking our skin. When his cock brushes my prostate again, I don't even have time to warn him before I'm coming hard over our abdomens and his hand, which is milking rope after rope of cum from me.

I'm still riding the wave of pleasure when I realize that my orgasm has pulled him over the edge with me, his hips jerking. I feel the heat of his release inside me, dribbling out of my ass when he pulls out as gently as he can. It's messy, and sticky, and cooling…and absolutely perfect.

"Shower?" he asks, having flopped down on the mattress beside me to catch his breath.

I turn my head, feeling boneless and sleepy, and kiss his shoulder. "Definitely."

And, when we get out of the shower and he starts slipping into his Little headspace, I'm once again overwhelmed by just how perfect he is for me.

* * *

I call my parents to tell them all about Asher the next day. It's something I've been putting off because Mom can be…*a lot.* I know I've gotten my caregiver tendencies from her, but she's loud and excitable and will probably try to smother Ash with adoration. Don't get me wrong: he deserves all the love in the world. But he's also kind of skittish, and my mother might just scare him off.

Still, we've officially exchanged I-love-yous now, and I have no reason to hide him from my family. In fact, I want to show him off, this beautiful man of mine.

When Mom picks up the phone, I can't help but smile at her infectious joy. "Well, if it isn't my firstborn," she answers, and I can picture the shit-eating grin on her face. "You finally remembered that you have parents, huh?"

"I texted you last week." I sigh dramatically, deliberately poking the bear.

"You sent a thumbs up when I texted to say hi."

"I can move on to GIFs instead of emojis if you'd like?"

"That does feel much more personalized."

I laugh and so does she, and I do have to acknowledge that I miss her, even if she does get a little suffocating sometimes. My dad's the calming influence, but he generally lets her do what she wants because it's easier and he likes to indulge her. Now that I've got Ash in my life, I can understand that more.

"So, how much money do you need?" Mom jokes. "Or do we finally need to bail you out of jail?"

"You're hilarious, Mom," I deadpan, and I lean back in my desk chair at the station. I've finished my shift, but I want to have this conversation where Ash can't hear. Not because I have anything to hide from him, but because it's a private moment for me. "How's that career in stand-up comedy working out for you?"

"Getting defensive?" she teases back. We honestly could do this all day. She snickers. "Oh, I know, this is finally the Oops-my-girlfriend-is-pregnant call! Tell me, how far along is she?"

I don't miss a beat, not taking the bait and instead turning it on her. "Just wait; Axel's gonna give you that call one day for sure."

Her gasp is dramatic, and I can imagine her pressing a hand to her chest, clutching at imaginary pearls. My mom's a bit of a drama queen. "You wash your mouth out with soap. My baby's a responsible boy."

I can't resist. "...For now." He's only eighteen. He's got time to prove her wrong.

"I'll tell him that his big brother has zero faith in him."

"Oh, don't worry; I text him that on a daily basis. Gotta keep his ego in check."

We both know that's a lie. I adore my youngest sibling. Mom's right: he can do no wrong.

"You're a terror," she accuses with another laugh. "Now, are you actually going to tell your poor, old mother why you called out of the blue, or do I have to keep guessing?"

I take a steadying breath, allowing the din of the station to fade into the background. Phones ringing, people talking, the guy at the desk to my left slurping his sludgy station-brew coffee…it all ceases to exist. "I'm in love, Mom. His name's Asher, we've been together for a few months…and I'm crazy about him."

It feels so good to say it out loud. Especially to my mother. I joke about how insane she makes me, but she's honestly the person whose opinion matters most to me. When I was growing up, she was my rock. Keeping Ash from her, and from the rest of my family, feels wrong on so many levels.

I know I should have said something earlier, but there was a part of me that worried it might not work out…and then life got busy, and I didn't prioritize telling them. That makes me feel guilty. But, to be fair, I've never done this before. I've never been serious enough with anyone to feel like I needed to tell them. Is four months too late? Not early enough?

What's done is done now, but…maybe I should have called sooner.

In the silence that follows my blurted confession, I check the screen of my phone to make sure the call is still connected. Then I start to get anxious. "Mom?"

"Oh, Charlie." She sniffles, which takes me completely by surprise. "I'm so happy for you."

Relief sweeps through me and my shoulders sag.

Then the torrent of questions comes down the line. Mom's voice escalates in pitch and speed as her excitement ramps up. "When can we meet him? Dinner tonight? Tomorrow? You can bring him over and I'll take care of everything. What's his favorite food? Does he have any allergies?"

Midway through her stream-of-consciousness style interrogation, I try to interrupt. "Mom…"

She steamrolls right over me. "Oh, would it be easier for your dad and I to come to you? You're probably tired from working so hard. Asher, that's such a sweet name. Tell me everything about him."

"Mom…"

"Is he younger than you? You've always liked them a bit younger, haven't you? Not that that's a problem. As long as you're both consenting adults and you're being safe, you know Dad and I won't judge you—"

"Jesus Christ, Mom." I facepalm and wonder why I decided to make this call in public. I know that nobody else can hear her, but I'm limited by how I can respond. "*Stop*. Just…stop."

I can understand her enthusiasm, though. This is the first time since high school that I've directly told her about one of my relationships. She's bound to know how serious it is for that reason alone. Additionally, she's only ever wanted her kids to be as disgustingly happy as she and Dad are. The funny thing is, I think Ash and I are, and I can see us staying that way. I've never thought that before. Not about my previous relationships, I mean. But with Ash, I can imagine forever with him. It should scare me, but it doesn't.

To be honest, it thrills me that my mom is as excited about my news as I am, even if I don't ramble on.

Not out loud, anyway.

"You're going to introduce us soon, right?"

"Of course, but…"

"But?! I know you're not ashamed of your mother, Charles Franklin Walker." I can picture her narrowing her eyes at me, and it makes me squirm even though she's a forty-five-minute drive away.

"Oh, I got the full name treatment." I try to verbally sidestep, not having thought this entire plan through. Because of course Mom's not going to accept the news that I've fallen in love without demanding to meet Ash instantly.

"*Charlie*." She's got her Mom voice down pat. It's very Domme. I'm pretty sure it's where I learned to sound like such a stern Daddy.

"Okay, so, here's the thing…" I begin, hoping that I can calm her down so

I can prepare Ash for the insanity that is my family. "Ash has been through a lot, and he's a bit…anxious about meeting new people. I'd like to ease him into the concept of meeting you guys."

"Ease him in?" Mom sounds insulted. "We're not going to mob the poor boy."

I remember exactly how she handled meeting my first boyfriend, and I scoff. "You can come on a bit strong at first is all I'm saying."

It takes a lot of convincing, but she eventually promises to wait until I'm ready to introduce them to the man I've fallen in love with. I just hope that she'll keep that promise. You never know with my mom, and it's best to be prepared for anything.

I'll broach the subject with Ash soon, but for now I'm content with having him to myself.

Chapter Thirteen – Asher

"Asher?" I freeze at the voice behind me. It's not one I thought I'd hear again, and it's not one I ever wanted to, either.

It's a Saturday, but Charlie and Josh are both working, so I decided to go shopping, formulating a plan in my head to surprise Charlie by cooking him dinner for once. The last time I'd wanted to do this, my car broke down. Maybe these are all signs from the universe that cooking for my Daddy is not in the cards for me.

"Asher." The voice is getting closer and it's just as gruff and unhappy as the last time I heard it. "Don't ignore me."

The urge to slip into my Little headspace to avoid the confrontation and stress is strong, but in this situation it'll only make things worse. With a deep breath, I square my shoulders and turn to face the person whose voice I least want to hear.

"Dad." I address him simply. No hello. No fake smile. No indication that I have any actual interest in talking to him. But I don't sound upset, either, which is something.

At least we're in public. He won't make a scene in public.

I hope.

He stops a few feet away from me, not the towering, fearsome figure from my memories any longer. He's still taller than me, still imposing and larger than life, but he doesn't inspire terror in me now. Maybe because he doesn't have any power over me. He can't threaten the roof over my head or my college degree anymore.

Dad looks me up and down with a sneer. "You landed on your feet, then?"

It shouldn't hurt. It shouldn't. But the implication that he was hoping that I wouldn't recover eats away at me. What kind of parent wants their kid to suffer? What did he hope would happen to me when he kicked me out? Actually, no, I don't want to know.

Folding my arms across my chest, I nod curtly. "I did." I refuse to give him any information. He's not going to learn about Charlie, or the friends I've made, or the job I've landed, or the plans I have to finish my degree after all.

"You disgust me," Dad says, leaning in to deliver the assessment. He's repeating some of the awful things he said the day he unknowingly set me free, and while the words hurt, I'm surprised that the voice in my head which once agreed with him is telling me he's wrong. Leaning closer to me, he spits out, "How can you stand there and look so proud of yourself? It's bad enough you were queer," he sneers the word like a slur, "but the freaky shit is beyond the pale. They should lock you up for that pedophile crap."

I feel myself blanch, but before I can refute him, I'm interrupted by a much more welcome voice.

"Ash." A large, tattooed arm slings around my shoulders and I sag into Matt's side. He's come out of nowhere, but I'm beyond relieved to have the support. I turn my head and crane my neck. He's looking down at me with concern and his phone is in his hand. "Is this guy giving you grief? Should I call Charlie?" He eyes my dad warily. "You know, your cop boyfriend?"

I'm guessing he was close enough to catch at least the tail end of my father's vitriol. A part of me curls in on itself. The thought of Matt hearing my father talk to me that way is beyond embarrassing. I feel genuine shame coursing through my veins.

"Fuck off," Dad hisses, not seeming to care that Matt's built like a linebacker and could probably lay him out with one punch. He also seems to have ignored the implicit threat of my dating a cop. The asshole always did think he was above the law. "This is between me and my son."

Matt's arm tenses around my shoulders and I know the jigsaw puzzle that is me and my anxiety issues is all falling into place for him.

But it's me that speaks, and I put this sudden burst of confidence down to my therapy and Charlie. "I stopped being your son when you kicked me out and left me homeless and alone." It feels so good to get this closure. Like a weight is being lifted from my shoulders. The albatross around my neck removed. And because I'm giddy and can't help myself from stirring the pot, I lean forward conspiratorially and tell him, "But because you did that, I found my Daddy and I've never been happier. So, really, maybe I should thank you for that. You did me a solid."

I offer him a sharp, shit-eating grin before I turn away, leaving him red-faced and sputtering, and Matt chortles at my side. "Holy shit, dude." He gives me an excited little shake, even though I'm starting to tremble as the shock of what the fuck I just did sets in. "That was incredible!"

My answering smile feels tremulous, but I'm aware that I've just had some sort of breakthrough. I mean, I just told the bigot that booted me out of my house that I have a Daddy. I said it in public. With pride. And I meant everything I said.

"Charlie's going to be so proud of you."

Except Daddy's also going to be worried. He's going to hate that I goaded my father. That I wasn't the bigger man, and that I didn't just walk away. I still let Dad's crap get under my skin, and who knows what that's going to do to my recovery from the trauma. Is it going to set me back? Are the nightmares —which have become few and far between— going to start back up again?

It's too late to voice any of this, though, because Matt's already typed out a text to Charlie. He's probably concerned that I've gone a little catatonic beside him. And though he's a strong, capable man when he's Big, he still doesn't have the Daddy vibes I need to settle my burst of anxiety.

"Where've you parked?" he asks me after what I assume is a reply from Charlie.

I rally enough to answer, "I caught the bus." I still haven't bought a new car, and I didn't want to risk mine dying again. "I was only going to buy a few things."

He taps away on his phone screen again, then slides it into his pocket and takes me to his car. He drives a white, late-model sedan, and I have a private laugh that it's not a motorcycle. His look screams "biker," but I know better than anyone not to stereotype. It's only as I'm buckling myself in that I start to come back to reality.

"Didn't you need to buy anything?"

Matt shakes his head. "Nothin' that can't wait."

I accept his words at face value, acknowledging that I'd do the same for him in a heartbeat, and let him drive me home. He hangs around and we talk about everything and nothing —how our fantasy football leagues are doing, our thoughts on the most recent NHL draft, who the best character on *Once Upon A Time* was— and by the time Charlie walks through the door, I'm pretty much back to my usual self.

Charlie claps Matt on the back and thanks him as he goes to leave, and I hug him and do the same. He shrugs our thanks off with a sheepish grin and leaves, and once again I find myself musing on how lucky I am to have stumbled into a life with these people. Charlie and his friends have become my found family. And having just faced the last of my biological family, I know that the grass is definitely greener on this side of the fence.

"You okay, baby?" Charlie asks me once he's closed the door. He's holding my face in his hands and looking me over as though I'd gotten into a physical fight.

I smile brightly at him. "I've never been better."

It's not even a lie.

* * *

It turns out that getting closure with my father was something I desperately needed. It was kind of like I had to physically face my fears, and once I did, all that self-loathing and those fears of being abnormal and embarrassed about what I wanted started to fall away faster.

It wasn't instantaneous, not by a long shot. But after publicly telling my asshole father that I'd found a Daddy, it's been easier with each passing day to tell Charlie when I need something.

"Daddy, I need cuddles." "Daddy, I want a bottle." "Daddy, play blocks with me." "Daddy, help me potty." "Daddy, I'm horny."

Okay, so that last one has always come pretty easily to me.

But every time I vocalize my needs, I watch Daddy's eyes light up and he tells me I'm a good boy. Nothing feels better than that. We even start going out to The Grove on Littles' Nights.

The club turns out to be nothing like the dingy, oppressive space I'd imagined. Instead, it's a huge warehouse space on the edge of the city, heading into the industrial part of town. It's unassuming from the outside, with its entrance on the side of the building: a plain black door with an olive tree imprinted on it.

The room we enter when we step inside is bright and kind of bland. It reminds me of the waiting room at my childhood dentist's office. There's a pretty woman working the counter, and she looks like a sexy librarian in her pencil skirt, blouse, and cat-eye glasses.

Charlie's a member and she greets him by name, handing over a selection of colored paper wristbands which he fastens to his right wrist. Then she turns to me.

"And you must be Ash," she says cheerily. "Your Daddy called to book you for tonight's session. Has he run through the rules?"

I nod because Charlie has been very thorough about the club's nondisclosure agreement, the house safe word (monitored electronically and by the moderators in each room), the whole "flagging" thing (hence his wristbands) and the sorts of things to expect once we're inside. I'm nervous but excited.

She beams and asks me to sign the NDA she's prepared. When Charlie called ahead to book us for the event, he gave all of my details ahead of time, so I don't need to fill in a temporary membership application for the night — though I do have to sign it, and the indemnity waivers, too. I hand over my ID and she passes me my wristbands to indicate my preferences.

Charlie helps me put them on. After she makes sure I know the house safe word ("turmeric"), she sends us through the two large metal doors on the far side of the room.

Once we pass through those, my jaw drops.

There must be significant soundproofing around the building, because the bass and general wave of sound from the music pumping into the large, open nightclub space in front of us is intense. There's a bar and a dance floor and dimly lit booths lining the walls. There's also an elevated stage at the far end of the space, and Charlie's already told me that they host scenes and demonstrations here.

There's a wide hallway that surrounds the club space, traveling around the entire building. It leads to the locker rooms and bathrooms, as well as the back staircase and elevators to the second floor, which is host to the playrooms. That's where we're heading.

We ride the elevator to the second floor, and it feels like a hotel up here. Two parallel hallways greet us, and the one we walk down is lined with doors to rooms Charlie says are themed playrooms. The other hallway is apparently the same. These spaces can be booked for specific scenes, and Charlie points out a couple as we walk past. There's a classroom, a corporate office and boardroom, and a sauna. Then there's the space we want: the littles' playroom.

When we walk in, I blink. It's a massive, brightly lit space, full of color and toys and everything a Little could want. It looks like it runs the entire width of the warehouse building and takes up at least a quarter of the top floor.

"Holy shit," I breathe, staring with wide eyes as the door closes behind us. "Is that a bouncy castle?"

It's at the far end of the space, taking up the bulk of the end of the room from ceiling to floor. It looks like it can only hold three or four adults comfortably at a time, but it's definitely a freaking bouncy castle.

"Yep," Charlie acknowledges. "Wanna bounce?"

I itch to, but I shake my head. Tonight, I'm not comfortable being Little. I just want to see what this place is all about. I look around a bit more.

Couches line the wall to my left, presumably for Mommies and Daddies who want to watch their littles play. In the middle of the carpeted floor, there are mats and rugs and buckets of toys. To my right, there's a massive train set, beanbags, and brightly colored tables laden with paints and crayons and markers. It's like a giant day care center…with a bouncy castle.

"There's a changing room across the hall," Charlie says. "Did you want to see that, too?"

I shake my head again. "I'm imagining it's like a giant nursery? Changing tables and all that jazz?"

"Pretty much."

"Good to know."

We're the first to arrive tonight, and I'm not wearing my Little clothes. I just wanted to see what the place was like. Charlie doesn't push me, and we settle into a corner as a group of littles and their caregivers enter the room, laughing and chatting.

For this first time, I'm too shy to do more than sit in a corner and watch the other littles play and participate in the evening's organized activities.

On the second Littles' Night we attend, I ask Daddy to dress me in my training pants, a onesie, and some play shorts. I join Josh, Matt, and Emma in some finger painting (which leads to an awesome bath time experience later that night because I *accidentally* manage to get paint *everywhere*).

On the third visit, I'm in another onesie, this time wearing a diaper I'm still not ready to use; but I'm playing with littles I've never met, and interacting with Mommies and Daddies that aren't Charlie or his friends.

This is when I finally realize that there is nothing shameful in my kinks. Most people have *something* that makes them tick, and to be ashamed of what I share with Charlie —with my Daddy— is unfair to him and to our relationship. I'm still not going to walk down the street broadcasting our lifestyle, but I no longer panic at the thought of someone discovering that I'm kinky, although the kink I'm into is sometimes looked down on even by others in the BDSM community, which I think is ridiculous.

When I see her next, my therapist says this is a huge breakthrough for me, and I suppose she's right. This is who I am, and I'm happy to embrace it.

So it's no surprise that, the next time Daddy has Ted and Chance over for beers and grown-up time, I'm beyond comfortable being Little. I'm kind of disappointed that Spencer and Emma couldn't make it, and that Josh and Matt had other plans, but I'm not disappointed enough to hide this part of me from the others. It's not like it's the first time they've seen me in Little space, anyway. It's become more and more regular, especially when they tend to visit at random. The fact that they're involved in the lifestyle helps, too.

Daddy and his friends are on the couch talking while I'm sprawled on my stomach on the play mat in front of them, kicking my socked feet back and forth in the air behind me. I'm thoroughly entertained by the water mat Ted bought me on a whim. It's like finger painting without the mess, and I'm mesmerized by it. I lose myself in play, and it's the deepest I've *ever* been into my Little space, to the point where I don't even notice just how far gone I am. It's glorious. It feels like complete freedom from my adult responsibilities and worries. I play, and I giggle, and I've tuned out everything Daddy and his friends are saying.

Every so often, one of them asks me to show them my latest picture, or joins me to play with a different toy for a while, or hands me a snack or my sippy cup; but they're all just as content to let me float in my happy space as I am to do it. It's a magical afternoon.

I'm so far into Little space that I don't even notice how badly I need to pee until I sit up. Lying on my stomach has dulled the urge and distracted me from needing to potty, but as soon as I'm vertical, gravity's not my friend. I'm on my knees, but as soon as I move one leg out to try to stand, my bladder gives way a bit.

I go straight back to my knees and bite my lip.

I'm diapered, as I happen to be more often than not when I'm in my Little space nowadays, but up to this point it's been a comfort thing. And that's probably part of how I got so far into Little space this time, really. I've let go and embraced my Little urges completely because I felt safe and relaxed.

Besides, Daddy's made it clear that he's got no issues when I do wet my diaper, or even if I have accidents in my training pants — I know that's *never* going to happen, because the thought of deliberately pushing that envelope when I'm a bigger Boy doesn't appeal; however, I've been good with the status quo. I'll admit that I have been curious to the point where we've both started saying "when" I use my diaper, not "if", but I've still never been in the right headspace to just let go and try.

Today, though, I've let myself get there…and it's not scary.

I know I could try and crawl to the bathroom, but I decide not to. I decide to just let go. And when it happens, I'm not hit with the panic or feeling of wrongness that I'd expected this moment would bring.

Instead, aside from the relief I feel as my bladder empties into the absorbent material, I feel the strangest surge of absolute freedom and a tiny bit of curious excitement. Maybe there is a mild bit of humiliation kink somewhere deep in my psyche, too. I know public humiliation isn't my thing, but maybe a bit of embarrassment in front of my Daddy does give me a thrill after all. Who knows? Either way, I know that Daddy's got this. He's going to change me, and it's going to be just another thing we do together. I trust him completely.

Was I planning on having this revelation with two other Daddies in the same room? No. But I'm not worried.

"Hey little lamb." Daddy's voice startles me because it's much closer than where he's been sitting on the couch. He's crouching beside me, his head tilted to the side, his blue eyes warm but cautious. "You okay? You've been sitting here really still for a minute."

I turn into him, hiding my face in his neck. "Daddy…" I whine because the situation in my diaper is now weighty, a bit damp, and becoming noticeably uncomfortable.

He rubs my back. "What's wrong, baby?"

Even though I know he's not going to react badly, the part of my brain that's still an adult knows that we haven't discussed this recently. The last time we did, I said I'd let him know when I felt ready.

I've blown past giving him the heads-up that it was potentially going to happen, haven't been able to warn him that I was ready today. And as my headspace clears with that knowledge, a tiny bit of embarrassment sneaks in after all. Maybe I should have waited until it was just the two of us? Too late now.

Burrowing my face farther into him and feeling my cheeks burn, I whisper, "I… Daddy, I… I *wet*."

Daddy doesn't miss a beat, but I imagine he's a little surprised —I'm sure he didn't think this would happen with company around, either— and his hand sneaks between us to pat the front of my diaper through the onesie. It's not a sexual touch, but I feel a short thrill of some convoluted, bubbly feeling at the action anyway.

"So you are," he observes, and I can hear him smiling. "You're such a good boy for telling me." Then he's pulling me to my feet and telling the others we'll be back in a minute.

Ted and Chance are both Daddies, too, and neither even blinks at the situation. It's perfectly normal to them, and my momentary embarrassment fades.

This is when I discover that walking in a heavy, wet diaper is not fun. I'm waddling worse than usual, and the sensation against my skin is not pleasant. Climbing the stairs is even worse, and I cringe my way through it.

Daddy spreads a towel out on the bed in my little boy room and then *lifts me* onto it, gently arranging me onto my back. That's new, too, but I kind of love the casual display of his strength, and the way it seems to affirm my littleness. "Baby, I'm so, *so* proud of you," Daddy tells me as he undoes the snaps holding the short legs of my onesie together. "I know this was a huge deal for you, and I love that you trust me so much to explore it."

And I do. I trust him implicitly. But I'm still feeling too Little to express that properly. All I can do is smile, wriggle my hips, and say, "Change now?"

The blinding smile he shoots me in return takes away any vestiges of awkwardness.

Yeah, I think as I lie back and Daddy wipes and changes me with efficiency, as though we've been doing this all along. *Daddy's got this.*

* * *

"Little lamb." Daddy kisses my neck after bath time, making me giggle. I'm wrapped in my towel, nice and dry, but his hands are still traveling over my body. "You were such a good boy today."

After Chance and Ted left, I took a nap, feeling oddly emotional after taking that final leap. Daddy napped with me, holding me close. I wondered if he was just as affected as I was. I got the feeling that the answer was yes.

When we woke up, Daddy took me out for dinner. I was Big, as I always am when we're in public, but for the first time I asked him to order for me, testing the waters for potentially slipping into Little habits more often. The surprised delight in his eyes was worth it. Plus, he ordered me a steak with mushroom sauce —my favorite— instead of something off the kid's menu, which I found relief in. We were still equals on our date, even if I was giving him a little more control. Still balanced and still in sync. It was just what I had needed after the afternoon's events.

I might have teased Daddy a little during the meal as a reward for just how perfect he had been. Between my hand inching up his thigh and the indecent way I treated every bite of food on my fork, I had watched as his pupils had dilated and his grip on his own cutlery had tightened. But it was my moans over the decadent chocolate mousse I'd ordered for dessert which had done him in.

Daddy had rushed us out of that restaurant so fast, I'd wanted to call him the Flash. But instead of pinning me against the car and kissing me senseless, he'd been a gentleman. Conversation on the drive home had remained just as easy as it had been over dinner, even though I could see the outline of his cock straining in his jeans. Mine was equally hard.

Daddy still didn't have his way with me when we got home, though. He'd just pinched my ass and told me it was bath time…and had restrained himself during all of that, too. Even washing my body with the washcloth, he didn't linger on my cock or play with my hole.

It took a while for me to realize that he was holding himself back to "punish" me. The sneaky bastard.

But now that I've been toweled off and I've slipped back into Little space, his touches have turned playful and naughty.

My cock is aching for him, leaking precum while he continues to avoid it. The only thing keeping me from complaining is the feel of his own hard length poking into my back through the layers of his clothes.

His words finally register in my brain. I was a good boy today. This is both a "punishment" for the restaurant and a reward for putting my trust in him, and I'm simultaneously hating and loving every second of it.

"Daddy…" I gasp as his tongue travels over the shell of my ear. "Daddy, I *need…"*

The towel falls, landing with a muted thud as it crumples on the mat at my feet. Some of the steam from my bath is still lingering in the air, warming the bathroom and fogging the glass of the mirror above the basin, so I can't see our reflections in it beyond the blur of our shapes.

"What do you need, little lamb?" Daddy's whisper is husky in my ear and my cock jumps, eliciting a deep chuckle that vibrates through me because his chest is pressed against my back.

"Daddy…"

I feel his lips curve into a smile against the skin of my jaw. "You need Daddy to take care of this?" His hand finally grasps my aching shaft and his thumb smooths over the head, smearing precum everywhere. I buck into his palm, nodding enthusiastically.

"Please."

"What else do you need, baby boy?"

My brain is mush. Words are too difficult. I whine.

Daddy trails wet, open-mouthed kisses down my neck and into the hollow of my throat from behind me, the hair of his beard scratching and tickling in the best ways. "I need you to tell me, Asher."

Fuck, that authoritative tone is the hottest thing ever. He knows what it does to me. Especially when I'm floating in Little space.

Bending over, I push my ass back at him, grinding against his insanely hard bulge. "Inside me, Daddy."

His hands move to my ass cheeks, fondling them, squeezing them, spreading them. A dry finger trails down my crack, teases my hole. "In here?"

"Please. *Please, please, please.*"

Daddy stills. "Please, *what*?"

I swear to God, I'm going to come without even touching myself if he keeps using that tone. "Please, *Daddy*."

"Good boy."

More precum dribbles from my tip and slides down my raging erection, but I know I can't stroke myself. I'm never allowed to when I'm Little. It's one of Daddy's rules. A whimper escapes me and I push back against his hand, trying to coerce him into teasing me again.

I almost cry when he takes the hand away completely. He laughs and smacks my ass lightly, a sign to get moving. "I don't have any lube in here, baby. Let's go to our room, okay?"

He doesn't need to tell me twice. I scamper out of the bathroom and across the carpeted living space, down the short hallway that leads to the primary suite. I dig out the lube from the bedside table and hold it out with both my arms extended in childlike glee as Daddy saunters through the bedroom door at a more sedate pace, those big fingers of his working the buttons of his sexy dress shirt.

He looks every bit a Daddy tonight. Pressed black trousers and a sky-blue dress shirt rolled to his elbows, a little damp and ruffled from having given me a bath. His blue eyes are dark with desire when he looks at me. Even though we've been together for months, the sight of him still takes my breath away.

"I love you, Daddy," I blurt out, unprompted.

His expression softens and he steps forward, abandoning his shirt buttons to kiss me sweetly. "I love you, too, little lamb."

My heart flutters as it always does when he says those words. After today, they seem even stronger somehow. Cemented by my absolute trust in him.

Our mouths meet again, and I lick at the seam of his lips, silently begging to deepen the connection. Daddy opens for me and our tongues dance together. His strong arms pull me flush against him as he takes over, dominating the kiss. I wriggle my hands between us, clumsily trying to undo his shirt, pulling away to cheer in victory when the fabric parts to reveal Daddy's muscular abdomen.

He laughs and takes half a step back, pulling his rolled-up sleeves back down to his wrists so I can push the shirt over his big, strong shoulders. The material slides off his arms and to the floor, then my hands fumble with Daddy's belt buckle.

"I've got this," he tells me, sounding amused when I make a sound of frustration at the back of my throat. He shoots me a smoldering look. "Get on the bed. On your hands and knees — butt up, head down."

I scramble to obey, climbing into position in the middle of the mattress and listening to the sounds of him shedding the rest of his clothing. The bed moves as he climbs on behind me and I shiver with anticipation at the feel of his big hands on my ass cheeks.

Instead of reaching for the lube I've helpfully left near my leg, Daddy spreads me open and I feel his hot breath ghosting over my hole. Swallowing convulsively, I wait for what's coming. He doesn't disappoint and I gasp at the warm, wet sensation of his tongue licking a stripe from my balls and over my taint before he teases my entrance.

I start babbling incoherently when he finally works his tongue inside me, spearing it in and out in a maddeningly slow rhythm. My cock is painfully hard now, leaking profusely, and I rock back against Daddy's face, not getting nearly enough stimulation out of the tongue-fucking, but not wanting it to stop, either. He works his tongue with practiced ease, loosening me up while he eats me out.

I start begging, completely lost to the exquisite torture of this experience, and I cry out when he pulls away to finally grab the lube.

"Easy, baby; Daddy's got you." His words are soothing, but his voice is tight with his own intense need. Thankfully, he doesn't drag the prep out further, but he praises me while he works two —and then three— fingers in. "You were so brave for me today, Ash. So brave, and your trust in me is so fucking hot. What you do to me…"

I can barely process the words, too horny to properly understand that he's talking about this afternoon. I moan loudly when he finally buries his cock inside me with one smooth push of his hips.

"My good boy." He pulls back out and thrusts in deep again, then leans over me, covering my body with his to snake his hand underneath us and grab my weeping dick. Then he tugs me up into a kneeling position, still pumping into me, holding me upright with my back to his chest and his other arm wrapped possessively around my front.

He uses my precum and the remnants of lube from slicking himself up to glide his hand up and down my length. Ecstasy bubbles beneath my skin while he brings his mouth to my ear again. "My sweet, perfect little lamb. I love you so much."

Oh, my heart.

"*Daddy*, I—" I don't even finish the warning. With a twist of his wrist on an upstroke and his cock brushing my prostate, I fly over the edge of my orgasm, coming so hard I think I white out for a moment.

When my brain reengages, Daddy's crying out his own release, holding me tightly while his cock swells and spurts inside me. It's perfect. Everything about today has been perfect.

We're panting, catching our breaths, and a giggle bursts from my lips. "Daddy," I complain playfully, "you got me all dirty again."

He snorts and presses a tired kiss to the sensitive spot behind my ear. "Are you really complaining, baby?"

"Nope."

Not now, not ever. I have lucked out with this man, and I know it.

Chapter Fourteen – Charlie

"You've got a spring in your step today," Max says with a laugh as we start our new shift. We've had the weekend off, which happens once a month, and we're on the early beat this week. It's ridiculously early —barely six a.m.— but I'm on cloud nine because life is good.

My boyfriend finally felt comfortable enough to tick the last thing off the list of Little experiences he had wanted to try; I know it sounds ridiculous to be so excited about that, but it was such a big deal for him. I don't have the words for how proud I am of him, or how humbled I am that he trusted me enough to finally let go and slide so deeply into Little space, but it meant everything to me. And seeing him so happy and confident as a Little only makes me happier.

Once Asher was Big again, I showed him just how happy he made me. The additional orgasms late into the night —and the quick blow jobs we exchanged this morning— are worth how tired I am now. Thank God for caffeine.

"Life is good, Max," I answer my partner as we walk away from our lockers and check in with the departing shift.

He chuckles and shakes his head. "And when am I gonna meet this boy of yours, then?"

I falter in my step because he says "boy" like it's more than just *boyfriend.*

And even though I don't care if he knows about my kinks, I know Ash is still hoping to keep it in the family, so to speak. He doesn't call me Daddy when we're on dates, and he doesn't slip into his Little headspace when we're out, either. And that's fine with me. It works for us.

Max claps me on the back. "I'm a cop, Charlie. And you're not subtle."

"Look, I don't care if you know," I tell him as I fall into step with him, "but Ash is…"

"Private." He finishes for me, sweeping his blond hair back off his forehead. "I get it. *Trust me.*"

I arch an eyebrow, but he doesn't elaborate. I've never seen him at The Grove, but that doesn't mean he's not kinky. Besides, The Grove isn't the only fetish club in the city, though it is the best for a number of reasons. It's exclusive, there's a vetting process for members, and all members must sign NDAs to attend. It's the safest space of its kind for people in the kink community. However, instead of pressing my partner for more information, I nod and go back to his original question. "He'd love to meet you, too."

It's not a lie. Ash has mentioned wanting to meet my "work husband" a few times now. He's proud of his nickname for Max, and I know there's not even a hint of jealousy behind it.

"So is there a reason you're keeping us apart? I mean, aside from the stuff I'm not supposed to know about?"

I roll my eyes at the teasing lilt to his voice. "I get it, subtlety is not my strong suit." We bump into the guys we're taking over for and exchange notes and pleasantries. As they walk away, I explain, "It's just been a hectic few months. I promise you'll get to meet him soon."

"I'm sure I'm gonna love him," Max replies as we slide into our seats in the patrol car. "How can I not, when he's the reason you've got that goofy-ass grin on your face most days?"

"Shut up," I say with a laugh. "Maybe I'm just this happy 'cause the Piranhas beat the Tigers?" I say, referencing our NHL teams who played a preseason game against each other over the weekend.

"That was sheer luck and a bad call from the ref." Max takes the bait, and we launch into a lighthearted debate over the game.

* * *

Things start going south near the end of our shift. It's early afternoon, and we're called to check out a robbery in progress because we're the closest unit to the scene. When we get to the jewelry store in question, there are three perps in masks and a handful of terrified store staff in what I can only call a hostage situation. The perps freak out the second they notice us in our uniforms.

There's yelling and gunfire before we can fall back and call for backup. A searing pain in my chest is surpassed only by the matching pain in my right thigh.

Then the world goes black.

Chapter Fifteen – Asher

"Josh." I smile, surprised as the man in question walks through to the admin team.

A couple of the women titter, and I hear Louise whisper "Hot damn" under her breath. I can't say I blame them. Like his older brother, Josh Walker is a very attractive man. He's in his uniform, which isn't a surprise because he and Charlie are on similar schedules despite working different beats.

It *is* a surprise that he doesn't smile back. I feel my face fall.

Josh cocks his head in the direction he's just come from. "Can you join me in Ted's office, Ash?"

There's something off about his tone. He's too calm. Too measured. I don't like it at all.

I swallow and nod, ignoring the stares of my colleagues around me. He puts his hand on my back as we walk down the hall to Ted's private office, a huge room with floor-to-ceiling windows that look out over the city toward the mountains.

When we get there, Ted's leaning against the window looking pensive. His hair's messed up, like he's been running his hands through it. His face is tense. His strong jaw is clenched, and stress lines pull his forehead down. Josh shuts the door behind me, and I look between both men, getting the distinct impression that they've already spoken.

This is confirmed by the silent conversation they seem to have, before Ted pushes off from the window and moves around his desk, leaning against the side of the glass and chrome monstrosity which is home to his laptop and not much else. Without speaking, Josh guides me into the seat right in front of Ted and then crouches at my side.

Red flags abound. My chest tightens.

"What's going on?" I ask, but my gut knows it's not going to be good news.

Josh swallows, and I'm finally noticing just how pale and shaken he looks. "There's been an…incident."

My heart speeds up and I put two and two together. "Where's Charlie?"

Josh's expression shutters and I *know*. It's bad news. It's bad news, and it's about Charlie.

"Josh…" My mouth is dry, and I can barely get the question out. "What happened? *Where's Charlie?*" This time I sound more demanding. Panicked, even.

While Josh starts to explain that Charlie and Max were responding to a call, I'm barely aware of Ted moving closer to me. When Josh tells me that Charlie was shot —*twice*— in a case of bad timing, I feel like I'm having an out of body experience.

"No…" I say and shake my head, refusing to believe the man in front of me. "No, it wasn't Charlie. I saw Charlie this morning. He… he…" He'd given me a very quick blow job because he was still riding the high from the weekend, still calling me his big, brave boy and thanking me for being everything he's ever wanted in a Little and a lover. For trusting him.

After returning the favor, I'd snuggled back into the pillows and gone back to sleep as he left for the early shift. I hadn't even told him that I loved him.

"He's in surgery," Josh says. He squeezes my thigh in what I assume is meant to be a reassuring gesture. "Mom and Dad are there. So are Maisy and Axel."

I haven't met any of Charlie's family yet. Not outside of Josh. Is that weird? We've been together for over six months now, and I've only met his friends from the kink community.

Oh, God, did he never want me to meet them? Has he even told them about me?

That makes my chest squeeze harder.

Am I that embarrassing?

Does he not feel the same way about this relationship as I do?

Because even if the world finds out that I'm his boy and he's my Daddy, as long as I have him it's okay. It's okay because he's worth the uncomfortable conversations. He's worth the momentary sting of judgment from people who don't get it but whose opinions ultimately don't matter. He's worth everything to me.

"I... Did you want me to stay away?" My voice breaks as I ask the question, but if Charlie hasn't told his family about me, it would make sense not to be there.

"What?" Josh frowns, and he almost sounds insulted. He pushes back to his feet, staring down at me incredulously. "Why?"

I want to try and explain the jumble of concerns in my head, but the tears are starting to flow. I'm scared for Charlie, and confused about his family, and can feel the anxiety building as my chest squeezes.

"Okay, kiddo, breathe," Ted says soothingly, pulling me up from the chair and into his hug. He's not Charlie, but I've spent enough time with him now that I'm comfortable with him when Daddy can't be there. Over the top of my head, he asks Josh, "Has Ash met any of your family?"

I sniffle and answer before Josh can. "No."

Josh groans. "And you think, what? You're Charlie's dirty little secret?" He sounds derisive and mean, like I'm an idiot for jumping to that conclusion.

I flinch.

"Josh," Ted snaps, and I press my face into his shoulder while I try to get my tears back under control. "I know you're stressed, but don't take it out on Ash."

There's a moment of silence before Josh sighs. "Sorry. I'm just..." He makes a frustrated sound. "Ash, Charlie loves you. *Of course* he's told Mom and Dad about you. And Maisy and Axel, too. But…our family is *a lot*, and he wanted to make sure you were comfortable before he unleashed them all on you." Then he chuckles a little. "I'm honestly surprised Mom hasn't just turned up on your doorstep yet."

"Really?" I look up and turn to face him, wanting to be sure he's not just giving me lip service.

He nods. "And, look, they don't know about the whole Daddy/boy BDSM thing, but that's partially because Charlie's never had anyone he's been serious enough with to explain it to them. Neither have I, for that matter."

"Oh." I think that through for a moment. It's not surprising. Not many people would want their parents knowing about their sex lives, vanilla or otherwise. "That's understandable," I finally respond. "I can stay Big. That's easy to do, especially around strangers."

Josh cocks an eyebrow at me. "How'd we meet again?"

I can't help snorting. "Those were extenuating circumstances."

"Yeah." His face falls, the amusement fading as quickly as it appeared. "But so are these."

He's got a point. Can I hold it together and not drop into Little space in front of his parents?

"It's not going to matter if you slip," he tells me, as though he's read my mind. "Charlie loves you and they're gonna love you."

Swallowing, I can only nod because I don't want to argue with him about my fears. Not when the bigger issue is whether the man I love is going to be okay or not. Suddenly, with that thought, I can't be here any longer. I need to be where Charlie is, even if he's not conscious. "Can we go to the hospital?"

When Josh nods, I turn back to Ted. I've never taken him up on his offer to stand in for Charlie when he's not able to be there for me —not without Charlie arranging it himself— but I don't think I can do this alone. "Will you come, too?"

Ted has babysat me, for lack of a better term, on evenings when Charlie's worked late, and he's been around the house a lot. Daddy's been trying to coax me into calling the other man Uncle Ted, but in the office that just feels weird. Still, if there's anyone I can rely on to be a caregiver in Charlie's absence, it's Ted, and I know Charlie trusts him, too. The fact that I know this makes it easier. There's no sexual or romantic aspect in our interactions, just pure comfort, and I need that now more than ever.

"I wouldn't be anywhere else, little one," he tells me, kissing the top of my head. "It's going to be okay."

"You can't promise that."

"For my sake," he confesses, and I feel selfish because he cares about Charlie, too. "I have to believe it."

* * *

At the hospital, Josh's uniformed presence helps get us moved straight back into the private waiting room for families awaiting news of ER patients. He strides in first and I watch as he's swarmed by the other four people already in the room, enveloped into an emotional group hug.

There's an older man who looks so much like him and Charlie that it takes my breath away, and a short, curvy woman with riotous, dark, curly hair who must be their mom. The younger woman's hair is straight and platinum blonde. She's a bit shorter than Josh and reed thin. I assume she's Maisy. She doesn't look much older than Josh, and she has the same nose as her brothers and shares the same blue eyes as Charlie and their dad. Then there's the younger guy, who must be Axel. He looks more like their mother than the others, shorter and stockier, his hair curly like hers.

I stand back, pressed up against Ted, my insecurities getting the better of me until Josh and Charlie's mom looks over and gasps.

"You must be Ash," she declares, already pulling away from the group to tug me into a hug. The top of her head barely reaches my shoulder. She's soft and warm and her hug makes my breathing hitch. My mom died when I was four, so I don't really remember this sort of maternal affection, but I love it.

"Oh, sweetheart." She reaches up and brushes back my curls which are getting a bit long. "I'm sorry we had to meet this way. You're just the sweetest thing, aren't you?"

"Mom," Josh says with a warning in his tone; but she waves him off, takes me by the hand and tugs me toward the rest of the family. Over her shoulder, she glances back at Ted. "Come on, Theodore; you too."

I want to laugh, because it's not often I see Ted get bossed around by anyone, let alone a short, matronly woman.

"I'm Marie," she introduces herself, then points to her husband, "and this is Grant. These are Charlie's sister and brother, Maisy and Axel. I've heard you know Josh."

I nod at everyone in turn. "Yes, ma'am."

"None of that. It's Marie or Mom," she insists, and I can definitely see where Charlie gets his take-charge, hold-no-prisoners attitude from. The same one that saw him inviting me to live with him almost instantly. I think I love this woman already for that reason alone.

"Okay," I answer, not using either name because I'm not ready yet.

"Let the poor boy breathe, Marie," Grant chides, but his tone is full of affection. Everything about this family radiates support and warmth, and it settles my nerves about meeting them.

There's a knock at the door, and we turn as a group to see a blond cop hovering at the threshold, his uniform stained and rumpled. Josh stomps over to him and wraps his arms around him. I blink. I don't hear the murmured words they exchange, but there's a lot of manly back thumping as they part.

Josh gestures between the group and the other cop. "Everyone, Max Dalton. Max, everyone."

Max. Charlie's partner. My gaze zeroes in on the stains on his shirt and pants. That's Charlie's blood, I'm betting. I feel woozy.

"Down he goes," Ted says, catching me as my knees buckle.

"Sorry." I feel my cheeks burn as he eases me into a chair. I can feel everyone's gazes on me. "I just…blood…" I swallow back bile.

"Shit," Max curses, looking down at himself. He looks over at me, genuinely apologetic. "I didn't think. The paramedics let me go; I had to give my statement and then I came straight here." He looks across to

Josh. "Any update?"

Josh shakes his head. "Not yet. I only just got here."

Max sinks into a chair by the door. And then we all wait. Marie peppers me with questions, and I can tell it's partially to distract us from the not-knowing, but also because she really is excited to meet me, even if the circumstances aren't ideal. They're not difficult questions —stuff like where I grew up, my favorite foods, whether I enjoy my job— and they help keep me from breaking down. When a doctor enters the room, though, we all fall silent.

"You're here for Charlie Walker?" the man asks, taking in the assembled group. We all nod.

"Okay, he's out of surgery, it went well" —there's a collective sigh of relief, and Marie and I both sob a little, clutching each other's hands— "and he's awake, but heavily medicated." He looks over us all and frowns. "I'm afraid we can only let two visitors in for now, and he'll need rest."

"You go," I tell his mother. "I'll come back tomorrow."

"That's not happening," Josh argues, shaking his head. "I know Charlie. He'll ask for you, Ash."

I want that. I desperately do. But it doesn't feel right. "Over his own parents? I can't…"

"You and Marie both go," Grant says in a tone that brooks no arguments. *Huh. Maybe Charlie gets a little of his Daddy vibe from him, after all.* "Then we'll all come back tomorrow and take shifts."

Have I mentioned that I love his parents?

Chapter Sixteen – Charlie

The antiseptic smell of the hospital hits me before I open my eyes. I wince against the bright lights and groan, disoriented. A doctor checks my vision briefly, asks me what I remember —getting out of the car, gunfire, yelling— and nods, explaining that I took two bullets. It feels surreal. I'm not the kind of cop that gets shot at. I'm not a detective. I don't even usually work Robbery and Homicide. My life isn't like an episode of *Law & Order*.

"You were lucky," the surgeon tells me. "The bullet in your thigh missed the femoral artery by a fraction of an inch. We were able to successfully remove the bullet intact. You suffered a femur fracture, though, for which we needed to insert a metal rod into the bone. You're going to need crutches for a while and a physical therapy regimen to regain full movement. Recovery's probably going to take a few months." He tilts his head to the side. "The second was to your right pectoral and was a clean shot through. No significant damage, but you'll have some scar tissue on your chest and shoulder blade. I expect you'll probably need physical therapy to prevent muscular atrophy in your chest and shoulder, too."

I nod as I take this in, my brain still fuzzy.

"Are you in any pain?"

I have a dull ache in my chest and my thigh, but other than that, I can't feel anything. I shake my head. "No." My mouth is dry and feels like it's been stuffed with cotton balls. I try to clear my throat, which hurts. I assume they put a tube down it during surgery. "Water?"

A nurse materializes from out of nowhere and hands me a cup with a straw. "Sip it to start," she instructs, and it's difficult not to slurp it all down, but I do as I'm told.

"They've got you on the good stuff, so I'm not surprised nothing hurts." The doctor carries on with an amused little smile. "And I wouldn't be surprised if you're still sleepy. You're going to need to rest for a bit." He pauses. "You've got quite the number of visitors out there. We can only send two people in, but I'll let them all know you're going to pull through."

I frown, the words taking a while to process. By the time I move to ask about Ash —who is probably going out of his mind with worry— the doctor's already gone.

I try to stay awake, but my eyes are heavy, and I doze off before the doctor comes back.

* * *

When I wake up again, I can feel the pain. My leg and chest hurt like a bitch. I groan, once again disoriented, and I blink as I get used to the light again.

"Charlie." My mother's voice, full of relief and love, makes me wince. I've got a headache, too, apparently. "Oh, sweetheart, you're awake."

"Mom," I moan. "Volume down. Jesus."

There's a gentle, tinkling —but still watery— giggle from the other side of the bed and I whip my head over, suddenly unconcerned with how bright everything is. I still squint, though. "Ash?"

He leans forward and grasps my hand, careful of the IV line attached to the back of it. "You scared me, Charlie," he murmurs, pressing a kiss to the inside of my palm. His soft lips against my skin are a healing balm for my soul.

"I'm so sorry, baby." What else can I say? Even though none of this was my fault, I left him alone and worried.

He smiles softly at me, then glances over my head. "So…I met your mom…"

"Yeah; I apologize for anything she's said or done while I've been out of it."

She smacks my uninjured left shoulder lightly. "Behave, Charles."

I make a face. "Ugh. Really? I almost *died*, Mom, you can let up with the 'Charles' crap." Even though it was meant to be a joke, I watch my mother's eyes fill with tears and hear the shaky inhalation from my boyfriend and… Alright, I'll admit it, my comedic timing sucks right now. Blame the morphine. "Shit. Sorry. I was trying to lighten the mood."

"You're an idiot," Ash observes.

I turn my head to face him and look him over properly. His eyes are red rimmed but sharp. There's no sense of Little Ash about him. I'm surprised that he's not even hovering near the brink of his Little headspace. I'm glad, but surprised.

"Ted talked me down from my anxiety attack," Ash offers, as though he can read my thoughts on my face. "And your family is amazing, too. I'm gonna keep your mom if it's all the same to you."

Above me to my left, my mother laughs and pats my shoulder. It's her sign that she's happy for me and that she approves of my boyfriend. A little "don't fuck this up" and a lot "we're keeping him, too." I blink back tears.

God, I love this man. He's worked through his issues with his boss seeing him Little because he knows how much Ted's friendship means to me. And his easy acceptance of my intense (but admittedly loving) family brings a lump of pure emotion to my throat.

I already knew that I loved him, but this…this is unlike anything I've ever felt before. It's an all-encompassing, soul-wrenching, gut-clenching feeling that lifts me up and terrifies me in equal measures. If I were to lose him now, it would destroy me.

Clearing my throat, I squeeze his fingers back. "I love you, Ash. So much."

His expression says it all, his eyes shining the way I know mine are, his full lips turned upward into a soft, emotional smile. He gets up and leans over me, still holding my hand, to bring our lips together. But, before they meet, he pauses. I can feel his breath on my lips. "I love you too, Charlie." Then he kisses me so carefully —soft, chaste, and sweet— and it's not enough. Not nearly enough. But it's also everything.

* * *

I'm moved into a private room the next day, and when visiting hours open, it feels like everyone I've ever met pours in through the doors. Naturally, my family and closest friends arrive first. Then Max, who is tearing himself up over the whole incident, even though neither of us had anticipated the events as they unfolded.

I do know that if he hadn't acted so quickly, compressing the blood flow and calling in the shooting, I would have bled out, so I tell him as much. I've never seen my partner as anything other than stoic or jovial, and it rattles me to see him this way. Josh steps in and repeats everything I've said, adding details that have made their way around the precinct in the hours since it all went down. Nobody blames Max, and we both did everything by the book.

Max has been put on desk duty, though, and needs a psych clearance before he can return to the beat. That's hardly a surprise to any of us —it's standard practice— but I can tell it's grating on him.

Then some of the other guys from the station come in, wanting to see for themselves that I'm alive, and things turn somber when my Captain joins us. I'm aware that my leg injury puts my future in the force on the line, but when he says it out loud, it's like I'm losing a part of me. With the metal rod in my leg, it's not likely I'll get medical clearance to return, even if I do get a full range of motion back; but he doesn't know for sure, and we all pretend to be hopeful.

I start making backup plans anyway.

At some point the stream of visitors abates, and I'm left alone with Ash for the first time in far too long. I shuffle toward the right side of my bed —my injured side— and pat the space I've opened on the left. "C'mere, little lamb."

Cautiously, he snuggles into my side, and we both sigh in contentment. In addition to my concerns about my career, I'm worried that my injuries are going to make it difficult for me to be the Daddy he needs. Sex is probably going to be off the table while my leg recovers, but it's the other stuff —crawling around on the floor with him during playtime, kneeling beside the tub for bath time, sitting him in my lap, lifting and carrying him— that I'm really concerned about. The next few months are going to suck, and I don't want to disappoint him.

I keep these thoughts to myself, though. Once I've spoken to the physical therapist, I'll know what I'm really working with. Until then, we're just going to have to get creative.

"I really do love your family," Ash says, breaking the silence that's descended between us. He nuzzles his head into the hollow of my throat and my arm tightens around him. "They are…" He pauses and weighs his words. "…boisterous, but they've been so sweet to include me in everything."

Josh has already told me that my family dragged Ash and Ted along with them to dinner last night, and that Maisy's been doing her best to keep Mom from smothering him with too much affection. Not that I think there is such a thing as too much affection when it comes to my boy. He soaks it up like a sponge, and I'm starting to guess that he never had enough of it growing up.

"Even Axel's showing his inner Daddy around him," Josh had teased.

I can see that being a thing. Ash has this air about him —even when he's Big— that seems to beg for love and protection. Considering those big, hazel eyes, the soft curls on his head, and his youthful face, it's hard not to want to wrap him in bubble wrap and keep him safe.

"Let me know if they get to be too much," I tell Ash as I pull myself out of my thoughts. "It happens. They drive me crazy and I'm used to them."

"I mean… Your mom asked me what size underwear I wear, so…I can see that."

I groan and close my eyes. "*Mom…*"

Ash giggles and attempts to snuggle closer. Unless he can somehow melt into me via osmosis, he's already as close as he can get. But the feel of him, warm and solid against me, is everything I need right now. "She means well. I think she wanted to bring me a change of clothes because I don't want to go home."

My heart sinks. "Baby, you're going to have to go eventually."

I feel him go tense. "I don't want to." I can't see his face, but I can hear him pouting. It's the first sign of Little Ash I've seen since I woke up here.

"Asher..."

"No."

I pause. I'm not exactly sure how to proceed here. He's pushing boundaries, but at the same time he's likely reacting to the fear and stress of yesterday's events. It's not fair to discipline him for that; however, the way he's channeling those feelings isn't appropriate. "Ash."

He shakes his head, pressing his face harder into me. His shoulders shake under my arm, and yeah, there's no way I'm going to get stern with him.

"Baby, I'm okay..." I say as the first tears hit the skin of my neck.

"I was so scared," he cries, and it breaks my heart all over again.

"I know."

"I thought I was going to lose you."

"I know."

"I don't know what I'd do if—"

"Ash, don't. I'm okay. I'm going to be back home before you know it." I'm not playing the game of what-ifs. I refuse.

He sniffles and I rub his back. "I need you, Daddy."

A tear escapes from the corner of my eye and runs down my cheek. My throat is clogged with emotion, and I can't promise him that I'll be the man he needs me to be. Not for a few months, maybe not ever again, depending on the damage to my leg. But I swallow over the lump and try to ignore those doubts. "You've got me, little lamb," I tell him, my voice tight and gruff. "You've got me."

He dozes off against me, and this is how Ted finds us an hour or so later. He knocks on the open door of my room and smiles indulgently at the scene he walks in on.

"I need you to look after him." The plea falls from my lips before Ted makes it even halfway across the room. "I don't know how long I'll be here, and he can't stay forever, and—"

"You don't even need to ask," Ted assures me, sitting in the seat to my right. The seat Ash has been using for the most part. He leans forward, narrowing his brown eyes, assessing me. "How are you doing? And I mean really, Charlie."

Double-checking that Ash is asleep, measuring the slow, even puffs of breath that coast over my chest, I sigh. "I don't know." I'm not used to admitting weakness or exposing my own vulnerability. But Ted's the big brother I never had, and I need his guidance as much as I did when I first met him.

He arches an eyebrow, and my worries all spill out. I tell him about the likely end of my career, of not knowing what the hell I'm going to do if that happens. I describe the few backup plans I've had that sound crazy to even my own ears and are probably morphine-induced ravings. Then I move on to my worries about how I'm going to be the person —the Daddy— Ash needs me to be while I'm physically unable to do the things we enjoy.

By the time I've vented all of my worries, I feel lighter for having shared them, but guilty for not having shared them with Ash. So then, on a whisper, I confess that to Ted as well.

He takes it all in, nodding and asking questions quietly as I ramble, then sits back and shakes his head at me when I'm done.

"Do you honestly think he's going to care that you can't crawl around on the floor with him?" he asks, bypassing my worries about my career entirely. I'm honestly glad that he does, because I think we both know that those are surface concerns at best. "Or that you'll probably be limited to blow jobs and hand jobs for a bit?" Ted cocks his head, giving me his best are-you-completely-stupid look. "If the tables were turned, would you care if he couldn't?"

"No," I answer without hesitation. I close my eyes and take a deep breath. "But...I'm supposed to—"

"I'm an adult." Ash's voice interrupts me, and I wonder just how long he's been awake. He sits up and gives me the exact same look Ted just did. "We're equals in this, Charlie. It's a give and take. And just because you're dominant doesn't mean you can't be vulnerable and need help sometimes. Just like my being submissive doesn't mean I'm weak and helpless."

I scramble to fix the mess I've just made. "I never said—"

"I know." His voice turns soft, and I relax because he's not angry with me or hurt by my assumptions. "But, Charlie, I don't love you *just* because you play with me, or because you're big and strong, or even because we're great in bed together. I love you for this." He splays his hand over my heart, which attempts to beat its way out of my chest when he touches it. The increased beeping on the monitor beside me gives me away and I blush. Ash continues sagely, "And I love you for the person you are inside. The rest is fun, but we can work around it. We can get creative."

The unknowing way he echoes my original attempt to console myself makes me smile. "Yeah?" I ask him, waggling my eyebrows suggestively.

He chuckles. "Yeah."

My tone dips low and flirtatious, and I'm already forgetting my worries. "I'd like to know what sort of creative ideas you have."

"I'm still in the room," Ted says through some obviously fake coughing, and the moment between me and Ash is broken, though we laugh about it.

Despite the lighter mood, I'm still concerned about Ash being alone at home while I'm stuck in a hospital bed. Bracing myself, I squeeze his hip and say, "You still need your Little time while I'm here, baby. And I know you don't enjoy it on your own."

I don't tell him that I know he can function without it, because I don't want him to have to try. It helps him manage his stress levels, and I can't help but think that he'll be even more stressed while I'm recovering from being shot. But I don't say any of this because he knows it already.

Instead of fighting me, he sighs. "What do you suggest?"

Chapter Seventeen – Asher

"I'll swing by my place, grab some stuff, and come back here if you're good with that," Ted says as he pulls his car up at home.

Charlie convinced me to come back here while conceding that there's nothing stopping me from visiting him every day. Well, nothing except for work, but seeing as my boss is now also my live-in babysitter, I feel like it's not going to be an issue.

Ted's going to be staying in the adult guest room for the next few nights. Just until Charlie's released from the hospital. We talked the whole plan through.

As much as I hate being away from Charlie, I know he's right. My Little time, even if it's only an hour or so a day, helps ground me. In addition to that, I'm most comfortable being Little at home, usually with a playmate or with my Daddy at my side. Without either of those things, Ted's not a bad stand-in. I'm used to his presence, and he's not bad at coloring or playing race cars with me. He's not a huge fan of teddy bear tea parties, but I'm working on changing that. His next Little will thank me.

When I'm with Ted, I don't go too deep into Little space. I don't want help changing or bathing, and I don't use —or even wear— diapers. I go just far enough to relax and enjoy playtime and story time, and I still like having a bottle and being cuddled to sleep. I've also told Ted that I don't feel right being put to bed in the primary suite without Charlie there, so

I'll be crashing in my kid's room for the time being.

Realizing that Ted is waiting for an answer, I nod. "Sorry, my mind was elsewhere."

He gives me a sad little smile and leans over to rub my shoulder. "It's okay, Ash. It's been a rough couple of days."

He sounds just as wrung out as I feel. Guilt lances through me. "You don't have to stay here," I rush to tell him. "Your job is stressful and busy enough as it is without having to be Uncle Ted." I offer him a rueful smile. "Charlie worries about me, but I *can* function on my own."

"Nobody's questioning that," he assures me seriously. "But someone you love is in the hospital, and being alone through that..." Ted gets a distant look in his eye. "Well, it sucks." Giving himself a little shake, he pins his best Uncle Ted stare on me again. "I want to be here. To be honest, I think it's as much for me as it is for you."

I don't question him. His best friend just got shot. If he says he needs company, I'm going to have to take his words at face value. "Okay," I answer softly. "Go get your stuff and I'll organize something for dinner." I don't tell him that if he weren't staying over, I would just have a bowl of cereal.

Looking left to right, Ted leans in again with a playful little grin. "*Or* we can get takeout and not tell your Daddy?"

For the first time in over twenty-four hours, I feel a spark of childish glee. With my eyes going wide and a genuine smile stretching across my face, I clap my hands. "This is why you're my favorite Uncle Ted."

"Hey! I'm your *only* Uncle Ted!" He darts out a hand and tickles me, and I squirm and squeal and leave the car feeling lighter than I imagined I could when I left the hospital earlier.

* * *

Ted drops me off at the hospital every morning on his way to work. He's arranged for me to have time off until Charlie's released —which should be in a couple more days— and I have to admit that having him staying with me has helped keep my mind off the fact that Charlie could have died.

Not that Ted's presence has helped keep the nightmares at bay, but he has cuddled with me on the couch, watching cartoons in the middle of the night, and he's carried me back to my bed when I've drifted off to sleep against him. He's been kind enough not to mention the nightmares after the fact, but I know he's itching for me to talk the issue through with him. I don't plan on doing that, but it's a comfort to know he's here for me.

Today's the fourth day of this new routine, and when I walk into Charlie's hospital room, his nurse is removing the IV line from his hand.

"Look, babe." He beams at me, his beard now reminding me of all my dirty lumberjack fantasies because he hasn't been able to trim it. "I'm losing the cords. One step closer to freedom."

His color is looking better, and his eyes have lost that drugged-up, glazed look. "They've taken you off the meds, huh?"

"Finally," Charlie says with a bob of his head. It's good to see him like this. For the past couple of days, he's been on edge and snappish, feeling trapped and useless and fidgety. We haven't fought, but our easy camaraderie hasn't been there either. "Tylenol only from here on out."

There's a part of me that wonders if that's going to be enough, but I know better than to question it out loud. Charlie's desperate to come home, and I'm not going to say anything that might suggest I don't think he's ready, even though I don't know how he'll manage getting up and down the stairs.

"No more monitors either?" I ask, watching as the nurse starts wheeling the equipment aside, having already removed the sensors that were taped to his chest and clipped to his finger. To my eyes, he immediately looks healthier without anything attached to him.

"Nope." Charlie's blue eyes glitter as the nurse leaves the room. "*And* I'll be able to take a piss by myself."

I can't help snorting. He's hated that he's had to rely on someone to come and help him drag his IV line and monitors everywhere while also using crutches because he can't put any weight on his right leg. To tease him, I lower my voice and say, "Sometimes having Daddy help is fun."

With fire in his eyes, Charlie groans. "Fuck, I miss you." His hand, now blessedly free of wires and tubes, goes to his crotch and he squeezes himself through the thin hospital blanket.

"*Charlie*." I shake my head, laughter bubbling up while I try to sound scandalized. "You're in a hospital bed."

A bit of unease sets in when he continues to fondle himself shamelessly.

Oblivious, he waggles his dark eyebrows at me. "So? We could play doctor."

My dick is on board. I am not. "I'm not into exhibitionism," I remind him. It was something we discussed when we went over our hard limits. The idea of someone walking in and catching us spikes my anxiety.

I don't even like secondhand embarrassment when I'm watching a movie.

The unease turns to something darker, tendrils of panic beginning to unfurl in my belly, but Charlie's still playful, unaware of the turn my thoughts are taking. "You can just watch me then."

My gaze flits to the open door, my heart hammering. No longer feeling amused at all, I shake my head. I *can't*.

Memories of being caught kissing my first boyfriend by my father —*just kissing*— have my palms sweaty and nausea churning in my gut.

I know this isn't the same thing, but the feelings are similar and there's no thrill in potentially being caught. Not for me. "Red light, Charlie."

He stops immediately, all merriment ceasing. I immediately feel guilty. I assume the feeling is written all over my face and I look to the ground, scuffing my worn sneaker over the linoleum.

"Ash, baby," Charlie reaches for me, tugging me onto the bed at his side and I go willingly, needing the comfort. "I'm proud of you for safe wording."

"It's so stupid," I mutter. "You were being sexy. It wasn't even *me* who would have been caught doing something naughty." But I would have been a party to it. My stomach is still churning with discomfort.

"You were uncomfortable and I pushed the envelope. I'm sorry."

He's full of remorse and I hate that, too.

"This is why safe words exist," I say as I relax into his side. "You were being playful, and it's not like you were asking me to get naked or fuck you or anything. But…the whole idea of getting caught doing anything sexual… It's a trigger for me." And not one we've had any reason to discuss.

Well, not until now. But instead of explaining why, I acknowledge, "I safe worded and you stopped straight away. That means everything to me, Charlie."

"Nobody in the lifestyle worth their salt wouldn't," he refutes gently, and I nod. But he continues, "And never *ever* feel guilty for safe wording. Never. It's not a weakness. The whole point of the games we play is that we enjoy ourselves. If one of us isn't into it —*especially* if it's making one of us uncomfortable— stopping is the *only* option."

"Okay," I answer quietly.

After another moment, Charlie cuddles me a little bit tighter and kisses the top of my head. "You don't need to explain why you safe worded, either. I mean, as your boyfriend and Daddy, I want to know so I don't accidentally trigger you in other ways, but it's your prerogative whether you want to tell me or not." His hand shifts from my side, sliding up over my bicep and into my hair. "But I know now that public displays of indecency for either of us are definitely a no-go."

"Yeah... I didn't think it would make me feel like it did, to be honest," I tell him with a shrug. "I just... It reminded me of the way I accidentally outed myself to my dad."

Charlie stiffens. Considering he knows that the man kicked me out of home for buying myself diapers, he knows the story doesn't end well.

I pick at a loose threat in the blanket on Charlie's stomach. "I was sixteen. He used to work late, so I invited Jack —my first boyfriend— over. We were making out on the couch, and I didn't hear Dad's truck pull into the driveway."

Even now, my heart thuds painfully with the memory of the door opening, of the screaming, of the way he threatened Jack and the fact that Jack never even looked at me again after that. The names Dad called me. The slap to my face. The threats of what would happen if he ever caught me with a boy again.

Haltingly, I tell Charlie all of it. I'm shaking a little by the end, but I haven't cried. I refuse to ever cry over my father again.

"Jesus." Charlie exhales the word, holding me tight. Instead of reiterating his thoughts that my father is an asshole —which I know he thinks, and I wholeheartedly agree with him— he gives me exactly what I need. He lightens the mood. "And here I thought having my mom sit me and my first boyfriend down at the kitchen table, handing us condoms and lube and talking about the best positions for first-time anal penetration was traumatizing."

Laughter bursts out of me, and I'm cackling so hard I can barely breathe. As I finally calm down, wiping tears from my eyes, I manage, "I want to say 'She didn't?!' but having met your mom… Yeah, I can totally imagine that."

"Oh, she did. But it was better than the time she sat Maisy down to watch a birthing video." Charlie shudders. "*Maisy's* birth, at that."

"Oh my God. *Why*?"

"Let's just say Mom's brand of sexual education is…disturbing at best. Pretty sure Maisy abstained until college. Honestly, I can acknowledge that Mom pushes things too far sometimes. She means well, and I love her, but I can admit that it's not okay to do the things she does."

"She's still a good person, and I like her." Snuggling against him and determined to get him to smile again, I follow my assessment with a demand to hear more of the ludicrous stories from his youth, and he indulges me like a good Daddy should.

Chapter Eighteen – Charlie

I shouldn't be surprised to find a billion people at home when I'm finally released from my sterile prison. Ted drove, because with my right leg out of action I can't drive without clearance from my physical therapist. I sat in the back seat with Ash, who is being a real mother hen. I want to ask him which of us is the Daddy, but I'm letting him have this for now because I get it. He almost lost me. I suspect that when he's Little for me, he's going to be clingy as fuck…and damn if that doesn't warm and excite me in all the possible ways. I love it when he's needy. It's a thrill to feel wanted by my boy.

I hobble up the front steps, relying on the handrail while Ash shoulders my bulk on the other side with his arm wrapped securely around my waist. I can already hear the cacophony of voices from inside. If the cars lining my usually quiet suburban street hadn't been a dead giveaway, the commotion is.

"Did you invite the entire city?" I ask Ash when we reach the top of the front steps and he hands me my crutches.

"Nah," he says. "Only, like, a quarter of it."

I'm getting better with the crutches, I have to admit. Putting my weight on my left leg and swinging forward with my right, I make my way through the doorway and down the short hall from the little foyer. My family's in the living area, and with a start I realize Ash's toys are neatly tucked into the corner next to the couch, on display for everyone to see. Hell, Josh is even sitting on the end of the couch, absentmindedly rolling one of Ash's toy cars over his thigh. There's no excuse for the toys' existence —I don't have any nieces or nephews, and my friends don't have kids— and I look back at Ash, gauging his reaction.

I'm surprised when he doesn't even blink at the concept of our secret lives being outed. Or maybe he hasn't made that connection yet?

At my arched eyebrow, he moves in close and says, "Your mom worked it out. She and your dad turned up here one night with a casserole…" He shrugs, like it's no big deal. "I was in my pj's and playing with my water mat, and Ted couldn't exactly turn them away."

I'm going to get the whole story out of him later, but he doesn't seem panicked or upset, so I'm going to just go with it. "Okay…"

"Ted kind of gave them the CliffsNotes version. They, uh, they know he's also part of the lifestyle…" His cheeks burn. "Having to explain that, no, I'm not sleeping with you *and* Ted was awkward."

I laugh at that, and the sound catches my parents' attention. Mom's off the couch like lightning, rushing forward and wrapping her arms around my middle like a short, plump linebacker going in for a tackle.

"Mom," I complain as she almost knocks me off balance, "it's almost as if you don't know I'm injured."

There's zero remorse from my mother. Instead, she says, "You're a big boy, Daddy, and you can take a hug from your mother."

"Please don't call me Daddy ever again." I cringe. "That's so wrong coming from you."

At the same time, her easy acceptance of my lifestyle choice feels good. She ushers me into my own living room and pushes me to sit on the couch. "I've been reading a lot about BDSM since Theodore explained the situation."

Flashbacks to her lectures on gay sex have me already struggling to get back to my feet so I can escape. My cheeks are on fire. "Mom. Stop." I look to Ash, who is covering his mouth with his hand, trying to stifle his amusement. *Traitor*. "Ash, help."

Mom shakes her head. "Oh, no, I think he needs to hear this, too..."

"Actually, sorry, I can hear Spencer calling for help with the grill," he says, flouncing out of the room.

That brat is getting the spanking of a lifetime for this. Or an hour in the corner.

Turning to my father, who looks mildly uncomfortable, I beg, "Come on, Dad. Stop her. This is madness."

"I've tried." He follows his words with the same beleaguered sigh that he gives every time she does something like this. "It's not like I want to hear about your sex life, either."

"I'm thirty-one! *Nobody* in this room needs to be talking about my sex life."

This. *This* is why I wanted to keep my family and Ash separate.

Josh snorts from the end of the couch, and I cast him a filthy look. If I weren't such a good brother, I'd consider outing him, too. But that is an epic douche move, and I wouldn't forgive myself if I did it, tempting as it is to turn my mother's "research" on him.

"I'll be honest, I'm going to second that," Chance says, leaning against the archway between the dining area and the living room. He lifts his bearded chin at me. "I've been sent to come resc—er...get you."

"Nice save," I respond dryly. "Very smooth."

He crosses the room and extends a hand, helping me to my feet and keeping me steady until I can get my crutches under my arms again. We make our way out through the dining area and kitchen to the deck out back. Not wanting to be left out, my family trails behind us.

The rest of the gang is here, and I'm not surprised to find Max at the table as well. Ash is leaning against the wall near the grill, chatting with Spencer, who is flipping burgers. When Ash sees me, he pulls the nearest chair out and gestures for me to sit, giving me a quick peck on the lips before leaning against the side of the chair. I want nothing more than to pull him into my lap, but with the wound from my surgery still pretty fresh, I can't.

Spence offers me a sympathetic grimace. "How long 'til the stitches come out?" he asks, guessing my predicament correctly.

"Not soon enough," I grumble.

Ash's hand runs through my hair in a soothing gesture. "We'll get through it, Daddy."

With how sweet and optimistic he sounds, I can't help but believe it.

* * *

Ash's cries wake me up in the middle of the night. I shoot up into a seated position against the headboard, regretting the rapid movement instantly. Pain radiates from my shoulder and thigh, and I grit my teeth.

Ted told me that Ash has been having nightmares, but a part of me had hoped that my being home again might relieve some of his anxiety. However, even though we're in the same bed, we're not spooned up together as we normally would be. I have to sleep on my back while I heal, and Ash is terrified of jostling and hurting me. So, instead of being pressed up against my side, he's curled in a fetal position on the far edge of the mattress. It's a king-size bed, and the distance between us makes my heart sink.

"Baby." I reach for him, rolling onto my uninjured side, my fingers skimming his tense shoulders. "Wake up. It's just a bad dream."

Ash comes to slowly, then turns to face me. I catch the sheen of tears on his cheeks, lit by the sliver of moonlight filtering in through the gap in the curtains. The guilt on his face breaks my heart, though.

"Sorry," he whispers into the silence. "I didn't mean to wake you."

He's never apologized for the nightmares. Not even on that first night when we were relative strangers. I can't explain why this hurts me so much to hear now, but it makes me ache inside. Swallowing roughly, I extend my arm. "Come here, little lamb."

He hesitates and it twists the knife a little further.

"Asher." He never fails to respond to my firm tone, but tonight it feels wrong to use it like this. "Come here."

As he finally rolls into my embrace, his head comes to rest on my shoulder.

He's not crying, but I can feel his shoulders trembling. Running my hand through his soft curls, I try to soothe us both. "Are we going to talk about it?"

He shakes his head.

In those early days of our relationship, I never pushed. But this feels bigger somehow. He apologized for no reason. I hate that. Earlier today, I thought that we'd be able to get through this, but maybe it's not the case.

I hate that my being injured has put limitations on our relationship. I hate that he no longer feels like he can wake me up when he has a bad dream. I hate that my fears of not being able to be the Daddy he needs appear to be coming true.

No. No, I refuse to accept that. I need to grow up and force the issue, even if it means I'm the one who has to be vulnerable first right now.

With a shaky inhale, I start talking. "I can't lose you, Ash. I know that things are going to suck for a while, that I can't do all the Daddy things—"

His body stiffens and he sounds horrified. "What? No, I don't care about—"

"I know," I assure him, "but…you had a nightmare, baby. And you pulled away instead of coming to me and…" My voice cracks and Ash's hold on me tightens. After a moment, when I feel calm enough, I try to get to the point. "I might not be able to do all the Daddy things, baby, but I'm still your Daddy and I'll never not be here to comfort you. I need to be able to do that, Asher. *I need to*. Please don't hold back like that."

The words are clumsy and I'm not sure that I'm even making any sense, but Ash rubs his face into my chest and sniffles. "You need your rest. You were *shot*, Charlie. Twice!"

It feels like all I've done since it happened is rest, but that's not what I focus on. "Is… Is that what your nightmare was about?" I don't know why I ask. Ash has always been adamant that he can't remember the details of his dreams, only the way they make him feel. Tonight feels different than all the other times, though.

"That's what they've all been about." His reply is quiet, but it seems to echo in the silence of the room. "Ever since it happened. I can't…" Ash clears his throat. "I know you're okay. Rationally, I know it. But I just keep thinking...I almost lost you. It feels like I just found you and then you were almost gone."

We've spoken about this before and there's nothing either of us can do to resolve these lingering fears. I just hold him closer, kissing the top of his head, and acknowledge the truth in them. "I know, baby. I know. But I'm still here, and I need you to not lock me out, okay? You said it earlier, when the guys were here: we are going to get through this. Together."

I don't know which of us I'm most trying to convince.

Chapter Nineteen – Asher

The first few weeks of Charlie's recovery are rough. He gets easily frustrated when simple tasks evade him because he can't balance without at least one crutch, or when he can't get anywhere as quickly as he'd like. He does his best not to lose his temper, but I've still felt like I've been walking on eggshells around him. When his stitches come out and he's allowed to start using a walking stick instead of crutches, though, a little of his frustration ebbs.

My Little time has been spent much the same way as it was with Ted. I've been getting myself dressed and taking showers instead of baths. I know it has been frustrating Daddy, but I won't risk his recovery.

Daddy and I have been playing games at the dining table —race cars, coloring, even some basic jigsaw puzzles— because he can't kneel on the floor yet. I've been having my bottles and snuggling in bed with him at night, but he needs to sleep on his back and I'm afraid of bumping his leg, so we're sleeping on opposite sides of the king-size mattress. The distance feels like a football field between us.

That said, if I'm being thankful for small mercies, having him with me seems to have staved off the nightmares again, but I desperately miss being wrapped in his arms during the night.

In terms of sex, hand jobs and blow jobs have been the order of the day. Not that either of us is complaining, but I know Charlie misses fucking me as badly as I miss him inside me. The day his physical therapist casually mentions that *certain positions* should be fine if Charlie's careful, we tumble into bed together as soon as we get home from the appointment. I couldn't even bring myself to be embarrassed that the doctor had raised the issue at all. I was too thankful. Too relieved.

Too horny.

We're both hard and aching as we kiss with an intensity that takes my breath away. We have been gentle and cautious up until this point, since Charlie's chest and shoulder are recovering from bullet wounds, but today all bets are off.

I'm giddy as Charlie's hands pull my clothes off roughly. His need makes me burn hotter for him, makes my dick dribble precum and jerk within the confines of my training pants. He's on his back on the mattress and I'm on my knees, leaning over him. His eyes are shining with myriad emotions. I can see his arousal, his love, his relief…and it's all intoxicating.

"Do you want me Big or Little?" I ask him, because honestly, I'm teetering on the edge of either right now. This is the closest we have felt to *us* in a long time, and I want everything with him.

He considers it for a moment, and I can see that he wants it all just as badly as I do. "Big," he eventually decides. His strong hands sweep over the muscles of my back, down to my hips, and tug my undone pants down my thighs, along with my underwear.

I climb off the bed with reluctance and push them the rest of the way down, hopping as my left foot gets caught in my underwear. We both laugh. I pause to remove the last of my clothes and then crawl back over my man. He's trimmed his beard back again to that length that's just a touch longer than stubble and I lean back over him, nuzzling his jaw before our lips reconnect.

Then I carefully unbutton his shirt, helping it over his injured shoulder, and he tugs it off the other side when I'm done. He balls it up and sends it sailing across the room. I shuffle down the mattress and tuck my fingers into the waistband of the sweatpants he's taken to wearing because they are loose fitting and don't put unnecessary pressure on his injury. He plants both feet on the bed, bearing most of his weight on his left leg, and lifts his hips so I can pull the pants and his boxer briefs down and off.

I toss them over the edge of the mattress and then stretch myself out next to him, pressing my naked body against his. This time when we kiss, it's sweeter.

"Hi," I say softly, smiling down at him. He's rolled to face me, resting on his left side, and I gasp as our cocks rub against each other.

"Hey," he responds, equally reverent.

"Did you want to just do this?" I ask him on a whisper, rocking my hips, our precum slicking the connection between us. "Or did you want me to ride you?"

Charlie groans. "Ride me, baby. It's been too long."

Nodding in agreement, I roll away to my bedside table and dig around for the lube in the drawer. I open the lid with a click and grin saucily. "Wanna prep me? Or wanna watch me do it?"

I'm not used to giving him options. He's usually the one who sets the pace and makes the decisions ahead of time. But as he said, it's been a while and he wanted me Big. His equal. His partner in this as much as everything else. To hazard a guess, I think he's in his head about his limitations and I want so desperately to make it all better for him.

"Your ass is mine," he answers in a sexy growl, and I don't need any further encouragement.

With him still propped on his side, I roll to my hands and knees and turn sideways across the bed so he doesn't have to pretzel himself into an awkward angle. I rest forward on my elbows, my ass in the air, and suck in a breath when I feel his lube-covered finger circle my hole. He teases for what feels like forever, circling the rim, barely pressing in. He smacks my ass when I try rocking back into him. The *zing* of it goes straight to my cock and I smother a groan.

I'm not usually big on impact play. Before Charlie was injured, we tried a couple of spanking scenes, but they felt awkward to me. Maybe I was too Little for it at the time, though, because the sting and the unexpected heat of his palm on my skin light me up from the inside this time.

Charlie definitely notices. "That's new," he observes, smoothing his hand over the spot he smacked.

"Uh-huh," I answer. Words are hard right now. "Explore later. Fuck me now."

With a chuckle, his finger probes gently at my hole again. "So impatient," he says accusingly, but I know that he's just as desperate for this as I am. Still, it's the first genuine glimpse of my playful Daddy that I've seen in weeks, and I go with it.

"Please Daddy," I whine, and I rock back against his probing digit again, forgetting my promise to remain Big. "Make me feel good."

"I'll get you there, baby." His voice is suddenly tight and gruff, and now I wonder if him asking me to stay Big was for other reasons. I know he hasn't felt whole in his Daddy role lately. I make a note to discuss it with him later.

Right now, sex.

"*Charlie*," I plead while I grind against his teasing finger, then I moan loudly as he gives me exactly what I've been begging for. He takes it slowly, twisting that one thick digit before eventually adding more lube and a second finger. It feels like he spends hours this way, too, scissoring them and stretching me while I babble and demand more. Crooking them, he grazes my prostate and I buck against him, and my cock jerks, precum practically pouring from me. "*Now*, Charlie, please."

He swats my ass again, taking me by surprise and I thrust backward, fucking myself on his fingers. He adds a third, no longer slow and teasing, just stretching and fucking me with his fingers until he deems me ready. When he pulls his fingers out, I whimper, but then I remember that I get to ride him, and I push up onto my knees with haste.

I turn to face Charlie, who has rolled onto his back and has drizzled more lube into his fist, stroking it over his impressive length. He looks impossibly hard, the head of his cock an angry red, and I push his hand away so I can gingerly straddle his hips.

I lock my gaze on his, the blue of his eyes so dark that I almost forget what I wanted to say. "You safe word out if I hurt your leg," I demand in a tone that brooks no argument. "Understood?" He might be the Daddy, but his safety and recovery is far more important to me than orgasms and our usual roles.

With a warm, understanding look on his handsome face, Charlie nods and grips my thighs. "I promise."

Nothing more needs to be said. I reach beneath me to guide him to my entrance and then slowly bear down, watching Charlie's face the entire time. He steels his jaw and slides his eyes shut when he bottoms out, exhaling heavily.

"Fuck, I've missed you, baby," he murmurs, so quietly that I almost don't hear it. "Missed being inside you."

"Me too," I whisper back, a knot of emotion in my throat.

Starting to move, I force myself to be slow and careful. Charlie's hand wraps around my shaft, still slick from the lube, and he starts rocking his hips and fucking up into me, setting a faster pace that I happily fall into.

I bend forward and tangle my hand in the hair at the back of his head, kissing him deeply and desperately. With the change in angle and the natural curve of his cock, he brushes my prostate with every quick thrust. I'm seeing stars, my balls drawing tight, electricity zapping along the base of my spine.

"I'm close," I warn him, my forehead pressed to his. "Charlie, I..."

He stares into my eyes. Beyond the fire in them, there's joy and intensity and that glimmer of relief again. "Come for me, baby."

And I do. I still my hips, my cock jerking in his hold as I spill over his fist and abdomen. Then he's groaning and I feel the warmth of his release inside me. We're both panting and I wince as I climb off him as cautiously as possible. I bend down for another kiss, back to languorous but with an edge of neediness that neither of us has completely shed yet.

"I'll just grab a washcloth," I tell him when I pull back, feeling the not-exactly-pleasant sensation of cum trickling out of me.

Charlie shakes his head and pushes himself up, swinging his legs over the edge of the bed. "Shower with me," he says, and I bite back my surprise. He's been forced to use a shower chair and hasn't wanted me to see him in it, even though it had given me some delightfully naughty ideas.

"I'd like that a lot," I answer. I hook my arm around his waist, and he leans on me instead of a crutch as we head into the ensuite.

Under the hot spray, we put some of my ideas into action after all. It's such a relief to see him return to his playful self that I find myself slipping back into my Little headspace when we finally make our way back to bed, cleaned off and satiated.

Once I'm there, cocooned in Daddy's sleepy-time hold for the first time in what feels like forever, the tension of the last few weeks melts away.

We're going to be okay, I realize before sleep claims me. We've gone through a lot together in such a short amount of time and come out stronger for it. And even though I've thought it before, I can't help but acknowledge just how lucky I am to have him with me. My Daddy. My partner. The answer to all my unspoken prayers. The man who opened his home to me when I was a broken shell of myself. The man who not only accepted the things I was most ashamed of but also celebrated them with me.

We still have a lot to discuss —numerous issues that we will have to face together, like his career and his obvious feelings of self-recrimination— but I know it's all going to be okay.

Daddy's got this, and I've got him.

Epilogue – Charlie

It's been just over a year since I got shot. Life has returned to some semblance of normal, and we're happy and thriving. Ash is still in therapy, but he's managing his anxiety with so much grace and strength that it blows me away. He even convinced me to see a therapist over my lingering frustration at the sudden end to my career, and I have to admit that it has helped a lot.

Being forced to retire threw me for a loop at first. I'd known it was possible, but I'd remained optimistic. Unfortunately, I still have a mild limp from the bullet I took to my thigh, and I didn't pass the medical to return to my usual duties. I did receive a disability retirement pension, though, having been injured in the line of duty. The backup plans I originally considered are still floating around in my mind, even if I feel like they're a pipe dream for the time being.

I want to do something for the kink community, particularly the age-regression subset. I'd like to potentially work in conjunction with The Grove to create a space that's a haven for at-risk people…like Asher was.

I want to know if it's possible to create a safe house for people in the kink community to stay in if they find themselves suddenly homeless. It happens more frequently than I'd imagined: apparently even Matt experienced this before we met him. Ash found that news particularly distressing, despite Matt being settled and safe now. So, ideally, this would be my main priority.

But I'd like to expand the idea further. To create a safe, welcoming, judgment-free zone where people interested in the BDSM lifestyle can meet, learn, and network with other members of the community without feeling like a kink nightclub or a public munch are their only options.

Ted is helping me sort through the legalities of the sort of things I want to achieve, but it's all hypothetical at the moment. Ash has also contributed some ideas of his own, and his perspective has me rethinking some of the plans.

But that's all still in the air. It's something to keep me busy while my beautiful man continues to find his footing at work and in study, and I'm content to let it happen slowly.

So today finds us hosting another get-together with our friends, and it's a far cry from the first time. Sadly, Spence and Emma broke up, so we're minus one Little, but everyone's seated around the large outdoor table laughing, drinking and eating, and it feels perfect. Ash is over by the grill, turning burgers and teasing Matt; Ted is regaling Chance, Josh, and Max with his plans to renovate the huge house he just bought; and Spence is at my side, debating whether he should get a pet to fill the void Emma left behind.

"Get a cat," I tell him, and from across the deck Ash turns to me with a grin.

"Kitty?" He bounces on his heels. "Oh, Daddy, please can we get a kitty?"

Spence laughs and nudges me. "Now you've done it."

"We're not getting a cat," I argue back playfully. "You're enough of a handful on your own."

"Pfft" —he waves the spatula in the air in front of him— "you love me and you know it."

I do. Everyone here knows just how in love I am with him. In fact, once the burgers are done and we're all seated and comfortable, I've got plans to formalize that. But, for now, while he's sassing me, I have to sass back.

Tapping my chin, I muse with exaggeration, "Hmm, do I?"

Ash gives me the finger and turns back to the grill, but he's wiggling his butt, so I know the cold shoulder is for show.

Smirking at his back, I put on my Daddy voice knowing just what it does to him. "Do you want a spanking, Asher?"

The look he throws me over his shoulder is smoldering. "Always, Daddy."

He really has come out of his shell and embraced our lifestyle. He no longer blushes at the chuckles and whistles from our friends, and when Chance declares that I'm letting my boy get bratty, Ash scowls and brandishes the spatula in Chance's direction. "For that, you're not getting dessert, Uncle Chance."

I know that our dynamic isn't exactly usual for Daddy/Little roles. I don't care about Ash's potty mouth or his attitude when he's Big, and he doesn't rely on me to resolve all his problems or do things for him. He likes to feel independent as an adult, and I enjoy having a lover and boyfriend to hang out with, even if I do like doting on him then, too.

But at the same time, things change when he slips into his Little space, which now tends to happen on a whim. We don't really plan for it, outside of the few dedicated hours after work where Ash needs the relaxation, and it blends effortlessly into our lives.

This is exactly the balance that I was looking for and thought was a myth. In my experience, not many littles have done well without strict routines; my exes wanted me to make all their life decisions for them and wanted to be Little more often than not. As much as I had liked taking care of them, it had wound up putting too much stress on me, especially when my job had thrown wrenches in the works.

I'd almost given up hope that there was a Little out there who would be okay with a more fluid situation — with more give and take, and more flexibility. I certainly hadn't expected to meet him outside of the kink community.

It's funny how life works sometimes.

When there's a spread of food on the table, Ash finally drops into my lap and snuggles into me with all sense of his bratty, bigger self gone. Once again I muse on my luck. I still can't believe that this gorgeous boy is mine. It really does look like I've found my unicorn, and the sensation of just how perfect we are together settles over me. It feels good and *right*. He makes me whole.

That thought spurs another on:

It's go time.

When I first planned this moment, I thought I'd be nervous. But, looking at Ash, seeing the way he fits so perfectly into my life and my world, I'm settled and confident. This is a formality and a confirmation of what we mean to each other. He's not going to reject me, not after everything we've been through together already.

Nudging him to sit up, I reach into my jacket pocket and pull out the ring box I'd stuffed in there earlier. As I hold it out in front of him, I'm dimly aware of the sounds around us stopping, the chatter and laughter from our friends turning to stunned silence, the clink of cutlery cut off.

"Wha—Charlie?" Ash's eyes are wide with surprise, but there's excitement and joy and love simmering beneath the expression. While I would have happily proposed to him in his Little space, I find relief in him coming back out of it to meet me as his partner again.

I had a whole speech prepared. Words about how much he means to me. The story of us consolidated into thirty seconds of justification for this moment. But I don't say any of it. I don't have to. He knows it all and then some. What I do say is "Little lamb, will you marry me?" and it's enough.

Asher squeals and shouts a very emphatic "Yes!" before he slams his lips to mine, and our friends hoot and holler. They start congratulating us as I slide the simple platinum band onto Ash's ring finger, and he holds it up with pride.

"Mom's going to kill you for not inviting them for this," Josh says with a laugh, from his spot between Max and Matt.

I roll my eyes. "If we could get away with eloping, I'd do that, too."

Holding his beer bottle up in the air in a salute, Josh tilts it forward and nods. "Fair. I just hope you realize what you're setting yourself up for."

I know he means Mom's enthusiasm for wedding planning (Maisy's dramatic ordeal still makes me shudder), but my brain goes elsewhere. Pinning Ash with a soft smile, I say, "A lifetime of happiness, I hope."

The guys cheer again and glasses clink, but Ash and I disappear into our own little bubble for a moment.

He kisses my lips tenderly before he pulls back, those plump lips curving upward in a gentle smile that mirrors mine. His hazel eyes are so full of love and assurance as he replies, "A lifetime of happiness for sure."

The End.

Matteo's Mettle - Preface

This is Book 2 of the *Littles & Lace* series, however it can be read as a standalone.

Please bear in mind that, while this is a low-angst, sweet & cute, instant-attraction romance, this book does contain brief mentions of cruelty and bigotry, as well as anxiety and panic attacks.

Similarly, this book is an MM Age Play/Age Regression romance between consenting adults with a **significant age gap** (younger Daddy, older Little) and **does** include ABDL and wetting, as well as descriptions of men wearing lingerie.

I am still a firm believer in not yucking someone else's yum, so if these kinks aren't for you, don't read them.

Life's too short to read something you don't enjoy.

Chapter One – Matteo

Just under two years ago, I reached the lowest point of my life. I'd turned forty-three and my Daddy, a man I'd been with for almost a decade, sat me down and told me that our relationship wasn't working for him anymore. Heartbroken didn't quite cover how I felt.

I'd given that man the prime years of my life and he was ending it without any warning. Hell, the night before had been just like any other. We'd had sex, exchanging words of affection as always, and then we'd gone through my little night-time routine. Bath time, diapering, a bedtime story, and a bottle as I snuggled up alongside him. It was the same routine he had set when we first got together, when I was new to the world of BDSM and kink play.

I was a late bloomer, I guess. Imagine being in your thirties and discovering sides of yourself you'd never known were there.

Ladies and gentlemen, I give you Matteo Brightman: dense as fuck.

So, yeah. Daddy had sat me down three weeks after my forty-third birthday and ended our relationship. Just like that. He'd been clinical and impassive about it, hinting that I wasn't the kind of little he wanted anymore. Not as I inched towards my mid-forties. Not with my bulky build and tattooed skin – changes I'd made over the course of the decade which he had been wholly supportive of at the time. I understood. I was graying at the temples, and I was physically too big and 'masculine' to fit the 'little' stereotype. Still, surely ten years of togetherness should have meant *something* to him?

Spoiler alert: it did not.

Unfortunately, nothing I said moved him. He hadn't reacted to my tears, either. That had cemented the whole breakup for me. If Daddy was impassive in the face of my tears, things really were over.

The only friends I had were all his to start with; people in the lifestyle he had introduced me to. None had been willing to 'get in the middle' of our breakup by allowing me to couch surf. I spent one night at a colleague's place, then called my dad and arranged to move back in with him until I could sort my shit out. The only issue with that was moving halfway across the country.

I'd seen it as a win, though. A fresh start away from the reminder of my shattered heart and ruined life. As an electrical engineer, finding another job near Dad's place wasn't too difficult. Starting my whole life over again at forty-three? That turned out to be much harder.

Especially when Dad died from a sudden heart attack three months after I moved in.

The only thing that consoled me in my grief was that I'd had those three months with him. If Trent -my Daddy- hadn't dumped me when he did, I would never have moved back home. In some ways, I was glad that the end of my relationship had given me those last few months with my father.

Following Dad's death, I threw myself into work. I'd inherited his house (the one I'd grown up in) and, when I wasn't working, I was doing small renovations. It was both rewarding and necessary. I had needed to make the space my own as part of my grieving process. Close to three months following his death, I discovered The Grove.

It had happened by complete accident. One of the guys at work had mentioned it under his breath. The Grove had hired our company to update their high-tech monitoring systems and the teams working on the project had all had to sign hefty non-disclosure agreements. Craig, a younger, kind of arrogant engineer, had been in the employee break room with another member of their team, muttering derisively about 'fetishists' and 'kinky freaks' under his breath while I'd been waiting for my lunch to heat up in the microwave.

My ears had perked up immediately, my stomach swooping with hope.

It had been six months since I had truly indulged my kinky urges. Before Dad had died, I'd tried a couple of BDSM clubs in the city, but my experiences had not been positive. It turned out Trent wasn't the only Daddy who thought I was too big and too old to be a little. I'd been beginning to wonder if maybe they were right.

Unfortunately, though, my heart (and dick) weren't giving up on my interests or my needs. This was who I was always going to be. A little. I had an inherent need to be cherished and cared for and, yeah, *babied*...for lack of a better word.

I loved having a Daddy to play with me, bathe me, diaper and dress me. I loved having my decisions -when I wasn't at work- taken care of for me. My food chosen and cut up for me, my entertainment arranged by someone else. It made the maelstrom of stressful thoughts in my head cease.

And the fact that I enjoyed the sexual aspect of the Daddy/little boy dynamic? That was the cherry on top.

Well, it had been in my thirties. Before I'd bulked up. Trent had been a gym rat and, with nothing else to do but follow along, I'd discovered that I enjoyed weight training, too. He had supported it. Had even said that he loved how big and strong I was becoming. He'd always had a thing for buff men. He hadn't ever complained that it made it more difficult to find onesies and little clothes that fit properly, or that I was beginning to look ridiculous wearing them.

Not until he dumped my sorry ass, anyway.

So heading back out into the community into a new city where I didn't know anybody else involved the lifestyle was rough. Most Daddies aren't into a boy who could bench press them, or who 'looks like a sad reject from *Sons of Anarchy*' if the guy I'd met at my first club's assessment was to be believed. I felt lost and alone, and indulging in cartoons at home in a diaper I'd put on myself was a cold comfort at best.

Would The Grove be able to offer anything that the other clubs had not? It had sounded like it was a more professional establishment, if the NDAs our company had needed to sign were any indication, but I was wary.

Still, I reached out to them anyway. Meg, one of the three women who manned the front desk, had been so sweet and helpful. She'd answered all my questions and invited me to the next dedicated Littles' Night where they would open the doors to non-members (after a vetting process) to check out the space and interact with other caregivers and littles. The club would also organize a variety of fun activities for the evening as part of the themed event. I signed up on the spot.

Even though I didn't meet any potential Daddies that night, I made a connection with another buff little. Josh Walker. When I'm little, I'm painfully shy, but that hadn't stopped the guy from plopping down beside me at the pottery station and chatting my ears off. By the end of the night, I'd left with a smile on my face and a new friend's contact number in my phone.

However, while Josh introduced me to his brother and his friends in kink community, I still longed to find a Daddy of my own.

Hell, eighteen months on from that and I'm still lonely as fuck.

Maybe it's just time to hang up my onesies and settle for a vanilla relationship. As much as I hate that idea, I hate the idea of being alone forever even more.

"Earth to Matt," my friend and fellow little, Ash, waves his hand in my face. I'm at the house he shares with his Daddy and fiancé, Charlie, and we've been playing with blocks in the lounge room.

These playdates have been happening ever since Josh introduced me to the guys. Charlie also happens to be Josh's older brother, and they have a close-knit social circle of kinky friends. Even now, I'm still amazed that they invited me to be a part of it.

Charlie, a former cop, has also been kind enough to be my caretaker during these playdates. He's a decade my junior, but he's got Daddy vibes for days. To be honest, I've always been a little envious of Asher (who is in his early twenties, has a slender, athletic frame and guileless wide hazel eyes) for his luck finding such a perfect Daddy. Not that I'd be Charlie's type, obviously, but I badly want what they share together.

I don't allow myself to regress too far with Charlie. I don't need him changing me or giving me a bottle. But he does cut up my meals while I'm here and cuddle me on the couch when the three of us enjoy story-time. It's the most bitter-sweet feeling: I get a taste of the life I want, but I also know this isn't mine to really enjoy.

"Matt?"

I give myself a little shake at Ash's repetition of my name. Biting my lip, I offer him a sheepish grin. "Sorry. I was just thinking."

Ash frowns and cocks his head. "About?"

He's not overly little today, either. He tends to be more fluid in the way he drifts in between his little and big personas, but it is unusual that he's not letting go during our playdate. I feel a bit guilty, because I can see his concern for me written all over his expressive face and I'm guessing that's what's keeping him from losing himself.

Great. Now I'm bringing him down, too.

With a sigh, I drop the orange cylindrical block I've been fiddling with for the last few minutes and shrug. "Nothing important."

His eyes narrow. After observing me for a moment longer, he looks up and over my shoulder, where Charlie's lounging on the couch with a book. "Charlie, we're done here," he declares without any trace of his little self in his words and unfolds himself from his cross-legged position with a grace I wish I could emulate. He climbs to his feet and dusts imaginary lint off his play shorts. Then he offers me his hand.

Taking it, I groan as he helps pull me to my feet where I tower over him. My knees and back protest painfully. Another sign that maybe I really am getting too old for this. I can't quite school my face in time, and I know that Ash catches the flicker of mourning I just felt.

Still eyeing me carefully, he says, "Let's get changed, then grab a beer." It's more a demand than a suggestion.

Nodding, I head towards the guest bathroom upstairs where I left my adult clothes and can hear Charlie and Ash murmuring quietly as I go.

When I meet them back in the kitchen a handful of minutes later, their combined worry for me is almost palpable.

I offer Charlie a grateful "Thank you" when he hands me a bottle of pale ale, the cap already popped.

Ash and Charlie let me take a deep draw from the amber bottle before Charlie asks, "What's going on?"

I look back across the kitchen island at him. He's got his arm wrapped around Ash, but his eyes are narrowed on me. He and I are close in height and build, where Ash is a handful of inches shorter. Charlie's got a neatly trimmed, thick dark beard and startlingly blue eyes. He's a handsome man, and Ash is equally pretty. Nestled together as they are, they make a beautiful couple and my heart aches with jealousy and loneliness even more.

Get it together, Brightman.

"It's nothing," I try to brush off the question, but these guys know me better than that by now.

While we might only have been in each other's lives for eighteen months or so, I like to think that we've gotten close. I would say that I have connected more with them and Josh than with the other guys in our social circle. It comes from spending so much time on playdates with Ash, I suppose.

As expected, Charlie scoffs. "*Matteo*," he goes full Daddy, all stern and expectant.

He's not my Daddy, but with all the time we've spent together with him as my proxy caretaker, I'm still wired to respond. "Ugh, that's a sneaky tactic, asshole," I tilt the neck of my beer bottle at him in accusation and he raises an eyebrow, not wavering. *Damn it.* Swallowing roughly, I look up at the ceiling. "I'm just all up in my head right now. I'm feeling…" *Lost. Alone. Hopeless. Broken. Pathetic.* "…tired."

Charlie's expression remains neutral as he continues to observe me in silence. I pick at the label on my beer bottle, averting my eyes under his scrutiny. But it's not him who speaks next. It's Ash.

"You're lonely."

Even though they're delivered softly and with obvious compassion, the words seem to echo around us and I flinch. My shoulders lift and droop in a shrug, and now I really can't meet either of their gazes.

Running my finger through the condensation dripping down the bottle in my hand, I try to brush the whole thing off. "It's just…I don't know…like a midlife crisis. It's stupid."

I'll be turning forty-five in another week, and I assume that's been a trigger for these feelings. Another birthday to spend on my own. Another sign that I'm aging out of the lifestyle I enjoy so deeply.

Forty-five. Fucking hell.

"It's not stupid," Ash argues, slipping out of Charlie's embrace and circling the kitchen island. He wraps one of his arms around me and pulls my head down to his shoulder. I hate myself for soaking up the affection like a sponge. "Have you thought about-"

"I'm not going back again." This I am firm on. "Every time I go, it's the same shit. I can't…"

Fuck it.

My voice breaks, and my throat clogs with tears. The truth is, I can't handle constantly being told what I know deep in my bones: I'm not a desirable little. And it stings all the more that I'm about to have this breakdown on the shoulder of a *perfect* little. I shouldn't resent him for his youth or his slimmer frame, but some part of me does, and that makes me feel like an incredibly shitty friend on top of everything else.

It's bad enough that I'm jealous of the relationship he and Charlie have, but being envious of his appearance? What am I, twelve? I give myself a mental shake and go back to the issue at hand.

The clientele at The Grove are certainly of a higher caliber than at the other clubs in the city, but the rejection there has been hurtful all the same. Even at The Grove, or in the online groups Josh and Ash suggested I join, the Daddies are looking for cute, sweet littles. *Littles like Ash.* They're usually kind about turning down my advances, but I don't have it in me to try anymore.

"I'm done." I say into the silence that has once again descended. My voice is shaky, and I can feel my heart breaking, already grieving the life I've decided to say goodbye to. "I'm giving up age play."

Ash gasps, and out of the corner of my eye I watch his hand fly to his mouth.

Across the kitchen island, Charlie's voice is low and equally surprised. "Matt…"

Forcing myself to look up, I steel my jaw. Looking between them, I shake my head. "I've been thinking about this for a while. I need to walk away from it."

I'm surprised by how convinced I sound to my own ears.

If only my heart would get with the program.

Chapter Two – London

"You are a life saver," my best friend, Cherie, tells me as she lets me in through the front door of her apartment. She looks harried, with dark circles under her brown eyes, and wisps of her honey blonde hair escaping from the messy bun on top of her head.

I pin her with a firm stare. "You need to find a new job."

She's currently working as a PA for a local politician and, as far as I am concerned, the guy is an epic douchebag. He calls her at all hours with outrageous demands, and because she can't afford not to work right now she jumps at his every beck and call. He's taking advantage, and I hate him.

Abject misery washes over her face. "I know. I've started applying."

"Thank fuck for that."

"London, language," she scolds, launching into what I call her 'Mommy mode'.

I chuckle and shake my head. "That might work on your cute little wife, Cher, but not on me."

Which brings us back to why I'm here at all. Cherie promised her wife, Kate, that she would take her to this month's Littles' Night at The Grove (which is happening tonight) and, naturally, her dickwad boss has jumped up and down with a last-minute emergency that Cherie needs to fix immediately. When she called me an hour ago, she sounded close to tears.

Never one to cope well with anyone being upset, let alone my best friend, I told her I'd happily take Kate. Being 'cool Uncle London' has always been fun, and it's about time I checked out the club that my girls are so fond of.

Cherie pins me with an intense stare. "Are you sure you're okay with this? It's one thing to be around Kate when she's little, but something completely different to go to a kink club for a themed night."

"Hey, you know me," I shrug. "I'm easy. Am I particularly kinky? No." Well, not that she's aware. My penchant for lace underwear is a secret nobody knows about. Not even my exes, and certainly not my best friend. It's something I indulge in in private. "But do I yuck other peoples' yum? Also no." My lips curl upwards into my standard winning grin. "Besides, Kate said it's Disney night tonight. I'm not missing that. My girl and I are going to get our Disney on together."

Cherie still doesn't look convinced. "I'm serious," she insists. "It can be a bit full-on. And I know you're good with our lifestyle, but you're still so young and-"

"Whoa," I hold up my index finger to silence her, then point it at her. "Since when has my age ever bothered you?" She's in her mid-thirties, while I'm twenty-six.

We met at college, where she was auditing one of my classes, and exchanged sarcastic barbs about the professor of the class while seated next to each other in the back row of the lecture hall. From there a friendship was born, with the two of us bonding over both being a part of the LGBTQ+ community in addition to loathing lazy college professors who read directly from the textbook.

I was the first person she introduced Kate to, the first person with whom they publicly explored their Mommy/girl relationship, and her Best Man at their wedding last year. As far as I'm aware, my age has never made a difference to her.

Hell, Kate's only two years older than me anyway.

As if Cherie can read all of these thoughts on my face, her own falls and she appears stricken at the words that left her own lips. She scrubs her perfectly manicured hand over her face. "I know, I know; I'm sorry. I don't even know why I said that."

I can't even stay mad at her. Pulling her into a hug, I justify it for her. "You're tired. Overworked. Overwhelmed. Stressed as fuck. And you feel guilty because you can't take your girl to the one thing she's been looking forward to for weeks."

Cherie allows herself one broken sob against me before she pulls back and puts herself back together. That shit's not healthy, either, but I'm not telling her that. She has to work tonight, after all.

Even if I was going to say something, the chance is broken by the loud squeal of my name from just down the hallway. "Uncle London!"

I turn, grinning at the sight of Kate in her costume for the evening. And that's what it is: an actual Disney costume. She's gone full princess, wearing a big, poofy yellow ballgown and has her dark brown hair piled atop her head with loose tendrils framing her rounded face.

Seeing as she's already in little mode, I'm down to play along.

"Excuse me, Belle, but I'm actually looking for my little niece, Katie. Have you seen her?"

Her giggles warm me from the inside and I share a fond look with Cherie, whose eyes glisten with telling tears. She really needs to leave that job.

"Uncle London, it *is* me," Kate insists in that exaggerated 'you're an idiot' tone that most three-year-olds have down pat. She spins around, the sweeping skirts of her dress fanning out with the movement. "Mommy had this made 'specially for me so I can be Belle."

When they first started exploring their kink, Cherie confessed that Kate was particularly self-conscious about being a plus-sized little. Finding little clothes was, in and of itself, a fairly niche market. Finding little clothes for plus-sized women -especially girls like Kate who loved all things Disney and princessy- was even more difficult. I've told Cherie on more than one occasion that she and I should go into business together to fill the hole in the market.

Shooting Cherie a quick glance that once again conveys this idea, I look back at Kate and smile indulgently. "It's perfect. You look *just* like Belle. But," I gasp dramatically, putting my hand on my chest, "if you're Beauty, does that make me the *Beast?*"

This earns me the desired reaction of loud peals of laughter, clapped hands and enthusiastic agreement. She throws her arms around me and stares up at me with her big, brown eyes. "Please, Uncle London? Can we be Beauty and the Beast? Even if you do look more like Gaston."

I'm never able to deny her. "I'll be your Beast, little one. But only because I love you." Then I cock my head to the side, as if I'm only just registering her last words, then I waggle my index finger at her. "But if you liken me to Gaston again, I don't know how long that love will last."

More giggles erupt from my little friend.

Cherie's expression is convoluted – a mixture of fond adoration and blatant guilt. Unwilling to make this harder on her, I gesture for Kate to head towards the door. "Alright, Mommy, I have a princess to take to the ball, and I don't want our carriage to turn into a pumpkin."

Kate snorts and tells me that's the wrong movie, but it gets us moving out into the hallway. I wave off Cherie's effusive thanks and tell her I'll have her girl back home in a few hours. Then Kate grabs my hand and drags me to my car, chattering about how much fun we're going to have for the entire drive to the club.

When we get to The Grove, Kate gets impatient at the reception desk. She's already a member, but I am not. As it is Littles' Night, I don't have to be, but I do have to sign the requisite non-disclosure agreements, listen to the club's rules, acknowledge the house safe word ('turmeric') and sign a temporary membership and indemnity form. I'm impressed by all of this, knowing how exclusive this club is, and it makes me glad that they take the safety of their members so seriously.

"*Katie*." My tone is firmer than I've ever had to use it when my best friend's wife tries pulling me away from the desk.

The woman at the reception desk has just finished explaining the 'flagging' system and is trying to wrap my chosen wristbands around my wrist. Kate put hers on when she signed in. I'm flagging as a Daddy, seeing as I'm Katie's caregiver for the evening, 'taken'/not interested in open play, and interested in men. It's a bit strange to literally wear it all on my sleeve like this, but I can understand the reasoning for the practice. No misunderstandings. Everyone stays comfortable and safe. It works.

When I turn back to face Kate, she's staring at me in awe.

"What?" I ask her.

"That was the best Daddy voice *ever*," she declares.

I shrug her observation off. "I learned it from your Mommy, I guess."

She shoots me a speculative look, but doesn't say anything more on the topic, distracted by the concierge telling us we're good to go through to the club.

It's an entire massive warehouse building on the edge of the city, right on the cusp of the industrial area. As soon as the large, metal door inside the reception space is opened, a wave of bass and music assaults us. Stepping through those doors, there's a central club space with a dance floor, dimly lit booths lining the walls, and a large stage at the end of the room. But, branching off to our left and right are two matching corridors which Kate says house the change rooms, lockers and bathrooms, and these wrap around the main club space to meet at the back of the building where we find a large staircase and two elevators to take us to the second floor.

We head up in one of the elevators and are greeted by a space that feels more reminiscent of a fancy hotel, with two parallel hallways directly in front of us. The rooms along here, Kate tells me as she tugs me along, are the playrooms. All themed and available for private play. At the end of the hallway, she pushes open a door and we step through into the littles' playroom.

My jaw drops. This space has to take up at least a quarter of the entire second floor of the warehouse, running the entire width of the building. At the far end from the door we've just entered through, there's an honest-to-God bouncy castle which fills up the space from floor to ceiling. It's clearly sturdy enough to hold at least three adults, if the people currently bouncing on it are any indication.

The rest of the room is brightly lit by warm yellow lighting suspended high above our heads. The walls are painted bright colors, there are toys and activity stations all over the space, and there's a line of couches down the left side of the room where caregivers are lounging and chatting, elevated from the expansive playroom floor, giving them a good view of their littles.

Tonight, Disney songs are playing through speakers mounted on the walls, but not so loud that the 'kids' (for lack of a better word) can't chatter and play together comfortably. And, because it's a themed littles' night, there are specific activities being manned by club staff, like the 'Princess Makeup' group Kate drags me into. She plops down on her presumably padded backside (I can't tell if she's wearing a diaper under the voluminous mass of her ballgown, but she usually does when she's little) next to a little dressed like Elsa, complete with wig. They appear masculine, but I'm not going to interrupt in order to clarify.

"Katie!" they squeal and hug her. "You're Belle!"

"Uh huh," she replies, beaming and smoothing her hands down the mass of tulle and satin, "Mommy got it 'specially for me."

"Your Mommy's the best," they sigh dreamily. They're probably about my age. Blonde bangs poke out from under the white wig, accompanied by bright green eyes, a cute button nose, and a five o'clock shadow across a soft, oval jawline. "My Daddy bought me the hair, but I made my dress myself."

"Benny, you need to start selling them," Kate insists, and it sounds like this is something she's told them before.

The woman running the makeup station (tall, reed thin, wearing kitten ears, a skin-tight black pleather leotard and a tail instead of a Disney costume) interrupts to give Kate a smock and a makeup palette. Seeing as she's settling in without any drama, I tell her I'm going to go sit with some of the other caregivers, and she waves me away without a backwards glance.

I take the opportunity to explore the space further first. It's kitted out like a giant day care center, and all the littles clearly love it. It's no wonder that the membership fees for this place are so high. The club itself, from what I've seen, has spared no expense in the experiences it provides its members. It's enough to make me curious about seeing some of the other themed rooms someday.

"...can't believe you've talked me into this," a deep voice, sounding incredibly petulant, catches my ear.

Another male voice, pitched a little higher, laughs. "Just enjoy your birthday like a good boy, Matty. I promise, if this last-ditch effort fails, Charlie, Ash and I will drop it and you can hang up your diapers for good, okay?"

"*Ugh*," the first voice grumbles, but I can't hear much heat in it. "Fine."

"I still think you're crazy for wanting to do that, you know."

This time, the first voice, Matty, growls and I can hear the frustration in his words, "Drop it, Josh."

I turn around from the elaborate train set I've been pretending to inspect, intrigued by the conversation I've accidentally eavesdropped on. My curiosity has been piqued. Scanning the area near the 'paint a plaster character' table, my eyes land on the two men I assume were the ones I just overheard.

Holy fuck, they're hot.

Neither one of them looks like any of the other littles in the room. They're both *built*, with giant-ass biceps and broad shoulders. The younger of the pair is wearing a tight Buzz Lightyear costume. His jaw is squared, covered in carefully trimmed stubble, and his eyes are dark brown. His hair is a standard 'short back and sides, slightly more on top' cut.

The older guy is wearing a onesie with Eeyore on the front. His face is rounder than the young guy's and he has a neat, dark beard that is liberally speckled with gray and silver which offset wide green eyes spectacularly. His hair is longer, too. A little shaggy around his ears and down towards his neck. It's also graying at the temples. His skin is a deliciously golden tanned color that makes my mouth water. And those huge arms of his? They're covered in a collection of dark ink, some faded and some clearly more recent. I want to get closer to check out the designs.

The older guy senses my stare and looks up to catch me appraising him. Considering how big and rugged he appears, I'm surprised by the blush that creeps over his cheeks and up the back of his neck. It's ridiculously adorable. He offers me the most beautiful, shy smile before he glances at his companion, then back to me. The smile falters then slides off his face.

My heart tugs painfully when he drops his eyes back down to his hands, which are fiddling with a plaster character I can't quite discern the shape of.

Frowning, I step forward, but I'm quickly distracted by Kate calling out for me. I sigh as I make my way back toward the makeup activity, hoping that I'll be able to seek out the guy in the Eeyore onesie again soon.

I just want to see that smile return to his face.

Chapter Three – Matteo

I feel like a dirty old man.

No, really, I am *a dirty old man.*

The kid I was just eyeing off can't be more than twenty-five. That's twenty years my junior. But, *hot damn,* he was attractive. From my spot on the floor, he appeared tall and solid. Not exactly gym-toned muscular, but stocky, with piercing blue eyes and thick black hair in a kind of coiffed style. His friendly face was squared and clean shaven, and home to his plump, kissable lips. And for a moment, the briefest moment, I thought he'd been checking me out.

But that's absurd. I'm sitting next to Josh, who convinced me that Littles' Night being scheduled for my birthday was *a sign,* and it's more likely that the hot young Daddy was checking him out considering he's much more age appropriate for the guy.

"Seen anyone you wanna play with?" Josh asks, his tongue poking out of the side of his mouth as he concentrates on painting the Mickey Mouse plaster figure he selected.

Yes. A hot as fuck Daddy who I'm probably old enough to have actually fathered. Y'know, if I'd ever swung that way.

I sigh. "No. It looks like the usual crowd."

Josh looks up and scans the room. It's gotten busy, which isn't a surprise considering the theme of the evening. He frowns before he turns to arch an eyebrow at me. "I see a few new faces."

"Can't you just leave it?" I haven't even started painting the Donald Duck figurine I chose. "It's my birthday, and I'm really not in the mood to be rejected tonight."

He rolls his eyes and points his paintbrush at me, a glob of red paint wobbling dangerously on the end. "Those are big words for someone who's s'posed to be little."

Tears sting the back of my eyes as a lump lodges in my throat. I'm at war within myself. I haven't been able to sink into my little headspace properly in months. I want to; I really, truly do. But months of hearing 'you're too old', 'you're too big', 'you look like a Dom' have taken their toll. I'm on edge here in the club, feeling the stares and judgment from those around me, but being little at home without a Daddy has lost its appeal, too.

"Fuck, Matt, I'm sorry," Josh tosses his paintbrush down, splattering the paper-covered table with red paint, and pulls me into a hug. "You can be as little or big as you want."

It takes me a moment to get my shit together, and when I pull away from his hug, I force a smile. "I'm just having a midlife crisis," I jest, repeating the same words I've been using to describe my dilemma for a while now, "don't mind me."

"It's your birthday; you can cry if you want to."

"I don't think that's the right lyric."

"I'm paraphrasing."

Josh's blasé attitude about misquoting a classic tune has my lips twitching with amusement. "Just let me paint my duck in peace, would you?"

"You're the boss." He settles back in to his masterpiece without further argument, for which I'm beyond thankful.

I forget all about the hot Daddy for the better part of the next hour, managing to finally slip into little space. Josh drags me from one activity to another, and eventually I have to admit that I'm having fun.

Can I really give this up?

I know the guys won't shun me if I take a step back from the lifestyle, but will I really be happy hanging out with them if I do? Will I be able to watch Ash being little for Charlie, or listen to Josh's outlandish stories of how bratty he can be without it feeling like torture? Not to mention how much harder it might become if Chance, Spence and Ted also find their forever littles. Can I really sit among that and not miss being a part of it?

No. I don't think I can.

Which means that walking away from being little includes walking away from the friends I've made here.

I don't want to do that. But, at the same time, I don't want to be living in limbo, either.

A loud, infectious laugh pulls me out of my spiraling thoughts. I instinctively turn towards the sound. My breath catches in my throat when I realize that the laughter is coming from the hot young Daddy I locked eyes with earlier.

"Who's that?" I can't help asking Josh, pointing in the Daddy's direction.

Josh puts down the Play-Doh he'd been shaping into a giant penis and *not* the Disney characters we're supposed to be building and follows the line from my index finger. Hot Young Daddy (as I am now calling him, because I'm clearly very creative) is standing with a group of caregivers, watching as a bunch of littles engage in a 'dance off' set to Disney songs.

Thankfully, Josh and I both agreed that that particular activity was not for us.

"*Hellooo Daddy*," my friend says, all low and husky as he drags the words out, his eyes lighting up as they land on the man in question. He lets out an appreciative whistle. "I've never seen him here before…and, believe me, I'd remember if I had."

I snort.

Casting me a sideways glance, Josh's expression turns sly. "I didn't know you liked 'em young, Matty. He's gotta be about my age."

I refuse to blush. I refuse to blush. I refuse to…damn it.

My cheeks flame.

"Shut up. I don't usually." And I don't. I mean, I appreciate attractive men of all ages, but I've never been into younger Daddies. Of course, at my age, most of the guys in the club are at least a decade my junior now, and I can't be upset at being rejected for my age while simultaneously rejecting potential Daddies for theirs. That's just hypocritical. Still, this guy is *young* young. Like he's probably still getting asked for his ID at bars young.

Josh turns to look Hot Young Daddy over again. "Pity his bands say he's not looking to play."

My gaze drifts to Hot Young Daddy's wrist and my heart sinks. I should have figured someone as attractive as him would be taken.

"But he's gay, so all is not lost." Josh observes. His tone takes on a hopeful lilt. "Maybe he's not actually with anyone? Maybe he just wanted to check out the club without pressure?"

I shake my head, arching an eyebrow. "You're an eternal optimist, aren't you?"

Josh shrugs but doesn't turn back to look at me. He's still staring unashamedly at Hot Young Daddy. Then his brows furrow. "If he's gay, why's he here with a girl?"

"What?" I swivel my head back around so quickly I'm surprised I don't give myself whiplash. Sure enough, Hot Young Daddy is now cuddling a curvaceous little in a stunning Belle ballgown costume. Whatever was left of my hopes crashes and burns. I sigh. "Maybe Meg handed him the wrong band."

"Hmm," Josh doesn't sound convinced. "Meg's attention to detail is second to none. I don't buy it."

"Either way," I try to drag him back into playing with the Play-Doh, "he's here with someone, so he's not worth thinking about."

I manage to convince Josh to drop it and we turn back to our creations until someone calls his name. A Daddy I've met before saunters over, barely says hi to me, then asks Josh if he's interested in 'doing a scene' with him. He might have just said "Hey, wanna fuck?" for all the good his attempt at subtlety does him. Josh bites his lip, clearly torn between wanting to blow off some steam with this guy or sticking with me.

"Go," I wave him off, "have fun. I'll text you tomorrow."

Josh wraps his arms around me in a grateful hug, wishes me a happy birthday one last time, then disappears into the crowd of caregivers and littles, holding the random Daddy's hand. I drop my lump of Play-Doh with a sigh. It lands with a heavy splat on the table in front of me.

Happy birthday to me, indeed.

After scanning the space around me and not finding any more familiar faces, I decide to throw in the towel. It hasn't been a bad night, but once again I'm heading home alone. Even a one-night stand would be welcome at this point, but it seems like I'm not even good enough for that anymore, either.

There's an ache in my chest that won't go away, and my vision blurs as I push to my feet and trudge towards the door on the far end of the room.

With my gaze directed to the floor, I'm so lost in my woeful thoughts that I bump into someone. "Damn, sorry." Mortification burns beneath my skin as I look up to properly apologize.

I don't recognize the Daddy I've bumped into, but I can read his expression very well as he looks me over and clearly finds me wanting. "Where's your Daddy?" he asks. His tone isn't particularly friendly.

Part of me wants to wave my wrist at him and tell him to learn the flags, because mine make it clear that I'm unattached, but I hold my tongue. I'm in the wrong here, after all. I wasn't looking, and I walked into him.

"I was just leaving. Sorry for bumping into you." Attempting to step around him, I'm surprised when he grabs my wrist.

I'm bigger than him, but I'm also pretty non-confrontational. Especially when I'm still coming out of my little headspace and am admittedly already emotional.

"Someone needs to teach you to apologize properly," he says.

I blink, then give myself a little shake. "Look, dude, I'm not in little space right now. I'm actually just heading home and-"

"Too bad, boy. We're going to talk about this."

Is this guy for real? I stare back at him, taking him in. He looks to be in his mid to late thirties. He's got slicked back, almost greasy looking blonde hair and pale skin, and his eyes are a cold blue color. He's at least half a foot shorter than me, and probably forty pounds lighter, but his grip on my wrist suggests that he's stronger than he looks.

I don't want to cause a scene, so I try again to defuse the situation. "Look, I'm sorry I wasn't paying attention and that I ran into you. Please let me go."

"Are you trying to tell me you're turning me down, boy?" He looks me over again, his lips curling. His Southern accent twangs with a sharpness that sours it for me, even though I'm normally all over a good, old-fashioned drawl. "You're, what, fifty? And huge. Littles like you don't get many prospects, and *you're* turning *me* down?"

Even though this guy is an absolute jackass, the appraisal hurts the same way it always does, and I was already emotional before this unexpected confrontation. My throat tightens, my eyes sting, and my skin burns as the humiliation rolls over me. "Please," I beg, my voice thick with unshed tears, "just…let me go."

The guy laughs in my face. My gut churns. "You gonna cry, boy? You think that's going to make you more appealing as a little?"

"Red light," I croak, trying to step back, but he follows my movement, caging me in.

"We're not playing right now," he dismisses. "There's nothing to safe word out of."

He's making me feel small in all the wrong ways. I should be able to stand up for myself. I should be able to use my larger body to rear up and intimidate him. But he's pressed all the right buttons to make me forget that I'm capable of it.

My hands shake as tears finally spill down my cheeks, and I close my eyes and beg for the ground to just open up and take me now.

"Back off," a new voice interjects, sounding beyond pissed off.

I open my eyes to watch as Hot Young Daddy slips himself neatly between my aggressor and me. It startles the other guy enough that he drops my wrist and I take an immediate step back, adding more distance.

"What the hell does this have to do with you?" my would-be tormentor demands.

Hot Young Daddy's shoulders are tense, but I can't see his face because he's facing the other guy and his back is to me. He still sounds furious as he answers, "He asked you to stop. He used his safe words. You need to back the fuck off."

Jackass -my new name for the asshole- scoffs and gestures at me over Hot Young Daddy's shoulder. "Just look at him. He wants the attention."

"He safe worded." My rescuer repeats, beyond seething now. "Fuck off. Or do I need to use the house safe word and get the moderator involved?"

My eyes widen. That's not necessary at all. We don't need to make an even bigger scene here. I couldn't take the additional attention, and I certainly don't want to ruin anyone else's night. Using the house safe word is not a trivial thing. I should know: my company engineered the monitoring system.

"Pfft," Jackass leans around Hot Young Daddy and gives me another degrading glance over, "he ain't worth it." Then he turns on his heel and heads off into the crowd on the other side of the room.

My heart is hammering in my chest and I clench my hands into fists at my sides, willing them to stop shaking. I look at the ground again. I feel so stupid. How can I be this physically imposing, as no Daddy ever fails to remind me, and yet still need to be rescued? And I just let the asshole wander off where he might upset someone else. I'm a coward. Absolutely pathetic.

"Hey," Hot Young Daddy's voice is gentle now. Warm, if tentative. It's also much closer than I anticipated.

When I look back up, he's directly in front of me, his blue eyes lined with concern. He's even more attractive up close. I hate myself a little for thinking that.

"Are you okay?" he asks softly.

I nod, finding it too difficult to use my words.

He cautiously lifts a hand to my cheek and uses his thumb to wipe away the evidence of my tears. His touch sends tingles up my spine and I swallow convulsively.

"You sure?" he double checks, and I lament the loss of his touch as he pulls his hand away.

I finally find my voice, hoarse though it might be. "Yeah," I hesitate.

"Thank you for stepping in." I'm man enough to admit that I needed the help, even if I should have been able to handle the situation myself.

I'm not the macho posturing type, the sort of man to argue that I had it covered when I clearly did not. That tends to surprise people, but not this guy. His eyes go all soft and understanding.

"You don't have to thank me, sweetheart."

Sweetheart. The endearment has my heart in my throat all over again. When was the last time anyone called me something so…so…affectionate? Oh, God, I'm going to cry all over again.

There's something seriously wrong with me.

"I'm London," he says, introducing himself while I struggle to get my shit together, and then extends the same hand that was cradling my face only moments ago.

I accept the handshake. His hand is a little smaller than my own, his fingertips calloused where mine are smooth. I'm betting he works with his hands. He's got that rugged, outdoorsman look about him, even if he is clean shaven and wearing business attire.

It takes me a moment to realize that he's still waiting for me to speak. "Matteo." I don't know why I give him my proper name. I much prefer Matt or, when I'm little, Matty.

London opens his mouth to say something else, but a loud call of "Uncle London!" has him turning to face the new voice.

It's the little in the Belle costume. She stomps up with a pout on her lips and barely glances my way. "You promised we'd dance again."

Instead of capitulating, London arches an eyebrow at her. "*Katie*," he says in an authoritative tone that has my dick twitching in interest, "you're being rude. I was talking to someone." Here, he gestures towards me, before telling her, "I know your Mommy wouldn't want to hear that you're going around interrupting conversations and being bratty."

Katie's eyes widen. "No. Don't tell Mommy. I'll be good." She turns to me and offers a sheepish grin. "Sorry. I just love dancing."

"Good girl," London praises, and fuck if I don't want him to call me 'good boy' in the same way.

She sticks out her hand and I'm quicker to shake hers than I was his. "I'm Katie."

"Matty," I answer, feeling myself relax back into my little space to meet her at the same level. She's really cute: buxom and dark haired, with round cheeks dusted with bright pink rouge and matching glossy pink lips. Her hair's a bit messy from her prior exuberant dancing. "I like your dress. Belle's my favorite princess."

Her eyes light up and she starts tugging me towards the little dance floor. "Mine too! I want a library. *And* a talking teacup."

"I want a Beast." The confession slips out of my lips easily, and I feel myself blush at London's answering laugh.

Katie, thankfully, steamrolls the conversation forward. "What about a closet that can tell you what to wear and help you get dressed?"

"Or a kitchen that cooks for you."

She giggles and I realize too late that I'm in the middle of the dance floor with her. "I don't dance," I tell her, but she rolls her eyes.

"You do now, Matty."

At least when I'm in little space, I'm not expected to have rhythm or moves. She takes my hands in hers and sways her ample hips from side to side, pulling me into following the motion.

We're halfway through *Under The Sea* when she leans towards me with a conspiratorial grin. "Uncle London *likes* you."

At my actual age, those words should not induce a swarm of butterflies in my belly, but they do. It takes all of my self-control to not turn and seek out the man in question with my eyes. Instead, I arch an eyebrow and wiggle my butt to the beat. Dancing this way has been surprisingly fun, and in my little space I've been able to avoid worrying about looking ridiculous. My refutation, when it comes, is mild. "I'm too old for that to be true."

"*Pfft*," Katie does an uncoordinated spin, "he likes older men." Her expression turns a little pensive. "But he's never been a Daddy before."

I stumble over my feet. "*What?*"

She shrugs, as if the bomb she just dropped doesn't change *everything*.

"He brought me tonight 'cos my Mommy had to work. He's not part of the whole…" she gestures wildly around the space, "…scene."

I can feel a part of me breaking at that. Clearly, despite my attempts to be rational, I'd started to hope that maybe I had forged some sort of connection with London. That maybe we could have had a fun night together, if not more than just that. But if he's not really a Daddy, even if he is kink-friendly enough to bring his friend here as a proxy caregiver for a night, I'm right back to where I started.

"*Katie*," London interrupts us, his tone back to that low, stern one that screams 'natural Daddy', but he's looking at me pointedly even while he addresses her. I don't know when he snuck up close enough to overhear our conversation, but I almost die when he adds, "I think that's something Matteo and I should discuss between us."

"Yes, Uncle London." Katie doesn't sound at all repentant. If anything, she looks pleased with herself.

I make a mental note to never introduce her to Josh.

London's lips curl with amusement, then he checks his watch. "It's getting late, kiddo. I promised your Mommy I'd bring you home before the spell wears off and your dress turns back into rags." The pout she wore earlier returns in full force, but before she can whine, he points his index finger at her. "No complaints or there'll be corner time."

For a guy who isn't a Daddy, he sure as fuck seems to know what he's doing.

Katie sighs and nods with resignation. "Yes, Uncle London."

"Good girl." London praises, then looks at me. "Where'd your friend go? Do you need a ride home, too?"

Josh drove us in, but with him otherwise occupied, my plan was to go get changed and order a Lyft. "I'm fine," I tell him, even though I really want to take him up on his offer. There's no point putting myself through that. In addition to me being far too old for him, he's not really a Daddy. I'd be setting myself up for disappointment.

"Not what I asked," he counters, pinning me with a knowing stare. I fight the urge to fidget under his gaze. "Do you have a ride?"

Willing my instant arousal to fuck right off, I shrug. "I'm going to order a Lyft."

London doesn't even hesitate. "Nope. You'll be waiting forever *and* will have to pay a premium for the neighborhood and peak rates. I'll drive you."

"And if I live on the other side of the city?"

His grin turns wolfish. "Then we'll have more time to talk."

Chapter Four – London

It took all my self-control not to flatten the asshole who had harassed Matteo. For fuck's sake, the guy was getting off on making Matt cry. Where the room moderator was, or why nobody else around us had stepped in remains a mystery to me, even though the altercation was taking place off to the side of the room. It was clear as day that Matt was uncomfortable, and when I got close enough to hear him safe word only for him to be ignored, I'd snapped.

I might not be involved in the BDSM world, but I know enough to know that ignoring a safe word is like a cardinal sin.

I probably should have reported that asshole for it. Sadly, it's too late now.

But, *oh,* Matt is somehow both everything and nothing like I'd thought he'd be. He's tall -taller than me, and I'm not exactly short at 6 feet tall- and big and brawny. *Those arms...* I want to lick over the lines of his tattoos, tracing the ink that highlights those bulging muscles. But, even though his physical appearance is undeniably tough and hyper masculine, he's a soft, shy soul.

We make our way out of the epic playroom, travel back down to the main club floor via the elevator and then swing by the locker rooms so Matt can grab his things and get changed. I barely bite back the urge to ask him if he needs help: I've never helped Kate get changed before, so why would I ask this man I've only just met? Especially when it's clear that he's not in little space anymore.

While Kate and I lean against the hallway wall, I feel her eyes studying me. "You really like him, don't you?"

"I only met him, like, an hour ago."

Her full lips twist into a wry, knowing smirk. "You've been sneaking glances at him all night."

She's more observant in her little space than I gave her credit for.

"You've seen the man," I shrug, gesturing vaguely towards the locker room. "He's hot as fuck."

"You remember that I'm into women, right?"

I snort. "Doesn't mean you're unable to appreciate beauty in all its forms, male or female. I'm not saying you'd be attracted to him; I'm saying his hotness is obvious."

"Touché," Kate laughs. "You're really defensive about this guy. It's cute."

"I've been called a lot of things in my time, but 'cute' isn't one of them."

"Yeah, well, I've never seen you have zero chill around a guy before, either, so I guess it's all new territory."

"I have chill." Yep. That's my genius response. *I. Have. Chill.* Ugh.

It's Kate's turn to snort and she reaches up to pat my shoulder condescendingly. "Sure you do, London."

"Shut up." Oh, I am on fire tonight. So quick-witted. The amused sparkle in Kate's eye tells me her thoughts have gone the same way, but then her expression sobers.

"He's a little," she says softly, and there's a world of subtext in the three words.

My sighed "Yeah" acknowledges it all.

I'm not a Daddy. I've never really considered being a Daddy. Outside of playing the Uncle London role with Kate, I've got zero experience with the kink or the lifestyle. So is being interested in a little -even one as hot and intriguing as Matteo- really going to end well for either of us?

Also...just how little does he get? He wears a diaper, that much I could see, but does he *use* them? Kate wears them for the feel and aesthetic only

-or, at least, that's as far as she goes around me- but I know that everyone's exploration of the kink is different.

Does he regress often or just occasionally for fun? Does he want a Daddy to take control of most of his day-to-day stuff, or does he just want a partner to play scenes with? From what I've observed of his personality, he's submissive, sensitive, and non-confrontational...and seems to soak up any affection or positive reinforcement like a sponge. I wouldn't be surprised if he's looking for a full-time Daddy.

Then there's the fact that he appears to be in his early forties and I'm not even thirty. Would he even want a Daddy so much younger than him?

Not that I am a Daddy.

Jesus, am I actually considering it?

When I'd overheard Kate telling him that I'm not a Daddy, my heart had seized. That was a conversation I had wanted to have with him. That, apparently, I *still* want to have with him. But I have no idea what I want to say.

Kate's right: I *am* interested in him. More than I should be for having just met the guy. But everything about this is new to me and I don't know if the lifestyle is something I genuinely want or if I'm only now considering it because of my attraction to Matteo.

Could I be a Daddy? I mean really? Without it feeling weird?

Playing with Kate is always entertaining, but that's the extent of my experience. Sometimes I'll cut up her food or give her a bottle, but there's none of the other caregiver stuff between us. I'm the fun 'Uncle'. That's it.

And yet the thought of bathing Matteo, of dressing him, of being the person who kisses his boo-boos and looks after him...Well, it's oddly satisfying, and there's no hint of 'nah, too awkward for me' vibes at all. In fact, it sets off butterflies in my belly.

Huh. Who knew?

Kate's staring at me expectantly.

"What?" I ask.

"You're actually thinking about it, aren't you?"

There's no point denying it. Not if Matteo proves to be as interested in me as I am in him. "I am." I swallow, glancing over at the door to the locker room. "I guess I'm gonna need to talk to you and Cherie. Pick your brains on what, exactly, I'm thinking of getting myself into."

Kate's expression softens. "You're kind of a natural already, you know? As Uncle London, I mean. The Daddy vibes are pretty strong. You've got the voice and the instincts down pat. From there, it's just about finding what works for the two of you...and having fun with it." She waggles her eyebrows and pitches her voice low for the last bit.

Matt strides out of the change room before I can reply, and I almost swallow my tongue. He's wearing painted on dark wash jeans and a tight black polo shirt which emphasize his strong thighs and bulging biceps respectively. He's got a black duffel bag slung over his shoulder, which I assume contains the onesie he'd been wearing earlier. To look at him now, you'd never know the guy was a little, or that he was at all sweet and submissive.

"Yeah, okay," Kate huffs and nudges me, murmuring, "you were right. I'm gay, not blind."

I chuckle and a feeling of warmth sweeps over me as Matteo's expression flits between Kate and I, his insecurity painted on his handsome face. "What'd I miss?"

"Nothing important," I'm sure to keep my voice light and even, then I gesture in the vague direction of the exit. "Shall we?"

Anywhere else, I'd say we would have made a strange looking group: the big, tattooed guy, me in dress pants and a button down, and Kate in her costume. But nobody gives us a second glance as we head back out of the main doors and into the stark little foyer.

"Oh! Matt!" We all turn as the woman behind the reception desk comes around it. She heads towards Matteo and wraps her arms around his waist, her head barely coming to his shoulders. "Happy birthday. I should have said it when you came in, but-"

"Josh is a distraction," he chuckles. "Sorry about him."

The woman pokes him in the chest with her index finger, "That boy is not your responsibility. He's been giving me grief longer than you've been a member." There's a fondness in her voice that belies the complaint. "Still, I hope you've had a good night?"

"Yeah," he scratches the back of his neck, suddenly realizing that he has an audience. His cheeks flush.

Her eyes widen as she takes me and Kate in, and then her lips pull into a knowing grin when she addresses him again. "Making new friends?"

"*Meg*," he says in warning.

She laughs and pushes him back towards us, making a shooing motion. "The night's still young. Go enjoy your birthday some more."

"So…" I grin as we step out into the cool night air. "Birthday, huh?"

It's only as I ask that I recall his friend, Josh, saying something about it when I was eavesdropping earlier.

Matteo looks distinctly uncomfortable. "Yeah."

The smile slips from my face when I do the math and realize that he'd clearly arrived with a friend (under duress, if the conversation I'd overheard was any indication) who had then disappeared and left him on his own. *On his birthday*. That doesn't sit right with me. Still, I don't know what to say to make it better.

Thankfully, Kate steps in. "Have you had cake? I maintain that it's not a real birthday without cake."

Matteo shakes his head. "Nah. No cake. I haven't really been in a celebrating mood for the last couple of birthdays." Then, as if he's ashamed of having brought the mood down, he forces a bright smile that doesn't quite meet his eyes and jokes, "I'm getting old. Losing count and shit."

Alarms blare in the back of my brain. *He's hurting*. He might be trying to cover it up, but there's pain in his eyes and something about the tense set of his shoulders has me wanting to wrap him in my arms and never let him go. I can't imagine why his friend would have left him like this. On his actual birthday, no less.

I know I should let it go myself, but I can't see that happening. Someone needs to look after this man.

"Please, you're, what, forty?" Kate asks, brazen as always.

"You're my new favorite," he points at her, then upturns his palm and makes a 'gimme' gesture, curling his fingers back towards himself a few times. "Keep the flattery coming."

She pushes, "There's no way you're much older than that."

"You're not subtle, you know that?" He might be calling her out, but he's grinning so her tactics appear to be working. "Forty-fucking-five, if you absolutely have to know."

Kate's gasp is over-the-top dramatic, but that's Kate for you. "No! You lie!"

"I wish."

"Okay," I intervene, chuckling at their antics as I fish my keys from my pocket. We've been walking towards the car, parked in the designated lot behind the warehouse. I click the button to unlock it and the orange lights flash twice in the darkness. The lot is lit by a couple of large floodlights, but it's not super bright. "Here we are."

"Matteo can ride shotgun," Kate declares, gathering up layers of tulle and satin in preparation of smooshing herself into the back of my Hyundai. "It's your birthday," she tells him when he moves to argue, "and you're taller than me. Your legs will thank you for it. Besides, London will drop me off first, so it saves you having to get out at my place."

He can't fault her logic, so he thanks her. Then, hesitantly, he says, "It's Matt."

She stares at him quizzically.

"I prefer Matt. Only my dad ever called me Matteo."

Past tense, I note. This guy's been through some shit, I can just tell.

"Noted," I acknowledge easily, and we all climb into our seats.

Kate keeps conversation flowing from her spot in the middle of the backseats, talking about how fun the night was and thanking me again for stepping in for Cherie. Then she explains to Matteo (*Matt*, I correct myself mentally) that her wife is her Mommy and was called into work last minute. Matt makes appropriate comments of commiseration, and then they compare notes about their favorite activities of the evening. By the time we pull up outside Kate and Cherie's place, the pair have exchanged numbers.

"You should totally come for a playdate," she demands of the big man, stars in her eyes at the thought. "I don't have many little friends. We, uh, we don't get to socialize very often."

My heart squeezes for her and Cherie, and I'm once again filled with the feeling that the latter desperately needs to find a new job.

Matt smiles a sad smile at her. "I, um…I'm stopping the little stuff," he says, full of apology and a jumble of emotions I can't pinpoint. "Tonight was a last hurrah, I guess."

"You…*what*?" Kate's frozen, her leg suspended out of the open car door, her bafflement palpable. "You can't just turn off your kinks, Matt. If being a little makes you half as happy and relaxed as it does me, you're going to be miserable."

"I'm alr-" He stops himself abruptly, but I fill in the rest in my head.

Already miserable.

Oof, my heart.

Kate doesn't miss it, either. Her eyes fill with compassion, then flit to me for a second before she says, "Just please think about it, Matt. You might find joy in it again." Yeah, she's really not subtle, but I kind of love her for that. Her attention turns back to me, clearly giving Matt a chance to process. "Thanks for tonight, Uncle London." Then, quieter, "Take care of him."

After I've watched her safely enter the building, I start the car again. The silence between Matt and me is awkward, and I hate that.

"So…" I start, wondering where my usual charisma has gone. I've always considered myself a natural conversationalist but, with this man, I feel tongue-tied and off my game.

"I appreciate you giving me a ride home."

Ugh. Strained small talk. I don't want this at all. I want the spark of connection we had in the club. I want to hold him and call him sweetheart again, because the way his eyes had lit up at the simple endearment was pure magic. I want to try things with him I've never done before. I want to see him smile and laugh again. I want to know what his lips feel like, what his tongue tastes like, what that scruffy beard feels like against my skin.

Jesus Christ, I've known him for barely a couple of hours and I'm infatuated.

He startles when I reach out and grab his hand, but he doesn't disengage from my hold. "Here's the thing," I tell him as I pull away from the curb, "I'm into you."

I feel him tense. "You're, what, twenty-five?"

"Twenty-six," like the extra year makes any difference, "but is that a deal-breaker?"

"You're not a Daddy."

I have to tread *so* carefully here. I'm not pointing out that only minutes ago he said he was giving up the lifestyle, because it's obvious that it's a part of his identity. And the longing in his voice makes me want to offer him the world, but it's not that simple.

"No," I answer slowly, "but…I'm finding myself interested in trying."

Matt whips his head around to face me, but with my eyes on the road, I can't meet his gaze. From the corner of my eye, I can see that he studies me closely as he asks, "Why?"

I'm not going to tell him that it's just because I'm into him, because that sounds a little crazy even to me. And, having had a little bit of time for some introspection on the topic in the last hour or so, I can honestly say that it's *not* just about him.

"I've watched Kate and Cherie's dynamic for a few years now," I explain, "and what they have is special, y'know?" I give him a quick glance as we roll to a stop at a red light, exchanging soft, understanding smiles. "I'll admit that I've been curious, I guess, but never really motivated to head to the club to play with strangers. But tonight…" I swallow, drumming my fingers over the top of the steering wheel. "Tonight, when I saw you…when that asshole was giving you shit…something inside me *shifted* and I felt…" Like I *needed* to defend and protect him. To hold him. To kiss him and take his pain away. But I'm struggling to put those feelings into words.

He does it for me.

"Like a Daddy."

I can still feel his eyes on me after that quiet, but awe-filled assessment.

My lips curl upwards. "Yeah," I nod.

We're both quiet for a few minutes after that, with Matt's directions to his place the only thing breaking the silence between us. It's not a tense silence, though. More contemplative than anything.

"You don't..." he starts, then stops. "Never mind."

"No, what?"

I shoot another quick look his way before setting my eyes back on the road. I'm still holding his hand, but he's fidgety.

I don't press him further, content to wait him out. After a little while longer, he asks, "You don't think I'm too old, or big, or tatted, or...or whatever? You know, to be a little?"

He sounds so meek and pained as he asks the questions that I fight back the surge of anger at whoever has hurt him. Men like that absolute fuckweasel in the club. Men who don't deserve a second's thought, but who have obviously inflicted a lot of damage.

"Absolutely not," my response is firm and without hesitation. "You're hot as fuck, Matt. And you look fucking adorable in a onesie."

"I...*what*?" The disbelief in his tone is palpable.

Instead of giving in to the urge to pull over so I can lean across the center console and wrap him in a strong hug, I squeeze his hand as tightly as I can. "You heard me."

"Yeah, but..."

I stay silent, waiting for him to get his thoughts together.

It takes a bit longer this time before he sighs heavily. "My ex introduced me to age play," he begins, and it's not what I was expecting, not by a long shot. "I was in my early thirties. Nowhere near this bulky. Only a couple of tatts."

"Okay..."

Turning his head to look out the window, he continues, "Obviously, I loved it. It was...freeing, I guess, and it spoke to me like nothing else I'd ever experienced. And it worked well for us. We, uh, we were together for almost ten years."

Whoa. "That's impressive."

"Yeah, well, it felt less than impressive when he dumped me. It felt more like a waste. Of my time, my youth, my…"

"Love?"

I catch his nod again out of the corner of my eye and give his hand another squeeze.

"I felt stupid. Especially because he was clear that, uh…"

Realization dawns. "He said you were too old and too buff." I frown. "But he was with you all that time."

"*Bingo*." Matt sounds resigned. "All those years where he pretended to be into the changes I was making…"

"Yeah, but you did that for you, not for him."

"And fucked myself over."

"Why? Because a bunch of close-minded dickwads said you don't look the part? Last time I checked, it takes all sorts to make the world go around. *I* love seeing you little. There's something about the contrast of such a huge, alpha-looking kind of dude looking all soft and cute and cuddly." It's word vomit. A stream-of-consciousness ramble that bypasses my filter. I feel my own cheeks heat after the words register in my brain. "Sorry. That was too much."

"You really meant that." He says after a moment, clearly stunned.

My head bobs. "Confession time," I acknowledge lightly. "I *may* have a type."

"Let me guess," there's a confidence in his voice now that I haven't heard from him yet, and it sends a thrill of arousal straight through me. "Your type is huge, alpha-looking kind of dudes with unexpected soft sides who are old enough to actually be your father?"

There's nineteen years between us, so technically he's not wrong.

"What do you know?" I drawl, finally managing to summon my usual flirtatious tone. "You got it in one."

Chapter Five – Matteo

"Would you, uh, like to come in?" I ask London when we pull up at my place. It's been too long since I brought someone home from the club, and we both know that I'm not asking him in just for coffee. But there's a part of me that wants to ask for more than just one night, too.

I have to smother those urges. I've always been the type to get ahead of myself, and tonight is proving to be no different.

Honestly, tonight has been surreal. This kid (this *man*, I correct myself) has been so unexpected. The things he said about his burgeoning interest in being a Daddy rattle around in my brain on repeat. I'm relieved he didn't say that it came on suddenly when he saw me, as powerful a rush as that would have given my ego. Sexual attraction to another person is not reason enough to throw yourself headfirst into a Daddy/little relationship, right? I mean, okay, I got into it for Trent, but we'd already been together for a few months at that stage.

Anyway, that's not the point. And it's not like London said he wants a relationship, even if that's where my thoughts keep drifting.

Ugh. My brain is a mess. I went into the club tonight thinking that it was the end of that part of my life, and then London turned up and suddenly I have *hope*. It's a dangerous feeling.

What does it say about me that I'm allowing myself to get so invested after a few hours with the guy? A guy who is almost twenty years my junior, at that. Not that age should matter between consenting adults, but I feel a kind of skeevy lusting after him all the same. Not to mention asking him into my home, openly inviting him in for sex.

London turns off the ignition and looks me in the eye. His blue eyes are warm but assessing. "Is that what you want?"

Okay, so physically he might be in his mid-twenties, but he's got maturity in spades. That deep, firm Daddy voice of his is going to do me in, especially when it's apparent that he's not aware that he's doing it. It's just him.

Fuck, that's hot.

"Please," I answer with a nod, biting back the honorific that my brain already wants to tack on to the end.

I'm rewarded with a genuine smile and he reaches to unbuckle his seatbelt. "I'd love to come in, then."

Don't read too far into that, Brightman. Just enjoy it as a one-night club hook-up.

My place is a standard suburban, ranch-style family home. Brick and tile, single story, three bedrooms, two bathrooms and a large backyard. I've been slowly renovating it, making it a little less like the ode to the 80s it had been, but the carpets are still a gross beige color and the walls -a hideous shade of brown- could use a facelift, too.

I lead the way from the front door, past what was the 'formal' living room in my parents' day on the right, the smallest bedroom (which I converted into an office) on the left, and into the open living-dining-kitchen space. The floors here are tiled -big, gleaming white squares- and the kitchen is shiny with new cupboards and appliances.

"Coffee?" I ask my guest, gesturing for him to take a seat wherever he wants. "Or a beer?"

It's been so long since I've dated that I'm pretty sure I'm already fucking this up.

Not that this is a date.

Fuck.

"Coffee sounds good," he answers, his eyes slowly traveling the space as I wander into the kitchen proper. Instead of sitting down in the living area or at the dining table, he follows me and leans against the kitchen counter, watching as I set up the French press.

"You're a coffee snob, then?" he sounds amused. "No pod machine for you?"

I grin. "Guilty as charged." There's something satisfying in using high quality beans and controlling the depth and strength of your own brew. I turn to the fridge. "Are you a cream and sugar guy?"

"Nope. Black coffee all the way for me."

"Be still my heart."

Trent always insisted on flavored creamers which, as far as I'm concerned, destroys a perfectly good cup of coffee. Especially with the copious amounts he used to use, the heathen.

London's chuckle is as deep and rich as the beverage I'm brewing, and it takes me right out of my musings about my ex. "You take your coffee seriously. Noted."

"You're taking notes, huh?"

There's no sign of embarrassment on his face. Instead, he just gives me a cheeky smirk that gives me butterflies. "I'm a quick study."

Even though his words could be interpreted as arrogant or cocky, I can tell he's being playful. Well, mostly. There's a quiet confidence about him that makes me want all sorts of things I'm sure he's not ready for, or that he's not even into.

When we take our steaming mugs into the living area, I sit on the end seat of my large, cushy brown leather couch and London surprises me by taking the seat directly beside me. I expected him to leave the middle spot free. He leaves a little space between us, enough so he can bring his knee up onto the cushion and turn to face me, placing his mug on the coffee table in front of us.

I rack my brain to think of something to say, but the spicy scent of his cologne is a distraction, as is the proximity of his body to mine. I'm suddenly all too aware that we're alone together, both of us sober, both of us already having admitted an interest in the other…albeit an implied interest on my own part. Hell, he brought me home from a BDSM club and accepted my invitation inside.

We both know where this is going.

Butterflies take up residence in my belly.

His eyes seem to darken as he watches me, then he says, "Tell me about what you enjoy doing when you're little."

It takes a moment or two for the words to register through the lusty fog in my head. Of all the things he could have said, I wasn't anticipating that. "I…huh?"

London's smile is kind. "Like I said before, I'm into you. And you being little is a big part of that. But I don't have a lot of experience with the lifestyle so…tell me about your little side." He cocks his head. "I know about the onesie and the diaper," he's matter of fact, without a hint of judgment, "but what else do you enjoy?"

"Playing. Y'know: toys, hide 'n seek, make believe…Uh, I love story-time, especially with cuddles. And bath-time…" I clear my throat. "With or without, uh, 'grown up' touches."

The corner of his lips quirks upwards, but he doesn't react otherwise. "Uh huh. What about being looked after? What do you want from your Daddy?"

Fuck, even him saying the word -not calling himself Daddy, but just asking hypothetically- has my dick twitching. I swallow. "That's the main draw for me, to be honest. Being cared for, I mean."

"I figured as much," he acknowledges, still warm and kind, but there's additional heat in his gaze that I hope to God I'm not imagining. "But what does that look like to you?"

"Attention," I blurt, feeling pathetic as the admission escapes me. "Like…a lot. I'm…I've been alone for a while and I just-"

"Want to be someone's priority?"

It's as good a way to phrase it as any other. I nod. "Yeah. So, like, having Daddy take control at home, making my decisions for me, giving me rules and structure and schedules. Lots of affection and reassurance, because I'm, well, a needy little boy." I look down at my lap, picking at my cuticles.

An index finger lifts my chin. London's expression is still open and free of judgment when I'm forced to look at him. "What else?"

"Uh," my thoughts are a jumbled mess, that simple touch doing more to me than I can process, "So, I like it when Daddy does stuff for me. Cuts up my food. Makes sure I've been drinking my water and eating healthy. Orders for me at restaurants…but not off the kids' menu. Uh, and I like it when he chooses my outfits and dresses me?"

"Why is that a question?"

My cheeks burn. "I don't know."

Except I do. I want to know his limits. How much of this would he actually be okay with? Because I'm willing to compromise on any of it. And there I go getting ahead of myself again. He's asking out of curiosity, not because he's decided to be my Daddy.

"*Matteo*."

Fuck me, Daddy voice is back. I don't even hate the use of my full first name when it's said that way. In fact, it's more arousing than I could have imagined. Funny how I've never felt that way when Charlie does it, though.

"I just…can you tell me if something's too much?" I cringe even as I say it. "Not that…not that I'm just assuming you want to be my…that you're considering…"

Those blue eyes light with understanding. "Oh, sweetheart," he reaches out and pulls me in for a hug, running thick fingers through my hair, "I thought it was obvious. That's why I'm asking."

The hope I was trying to stomp down inside me breaks free, tendrils of it curling through my veins and into my heart and head, making me giddy. Could it be that he does want more than a one-night club hook-up? With me, of all people?

"You're not freaked out by this?"

"Not in the least. Honestly, I assumed most of it anyway, having seen Cherie and Kate's dynamic. But I know everyone's a bit different, so I just wanted to know what *you* want as a little." He cocks his head. "The dressing thing…do you prefer diapers or training pants or-"

"You know more about this than you said you do." I cut in, pulling out of his embrace and settling back in my seat, facing him again. I realize how silly the sentence sounds once it's out, but London seems to understand my meaning.

"I did a bit of research back when Cherie first told me about her and Kate. I wanted to make sure I wasn't gonna put my foot in my mouth or be taken completely by surprise."

I wonder if there's more to it than that, but I accept the explanation readily enough.

Then he repeats the question about my preferences.

I sigh, feeling my cheeks heat even before I answer him. "I like the diaper. It…uh, it helps me sink deeper into little space faster." Taking a steadying breath, I might as well go all in. "And the whole changing routine does that, too. Like being laid out and powdered and having it wrapped around me and secured…it's more intimate than just stepping into a pair of tight underwear, I guess."

"I can see that," London's voice is still steady and kind. "Do you use them? Or is it more a sensory thing for you?"

I wish I could get even a hint of his feelings on the topic. It's understandable that this is a hard limit for a lot of people, littles and Daddies alike. For me, it's not a deal-breaker, though I won't lie and say that the level of trust and intimacy involved isn't heady, nor that being able to sink so deeply into little space isn't incredibly freeing. Still, it's never been something I've indulged in often, either. Trent only went with it to humor me whenever I was incredibly stressed and needed the additional release, if you'll forgive the pun.

"Not for years, and never often. Usually only when I've been so stressed that I needed to go real deep into little space." I eventually answer, studying him closely for any sign of discomfort, "But wetting isn't something I desperately need as part of my little experience if it's a hard limit for my partner, and it's also not something I'm comfortable trying early on with a Daddy, either."

If he's relieved, or even disgusted, he doesn't show it. He just bobs his head. "That makes sense. And, honestly, I don't know that I'd be ready to jump straight into it from a Daddy perspective, either. I'd want a bit more practice with the diapering process first. For us both to be comfortable with each other. To trust each other implicitly."

My heart leaps into my throat. He seems so confident about this, even though it's all new to him. It's like he's made the decision to jump in feet first and that's that.

It's everything I've been wanting, that I've been dreaming of, for *years*. And now it's within my grasp and...I'm afraid. Afraid that I'm going to get attached too quickly. Afraid that he will hate it, though he obviously has every right to. Afraid it's not going to work out and that he has the potential to hurt me more than any of the jackasses in the clubs have, if only because my hopes are climbing too high now. But, mostly, I'm afraid that I won't recover if it doesn't work out.

"Hey, you're shaking," London's concerned now, reaching out for me again. I go willingly into another hug, tensing when he asks me to explain where my thoughts had gone.

This strange, almost instant connection I feel with him only serves to fuel my inner turmoil. It's ridiculous that I should feel so strongly after knowing the guy for barely a few hours. Am I so desperate for affection that I'm latching on to the first person to show me the kind of attention I've been yearning for for years? I don't want to use the guy. He's too good for that.

"*Matteo*." Damn it, I'm almost certain he knows exactly what he's doing now, even if he didn't earlier. "Talk to me, sweetheart."

The dam bursts and my thoughts pour forth from my mouth, bypassing my filter entirely. There's no rhyme or reason to them. No order. I just blurt out all of my concerns, my fears, and my hopes in a barrage of rapid-fire statements.

Despite my embarrassment, I tell him about how badly I would love for him to try being my Daddy. About how much I miss having someone who understands my needs. About how I desperately want to find someone who genuinely cares and wants to look after me, and for whom, in turn, I can be a good boy. The best boy.

This rambles into my snowballing feelings of inadequacy. My voice shakes as I tell him about how lonely and utterly pathetic I've felt; the rejected boy, not good enough for any Daddy. Lastly, I go into how miserable I've been, knowing that it's the choices I've made which have made me so undesirable.

It's like the last two years' worth just explodes out of me. Even though I've vented to my friends, it's never been quite like this. I've always held back with them, not wanting to burden them or make them feel awkward. But with London, this veritable stranger, I let it all out.

I realize that unloading like this is the least sexy thing I could do when I originally invited the guy in for a hook-up, but there's no stopping the flow of words, and I find the entire experience cathartic.

London holds me through it, carding fingers through my hair and squeezing me reassuringly. He doesn't interrupt once. Occasionally, I feel him make a sound of commiseration or understanding, but it's not until I've said the last of it and have then reiterated that I don't want to use him simply because he's the only man to show me even close to the attention that I crave that he finally says anything.

But what he says isn't anything I expected at all.

"Can I give you a bath?"

Chapter Six – London

After his outpouring of information, I can see Matt is emotionally and physically exhausted. The poor guy's clearly been holding most of that in, struggling away on his own for the last couple of years. Oh, and then there's the fact that it's his fucking birthday and, if not for my being here with him, he'd be alone for it.

It tugs at my heart, making it squeeze painfully in my chest. I'm overwhelmed by the same feeling I had when that asshole in the club made him cry. This time, though, I *am* able to wrap my arms around him, offering him what comfort I can, but I want to take away his hurt. I want to make him smile. I want to look after him and cherish him and, well, be the Daddy he so clearly needs.

Sure, there's the slight complication that I've never been anyone's Daddy before, as well as the fact that I've kept my lingerie secret to myself, but instinct will assist with the former and I get the feeling the latter won't bother him too much. I mean, he's a forty-five-year-old man who wears diapers for fun: if anyone will understand me wanting to wear panties because they make me feel good, I think it'll be him.

But would he *mind* having a Daddy who indulges in what's traditionally seen as a more effeminate kink?

Considering how beefy he is, would he prefer his Daddy to be the same? I'm solidly built (no abs to speak of but no beer gut either, though I can't deny there's a little softness around my middle) with a frame that rivals his, even if I am a little shorter. As much as I hate labels, I fit that whole 'masculine' vibe. You know, aside from my penchant for satin and lace.

But I'm getting way ahead of myself right now. Something about Matt inspires that from me. His vulnerability calls to me in ways I can't quite put into words.

So, instead of reacting to any of his emotional outburst (as desperately as I might want to address his specific concerns about me or the spark between us), I ask to give him a bath.

He blinks at me. "A...bath?"

I know I could have picked a far less intimate activity -one not involving nudity- but we met at a BDSM club, for fuck's sake. I'm also pretty sure he invited me in for a hook-up anyway, and this entire discussion has been dancing around our mutual desires to explore our connection, for lack of a better word. Besides, he's emotionally worked up and a bath will be relaxing if nothing else.

I nod decisively. "A bath, yes."

"Like...as a Daddy?" His question is tentative and spoken so quietly that I have to strain to hear it. There's a world of emotion packed into those few words -hope, longing, disbelief- and I want nothing more than to reassure him.

"Yes. If you're okay with that."

Wide green eyes look at me with that same 'are you stupid' expression Kate gave me earlier this evening. "I am *more* than okay with that."

Which is how I find myself standing next to a giant-ass bathtub in the master bathroom. Unlike most of the house, this space has clearly been renovated recently. The tiles are modern white subway tiles with glossy black accents. The shower, like the tub, is spacious enough to easily hold two adult bodies (even those as big as ours), and the toilet is positioned comfortably between the two, with a double vanity on the opposite wall.

I'd half expected to feel nervous for this moment, but a sense of how right this feels settles over me instead, and I'm calm and confident when I ask Matt if I can undress him.

"You really want to do this?" He double checks, even as he comes to stand in front of me while the tub fills. "This scene?"

I grin. "I really do." Excitement simmers beneath my skin. Not just at the prospect of getting him naked, even though my cock stirs valiantly at the thought, but excitement at seeing if the Daddy/boy dynamic will work for me.

For us.

"Safe words?" He prompts. "I usually use the stoplight system."

That much I had gathered at the club, but I nod. "Perfect."

Matt hesitates for barely a moment before he shakes out his shoulders and closes his eyes, exhaling with only a hint of shakiness. When he opens them again, he smiles, and it almost takes my breath away.

"Okay, sweetheart, arms up." My hands move to the hem of his polo shirt and I'm gentle as I pull it up and over his head. He's only a couple of inches taller than me, so it's not as awkward a maneuver as I'd anticipated.

I turn to toss the shirt at the hamper in the corner nearest to the bedroom and then allow my gaze to rake over his body. He's muscular and toned, no six-pack, but with definition beneath those big, sculpted pecs of his regardless. His olive skin is damn near flawless, and his chest hair is dark and silver streaked. It's not copious, stretching out across his pecs and thinning as it tapers down his abdomen and into his happy trail, creating a natural arrow towards his belly button and beyond.

"You are beautiful, sweet boy," I tell him after drinking him in, allowing my hands to coast over his broad shoulders and down his front, raking through the coarse hair on their journey to the waistband of his jeans.

"Thank you," he breathes, then hesitates.

I clear my throat. "You, uh, you can call me Daddy if you want to." Though I did read once that it's a title that has to be earned, so I quickly add, "Unless that's too much for now, or too fast." Suddenly, I'm not feeling as confident as I was only minutes ago. Have I fucked this up already? "It's just…I don't like 'Sir' or anything like that, so…I mean…Daddy or London are good for me."

Yep. I've ruined it. That has to be some sort of record, right? 'World's shortest stint as a Daddy' or something?

Surprising me, Matt seems to relax at my fumbling. He presses his forehead to mine and lets out a happy little sigh. "I want to call you Daddy."

It's like fireworks explode inside me. I feel lit up from the inside, elated and energized. I chuckle and can't resist pressing my lips to his in a short, chaste kiss which only makes the ecstatic buzz inside me last longer. "We probably should have discussed it before we started, huh?"

"Meh," Matt shrugs, then rubs his bearded cheek against my clean-shaven one, though he can probably feel the prickle of a day's worth of growth there now. "We can make it up as we go."

"I like the sound of that." The pressure is off that way. This is an agreement to learn and explore together. Even though he's got years of experience as a little, I don't feel like he has any expectations on how we should interact with each other in these roles. It feels like a clean slate for both of us, and that seems to reset my confidence.

He wiggles his hips from side to side with growing impatience, and I laugh. "Okay, I get the hint."

He's not wearing a belt, so I pop the button above his fly and then unzip him, hooking my fingers into the waistband and then dropping to my knees to tug the thick denim down. His legs are just as I remember them from seeing him romping around in his onesie, strong thighs and calves covered by a light carpet of dark hair. But the bulge straining against the front of tight black boxer briefs -and currently at my eye level- draws my attention, even as I help him step out of his jeans, thankful that we'd both kicked our shoes and socks off earlier.

Staying in this position, I reach for the band of his underwear and look up at him. "Color?" my voice is tight.

"Green," Matt's reply is quick.

I pull his boxer briefs down slowly, watching his cock spring free. I practically salivate as I visually take him in. He's thick and long and gorgeous, a bead of pearly liquid gathering at the tip of his purpling head as I watch.

Another conversation we did not have springs to mind as I contemplate leaning forward and licking that drop of precum off him. "Have you been tested recently?"

"Yes, Daddy." He sounds as affected as I am, and I can't even describe the reaction I feel to finally being called that name directly. It's like a bolt of lightning straight to my cock. I barely register that he's still talking. "Last week. Tests were negative, and I'm on PrEP. I can show y-"

"I trust you, sweetheart," I interrupt before indulging in the temptation in front of me, bringing my mouth to the crown of his cock. "And I'm the same." That's all I say before I give into the urge to I tease him, sucking the precum from him, and he proves to be delightfully responsive, sweet moans egging me on. "You taste so good."

So good, in fact, that I'm tempted to forget the bath plan and suck him dry, but I force myself to pull back and push myself back to my feet. I glance at the tub and decide it can still run for another minute or two.

Asking Matt to stay put, I stride over to the vanity and start opening the cupboards beneath the sink. I grin when I find what I'm looking for, pulling out a small basket of bath toys and a red loofah with a plastic Elmo head attached to it. There's also a bottle of baby wash, so I grab that, too.

Setting my collection down on the floor beside the tub, I unbutton the cuffs of my shirt and roll the sleeves to my elbows. Matt lets out a needy whimper, and I turn to watch his pupils dilating as he fixates on my forearms, then looks me over.

"Perfect, Daddy," he says when his gaze finally meets mine. His cheeks are flushed, his green eyes glazing over. "You look...*whoa*."

I glance past him and into the mirror above the vanity, immediately understanding that the business pants in combination with the rolled-up sleeves of my button down really do work for the Daddy vibes. It wasn't intentional – I'd just gone directly to pick up Kate after I finished work. But I'm glad for the outfit choice now. With a smile, I lean over the tub and turn off the faucet, dipping my hand through a mountain of bubbles to test the temperature of the water below.

I right myself and offer Matt my dry hand. "Alright, sweet boy, I'll help you in."

He climbs over and sinks into the welcoming warmth with a deep sigh.

I observe him for a quiet moment. With his eyes closed and bubbles caught in his beard, his vulnerability seems even more obvious, and my heart gives a funny squeeze. Was it really only a few hours ago that we met? It feels longer.

"Which is your favorite toy?" I ask him when his eyes drift open, possibly at sensing my stare.

"Um," he bites his lip, a gesture which should look strange on such a strong-looking man, but that I can only think of as adorable, "duckies, please Daddy. I have two."

It doesn't escape my notice that he uses the honorific every time he addresses me. I don't know if that's because it was a rule with his last Daddy, or if it's because it's been a while since he's had the chance to call anyone by the title, but if it makes him half as happy as it makes me, I'm more than glad for him to do so.

Digging through the little basket of toys, I locate the two rubber ducks. One is your standard yellow rubber ducky. The other is pink with multi-colored polka dots. His eyes light up as I hand them over, and it's a joy to watch him dunking them beneath the bubbles, splashing about as he creates a story where the two ducks go adventuring together. When I pick up a toy frog and join in, he blinks back surprised tears that make me angry at all those other men all over again, but I have him giggling within minutes.

"Daddy, it's a frog, not a dragon," he declares when I, as the frog, attempt to hold the little yellow duck prisoner in my tower of bubbles.

"This is a magical frog," I argue, "who can breathe fire."

Matt laughs and brandishes the other duck, waving him at me. "Then Sir Pinkie is a knight. And he's gonna beat your dragon frog and rescue Prince Quacker."

A dramatic fight scene ensues wherein, sure enough, the evil dragon frog is defeated by the pink duck, thereby allowing the prince to ride off into the sunset with the knight.

My shirt is damp, the remnants of dissolving bubbles and splashes of water soaking into my sleeves and chest, but it doesn't bother me at all. I wear the watermarks with pride, having genuinely enjoyed the imaginative play, and I reflect on that for a moment.

Should I have felt strange playing so childishly with another grown man? Especially one who was a stranger until a few hours ago? None of it felt awkward or forced. It felt natural. Just like it does when I'm playing with Kate when she's little. I take it as another sign that maybe I really am meant to be a Daddy and I just never realized it.

Speaking of...

"Alright, baby, the water's cooling down so let's get you all washed, okay?"

Matt bobs his head, still beaming at me. He's well and truly in little space now, and I'm thrilled that this is something I've been able to give him, considering how hurt and lonely it sounds like he has been. With a generous squirt of the baby wash onto the Elmo loofah, I scrub gently over his muscular, tattooed arms first, then over his strong chest and down his stomach. The water is deep, so I ask him to stand so I can properly wash his lower body.

He's not hard anymore, but that cock of his is still impressive even like this. All I do is wash him, though, scrubbing the foaming soap over his thighs and calf muscles, then getting him to turn so I can do the backs of his legs and up to his perfect ass. I don't tease him here, either, as tempted as I am. It's not the right moment for it. Not this time, anyway. Having him sit back down, I go over the rippling muscles of his back and then rinse him off.

"Time to get out," I declare, smiling when he makes a sound of complaint. "We've gotta get you dry and dressed and, if you're good, I'll read you a bedtime story."

Once again, his eyes turn suspiciously moist, and he blinks rapidly to clear them. "Okay, Daddy."

I'm fairly certain that telling myself to be rational and take things slowly right now is pointless, because my heart lurches yet again. I can't quite explain it, but something about this man pulls me in like nobody else I've ever met. I want to take away his hurt and make his days brighter. I want to worship him and show him that he's worthy of affection and attention. I want to be his Daddy for more than just tonight, even if that means letting him in in a way I've never allowed anyone else, sharing my own secrets and hang-ups like he's been brave enough to do with me.

But the strangest thing is that that revelation doesn't scare me. It should. I should be slapping myself for jumping in so deep, so fast. For not even questioning these urges to explore completely new and insanely intimate experiences with a man I met only a handful of hours ago. And yet I'm at peace with how fast this is going. It feels *right*.

He might have only invited me inside with the intention of a single night of fun, but I think we both know this is going to be more than that. Just how much more, though, is yet to be seen.

I towel him dry and then lead him into his bedroom. Nothing about this space even hints that he's a little. It's tastefully decorated with a king-sized bed decked out in a navy blue comforter and a couple of gray cushions. The bedside tables are plain and painted black, and I spy a matching chest of drawers through the open door of the walk-in robe.

"What do you like to sleep in, sweetheart?" I ask, already moving towards the walk-in robe as though I do this every night.

I push back the rising hope that we might get to that point sooner rather than later.

"Just loose boxer shorts," he answers. "Top left-hand drawer."

I don't know if the adult choice is his actual preference or if he's holding back for my benefit, but I don't push him. I select a pair of satin boxer shorts with an angry-looking cartoon squirrel emblazoned on the front, a pun about not touching his nuts printed on the right thigh. Matt chuckles when I hold them up.

"A gift from Josh," he explains, sounding fond and exasperated all at once.

"He sounds like a character." *Look at me not outwardly judging the guy for just abandoning his friend at the club on his birthday.* Not that I'm complaining about that too much – it led to me being able to hang out with Matt, after all. *Hmm, maybe I should thank this Josh guy...*

"He is."

I kneel in front of Matt and he places his hands on my shoulders, stepping into the shorts and allowing me to pull them up, standing back up along the way. Once I've made sure the waistband is sitting correctly and untwisted around his hips, I step back and look him over. "They suit you."

He grins at me. "Yeah, I kinda' love them."

I lead him to the bed and gesture for him to get in. "Do you have any storybooks?"

He briefly hesitates before he answers, "In the spare bedroom, three doors down the hallway on the left. There's a bookshelf…you'll find 'em."

I follow his instructions and find a room that is *much* more suited to a little. The bed in here is twin-sized, the room itself much smaller than the master suite, and the bedding is super-hero themed. The promised bookshelf is stationed against the far wall, tucked into the corner. Next to it is a small desk with coloring books and crayons spread out across the surface. There are a few stuffed toys propped up against the pillows on the bed, and a wooden toy box at the foot of the bed that I discover contains blocks and a train set.

Having crossed the space to poke around, I look through the selection of books, all for children, and choose one titled *'Elmo's Circle of Friends'* with a grin. I'm guessing I know his favorite *Sesame Street* character for sure, now. I hold the book up for Matt's inspection when I return to the master bedroom.

He cocks his head at me when I ask him to scoot over. "Are you staying the night?"

Now the awkwardness that I should have felt before surfaces. Aside from the tiniest bit of attention paid to his cock earlier, we haven't engaged in anything sexual, not that I expected us to following his unleashing of emotion. And yet giving him a bath has felt even more personal than if we had.

We're in a strange sort of limbo right now.

"I didn't want to assume." But, oh, how I want to spend the night in his arms, or with him in mine…and I really do want more than just the one night if I'm being completely honest.

“I’d like it if you did, but I don’t want you to feel, like, obligated or-”
I silence him with a kiss.

Chapter Seven – Matteo

London brings our lips together for the second time tonight. The first kiss was sweet, chaste and quick, but this one heats up quickly when I open my mouth to his, inviting his tongue to meet mine. We kiss slowly, exploring each other. His tongue is hot and sweet against mine, his lips just as soft as they look. When we finally pull apart, I can't help but let out a happy sigh.

"Mmm," he agrees.

"So…does that mean you're staying?" I feel ridiculous asking, like I'm a teenager again. I haven't felt this way about another man in over a decade. I'm giddy and a little nervous. Obviously, a large part of that is because tonight has been perfect. *He* has been perfect. I almost don't believe that he's never been a Daddy before.

He gives me a soft look and it gives me butterflies. "I'd love to."

"You can borrow a T-shirt and boxers if you want. Or sleep naked." I waggle my eyebrows at him.

"Don't tempt me," he laughs, the sound deep and rich, even as he wanders into my wardrobe. He returns wearing a plain black tee and a pair of loose cotton boxer shorts, the clothes he'd been wearing folded neatly over his arm. He hangs them over the armrest of the chair near the window, then slips into bed beside me with an endearingly unsure expression on his face.

"What?"

"You're out of little space," he begins, then lifts the book he'd discarded on top of the covers earlier. "Should we maybe table this and talk?"

There's a part of me that wants to say no and demand my bedtime story and snuggles, but I push that down. Talking is more important. I basically unloaded on him earlier, and instead of addressing any of those issues, or potentially even to buy himself some time to think about them properly, we went straight into a pretty personal scene to test the waters of a Daddy/boy relationship. It's the strangest, most unexpected turn of events, but I have zero complaints about it.

"Can we still cuddle while we talk?"

Eyes lighting up, he opens his arms and I move into his embrace, rolled onto my side with my cheek pressed against his chest and his chin on the top of my head. It doesn't escape my notice that we seem to fit together perfectly like this, either. Like jigsaw pieces clicking into place.

"How did you feel about the bath?" London asks once I'm settled. Then he starts answering his own question, like he knows I need time to process my feelings.

I appreciate that more than he can know.

"From my perspective," he says, "I thought it went well. It felt good. *Natural.* I liked being your Daddy." He clears his throat. "Did it help with your concerns? Or did it make them worse?"

"You're definitely a natural," I assure him, then realize that's not the part which is worrying him the most. I fight the urge to facepalm. "I'm less concerned now that you're not actually going to be into it."

His lips find my forehead, kissing it gently. "What about your fear that you're only going to get attached because I'm the first guy in a long time to do this with you?"

"You've proven me wrong on that front, too." I don't hesitate to answer.

From the second he started undressing me, that particular fear evaporated. I don't want him just because he's giving me what I crave. I want him for him.

I pull back a little so I can look him in the eye. "I think the connection we've got, this…this *spark* between us…is real. We had genuine fun playing in the tub, right? And that kiss just before was so hot." Not to mention the way he'd sucked the crown of my dick for a few seconds before my bath. I understand why a blow job never materialized; we had to explore the Daddy dynamic first. And, now that we know that works, there's no reason to rush things.

Well, not unless this is *just a one-night club hook-up type thing for him after all.*

My heart sinks at that thought, and I'm almost certain my expression mirrors my mounting worries.

"Hey, where'd you just go?"

"What do you want to get out of this?" I'm blurting the question before I can properly phrase it. "Because I don't think I can do casual, even if I thought I did when I asked you to come in tonight. I'm really an all-in kind of guy."

London's eyes are warm and his smile is fond. "I figured as much. From what I've read, and what I've seen -and, hell, what I just experienced as well- this sort of thing involves trust and familiarity that a casual relationship isn't generally cut out for. Well, at least for most people. And, to be honest, I'm an all-in kind of guy, too. So…" There's vulnerability on his face again, reminding me that we're equals in this. It steadies my nerves. "I'd like to date you. Exclusively. To be your Daddy…if that's what you want."

"This isn't going too fast for you? Like, you're not just doing this for my benefit, right?"

I hate how insecure I sound.

Another fear is that he's just saying what I want to hear and then I won't hear from him again after tomorrow. But he honestly doesn't strike me as the type of guy to pull that sort of stunt. I can't know that for sure, but I want to give him the benefit of the doubt. I need to.

The covers rustle as he gets more comfortable, wriggling closer, pressing our bodies together. He's hard, his bulge grinding into mine, eliciting a soft gasp from my lips. "This is perfect, sweetheart. And I'm benefiting, too."

How is it that he is so damn mature? When I was in my mid-twenties, I was a fucking mess. And that was *before* I discovered my kinky side.

I've got one arm trapped beneath him, but the other coasts down his strong back, sneaking under his shirt, teasing his skin before dipping towards the band of his borrowed boxers. He stills then exhales, "There's one more thing."

With our chests against each other, I can feel his heart rate picking up. Concerned, I pull my head back, watching him closely as I ask, "What's wrong?"

London swallows roughly, spots of pink on his cheeks. "I…" He clears his throat but doesn't look away. "I like to wear lingerie. Namely panties. Lace and satin do it for me."

Huh. I wouldn't have picked that from his big, rugged frame. But now the image of him wearing a strap of lace and nothing else forms in my brain and my cock gets impossibly harder. "That's fucking sexy."

"Really?" He sounds bewildered, like this was not the reaction he was expecting. I can't imagine why, considering I think my kink is even more taboo, socially speaking.

My fingers tease at the top of the boxers again. "Are you wearing a pair now?"

His resulting nod is slow and hesitant. Gone is the bold, confident man I've seen all evening, and in his place is someone wholly relatable.

"Can I see you?"

If I hadn't been so focused on him, I think I might have missed the panic on his face in the dim lighting. "I've never…" He trails off, averting his gaze.

"Never what?"

"I…I've kept it to myself." He bites his lip. "I've never let anyone else see me wearing them. I've never worn them if I even thought someone else might see them."

I blink, surprised by that. "Really?"

London bobs his head in affirmation, blushing in the dim lighting.

Holy shit.

Even though I've been enamored with his self-assurance until now, this vulnerability is somehow even sexier. The idea that he feels comfortable enough to share this secret of his with me, a veritable stranger, is heady. Maybe he sees it as a mutual thing, though, considering the way I spilled my own secrets to him earlier tonight.

"I'm the luckiest boy *ever*." I blurt, then realize that he hasn't actually agreed to show me. I rush to fix my presumption. "I mean, I will be when you're comfortable showing me. *If*. If you're comfortable. There's no pressure."

London's shoulders relax, the tension in his body fading while I babble. Then he's kissing me again, cutting off my ramble and rolling me onto my back. This kiss is even more intense than the last. It's sloppier, harder, less coordinated. London ruts against me, grinding his cock against mine while our tongues twist together. I pant into his mouth while I rock my hips up to meet his movements.

"Fuck me," I breathe, managing to get the thought out through the lust-induced fog in my brain. "Please, Daddy."

London groans, a deep sound full of pleasure that rockets straight through me. "God, hearing you call me Daddy is something else."

I don't need to beg him any further, though. He rolls off me, kneeling on the mattress to pull his borrowed shirt over his head, and I watch through hooded eyes as his thumbs tuck into to the waistband of his shorts. After taking a steadying breath, he pushes the cotton down where it catches around his thick thighs, revealing the black elastane and lace through which his cock is making a bid for freedom, straining against the fabric.

His blue eyes are pinned on me, watching me for my reaction. He has nothing to worry about, though. If anything, seeing him like this turns me on more. I lick my lips, reaching for him. My fingertips brush against the smooth, silky front which is edged by soft lace scallops. His dick jumps at the touch.

"Gorgeous," I murmur, palming him properly now through the material. There's a damp spot forming over the head of his cock, as though I needed any further proof of how much he's enjoying this. Thumbing over it, I relish in the sounds he's making.

"You're killing me, sweetheart," London says after allowing me to tease him for a while longer.

I'm aching and leaking precum in my own shorts, ignored by both of us to this point. "*Daddy*," I practically whine, and I can feel the jolt of arousal that shoots through his cock when I do. Grinning, I file that information away, beyond pleased to have proof that he really does enjoy it when I use the title on him.

Whatever lingering fear I harbored that he might just be playing along for my sake evaporates completely and I'm elated because my birthday wish seems to have come true. I've found a Daddy. A super hot Daddy, at that.

Oh, sure, we don't actually know each other, and the age gap isn't ideal, but those are issues to discuss later. For now, I just want to enjoy the moment. It's been far too long since I've been with another man, and even longer since I felt truly free to let go and be myself in bed.

But with London I don't feel any reason to hold back. I can call him Daddy. I can let him take control. He doesn't expect me to top, or to dominate, or to boss him around (not that I don't enjoy being a bossy bottom every now and again). London knows that I'm needy, that I'm starved for affection, that I want to be looked after and have my decisions made for me. And I trust him to give me what I need. I trust him when he says he wants more than just tonight.

Lunging, London rolls me onto my back again, kissing me while he struggles to push his shorts the rest of the way off. It's an awkward maneuver, but we're both worked up now and neither one of us has the capacity to be suave.

His hands tug at my boxers next, and I lift my hips, my mouth still connected to his, helping him remove them to a point where I can kick them free. I don't care where they land after that.

The only clothing separating us now are those sexy as hell panties he wears, and my hands slide over his perfect, firm ass, squeezing the smooth skin I find there. It turns out the pants are cut like cheeky boy shorts, the scalloped lace fanning out from his crack in graceful arches, feeling like they frame the globes of his cheeks to perfection. I want to demand that he stand up and show me, but that would involve stopping the kiss – not something I'm inclined to do.

"They're gonna have to come off if you want me to fuck you," London all but growls against my lips. I've been toying with the edges of the lace and squeezing his ass, so I'm not surprised that he's thinking along the same lines as I am.

"You strip, I'll grab the lube."

"I like the way you think."

We're a mess of limbs and movement for a brief interlude, each of us dedicated to our respective tasks, and when we meet back up in the middle of the bed again, there's no longer anything between us. He's gloriously naked and I drink in every inch of him, my hand gravitating to his hard length.

His cock is shorter than mine, but he's fucking thick. Just imagining the delicious stretch and burn of something that size inside me has me steadily leaking precum. The idea of him being inside me without even the thinnest barrier is even hotter.

"You sure you're good without a condom?" I double check. It was one thing to confirm we were both free of STIs before he licked my dick earlier, but this takes that implicit trust to a whole new level. I haven't gone bare since my relationship ended. But this thing between London and me isn't a one-night stand. It's the start of something new. Something serious. "We're going to be exclusive, right?" He'd said that earlier, hadn't he? Or am I just imagining the things I want to hear?

I feel only a little bit awkward as I ask these questions, like a fumbling teenager instead of a grown man. But it's important that we're on the same page. Especially when we're talking about unprotected sex. I get tested regularly and I'm on PrEP, but you can never be too careful.

London nods. "Definitely exclusive, sweetheart." As if reading my thoughts, he adds, "Like I said before, my tests have been negative, I haven't been with anyone since my last test, and I'm also taking PrEP." His lips curl upwards and he bumps our noses together. "And I want to see my cum dripping out of your tight, little hole."

Holy fuck.

Yeah, I'm done talking.

I lunge for his mouth, pulling him against me until our bodies are flush against each other. Wriggling my hand between us, I wrap it around both our cocks as best I can, pumping them together with our combined precum aiding the glide of flesh against flesh. This kiss is rough and needy, and I can't distinguish which moans and groans belong to him, or which have come from me. His hands feel like they're everywhere, exploring my body, tugging at my hair, driving me crazy for him. Then he picks up the lube from where I dropped it at my side.

I spread my legs for London without instruction, far too desperate to make him work for it. I can feel him smiling into our kiss and hear the click of the bottle lid opening. He manages to work some lube onto his fingers in a one-handed movement that has to be well practiced, then snaps the lid shut again, dropping the bottle back where he found it before bringing his coated fingers to my hole, all without breaking our kiss.

He doesn't tease me or draw out the prep, something I'm grateful for in this moment. There'll be time for slow and romantic later. Tonight, we're both too wound up. I bear down as he's adding a third finger, already babbling obscenities and begging for his cock.

"Fuck me already," I demand in a flash of lucidity, "please, Daddy."

The magic words have him stroking more lube over his cock. We make matching sounds of pleasure as he notches the head against my entrance and slowly sinks in, stretching me further with short, careful thrusts until he bottoms out. He gives me a moment to adjust and, once I've relaxed properly and the burn is less pain and more bliss, he pulls back out and then thrusts back in again in one smooth move.

It's not long before we find our rhythm, London spread over me so we can kiss as feverishly as we're fucking. My hands grip his shoulder blades, slipping over sweat-slicked skin, and a gasp is torn from my lips as he grazes my prostate.

"*Daddy*," I plead, hoping he'll hit that same angle again.

"*Fuck*," he draws the word out, his voice thick and gravelly, "you feel so fucking good, sweetheart. So tight and hot for Daddy."

I almost come at that. If he thinks me calling him Daddy is hot, it's nothing on hearing him refer to himself that way. My hips rock upwards, out of sync, my cock seeking friction.

"Please," I'm back to babbled begging, my heart hammering and my breath coming out in pants as the tension builds. I'm so fucking close, but I need more. "I need…" I don't know what I need. Not really. All I know is I'm cresting the wave, but my orgasm is just out of reach.

London shifts his weight onto his left arm, resting on his elbow and forearm so he can slip his right hand between our bodies. When his hand wraps around my leaking cock, I almost sob with relief. "Is this what you need, sweetheart?" He begins pumping me in time with his thrusts.

I don't answer. I'm unable to. Instead, I manage to partially warn, "I'm gonna-" My words cut off with a grunt as his dick pistons over my prostate again and I come hard, spurting over his hand and coating both our bellies.

He rides me through it, his movement becoming jerky before he curses and slams back in one last time, his hips stilling while the heat of his release fills me. When he pulls out slowly, I wince only a little. He presses a gentle kiss to my left pec, then flops onto his back at my side, catching his breath.

The silence between us is comfortable, but soon enough the sensation of his cum trickling out of me makes me squirm. London catches my movement and rolls out of bed, heading into the bathroom. I hear the cupboard open and shut, then the sound of running water. When he returns with a wet washcloth and cleans me up, my heart flutters.

It's a stupid thing to get emotional about, but he's the first man to ever do this for me. Trent would always insist we shower, and I'd be out of bed and dressing myself during condom disposal after any of my rare hook-ups. But this tender, sweet action from London feels like the most intimate thing we've done all night.

I barely register him tossing the cloth back through the bathroom door, or manhandling me against the pillows, but I do pay attention to the soft kiss he delivers just behind my ear.

"Sleep, sweetheart," he says, spooned up against my back. My eyes grow heavy, as though following his instructions is instinctive.

Best. Birthday. Ever.

Chapter Eight – London

"I want *all* the details," Cherie demands when I answer her call.

It's been three days since I took Kate to Littles' Night. Three days since I met Matteo. Three days since I discovered that I'm not as impartial to the lifestyle as I'd assumed. Three little days…and my whole world has changed.

"Honestly, I'm surprised it's taken you this long to hound me," I tell her, knowing she can hear the smirk in my voice.

Matt and I have texted every day. At night, I call him and read him a bedtime story. We haven't seen each other in person, but our connection feels just as strong as it did when we met. And hearing him call me Daddy still never fails to send a thrill of emotions straight through me.

"That's because I was waiting for you to come to me, jackass," Cherie interrupts my thoughts. "Kate came home telling me that you found yourself a little of your own. *That you're considering being a Daddy.* And I just assumed you'd come talk it through when you were ready."

I can hear the hurt behind her words. Becoming serious, I respond, "I was going to, Cher, I swear. But, not gonna lie: this Daddy thing hasn't been as complicated as I thought it would be. Like…it's just been easy, y'know? Instinctive? So, I didn't really have any questions or anything after all." And the ones I did have -the ones more specific to Daddy/little boy play- Google has helped with. "And I know you've been swamped with work, so I was gonna wait until you were free to chat."

"Hmm."

"*Hmm*? What '*hmm*'?"

I spin my chair around from my desk. I'm a landscaper by trade, but I work for a company that provides landscaping to large businesses and corporations -hospitals, schools, resorts, that sort of thing- and, more often than not, find myself seated at a desk sketching plans and working around budgets than toiling outside on a job site. Considering I majored in psychology, this was not where I saw myself when I graduated college. But my part-time college job as a laborer helping at sites turned into a full-time job, which turned into a promotion and…here I am.

I share my office with another guy, Tom, but today he's on site supervising one of his projects. Our two desks are pressed together in the middle of the room, surrounded by glass walls. Three of them look out into the other offices and reception area. There's also a boardroom three doors down, but the glass walls there are frosted. That's generally where we host pitch meetings for clients, as well as our monthly staff meetings.

The fourth wall is a window that looks out over the city. From where I sit, I have the perfect view of the manicured grounds of the local college. It serves as a reminder of how far I've come and how different life is to what I'd imagined for myself only a few years ago.

"I should have seen it earlier," Cherie muses, finally answering my question. I always allow her the time to think before she speaks, and she affords me the same courtesy. We're very similar, and we understand each other's limitations. This is why we work so well as friends. "That you're a Daddy, I mean."

"Oh?"

Her laughter is tinkling. "London, you've always been a natural with Kate. You barely even blinked when I told you what we were into. You just rolled with it."

"Yeah," I say, drawing out the word as if she's slow on the uptake, "because you're my best friend."

"It's more than that. It's always been more than that, now that I really think about it."

"Cher…"

"No," she cuts me off sharply, and I can picture her shaking her head. "None of my other friends outside of the lifestyle, or my family for that matter, really get it. But from the first time you saw Kate in little space, you just went with it. Zero judgment, zero hesitation. You just called yourself Uncle London and stepped in as a caregiver. Hell, you even enjoyed it."

She's got me there. "I did. I do."

Playing with Katie was always something I had fun with, as though it filled a need I didn't know I had. And, obviously, it had scratched the itch enough to keep me from realizing that I was actually into the lifestyle itself. Until I met Matt.

Her exhale is heavy as it travels down the phone line. "So, all this time, you've been a Daddy and neither of us realized it."

"Honestly, Cher, I don't think I was ready to realize it."

"Not until you met someone worth stepping out of your comfort zone for, anyway." Cherie's definitely got my number.

"Exactly."

"And this guy is worth it?" There's an edge to her voice again, a protective sort of bite that makes me smile.

I think of my big, buff, tattooed, bearded boy and my heart skips a beat. It's been three days, but I'm so fucking attached already, it's bizarre. But, strangely, I'm not panicked about that. This thing between him and me? It feels right in a way I can't put words to. Like we're two pieces of a puzzle that just fit. He's got the capacity to break me, but I'm more than aware of how fragile he is in return.

I think of the look in his eyes when I shared my own secret. Beneath the desire, I'd seen his understanding and his unwavering support. It should be weird that a complete stranger's acceptance had meant so much to me, but it had bolstered me, given me the courage to truly be myself with him, and it had been freeing in ways I've never experienced before.

I don't even hesitate with my reply. "He so is."

* * *

'Dinner at my place tonight?' Matt's message pops up on my phone screen just after lunch and my lips immediately pull into a wide smile. One of the guys on my crew arches an eyebrow and I shake my head at him. He'll probably give me shit later, but I don't care.

'What can I bring?'

The animated ellipsis pops up almost immediately, then disappears and reappears a couple of times. Finally, Matt's reply comes through. *'An overnight bag.'*

I chuckle, wondering just how much overthinking Matt did before he worked up the nerve to press send. My boy is one of the shy ones and I love to push the envelope with him. Getting Matt to blush and squirm is rapidly becoming one of my favorite things. I hope my flirtatious tone is conveyed in my next message back. *'Do you have plans for me, sweetheart?'*

'You don't have to stay over. I'm sorry if that was too forward.'

Smile slipping, I click on Matt's name and press the call button, bringing my phone to my ear. I step away from the guys working on my latest project (a community garden paid for by the local council) while I wait for Matt to pick up. When he does, I barely give him a chance to say hello before I launch into my gentle admonishment. "There's no such thing as too forward with me, baby."

All I can hear on the other end of the call is his soft breathing before Matt eventually admits, "I just don't want to come off too clingy."

"Oh, Matt," I sigh, having forgotten that he's been hurt to this extent. That other men have made him feel like his 'neediness' (his word, not mine) is something to apologize for, or to smother. But the thing is, I love being reminded of how much he wants me around. How much he desires my affection and my care. Honestly, I'm just as needy (for lack of a better word) as he is in this relationship. "You will never be too clingy for me, I promise."

Matt's response to my declaration is a dry, self-deprecating chuckle. "You say that now…" He lets the sentence hang.

It's only been four days since we met, since we fucked, since we agreed that he'd be my boy and I'd be his Daddy, but I'm already all in. If anything, I've been champing at the bit to spend more time with him, but I've been resolved to let him set the pace, knowing that he's got concerns of his own to work through first.

Then his words from that first night come back to me. He wanted a Daddy to take control, to make the decisions and allow him to relax. Maybe waiting was a mistake. Maybe he needed me to take control with this, too, and I failed at that.

Ugh. So much for 'I feel like a natural at this'.

"Okay, I'm pretty sure I've fucked up," I blurt out before I can think better of it.

"What? How?"

I wander further away from the guys, then lower my voice for additional privacy. I mightn't be ashamed of my proclivities, but I don't need to become water cooler gossip fodder. "I've been giving you space, I guess. Letting you set the pace because I know you were worried that you might just be getting over excited at the idea of having a Daddy again. And I know my age bothers you, too." He makes a sound of protest, but I steamroll right over it. "And that's all totally fair. But you said you wanted your Daddy to take control, right? And, well, I didn't do that, did I? I left the ball in your court, and I'm sorry."

There's a whoosh of air down the line, and it takes me a moment to realize that it's an exhalation of relief. I curse myself a little more for dropping the ball like this so early into our relationship, but Matt's words are reassuring. "You're new at this," he says, quiet but firm. "And we didn't exactly talk things through as much as we should have before we…" He stops and clears his throat, and I imagine spots of pink appearing on those sexy bearded cheeks of his.

"We're going to sit down and set rules tonight," I say definitively. "Proper negotiation. I want this to work so badly, Matt."

I barely manage to stop myself from telling him that I'm crazy about him. It's been four days. We've seen each other in person once, and all other contact has been via text, calls and two Facetime sessions. As comfortable as I am with how quickly I've become attached, I don't want to sound like a raving lunatic.

"Yeah, I do, too." Am I imagining it, or does he sound as wistful as I feel?

"Good." There's not much else to say beyond that. Jake, one of the youngest guys on my crew, is waving from across the expanse of recently laid turf, trying to get my attention. I sigh. "I've gotta go, sweetheart. I'll see you tonight." Those words send sparks of anticipation shooting up my spine.

"I can't wait." I can hear the smile in his voice and I grin.

"Me either."

* * *

At five minutes to six, I park my car behind Matt's in his driveway. We live a twenty-minute drive apart when there's no traffic, but it came closer to forty tonight. I caught every red light, and it was rush hour. All I've thought about since we ended our call this afternoon is wrapping my sexy man in my arms and kissing him senseless.

Well, that's a lie. I've thought about taking things further after the kissing, too.

But we've got things to discuss first. Everything I've read (and re-read) about the lifestyle says that limits, rules and expectations need to be set in stone. I don't want to repeat my mistake. Matt is a grown man, but he's already told me that he wants (no, *needs*) a full-time Daddy. I'm up for the job, but I want us both on the same page about what that entails. I need to know exactly how much leeway he wants me to give him, if any.

When he opens the door, my breath catches in my throat. He's wearing business attire, which doesn't surprise me given that he works for a Fortune 500 company (even though he's adamant that as an electrical engineer he shouldn't have to dress in such a corporate fashion), and it looks like it's been tailored to his large, muscular frame, fitting him like a second skin. His hair is tamed with gel, and his beard, while still more beard than scruff, is trimmed neatly.

"Fuck me," I say by way of greeting, and his grin turns predatory.

"I'm sure we can arrange that one day."

Oh, fuck yes. I don't know where this confidence has come from, but I love it almost as much as I love his usual shyness and vulnerability.

I step into his personal space and wrap my free arm around his back, reaching up behind his head to guide him towards me so our lips can finally become reacquainted. I drop my overnight bag at our feet as he deepens the kiss so I can use that arm to pull him flush against me. I don't care that we're making out like teenagers in the open doorway of his house. I couldn't wait a second longer for this kiss.

When we finally part, both of us breathing heavily and readjusting ourselves with matching smirks, Matt steps aside and closes the door behind me. I leave my bag where it is, figuring I'll grab it later, and follow him into the kitchen-dining-lounge area, which smells amazing and I tell him so.

"It's just pulled pork," he says, lifting the lid off a crockpot and stirring the mixture inside. "I've got some slaw and fresh burger buns. Figured it was nice and easy."

"It sounds awesome," I insist.

"It's still got a little more to go," he adds some extra seasoning and barbecue sauce to the mix and then puts the lid back on. He turns to smile at me. "Did you want a drink?"

"I'm good for now." Now that it appears he's not cooking, I close the space between us again, wrapping my arms around him. He sinks into my embrace and rests his head on my shoulder. "I've missed you."

"Mmm," he agrees, "me too."

I can sense his exhaustion and, even though I know we need to talk, instinct drives me to say, "Let's get you changed into something more comfortable. Okay, sweet boy?"

Instead of waiting for his response, I lead him by the hand to the spare room which contains all his little paraphernalia. There's a dresser against the wall to my left, across from the bed, and I release Matt's hand so I can rifle through it. I dig out a set of pjs covered in cartoon ducks, and then open another drawer to find training pants. My hand hovers over them for a moment before I shake my head and open the next drawer down.

Bingo.

Pulling a diaper from the packet, I turn to face Matt with my selection on display. The minute widening of his eyes is the only sign of his surprise. "Color?"

It takes him half a second to understand what I'm asking. "Green." He cocks his head at me, then jerks his chin at the diaper. "Color?"

"Green." I appreciate that he's checking in with me, too. He knows this is new for me and, as confident as I like to pretend I am, we both know that it's a big leap into Daddy play. I smile and wave towards the bed. "Let's get you changed, huh?"

We move over to the bed and I drop the clothes I've chosen for him on top of the covers. He allows me to unbutton his shirt and tug it loose from his pants, helping to slip it off once I've pushed the sleeves back over his shoulders. His belt goes next, then I divest him of his pants and underwear.

"Let's get the shirt on first, then you can climb up on the bed for me, yeah?"

As soon as I help him get the cotton t-shirt over his head, I can see the change in him. He's not little, but he's immediately more relaxed.

Landing a gentle love tap to his perfect bare ass, I direct him to lie back across the mattress and then reach for the diaper, unfolding it and turning it into the direction I need. "Butt up, baby," I instruct, and he complies, creating a bridge with his body, his strong thigh muscles emphasized by this position. "You're gorgeous," I can't help but tell him, delighting in the flush that creeps over his skin. I slide the diaper underneath him and, when I'm happy that it's positioned where I need it, I get him to drop his ass back down, legs spread and bent at the knees. His cock is at half-mast, but this isn't about sex right now, so I ignore it, even though my own fills at the sight.

Ignoring my arousal, I ask, "I know you're not planning on using this," I tap the open diaper, making it crinkle dully. It's like a mixture of cotton and plastic, which makes sense to me, considering its purpose, "but do you want a barrier cream, or some powder? The whole changing experience?"

"Someone's been reading up," he teases, and I grin unabashedly.

"Damn straight." We'll talk about this soon, but I want to do everything right. So, yeah, I have been doing some research on the stuff I've got zero practical experience with.

Matt's smile turns soft and understanding. He wriggles his hips. "Powder would be great. I don't know if it actually helps, but I like to think it prevents chafing." He gestures to the dresser. "Top right-hand drawer."

I find the little bottle of baby powder exactly where he said it was and return to my task. Pulling the front up and closing the sticky, velcro-like tabs is a simple enough process, and it's not long before I'm getting him to lift his hips again so I can tug his pajama bottoms up over his adorably padded butt.

"Better?" I ask, offering him both hands to pull him up from his reclined position.

He beams at me, the expression lighting up his face. "So much better. Thank you, Daddy."

I can't resist kissing him. I don't think that urge is ever going to disappear.

Chapter Nine – Matteo

Just over three weeks later, barring a few little stumbles due to miscommunication in those first few days, my relationship with London seems to barrel along with ease. He spends every second night at my place, and we've gotten into a proper routine. I indulge in little time after dinner on those nights, and I've become used to sleeping with him spooned against my back. It's crazy to think that I was miserable and lonely a month ago. It feels like a different time entirely.

A knock on my front door has me frowning. I'm not expecting London this evening, or any deliveries come to think of it. When I swing the timber aside, Ash and Josh push their way past me.

"Hello," I greet sarcastically, turning to follow them down the short hallway after shutting the door in their wake, "how are you? Please, make yourselves at home."

"This is a welfare check," Ash declares, dropping down on my couch and arching an eyebrow at me. "You've been M.I.A since before your birthday, and you've only been dropping emojis in the group chat. No words," he emphasizes and points at me sternly, "*just* emojis."

Alright, I'll admit it: that's not really like me. It's not like my responses are usually long and flowery, but I've been distracted.

Feeling a little miffed that it has taken my friends close to a month to notice my withdrawal, though, I fold my arms defensively. "I've been busy."

I feel marginally guilty for being combative, but I do feel a bit like they could have made an effort with me, too. I know it's a two-way street, but they knew I was struggling.

Then again, they both work full-time (and Josh, like his older brother was, is a cop, so his schedule can be unpredictable), and I *had* asked them to give me space.

Josh looks like he wants to argue, but Ash puts his hand on his soon-to-be brother-in-law's arm and shakes his head. Then he turns to me, empathetic but firm. "You asked us to back off. We gave you a month." His expression softens. "We were worried, Matt. And I miss our playdates. Don't you miss your little time?"

More guilt begins to creep into my gut, and I fight back a blush. London's told his friends and family about me. I even met his Mom via Facetime last week, which went surprisingly well considering she's only a few years older than me. However, I've kept him a secret from my friends. Not intentionally, mind you. But I haven't gone out of my way to casually drop his existence into the group chat, either. He hasn't pushed me to introduce him, but now I wonder if he's noticed that I've been keeping him all to myself. I make a note to talk to him about it. The last thing I want to do is hurt his feelings.

Swallowing, I look down at my socked feet and scuff my toe over a mark on the tiles. "Uh…I've kinda been getting my little time in at home." I really can't look at them. "With my new Daddy." I'm significantly older than both these men, but right now I feel like an errant teenager caught fooling around with the boy next door.

There's a moment of stunned silence before both Ash and Josh start firing a jumble of questions at me. When I look up to interrupt and attempt to answer them, the hurt on Ash's face makes me feel even guiltier.

He's half my age but he's become my best friend and keeping this from him probably seems like a betrayal from his perspective.

"It's really new," I try to explain. "I mean, I only met him on my birthday-"

"I was *with you* on your birthday," Josh argues, sounding bewildered.

I shrug. "Until you left me on my own because you found someone to fuck." The words come out harsher than I intended, but it doesn't make them any less truthful.

Ash turns to Josh and smacks his bicep. Hard. "*Really*?"

"Ow!" Josh pouts and rubs at the site of impact. Then he has the grace to appear sheepish. "Look, that wasn't my best moment, but Matty said it was fine."

Ash hits him again, punctuating every word in his next sentence with a whack of his open palm. "It. Was. His. Birthday. You. Dick."

"I know! I'm sorry!" Josh holds his hands up in surrender.

With an exaggerated sigh, Ash turns back to me. "Okay, so I can understand why you'd be avoiding us, considering Captain Oblivious here totally didn't help matters, but this is the sort of news I want to celebrate with you." His gaze turns imploring. "I was afraid I was losing my playmate. My best friend."

Well, that hurts to think about. Ash didn't exactly have an easy start in the lifestyle, and he'd be just as lonely without the guys as I would. "Shit," I rub the spot between my eyes, wincing. "I'm sorry. I just got caught up in the honeymoon period, I guess."

I'd wanted to stay in my happy little bubble with London. Wanted to indulge in something that was just for me. But I could have done that while letting the guys know that I'd met someone. Hell, I should have said something, and then they wouldn't have been worried about me.

I watch as a slow, smug smile stretches Ash's lips. He shakes his head, his curls flopping into his eyes. He brushes them back with the side of his hand. "Honeymoon period, huh?" He makes a 'gimme' motion. "C'mon. Spill. I want to know about this guy."

I grab beers for the three of us and drop down in one of the armchairs kitty-corner to the couch after handing the guys their drinks. "His name is London," I start, then jut my chin at Josh. "The hot young Daddy who was there with the girl in the Belle costume."

Josh's brown eyes widen and then he hoots and leans over the arm of the couch with his hand raised for a high-five. "Damn," he whistles, "nice catch, my man."

Laughing, I slap his palm, because, yeah, London's definitely a catch. "I'm waiting for the other shoe to drop," I confess, then I lick my lips. "He's…well, he's perfect for me." Even with the age gap, but I don't mention this to them. They're not going to judge me for dating someone their age.

"You've got me at a disadvantage here," Ash complains, "because I wasn't there, and I have no idea who this guy is." He scowls. "Stupid Charlie scheduling meetings on your birthday."

"You should have let Ted bring you," Josh rolls his eyes. "Or Chance. Or even Spence."

Ash starts listing reasons this was impossible by counting fingers. "Ted had a date, Chance was out of town, and Spence had a late recording session." He fidgets in his seat. "And you know I'm not used to being little in public without a caregiver. I'm just not comfortable with that."

Josh has the grace to appear both apologetic and understanding. He gentles his tone and reaches out to squeeze Ash's shoulder. "I know, I'm sorry."

Ash waves the apology off. "It's fine. But I need to know *everything* about this 'hot young Daddy'." He waggles his brows and pulls out his phone. "What's his last name? I'm gonna Facebook stalk him."

"Don't be stupid," I tug my own phone from my pocket. There's a text from London waiting on the screen and I swipe it away before I open my photos app and turn the screen to face my friends. "Here."

Ash grabs for it, closely inspecting the selfie I took on my last date with London. "Wow," he says after a moment, "you weren't exaggerating. Look at that jawline."

"Like Charlie's isn't just as pretty," I tease, and Josh scoffs.

"I'm prettier."

Josh and Charlie look so similar that I honestly can't agree with him or deny it. Thankfully, Ash just shoves Josh and tells him to fuck off. He hands my phone back to me and probes for more information. "Okay, so his name is London and he's hot. I feel like there's more to him than that?"

It's not hard for me to take the bait, and I spend a few more minutes telling them about how we met (Ash hits Josh again when I describe the creep London rescued me from, blaming him for having left me alone) and giving a brief summary of our relationship to date. We've gone out a few times, but generally spend time here at my place.

I've been over to his apartment twice, but it's spartan and doesn't really lend itself to my little time, so we've mostly hung out here at home. I get the feeling he likes it better here anyway. And it turns out that he shares my love of gaming, too, so when I'm not little -and we're not otherwise indisposed- we're going on campaigns through *WoW* or shooting up zombies together. We share an easy camaraderie which makes it feel like we've been together for longer than just a month.

When my phone rings, I belatedly remember the message I ignored in preference of calming the guys down. I cringe a little and answer London's call, much to Ash and Josh's combined amusement. "Hi, Daddy," I say sweetly. I'm not above a little emotional manipulation to save myself from getting in trouble.

He's onto me, though. Sounding amused, he replies, "Hi, sweetheart." He pauses for a moment, and I ignore the guys leaning closer, trying to listen in. They're worse than a pair of sixteen-year-old girls, literally hanging onto the edge of their seats for gossip material. "Did you get my message?"

It sounds a little like he's driving, the echo of the call telling me that he's got me on speaker through the Bluetooth connection to his stereo, and I check my watch, knowing that he's been working late at the office recently. "I saw it, but Ash and Josh are here so I haven't had a chance to read it."

"Ah, that makes sense then." I can't quite read his tone. Then he sighs. "I got off early today, so I texted to see if you minded me coming over, but-"

"No! No buts, I mean." I interrupt, wanting to facepalm when I realize that he might think I'm telling him not to come. "Please come over." Across from me, my friends sit up straighter, grinning and nodding. "The guys wanna meet you anyway, and..." I feel my cheeks heat, "I miss you."

Which is ridiculous. I saw him this morning because he stayed the night last night. However, I'm still in that honeymoon phase of our relationship where I want all the time with him I can get. Even if it means subjecting him to the Spanish Inquisition by way of two of my closest friends.

"I miss you too, sweetheart," he says, his tone warm and relaxed again. "I'm about ten minutes away. I'll see you soon."

Ash and Josh race to the door like the overgrown toddlers they are as soon as London knocks. He knows it's unlocked and that he can let himself in, but he never does. I loiter in the hallway and clear my throat, waiting for them to move aside so he can come in. They have the grace to appear sheepish, but it doesn't prevent them from eyeing my boyfriend with open curiosity.

London takes it in stride, chuckling and greeting them with an outstretched hand. "You must be Ash," he turns to my best friend, shaking his hand first, then to Josh. His smile doesn't seem as warm as he steps towards the cop, even though his tone hasn't changed as they shake hands, "And the infamous Josh."

"Fair warning," I inform him as I accept my greeting kiss, "Ash got on the group chat and now the whole gang's on their way. So, you know, brace yourself for the interrogation."

"Charlie's just getting out of a meeting with some city planners and the guys who own The Grove, though, so he'll be a bit late." Ash laments as he tucks his phone back into his hip pocket.

"City planners?" London asks as we make our way back into the main living area. He takes my favorite armchair and pulls me onto his lap, which probably looks silly considering we're both big, bulky men. Still, I relax against him, and he rests his chin on my shoulder.

Ash is busy explaining Charlie's desire to build some community spaces and resources specifically for people in the BDSM lifestyle who need help. Ash was one of those people once upon a time, and if I hadn't had my dad to come home to after my breakup, I would have been, too.

With the arm wrapped around my waist, London gives me a knowing squeeze. "That's such a commendable project," he tells Ash. "The company I work for provides large-scale landscaping solutions for businesses and stuff. Maybe I can talk to them about whether we can help out?"

"I'm sure Charlie would appreciate that," Ash grins.

Josh derails the conversation, barreling in without any tact. Classic Josh.

"So, London, how come we've never seen you at The Grove before? You new to town? Or do you usually go to one of the lesser clubs?"

"Actually, I'm new to the lifestyle," London answers easily. "My friends are in a Mommy/little girl relationship, but until I stepped in for Cherie as a favor, I never considered how good a fit it would be for me."

"Wait, hold up," Josh is gaping at us now, his eyes darting from mine to London's and back, before fixing on London's firmly. His expression becomes hard. Protective. "Is this experimentation for you?"

"For fuck's sake," I huff at the same time as London calmly answers, "Absolutely not."

Then he quietly admonishes me for cussing.

His arm squeezes me tightly again, and I can feel him tensing. Before I can tell Josh to back off, though, my boyfriend's tone turns saccharine sweet. "I should probably thank you, though. If you hadn't abandoned Matt, I probably wouldn't have met him or realized how much I enjoy being a Daddy. His Daddy, actually."

"I didn't *abandon* him," Josh bites back, defensive and snarkier than usual. "He's a grown ass man. He's twenty years older than you and me, my dude. He can handle himself just fine."

Ash intervenes, smacking Josh just as he had earlier. "Except it was his birthday, we all knew he wasn't in a great place emotionally or mentally, and Matt told us that the only reason he and London even got to talking was because some other asswipe was getting in his face, which wouldn't have happened *if you'd been there*."

"Ah, so Josh is getting himself in trouble again, there's a surprise," Chance observes as he and Ted casually saunter into the room. Unlike London, they have no qualms just letting themselves into my house. To be honest, I don't usually have an issue with it. But, now that I'm seeing someone, maybe I need to set boundaries. I wouldn't want them to walk in on something private, after all.

Or I could just start locking the front door like a normal person.

Chance is a pretty affable guy. He's in his late thirties and, like Asher, has never been a gym rat. He's confident in his dad bod, scruffy reddish beard and near buzz cut, and more power to him for that. Ted is about my age and also happens to be Ash's boss – a senior partner at a local law firm. He's got a real silver fox vibe about him, and I think he looks kind of like George Clooney, with his brown hair liberally streaked with gray, and his athletic build still well kept. They're both wearing jeans and t-shirts: not a surprise in Chance's case, but Ted usually appears at our get-togethers in a suit on a worknight. I suppose that he might have gone to the gym or something after work, but it still takes me a minute to process the unexpected outfit.

"Fuck you," Josh rolls his eyes, but he's smirking at our friends. Then he addresses Ash with a sigh. "But, yeah, okay, you're right. I messed up. I'm sorry."

"Apologize to Matt, dumbass, not me."

I flick a hand in the air to prevent Josh from doing that before I make the introductions between the newcomers and London. "Chance and Ted, this is London Hayes. London, these are my friends, Chance Baker and Ted Masters." I don't get off London's lap, though, so he's left to just nod at the guys, and they chuckle and nod back.

"Forgive me," Ted says, dragging one of the dining chairs out into the living room and situating it between the couch and the armchair London and I have commandeered, "but you're not at all what I expected when Ash said Matt had a new Daddy."

"Ted..." I growl in warning.

He laughs, all blinding white teeth and knowing eyes. As far as I'm aware, he never told anyone about the time I asked him if he'd be interested in being my Daddy not long after I was first introduced to the group and I'm grateful for that.

It was only awkward for a little while, and he was very kind about explaining, as most Daddies had, that I wasn't his type. To be honest, I don't think it would have worked out even if he had been interested. He's too polished, and our personalities would have clashed as Daddy and boy. I much prefer him as a friend.

With hands up in surrender, Ted shakes his head. "It's just an observation, Matt."

"Is it the age thing?" London asks in a neutral tone. "Or does my boy have a type I'm not aware of?"

"Mostly the age thing," Ted answers easily. He shrugs. "However, Matt's never brought anyone new into the group, so I'll admit that I've made assumptions where I probably shouldn't have."

"You think?" I scoff.

"Aww, c'mon, Matt," Chance has dropped into the armchair at my other side, "you're such a private person. I don't think I've even seen you little more than a handful of times, and you never talk about what kind of Daddies you're into."

I can feel my cheeks burning again.

Why did I ever think introducing them all to London was a good idea?

Chapter Ten – London

I can feel Matt getting increasingly more agitated with his friends and their not-at-all subtle probing as the conversation continues. They seem like nice enough guys, even if I still resent Josh for the way he'd treated Matt on his birthday, regardless of the fact that I probably wouldn't be with Matt if he hadn't been left alone.

Matt's best friend, Ash, is a couple of years younger than me, but it's obvious that he cares a lot about my boy, and that makes me appreciate him even more for it. And, when Ash's fiancé, Charlie, turns up, I find myself easily drawn into conversation with the guy. He looks a lot like Josh, which isn't a surprise as they're brothers, but is older and gives off a much more authoritative vibe.

"Charlie was also a cop," Matt explains as if he's reading my mind, "but…" He trails off uncertainly.

Charlie gives him a crooked smile. He's sitting on the couch and has Ash in his lap, a mirror image of Matt and I. I know they're also in a Daddy/little relationship, and that Charlie has stood in as a caregiver for Matt over the last couple of years so the two littles could have playdates. It's obvious that he also genuinely cares about Matt, and I don't know how to express gratitude for that. He finishes Matt's story for him with an easy shrug. "But a GSW brought an early end to my career, and now I'm trying to get some new businesses off the ground."

"Yikes," I blink, having been unaware of that. "That sounds like some scary shit. But Ash was telling me about the kind of community hub you want to get up and running, and I'm kind of in awe of that." I repeat my offer to see if the company I work for can assist with any landscaping needs. We probably can't do it for free, but maybe we could offer some sort of price cut. Hell, I'm even happy to sketch up plans and do a budget for them in my down time.

While Charlie and I chat about that, Matt relaxes back into me some more. I had been beginning to worry that he was keeping me separate from his friends for some reason, but I realize now that it wasn't a conscious act on his part. His friends are a big, boisterous bunch: all nosy and more than happy to intrude into Matt's personal life without shame. The last of the crew, a guy named Spencer, joins us just as talk of ordering pizza starts up.

Spencer and I receive a hasty introduction and he makes no secret of the way he eyes me up and down. He's tall and lean, his skin pale and a mop of wild dark brown hair atop his head. At a guess, I'd say he's in his late thirties or early forties, and the rectangular, wire-rimmed glasses framing his gray-blue eyes suit him well.

"I'll be damned," he says to Matt, "I didn't take you for the cradle robbing type."

"Why's our age gap any different to yours and Emma's?" Matt challenges, and I watch a flash of hurt cross Spencer's face.

"Considering she left me," the other man grits out, "I wouldn't say using her and me as an example helps you here, man."

I bristle a little at this conversation. Spencer is the second of Matt's Daddy friends to raise these concerns directly in front of me. That said, I suppose I prefer them to be open about it than try to railroad him behind my back. At least Ted was kinder about it, though.

"I'm an adult and this dynamic works for us. If he doesn't mind that I'm twenty years his junior, that's all that matters to me." Offering the guy what I hope is an understanding smile, I add, "But I'm glad you guys care about him and aren't afraid to show it." Macho posturing drives me a little bit nuts, but none of these guys seem to be the type for it. Not even Josh, even if he does seem a little bit bratty. Or maybe that's me projecting again.

Spencer stares me down for another moment before he grins and offers me a fist to bump. "You're gonna fit in just fine," he decides.

Matt snorts.

* * *

After ordering -and eating- enough pizzas to feed a small army, Matt's friends start ambling out of his house, each one of them patting me on the back and telling me they're happy that I'm a part of the group now. It's not lip service, either. They've already added me to their group chat and are treating me as though I've been one of them since the start. Ash and Charlie are the last to leave, and the former pulls me in for a hug.

"You're good for him," he says quietly, "I've never seen him so happy or relaxed." Stepping out of the quick embrace, he looks to Charlie, reaching to hold the other man's hand. He swings their clasped hands between them and begs, "Daddy, can we have a playdate soon?"

Charlie and I have already exchanged numbers and we agree readily. Matt nibbles his bottom lip. "Maybe we can invite Kate and Cherie, too?" He asks me. "I know Katie wishes she had more friends like me and Ash."

My heart swells. My precious, sweet boy. He seems to always be considering others and their needs. "I think that's a great idea, sweetheart." I wrap my arm around him and kiss his cheek. "We'll make it happen."

Charlie and Ash leave after exchanging final goodbyes and Matt and I are finally left alone. He hasn't had any time in little space tonight and, even though he was with his friends, the change from routine is showing in the tense set of his shoulders. While he wouldn't have had supervised little time tonight anyway, I know he would have spent some time coloring or playing with blocks on his own before I called to read him his bedtime story. He sags against me when I direct him to head to the bedroom, forgoing bath time.

I stop by the room I've dubbed his 'Little Room' and grab a set of pajamas with a teddy bear print, a diaper and the baby powder. His eyes light up when I join him in the master bedroom and he sees the items in my hands.

"You're the best, Daddy," he declares, before his face slowly falls and he averts his gaze.

I'm on him in a second, lifting his chin gently. "What's wrong?"

"I…you're so good to me, so perfect, and I…I kept you a secret from my friends. Not because I was embarrassed or anything," the last bit is rushed out, and I know he's worried that he might have offended me, "but…I was being selfish. I didn't want to burst our bubble." His shoulders droop and he looks away, studying the wall. "It hurt Ash's feelings; I know that much."

A part of me is elated. Wanting to keep me all to himself is actually a very sweet motive. However, he's beating himself up right now, feeling guilty about upsetting his friend and also the possibility of offending me, and it hits me that this is one of those moments where I've got a choice to make.

When Matt and I first sat down and spoke about rules and limits, the topic of discipline was glossed over. He promised me that he wasn't a bratty boy, but that he would sometimes appreciate a spanking to get him out of his head. We haven't tried impact play for fun yet, but I can't help but think this is the sort of situation he meant during that discussion. Domestic discipline to settle him, not arouse him.

My instincts haven't let me down yet, so I bite the bullet.

"You're right," I tell him softly, but with an edge to my voice that has those beautiful eyes of his flicking straight back to meet mine. "Keeping information from your friends had the potential to hurt a lot of feelings, mine included. It didn't hurt mine," I add, reassuring him that we're okay, "but I can understand why Ash might be upset. And I'm proud of you for knowing that you made the mistake. But I think you need to feel consequences for this. Am I right?"

It takes Matt a moment to understand what I'm asking, and I help his thoughts along by resting my hand over the curve of his ass, patting him gently. The strips of skin visible over his cheekbones turn pink, but he nods. "Yes, Daddy. Please." He all but exhales the words.

"Good boy," I praise. While allowing that to sink in, I step towards the edge of the bed and sit down, tossing the things I'd gathered earlier onto the mattress behind me. "Pants down, Matt. Then I want you over my lap."

He all but scrambles to obey, his slacks and underwear pooling around his ankles in record time. He kicks them off, sending them flying in the direction of the bathroom. Then he drapes himself over my lap and I take a moment to get him positioned so we're both more comfortable and that he's not going to put out his back.

I rub the perfect globes of his ass with my open palm. "After this, you're going to forgive yourself, okay? This is the consequence for your behavior. It's a clean slate after that. Do you understand?"

"Yes, Daddy."

I've never done this before, but I've done my research as thoroughly as I can. I'm not planning on going too hard on him, especially when I don't think he's done anything wrong. However, I can tell that he needs this and, after a month together without having to discipline him at all, even I feel like it's a necessity for us to experience this. Hell, maybe he needs it more often than I thought, but he doesn't know to ask for it.

Should he have to ask for it, though, or is it my job as his Daddy to know when he needs it?

I'm getting too lost in my thoughts.

"Color?" I check.

He doesn't hesitate, even if his back is ramrod straight. "Green."

After getting the circulation going beneath his skin, I pull back my hand and land the first slap. The skin meeting skin sounds out with a louder *crack* in the room than I'd expected. My palm stings a little with the impact, and I admire the pink outline I've left behind on olive skin that's a few shades lighter than the rest of him. I deliver the next smack to the other cheek, then return to the first for the third.

Matt flinches after the fifth smack, the skin on his ass cheeks now red and tender, but his back is still rigid with tension. My aim is to see him let go, so I rain down a handful more swats until I see his shoulders shake and hear the first of his muted whimpers.

Even though I know this is supposed to happen, it hurts my heart to hear him upset. But this is just another facet of the Daddy role and, while it's not fun, I'll do what Matt needs me to.

I spank him a little longer and, once he's practically boneless and sobbing properly, I stop to rub gently over the heated flesh.

"That's it, sweetheart. Let it out." I pull him back up for a cuddle, holding him tightly as he cries into the crook of my neck. "You're such a good boy for Daddy, Matty."

He clutches at me and sobs harder. I'm not stupid enough to think that this is just about his conflicted feelings over not disclosing our relationship to his friends. He hasn't had a Daddy in years, and I have my suspicions that his last long-term relationship wasn't as balanced as it should have been. He's been deprived of proper care and nurture for too long, and I can only hope that I'm starting to fill that void for him.

As he starts to calm, I kiss his temple. "Let's get some lotion on that perfect ass of yours, get dressed and snuggle, yeah?"

Matt takes a shuddering breath before he nods. He's quiet through the aftercare - contemplative and boneless. But the tension he was carrying is gone and he seems genuinely relaxed, so I'm convinced I made the right decision.

Once we're in bed and he's clinging to me like a spider monkey, he finally breaks his silence. "Thank you, Daddy," he murmurs into my chest. I rub my hand up and down his back soothingly. "I needed that. More than I realized."

"Mmm," I acknowledge sleepily. "Did you wanna talk about it?"

"Not really," he answers a few beats later. "I just…I…" A guttural sound of frustration travels up his chest and out of his throat. I wait, knowing that he's struggling to express himself. "It's been a while. A long while. I've always known that it helps me to work through my issues, in my own twisted way-"

"It's not twisted," I cut in, frowning. "It's a proven technique. I mean, I've read a bunch about spanking therapy online, and heaps of people find that it's useful to help process negative thoughts and emotions and stuff."

There's actually a whole lot of psychology behind it, which I found fascinating, but I don't bother going into that with Matt. That would derail the conversation and I can't risk that happening right now. Clearing my throat, I urge, "Anyway, you were saying?"

"I just didn't think it was going to feel like that," he admits. "Like…like I was drowning and finally coming up for air."

I card my fingers through his hair. "You probably had more stress to work through than you thought," I suggest slowly. "And maybe…maybe we need to talk about regular spankings to deal with that build up. Like…once a month?"

His index finger teases my nipple through the thin cotton of my t-shirt. "Could I still have sexy spankings, too?"

A smile stretches my face. That sounds much more enjoyable for both of us. "Of course, babe."

* * *

"So, you met the friends, huh?" Cherie grins at me from across the table. We're grabbing a bite to eat at a local café on our lunch breaks, which have miraculously aligned for once. She takes a delicate sip from her soda through the straw and then cocks her head. "Does this mean things are getting serious?"

Around us, there's a general buzz of conversations. The café itself is small, but bustling. We've nabbed a booth in the back of the space, and there are two others along this same wall, and three matching booths on the opposite side of the café. In the space in the middle, there are a few small, round tables and chair settings that barely seat two people each. It's busy enough that our conversation won't carry.

"Things have felt pretty serious since the start," I answer, scratching the back of my neck. "Which is new for me, I'll admit."

"It comes with the lifestyle." There's no teasing in her voice now. "Sure, there are some people who just enjoy the odd scene or two to scratch an itch, but most of us…" Bobbing her head from side to side, she searches for the best way to phrase her thoughts. "What we're doing is being really quite vulnerable with each other, right? We get that our kinks aren't exactly socially accepted, so to trust someone else to explore them with in depth is usually a serious thing."

Having taken the opportunity while she spoke to bite down into my chicken sandwich, I chew and swallow while I nod. "Yeah, that all makes a lot of sense. I mean, it's probably more acceptable for me, as a Daddy, to explore my kinks than for Matt, or even for you and Kate, but it's still one of those taboo things." I think of the chat I've been invited into (which I've had to mute because the guys talk a lot of shit) and smile. "But Matt's friends have welcomed me into their group and that's kinda' nice. I mean, we're all the same, y'know? So nothing's really taboo with them. We can just *be*." Then I realize who I'm talking to, and add, "Which we get when we hang out with you and Kate, too."

Cherie lifts her glass again, holding the straw in place between her index and middle fingers before she moves to wrap her bright red lips around it. "But it's different because they're Daddies and boys. They're more relatable."

"Well, Spencer's bi -his last relationship was with a woman- but…yeah." I frown down at my half-eaten meal. "It shouldn't make a difference, but it's still nice to talk to other men about this stuff."

"Hon, I get it. I'm not hurt that you want to talk to other Daddies for their perspective, too."

I really lucked out to have this woman as my best friend and I tell her so. "So, anyway," I shift the subject back, away from the unusual exchange of warm and fuzzy feelings, "Matt asked me to set up a playdate for him, Ash and Kate. You in?"

"Kate would love that," Cherie's face falls, "but with my schedule so up in the air, I've given up on trying to make plans."

"Seriously, you need to find another job."

She pushes her plate away and folds her arms over the Formica tabletop, then drops her forehead on top of them. Her voice is muffled when she laments, "I've been applying for *months,* London. Months, and not one interview."

It's rough seeing her like this, but I'd prefer her to vent her frustrations and reach out for help than bottle it all up inside. Unfortunately, I don't know what help I can offer her. "I know you don't have a lot of free time or personal time, but maybe you really should try to get your own business off the ground as a side hustle for now?" I suggest. "I still think there's a niche market for clothes and accessories for littles who don't fit the standard mold." Kate and Matt are both great examples. "And I'd still happily be your partner in that sort of endeavor." I just have no idea where to start to try and get something like that off the ground.

Cherie sighs heavily and sits up, toying with the corner of her paper napkin. "It's a great idea in theory," she says, "but think of all the startup costs."

"We could take out a loan."

"Oh, *sure*," she stretches the word out with liberal sarcasm. "Imagine pitching that idea to the bank. 'Oh, hi, Mister Uptight Bank Lender Man, we'd like to start a business specifically to cater for plus-sized adults who like to dress as babies. Please give us all your money.' *Pfft*." She scoffs after acting out her little monologue. "Like anyone would take it seriously."

I laugh. "Well, not if you pitched it like that."

She balls the napkin up and throws it at me. It lands on my plate. "Okay," I hold my hands up in surrender, "let's table the golden business idea again for now and go back to my original question. Matt and I are both kinda' homebodies, so our weekends are always pretty free. So, how's about I call you on Saturday and see what your day looks like?"

And that's what we do.

Miraculously, Cherie and Kate have Saturday afternoon free when I call. Matt calls Ash and is ecstatic to discover that they, too, are available. He's practically bouncing off the walls by the time the first knock at the door sounds.

Today he's dressed in an adorable pair of footie pajamas, his perfect butt rounded with the additional padding of his diaper. His lounge room is already strewn with toys and blocks, brought out from his Little Room.

"I've never had playdates here," Matt explains as he grabs me by the hand and drags me to the front door, "I've only ever gone to Ash's house." He's sinking into little space slowly, and I expect that's because he's not yet comfortable with Cherie and Kate. After today, I hope that changes.

I know my expression is indulgent when I reply, "Well, this'll be the first of many here, I'm sure."

He swings the front door wide open and, before I know it, turns shy, ducking behind me. Cherie grins at me, while Kate bounces on her heels at her side.

"Hi, Uncle London," Kate says excitedly, "we bought cupcakes! Mommy won't let me carry 'em, though." She pouts for only a moment before she leans over the threshold and sideways. "Hi, Matty!"

He's absolutely adorable, flushing pink and barely squeaking out his return greeting.

Ushering our guests into his home, I give him a squeeze. "Why don't you go show Katie around, sweetheart? I'm sure she's excited to see your train set."

Bless her, she plays along immediately, grabbing his hand and tugging him back through the house, chattering about how she can't wait to see what his toys are like. Cherie and I follow at a more sedate pace, sitting down on the couch and letting the other two do their thing. She seems a bit more relaxed than she did earlier in the week, the dark circles beneath her eyes no longer as noticeable.

We talk a little about how the rest of our respective weeks panned out, and then there's another knock at the door. One glance over at Matt and Kate, both focused on building a tower with the blocks, tells me neither has heard it, so I get up and let Charlie and Ash inside.

"The other two are playing with blocks right now," I tell Ash, who is dressed similarly to Matt, "so go nuts."

"Ugh, don't tell him that," Charlie jokes lightly as his fiancé scampers away, "or he'll wind up needing corner time."

From what I've seen of Ash, he looks like butter wouldn't melt in his mouth, but I wouldn't be surprised if he had a bratty streak. Thankfully, Matt does not. Which amuses me, considering his need for regular spankings and also his whole 'bad boy' aesthetic.

Still, I chuckle and introduce Charlie to Cherie. I travel back and forth between the kitchen and lounge for a bit, bringing out coffees for us adults and sippy cups of juice for the littles, then settle back into one of the two armchairs facing the couch.

Cherie and Charlie seem to be having an in-depth discussion about Charlie's plans for the kink community safe space and I don't want to interrupt. Instead, I watch the others as they play. Matt seems to have slipped comfortably into little space, and the other two are right there with him. They each have a stuffed toy in hand and are enacting some sort of story. Kate's decided that Ash's stuffed penguin is the princess and that she and Matt, armed with a teddy bear and a plush sheep respectively, are on some sort of valiant quest to rescue the penguin.

"They're kind of adorable, huh?" Charlie asks, and it takes me a moment to work out that he's talking to me.

I tear my eyes away from the imaginative play and grin at him. "Every time I think 'this is it; he's reached peak cute little-ness', I see him doing something new that's even cuter."

"And none of this is weird to you?" Charlie's gaze is sharp and assessing, even though his demeanor is relaxed. "Josh said you've never done the Daddy thing before. And, I'll admit, my own first Daddy-boy relationship was eye opening. It took me a while to get past some of my own prejudices, even though I was enjoying it…if that makes sense."

I shrug. "Honestly, if someone had told me that I'd be into this, even a few months ago, I might have laughed it off as not my thing." I shoot an apologetic glance in Cherie's direction. "Like, I've never judged anyone for it. To each their own and whatever. But, yeah, the concept itself does come off a bit…" I trail off, not actually wanting to label it negatively. Clearing my throat, I shake my head. "Still, living it feels as natural as breathing."

Charlie nods, scratching his stubbled chin as his expression becomes speculative. "Have you struggled with any of it? Like…for me, I never really got the bottles of milk thing when I started out. Weird, right? Totally down with the diapers and even the pacifiers, but I could *not* wrap my head around bottles." He chuckles, the sound pleasant and a little self-deprecating. "I'm good with them now, but it took a while."

"It was discipline for me," Cherie pipes in, gently placing her half-drunk coffee down on the coffee table in front of the couch. She leans forward around Charlie so she can address the both of us. "It took me a while to understand that, even though Kate's a grown woman, when she's in little space she needs the rules and the consequences just as much as she needs the fun and the comfort." She wrinkles her nose. "Spanking's a hard limit for me, so we do corner time and writing lines, mainly."

"I haven't really come up against anything yet," I shrug. "Maybe because I'd already seen so much of what to anticipate when I spent time with you and Kate," I gesture towards Cherie, "and I didn't really have any ideas or expectations going into this? I don't know. I mean, it's not like we've tried it all yet. And, sure, it took me some trial and error at the beginning to work out exactly how much control he needed me to take but, even then, I wouldn't say it was a struggle."

"Huh," Charlie sits back. "Well," he says after a long moment, "if that changes, any of us are more than willing to talk it out with you. Ted was kind of my mentor when I first joined the scene."

"I appreciate that. And, hey, maybe that's something your community center can look into arranging? Like...Q&A sessions, or mentorships, or stuff like that?"

"The Grove already has something similar in place for Doms in training," Charlie muses, "but not so much for Daddies who aren't Doms. At least, not that I know of." Cocking his head, he stares off into space. "Considering how much Ted helped me, I think it's a great idea."

The three of us talk about it some more, with Cherie adding in her thoughts about the pros and cons of Q&A sessions open to all walks of the BDSM lifestyle verse niche sessions. It's so good to see her putting her analytic mind and planning skills to work with such enthusiasm. I stow my observations away in my brain, but once the center is up and running, I make a note to suggest that she ask Charlie for a job there. She'd enjoy it a hell of a lot more than working for her piece of shit politician guy.

"Mommy," Kate interrupts the conversation a little while later, jiggling in a tell-tale way that has me hiding my smile behind my hand, "I've gotta go potty."

I give Cherie and Kate directions to the bathroom and catch the curious expression on Matt's face before he schools it.

I make another mental note to discuss that with him later. For now, I'm content to let him enjoy his playdate.

Chapter Eleven – Matteo

"Today was the best day ever," I declare long after our guests have left. I'm still coming out of little space, riding the wave of endorphins from a very successful playdate – the first I've had with my Daddy supervising me. It's also the first I've ever hosted in my own home.

The whole experience seems to have cemented how real this all is, and I can't help but think that even when I was with Trent, it was something I was missing.

Daddy's lips curl upwards and he leans across the kitchen bench, where he's currently cutting up veggies for a stir-fry, to kiss me chastely. "I'm glad, sweetheart."

"Did you have fun with Ash's Daddy and Katie's Mommy?"

"I did," his voice is filled with fond amusement. "It was good to see them getting along, too."

"Mmm," I agree, nodding. "Charlie added them to the group chat."

London looks up from slicing a bell pepper, his eyes bright and happy. "That's awesome. They don't really get to socialize much."

"I know," my own face falls a little. "Katie's a bit lonely, I think." It's something I can relate to. Not all that long ago, that loneliness was suffocating, and I had friends to talk to at the time. She seems a bit isolated and that tugs at my heartstrings. I know she and Cherie have London, and he's wonderful, but bringing them in to our rag-tag group means giving them some additional emotional support, which is never a bad thing.

"I'm going to try and convince Cherie to work with Charlie, once his community center is up and running," London tells me after a beat. "I'm sure Charlie would benefit from that, too."

"And it would mean more regular hours and less stress for Cherie."

It's actually kind of genius. I can't see Charlie having an issue with it, especially not now that she's officially part of the group, even if she hasn't met the other guys yet.

We continue to chat about the afternoon just gone, with London more than happy to let me give him a play-by-play of my activities. He doesn't seem to mind, even though he was sitting in the same room for the entire experience and my stories aren't exactly riveting. Nevertheless, he smiles and asks questions and I'm filled with warmth I've never really felt before.

"So," he says when we're at the dining table, steaming bowls of veggies, meat and rice in front of us, "I noticed that you seemed *interested-"* he draws the word out carefully "-when Kate asked Cherie for help in the bathroom." He picks up his fork and digs into his dish with a forced nonchalance that has me cocking my head. After he chews and swallows his first bite, he asks, "Wanna talk about that?"

No longer in little space, I take my own bite of the meal he just prepared, barely stifling a moan as the flavorsome sauce hits my tongue. It buys me some time to get my thoughts in order. "It's, um, it's not something I've ever done with a Daddy," I eventually tell him.

"But you'd like to?" As usual, there's zero judgment or expectation in his voice or on his handsome face. There's also no hint of his interest, or disinterest, either. Still, without knowing where his thoughts are at, I'm uncomfortable discussing it.

I shrug. "Look, I've done the diaper wetting thing..."

"Matteo," Daddy-voice comes out in force in response to my dismissive, vaguely defensive attitude. He softens when I look up and across the table at him. "We're talking about two different situations. Sure, there's an element of embarrassment and trust inherent in both, but asking Daddy

to help you pee is different to being changed."

I deflate. "I know," I sigh. "I'm just…I'm aware that it's a lot, you know? You've taken all of this-" I wave my hand around, trying to encapsulate the entire lifestyle "-in stride, but I'm worried that something like that is going to be too far out of your comfort zone. Too much, too fast."

Setting his fork down, London frowns. "We have safe words, Matt. They're not just for you. If I'm not comfortable, I'll use them."

"But…"

He sits back in his seat now, and I can tell I've offended him. "Don't you trust me to be honest with you?" When I don't refute the accusation immediately, hurt flashes across his face before his expression falls. "I see."

"It's not that I don't trust that you're being honest," I rush to try and fix my faux pas, pushing my bowl aside so I can lean across the table and reach for his hand. He lets me take it in mine, which is a relief. "This is all going so quickly between us, and I guess I'm still waiting for the other shoe to drop. You're kind of perfect, London. I don't want to jeopardize what we have. And I'm…I'm afraid that if I push you too far…if I make you safe word…" I look down, my throat suddenly tight. I can't even say it.

His hand squeezes mine. "You think that if I safe word, I won't be as into you anymore."

I tremble at the very suggestion but bob my head, still unable to look at him.

He lets out a breath and pulls his hand out from mine and my heart thuds hard in my chest. Then I hear his chair scraping back against the tile. I'm aware of him rounding the table and dropping into the seat beside me before he pulls me against him, holding me in a tight hug. "That's not going to happen, sweetheart," he murmurs, kissing the top of my head. "If I ask you to try something new and you safe word because it's not working for you, would you think less of me for suggesting the experience?"

Understanding dawns inside me and I feel stupid. "No."

"So why would you assume I would reject you in the case of my having to safe word out because I don't like the new experience?"

"I don't know."

He's silent for a moment, and I breathe in the spicy scent of his cologne. "I think you do," he tells me quietly.

I gnaw on my bottom lip. I'm terrified of rejection, that's hardly a secret. And from the very start of this, I told him all my concerns about a potential relationship between us. "I suppose part of me still thinks I'm not good enough for you."

London's body tenses and he hugs me tighter. "I don't know how to convince you that you're wrong. But, if it helps, I sometimes doubt that I'm good enough for you, too."

"Wait," I sit up straighter, twisting in my chair to look at him in surprise, "what?"

He rolls his eyes, but a smile tugs at his lips. His hand comes up to cup my bearded jaw, his thumb smoothing over the strip of skin of my cheekbone, just beneath my eye. "You're fucking hot, Matt. You're also successful, own your own home and are super sweet. And I'm a lot younger than you. I'm barely starting out in my career. I rent a crappy little apartment, drive a shitty little car…" he huffs out a breath that could almost be a short laugh, "and I wear lingerie. Pretty sure it looks ridiculous on a body like mine. I'm hardly a catch for a man like you."

Blinking, I struggle to process his words. "You're not serious." London stays silent. "You're also fucking hot," I dispute his logic, ignoring his muttered admonishment about my cussing despite the fact that he started it, "and you've gone from a laborer to a planner in, what, a couple of years? So you're successful in my opinion. Not that it matters where you are in your career. Not to me. Your age means jack shit to me, too, and-"

"Seriously, Matt, language," he interrupts again, but with enough amusement that I know I'm still safe from punishment.

"And," I continue on as though he didn't cut me off, "I don't care where you're living as long as it's safe. Besides, the only reason I own this place is because my dad left it to me. I didn't make great life choices before Trent dumped me, y'know?"

I shake my head, realizing that I'm getting off topic before I continue, "Not the point." Now I let my hands slide down his sides, my thumbs tucking into the waistband of his jeans, teasing the silky material they find underneath the denim. "Finally, I *love* your panties. Just thinking about you in them gets me all hot and bothered. And if you wanted to try out camisoles or corsets or negligees or whatever-" grabbing his hand, I place it right over my hardening cock which is pushing against the cargo shorts I changed into after our friends left earlier "-*this* is exactly what I think about that."

His fingers tighten over my erection, an almost inaudible groan issuing from his lips. "Yeah?"

He's usually so confident that this vulnerability -somehow even more obvious than it was on that first night we spent together- throws me for a loop at first. "Daddy," I bring our foreheads together, "I told you. You're perfect."

London's mouth is on mine before anything more can be said. Dinner is forgotten as our tongues twine together and our hands slip beneath shirts and undo the buttons and flies of our pants. Somewhere along the way, I've swiveled sideways in my seat so we're facing each other properly, and London slips off his chair and sinks to his knees in front of me.

His large hands rest on my thighs, his calloused fingertips toying with the open waistband of my shorts. He looks up at me through thick, dark lashes, the blue of his irises having darkened with his desire. "Can I?"

Lifting my hips in a gesture of silent invitation, I nod.

He doesn't need any further prompting and it's not long before my shorts and underwear are tugged down my legs and thrown aside unceremoniously.

My cock stands at attention for him and I groan when the warmth of his palm wraps around it. London gives it a couple of light pumps before he leans forward and the sweet, wet heat of his mouth envelops the head.

He suckles teasingly, the hand that had gripped me now trailing light, tickling trails up and down my shaft and over my balls with the tips of his fingers. I want to buck my hips, but I know from experience that he'll only pull off if I do.

London tongues the underside of the crown, putting pressure on my frenulum, driving circles into that sensitive spot with his deliciously devious muscle before licking back up and through the slit.

"*Daddy*," I whine plaintively. "*Please*."

He takes his wicked time, repeating his actions before slowly taking more of my cock into his mouth until he can't go further. Then he drags back off as torturously slowly, sucking as he goes. These long, languid bobs of his head have me fighting the urge to fuck up into his mouth. My balls draw up and ache with the need to unload, but he's not stimulating me enough to push me over the edge.

I'm a babbling mess of pleas and throbbing desire by the time he finally (*fucking finally*) wraps his hand around the base of my cock and takes pity on me, pumping with firm strokes and hollowing his cheeks. His other hand reaches for my balls, rolling and squeezing them, then moves further back, over the sensitive stretch of skin behind them and then to my needy hole where he slowly rubs his index finger around the rim.

The touch disappears, and I keen desperately, only for him to reach up and place that same finger at my lips. I suck it and his middle finger into my mouth, slicking both up as best I can. He groans around my dick, the vibrations traveling through me with frissons of bliss, then he removes those fingers from my mouth and sends them right back to where I want them the most.

I'm so far gone in the enjoyment of his ministrations that the first finger slips in with very little resistance. The second, lubed only with my spit, burns a bit as he stretches me, but it's a good kind of burn and I shift, spreading my legs wider and leaning back in the chair to give him better access. It's uncomfortable and my back won't thank me for it, but right now I don't care.

I reach out and grip the edge of the dining table when he crooks his fingers and finds my prostate with practiced accuracy.

"London," I breathe. "*Daddy*. I'm so fucking close."

He growls -actually growls- around my cock.

Oh. Right. Language. Whoops.

"S-sorry," I inhale sharply as he twists his tongue and teases the sensitive head of my dick on his next upwards movement. He can spank me later for this final slip of my tongue.

That thought is almost enough to send me over the edge, but I manage to last a few more bobs of his head and curls of his fingers before I unravel, crying out something unintelligible as I spend myself in his mouth.

I don't know what I ever did to deserve this man, this perfect Daddy, but I'll do everything in my power to keep him.

Chapter Twelve – London

"Hayes, you got a minute?" My boss, Stanley, asks, poking his head into my shared office space.

I know there's only one real way to answer that question, so I smother a rueful glance at the half-completed budget estimation for my next project and paste on a solicitous smile. "Sure."

I push back my chair and get to my feet, following him into his office. His is surrounded by the same frosted glass as the boardroom, affording him additional privacy. I close the solid door -painted white like all the others- behind me and take one of the two uncomfortable seats in front of his desk.

Stan steeples his fingers together, seeming to channel Monty Burns as he observes me from the other side of the glass and chrome surface. "You've been kicking goals left and right since you moved into the planner role," he begins, and a part of me relaxes at the compliment.

I'm not being fired. This is a good thing.

"I try," I shrug.

His thin lips quirk upwards. Stan's in his late sixties now and he reminds me a lot of my grandfather. He's short, balding, and stocky. His eyes are a watery sort of blue color, and he's not exactly an imposing figure. Still, he holds all the power here even if he is a pretty good boss, all things considered.

"I've noticed," he tells me after an almost awkward stretch of silence. "Which is why we're lookin' to move you to the new office."

I blink. "What?"

He seems to take my shock as a good sign, even though it's really not. "We're lookin' for someone to manage the team over there. Someone who knows what the company expects of its staff, and who has shown themselves to be a real go-getter. I can't think of anyone better to represent us, London."

This is high praise, especially coming from Stan, but my gut churns with indecision. On the one hand, another promotion so early into my career is kind of amazing. On the other? Taking it means moving to the other side of the country. Away from my friends and my life here.

Away from Matt.

Sure, we've only been together three months at this point, but just the thought of walking away from him makes me feel sick.

"I...I don't know what to say, Stan."

He chortles, missing my blatant reluctance to accept the offer. He'd probably think me insane to turn it down. Part of me knows that it would be crazy if I did. "I know you've only been a planner for a little while, but -let's be honest- you're runnin' rings around Tom, and we know you'll be a good fit for the new site."

"I appreciate that you think so. Really, I do..."

Now my boss's expression begins to fall. He stares back at me, incredulous. "So, what's the problem?"

"You want me to move across the country, right?" He nods. My shoulders slump. "I..." I lick my lips. "My partner is here. I don't think he'll move with me."

There's a flash of surprise on Stan's face, and I realize belatedly that he probably had no idea I was gay. I've always been private about my love life. I don't anticipate any sort of discrimination or anything, but I guess I figured it was easier to remain discreet. Still, even if I was dating a woman, I'd raise the same issue.

Stan leans back in his chair, rubbing his chin and jaw with his palm contemplatively. "I didn't realize you had a relationship to consider, to be honest." He sighs. "That does throw a spanner into the works, doesn't it?"

"Yeah," I exhale. I offer him an apologetic grimace. "I'm sorry. I really would love the job, but…" I trail off.

Once again I remind myself that I've only known Matt for three months. It seems like no time at all in the grand scheme of things. Will I regret turning down this epic career opportunity for something that could end tomorrow?

Guilt washes over me almost immediately at that thought. Matt and I are solid. Yeah, our relationship got serious really quickly, but that's the nature of the lifestyle. And I get far more out of being with him than I ever will from a job. A job I never really planned on having to begin with. I did a psych degree, for fuck's sake!

"Talk to your partner before you turn me down, son." Stan interrupts the whirlpool of thoughts in my head. His tone is understanding and patient. "And I'll see what sort of flexibility we've got up our sleeves here."

Really? Does Stan have that much faith in me that he'd even consider turning the role into something more flexible? Just him saying as much sends a *zing* of pride up my spine.

No, I mightn't have seen myself in this kind of job when I graduated college, but I'm damn good at what I do.

"Okay," I lower my chin, tilting my head appreciatively. "Thank you. I'll talk to him tonight."

Anticipation simmers beneath my skin for the rest of the day.

* * *

"I've got a surprise for you," Matt says by way of greeting when he opens the front door to his place.

He gave me a key last week, but I haven't used it yet. To be honest, while it feels like I've practically moved in, I still don't feel right just waltzing on in. Besides, watching his eyes light up every time he opens the door to find me on the other side makes the idea of using the key less inviting.

We kiss before I say, "And I kinda' have one for you, too."

His brow furrows as he registers my hesitance. "What's wrong?"

"Nothing." That much is certain. I've given it a lot of thought over the course of the day, and no matter what happens with my job, I'm not leaving Matt. "I just need to talk something over with you."

"That sounds fucking ominous."

"Language."

Beneath his beard, his lips quirk. "Sorry, Daddy."

We move into the living room and sit together on the couch. Usually, I'd pull him into my lap or kiss him senseless after a day of separation, but I need to face him right now. I need to see his thoughts play out in his expressions because I know him well enough that he'll try and keep any negative ones from me, still so afraid that I'll walk away if things get too difficult.

"What's going on?" he prods while I consider how to broach the subject.

"So…Stan called me into his office today," I begin, then forge on before he can leap to any incorrect conclusions, "and offered me a pretty big promotion."

The worry which had begun to build in his eyes clears immediately. "That's awesome!"

"Yeah…" Scratching the back of my neck, I watch his face fall again.

"Why aren't you excited about this?"

With a heavy sigh, I admit, "Because they want me to take the Office Manager position at the new location."

"The new…*oh*." Matt knows about the company's expansion because I've mentioned it a couple of times in passing. His face falls and I know where his thoughts are going. I expected as much. Hell, mine would have gone the same way if our roles were reversed.

I reach for his hand, squeezing it. "I'm not leaving, sweetheart."

Confusion contorts his handsome face. "Really?"

"Really."

Now there's guilt in those green eyes of his and it pains me to see it. "But-"

"No. No buts. I've already told my boss I'm not ending my relationship and my life here for a promotion." Running my free hand through my hair, I shrug. "I didn't want to keep this from you, though."

Secrets tend to ruin relationships. I've seen it enough in my life. Secrets, albeit in regard to infidelity, destroyed my parents' marriage. Having watched them fail spectacularly at communicating, I've never wanted to repeat those mistakes. So far, I think Matt and I have done well not to fall into that trap. Now's not the time to start.

"*London…*" Matt shakes his head in disbelief. He sounds awed and horrified all at once. "This is too good an opportunity for you. You work so hard. You shouldn't let it go."

"I'm not taking the job if it means having to let you go," I reiterate, warmed by the relief that flickers over his face. "Stan said that they'd look into how flexible they could be. Maybe that means fly-in fly-out or working remotely or something. But if they can't, I'm still choosing you, sweetheart." I can't help grinning at him now, because this is the part that I've been focused on all day. The pinnacle that everything has boiled down to. "I love you, Matt."

A myriad of emotions swim in his eyes at my declaration, but he doesn't leave me hanging. A huge smile tugs his lips upwards, and he brings our foreheads together. "I love you, too."

We're kissing before anything more can be said. Even though these feelings have been building for months, putting the words out there seems to add even more intensity to the meeting of our lips. We kiss slowly and deeply, as though rediscovering each other. I pull Matt into my lap, guiding his strong thighs to straddle mine, gripping and squeezing his ass over his jeans as I grind up against him with our mouths fused together. Beard burn be damned, I never want this kiss to end.

Most evenings when I come over after work, I help Matt get into his little space and we're content to spend the most of our time together as Daddy and boy. But today I'm glad he's big. I'm glad we've been able to talk and exchange mutual declarations of our feelings.

Don't get me wrong: I enjoy being his Daddy, and I don't mind if he's little more often than not (even if having sex with him in little space was something I did first reach out to talk to Charlie about because it turned out *that* was where I became a bit conflicted with the lifestyle) but I'm pleased we were on equal footing when I told him that I loved him for the first time.

"Oh," Matt's almost surprised murmur pulls me from my thoughts at the same time he disengages from the kiss, "I almost forgot *my* surprise for *you*."

With my cock aching between too many layers of fabric, I'm half tempted to tell him it can wait. But then I look into his eyes which are practically dancing with excitement, and I can't deny him. Especially not when it's something he's arranged for me.

Still, I do complain as he climbs off my lap and tugs me to my feet, ushering me into the master bedroom. "I do like bedroom surprises," I joke with a laugh as he enthusiastically drags me along by the hand.

"Well, this is kind of for me as much as it is for you," Matt says, suddenly sounding a little uncertain before he steps aside and I finally see the bed. Or, rather, the carefully laid out lingerie on top of the bed.

An array of satin and lace has been carefully arranged over the navy bedspread in a veritable rainbow of colors. There are panties and thongs, a couple of camisoles, a sheer black negligee and even a stunning corset. As I step in for a closer look, I can tell that he's picked out quality items, many of which I've had sitting in my online wish list, that I know have cost him a small fortune.

"*Matt*…" I breathe, not knowing what to say. "This is…" Beautiful. Amazing. Too much. Perfect. "*Wow*."

"You like them?" His voice is smaller again. Uncertain. He's not Little Matty right now, but he's not used to taking charge or making grand gestures like this (that's more my role) and my stunned silence is probably doing more harm than good in this situation.

"Sweetheart, I love them," I reach out to finger the sheer negligee, the material softer and smoother under my fingertips than I anticipated. I want nothing more than to strip off my business attire and slip it on instead.

Somehow, I refrain. Turning to Matt, I ask in wonderment, "But…why?"

The vulnerability and insecurity melts away from his expression. "I just wanted to do something nice for you," he explains with a shrug. "And, like I said, seeing you wearing them is a gift to myself, really." He reaches across in front of me and picks up a lacy red camisole and matching thong. "This is my favorite of the lot. I think it'll look hot as fu…er…*sin* on you."

"Good boy," I praise his self-censoring, then reach for the items he's holding. "Then I guess I shouldn't keep you waiting, huh? Better make sure they fit at the very least."

Matt nods enthusiastically and practically shoves the set into my hands, pushing me towards the bathroom to change. Through the partially closed door that separates us, I can hear him hurriedly removing the rest of the lingerie from the bed, and he loudly declares that he's putting it all away in my underwear drawer (the one he cleared out for me a couple of months earlier) for me to sort through later.

I toss the clothes I had been wearing into the hamper before I carefully pull on the scrap of thin material masquerading as a thong, adjusting my balls and still hard cock inside the lace. I don't glance into the mirror above the sink until I've also slipped the camisole over my head.

I've never gone beyond just panties and thongs, so the silky, thin material across my pecs and spaghetti straps over my shoulders feel foreign to me. I'm concerned that my reflection will appear ridiculous, but after fiddling with the straps so that the cami hangs comfortably, I finally look at myself.

Whoa.

Matt was right. The bright red pops against my pale skin and black hair, and it seems to make my eyes bluer. I still look like a stocky man wearing delicate, effeminate clothing, but I can't say that it looks *bad*. Just…different.

Lifting the hem of my camisole, I turn to the side, admiring my tight ass cheek and the sliver of red material peeking out from my crack and stretching over my hip. Facing forward again, I can see the tip of my cock peeking out from the top band of the front of the thong, glistening with precum. I drop the thin, almost see-through material and the hem reaches to just above the tops of my thighs, the material fluttering against the tip of my cock as I move.

"*Daddy*," the plaintive whine from the bedroom jerks me from my thoughts. "Are you dressed yet? I'm dying here."

I can't help but chuckle. We were both worked up before I stepped away to try on some of his gifts, and 'patient' isn't exactly a word I'd use to describe my boy at the best of times.

"Coming, sweetheart," I call back.

"That's the plan!"

I want to spank him a little for the sass, but I'm too horny and too excited to see his reaction to me wearing the lingerie he picked out to act on that urge. Instead, I take one last look in the mirror and stride to the door, swinging it open and striding into the bedroom with purpose.

Matt's already on the bed, naked, lying on his side with his head propped on his hand, his other hand palming his leaking cock. When he sees me, his jaw goes slack. "Holy shit," he growls out, his voice low and needy.

"Language."

"Sorry, but have you seen yourself?" He spreads precum over the head of his cock and then down the shaft, squeezing himself on his next upstroke. His eyes are practically blazing with desire. "That was justified cussing."

"Oh, was it now?" I stalk forward, my amusement warring with my need to replace his hand with mine. Or with my mouth. Or to roll him onto his back and pound into him with abandon. Or…well, anything that would lead to the intense orgasms I know we're going to share soon. "Pretty sure it's still breaking the rules, baby."

Matt remains unrepentant, those green eyes of his traveling over my body shamelessly. "I think I should get a pass this time," he argues, cocking an eyebrow at me when he finally looks up at my face again. "Because you love me…and I bought you all those pretty things."

The uncharacteristic mischief in his voice and his playfully bratty behavior tells me he's been spending time with Josh. I don't envy the Daddy who gets to take that boy in hand, even if I do consider Josh a friend these days.

Still, I'm not letting Matt push the boundaries too far, even if I do want to laugh and pin him to the mattress.

"*Matteo*," I warn, smirking when he groans and closes his eyes.

"Sorry, Daddy."

"Good boy."

Another moan escapes him. "*London*," he pleads, "you're killing me."

Taking pity on him, or, really, on myself, because I can't remember the last time I was this hard, I close the distance between us and roll him onto his back so I can crawl over him, allowing his hands to roam over the camisole he bought for me. He obediently spreads his legs and I grind my cock against his, the soft lace between us becoming wet with the evidence of our mutual arousal.

"I love the lingerie, sweetheart," I whisper against his lips, my breath teasing him, knowing that he wants me to close that last little bit of distance and kiss him stupid.

"Me too," he agrees, teasing my nipples through the silky soft fabric that covers them. "It's like wrapping paper for the world's best present."

This time, I can't contain my chuckles. "God, I love you." It's a thrill to say those words again, this time pressed against him in bed as we are, practically naked and writhing.

This seems to push him beyond the limits of his control and he surges forward, capturing my lips and rolling us until we've switched positions. Then his hands pull down the thong I'm wearing, throwing it across the room, and he straddles my hips.

"*Whoa*," I wrench our lips apart when he guides the tip of my cock to his hole. "Stop. Lube, babe."

Sitting up, still straddling me, Matt smirks down at me and gestures to the open bottle of lube on the bedside table. "You were taking your time getting changed," he explains, "so…I took a little initiative."

He prepped for me. I smother a groan. "Next time, I want to watch," I tell him, hearing the gravelly quality of my own voice while my dick jerks at the images my brain has conjured. "But, fuck, sweetheart, if that's not the hottest thing ever…"

Still, my fingers travel beneath him, wanting to be sure that he's ready to go. I sink two in with very little resistance and scissor them while he works his hips.

"Please..." Matt practically whimpers when I deliberately graze his prostate.

"Okay, baby. Okay." I grab for the lube and slick my cock up, clicking the cap shut and tossing the bottle back in the general direction of Matt's side of the bed. "Ride me, sweetheart."

He doesn't need to be told twice. We both moan as he slowly sinks down on top of me until I've bottomed out. I give him a moment to breathe and adjust, and then he begins to move, bouncing on my cock in earnest.

I love watching him like this. His golden skin glistens with a thin sheen of sweat, and his muscles ripple with every movement. But the best part is watching him control his own pleasure. He sets the pace, clenching around my cock on every upward motion, swiveling his hips and taking what he needs from me while I rock my own hips up to meet him at the rhythm he's setting.

When my hand closes around his cock, pumping him in time with his bouncing, he throws his head back, his mouth falling open as his eyes drift shut. His hands drift over my camisole, though, traveling the peaks and valleys of my skin over the now sweat-dampened fabric.

I can tell he's getting close, knowing the signs of his impending orgasm as well as I know my own now. His breathing hitches and his fingers clench in the lace over my pecs while he picks up speed with his hips.

"Da...Daddy," he pants, "London...fu...uuuhhh," I want to chuckle at the way he only just manages to censor himself, but I'm about to go over the edge myself. "Coming. I'm...*ungh...* I'm *coming*."

I love the way he makes the declaration, despite the fact that it's not something I can miss happening. I don't even think he knows he's doing it. He's just vocal and it's all sorts of hot and endearing all at once.

I shout incoherently as his orgasm pulls mine from me, the clenching around my cock milking everything I've got. He slumps down on top of me, my cock still inside him, while we catch our breaths. We're a sweaty, sticky, sated mess and I'm awash in the afterglow of our exuberant love making.

It just reaffirms my decision to choose my relationship over my potential promotion. Work could never make me feel this content.

"I love you," Matt says, nuzzling his bearded face into the crook of my neck. "You said it again and I didn't."

Snickering, I rub my hand soothingly over his back. "We're not keeping score, baby. But I do like hearing you say it."

"Mmm," he nibbles at my skin, almost as if he can't get enough of me. "Then I'll say it every chance I get."

"Me too, sweetheart. I promise."

Chapter Thirteen – Matteo

I should feel guilty that London turned down a promotion for me. I really should. But, instead, all I can feel is relief. It's a strange sensation to be someone's priority, but an addictive one all the same. That said, we talked about it some more over dinner last night, and I made it clear that if his company is willing to be flexible, London should still consider his options.

I'd love to be able to make some sort of grand gesture of my own, to offer to move with him and uproot my own life, but that's not really feasible. I've only just settled in here. I have close friends for the first time in over a decade. I have a job I enjoy, and I love living in the home I grew up in. I felt insanely selfish for telling him these things, but London just shook his head and gave me one of his indulgent smiles and reassured me that he understood.

I've really lucked out with him.

I float through my workday, riding on the endorphins from last night. Between finally saying those three little words to each other, hearing London tell me that he'll choose me over his job and then seeing him rock the sexy as hell lingerie I bought for him, I honestly feel like maybe I'm dreaming. If I am, though, I don't want to wake up.

When Ash calls me after I finish work, we agree to meet for beers at a little hole in the wall bar that's roughly halfway between our houses.

It's a relaxed space, with scuffed cement floors and a hipster-industrial atmosphere. I get there before Ash and find a tall table with high, wrought-iron bar stools, snagging it for us and ordering two of the daily special brews, seeing as the drinks menu here rotates frequently.

Jesse, the guy behind the bar, grins at me as he hands over two tall glasses of pale ale, his dirty-blonde man-bun wobbling on top of his head as he excitedly tells me all about the brew I'm about to try. I'm not all that interested in hearing about the hops or the fruity infusion or whatever, but his passion for supporting local micro-breweries is actually kind of sweet, so I nod and make appropriate sounds of appreciation as required.

I'm still relieved when Ash saunters through the door and waves at me.

"That's my cue," I tell Jesse with feigned regret, lifting the beers in a gesture of thanks before sliding back over to the table I commandeered earlier. "Thanks."

He waves me off and I set the glasses down on the worn timber table top before greeting Ash with a quick hug. He slips his messenger bag from his shoulder and drops it on top of the table next to his beer with a grateful sigh.

"Long day?" I ask.

He's gone back to only working part time at Ted's firm so that he can work on finishing his college degree. I know he hates studying, but with only two semesters to go at part-time (or one at full-time), Ash decided it made no sense not to see it out to the end. Besides, once he realized that he could put the knowledge and skills to work with Charlie's business plans, that has only made him more determined to graduate.

"My statistics professor can kiss my ass," he complains, dropping onto the stool across the table from me with a huff. "The assignment he's set is worth fifty percent of my grade and it's brutal."

"Do you need help?" It's no secret that I'm good with numbers, data and extrapolation. "I can look over your work before you submit it if you want."

Ash's smile turns grateful. "I'd love that. All my other classes are fine, but stats aren't my thing."

We chat about the parameters of his assignment for a little while and I offer him some pointers before he drains his glass and hisses through his teeth. "Okay, no more college talk. My brain is fried. I can't handle it."

I chuckle and nod, finishing the last of my drink as well. "That's fair, dude. Take a break; it sounds like you've earned it."

"Amen to that." He swings around on his stool, slinking off it with the grace of youth and his slimmer frame. Snagging our glasses, he tells me the next round is on him and he crosses the narrow walkway between our table and the bar before I can argue.

I watch him banter with Jesse for a minute before he returns with two new glasses brimming with golden liquid and the perfect froth ratio. I thank him as I take my first drag from the new glass. The liquid is crisp and refreshing, even though I've already polished off one glass already.

"Okay, so I've whined enough about my day," Ash settles himself back on his seat, running his finger through the condensation on the side of his glass while he cocks his head at me. "Your turn. How's your week going?"

I can't suppress the wide, happy smile that splits my face as I remember yesterday all over again.

"Well," my best friend's expression brightens to match mine, "that good, huh?" He leans across the table and places his hand over my forearm. "I'm glad to see it, Matt. Really. London's perfect for you."

"He is," I agree. "We, uh, we did the whole 'I love you' thing yesterday." I can feel my cheeks turning pink. "This whole thing has felt kind of surreal, but..." I trail off, shaking my head, unable to really put my jumbled mess of feelings and thoughts into words.

"Hey, I get it," Ash laughs. "Remember, it wasn't that long ago I was in the same boat. Well, maybe a similar boat." He takes another sip of his drink then licks his lips contemplatively. He's a couple of years younger than London, but has the same mature outlook on life. I know that, in his case, it's because he had a rough upbringing with his asshole dad...and that makes me wonder whether London's the same.

London and I have obviously spoken about our pasts and our personal baggage some, but he hasn't really gone into detail about his childhood.

I know he's the child of a messy divorce, and that he adores his mother beyond words, but, to be honest, he doesn't mention his dad very often. There's a tiny part of me that worries he's into me (or older men in general) because he's got Daddy issues. Which, okay, given our kinky relationship and the roles we play, is really kind of hilarious.

"...fast, right?"

I shake my head, offering my friend a sheepish smile. "Sorry," I apologize. "I got lost in thought for a minute there." I lift my glass and eye him over the rim. "You were saying?"

Asher's smile is understanding, as though he can guess where my thoughts went. He wouldn't be completely wrong, even if he thought I was thinking naughtier thoughts about my man than I actually was.

"I was just saying that it feels like things are going fast, right? Like...things got serious kinda' quickly?" Ash shrugs and sets down his beer, staring into it with a more serious expression on his face while he continues to muse aloud. "Things *really* flew with Charlie. In hindsight, it was almost scary how we went from complete strangers to falling for each other within weeks. Maybe even days. But," he looks back up at me, a secretive little grin toying with the corners of his lips, "I've read, and the guys have all agreed, that it's not wholly unexpected in the lifestyle, y'know? I mean, Charlie and I did go a lot faster than most, I think, but I...I needed that. I needed to feel wanted and grounded and looked after."

"I can relate to that," I nod. "And as long as you were both comfortable with it, who cares how fast you guys went? I mean, I gave London a key a month ago, when we'd only been together for two months."

I know that Ash moved in with Charlie the day they met, but those were extenuating circumstances.

He bobs his head. "Like I said, I think a lot of it comes down to the lifestyle. As littles, we put a lot of trust in these guys and get attached to them in ways more traditional or vanilla relationships take additional time to develop or whatever."

I can see his point. It's not even the careful balance of power between the Daddy and boy roles, either. At least, not to me. Giving him control isn't about being bossed around, but about letting him handle all the things that stress me out. There's something about the amount of emotion that builds when Daddy's being so nurturing. Something about letting go and being insanely vulnerable, and knowing that Daddy not only cares about my little side, but genuinely enjoys being my caretaker as much as I love having someone look after me like he does.

But with London there's the additional level of trust he puts in me. I know that he has his hang ups about being a big, strong man who gets off on wearing frilly, lacy underwear, but he still lets me see him as he explores his kink. The feeling I get knowing that I'm the only person to ever see him do so is intoxicating.

There's a real give and take between us, and that's definitely helped to shuttle us along in our relationship.

"You're right," I tell Ash in response to his musings. "And I'm okay with that. We're still taking things step-by-step, even if the steps are coming on quickly."

Ash clinks our glasses together, his shiny engagement ring glinting with the movement. He winks. "I'll drink to that."

* * *

"Daddy?" I squirm when London looks at me from over the top of his book.

It's finally Saturday and we're chilling at home; he's reading while I play with my blocks on the mat in front of the couch. His bosses are still discussing just how flexible they can be with the position they've offered him, so we haven't had to revisit the discussion about his job and what those changes might mean for us. Still, it's lurking in the back of my brain constantly and, even though I know he loves me, I've started to let doubts creep in about his choices. Because he can read me as well as the fantasy novels he enjoys so much, London insisted I let go and get some additional little time in to try and settle my anxieties.

"What's up, sweetheart?"

I bite my lip, second-guessing the urge that overtook me enough to interrupt his reading. We've talked about this before, but I've never worked up the courage to ask for it. Something about our exchange earlier in the week, knowing that he loves me, pushed me enough to get his attention, though. And with how deeply little I want to get around him, if I can get the words out, I think it'll help me.

"Matt?" Daddy prompts, sliding his bookmark in between the pages of his novel and setting the book aside so he can give me his full attention.

I wriggle in place, wondering why it's so difficult to ask for what I want. I remind myself that he'll safe word if he's at all uncomfortable. He loves me. He trusts me. And I trust him. Still, I avert my gaze as I ask, "*Can-you-help-me-potty*?" all in one breath.

I can hear the sounds of his clothes rustling and the soft footsteps he takes before his bare feet enter my field of vision. Then he crouches down in front of me, tilting my chin up so I have to look him in the eye. He smiles at me and kisses me on the forehead. "I'm proud of you for asking, baby." Then he stands and offers me his hand. I take it and he helps me to my feet.

"Traffic light?" I ask him, searching those blue eyes for even a hint of discomfort or disgust.

"Green." He replies without hesitation. "You?"

I love that he still asks me, even though I'm the one who suggested trying this new thing. "Green."

Guiding me to the bathroom, he leads me to the toilet and helps me pull down the play shorts and training pants he dressed me in earlier. Then he steps in close behind me, pressing his chest against my back, and holds his hand over mine while he helps me aim over the bowl as I pee.

"Good boy," he praises after giving me a couple of quick shakes, reaching for a couple of squares of toilet paper to give me a brief dab before tucking my cock back into my training pants, resettling my shorts around my hips.

We wash and dry our hands and, after he leads me back into the living room, he tugs me into his lap.

The entire experience was over within a couple of minutes at most, and I'm bewildered to feel like it was *normal*. A complete non-event.

I mean, yeah, having someone else's hands on me while I peed did feel a bit strange, but I was expecting to feel more embarrassment or *something*. Instead, it just felt exactly like what it was: Daddy helping his boy. Nothing beyond that. Hell, the diapering process is more intimate and confronting than this was.

"You okay, baby?" Daddy asks, nuzzling the back of my neck with his nose.

I snort. "I guess I expected that to feel weirder than it did." I turn, trying to meet his gaze. "Was it weird for you at all?"

"Nope." Again, there's no hesitation in his response. "Did you want it to feel differently?"

I consider the question before I shake my head in the negative. "No. Not really." I scrunch my nose. "I thought it would be something bigger, y'know? But it was...nice? That's not the right word. It..." I huff out a breath, frustrated that I can't quite express what I'm feeling. "I think it'll help me stay little next time. I mean... if you're comfortable with it."

His lips find my temple. "I am," he assures me, his voice rumbling up his chest. "And if you decide to take it further...if you want to use your diapers...I'm okay with that, too."

Huh.

"Is that something *you're* curious about?"

London pauses for a moment, but I don't sense any indecision. If anything, the silence is thoughtful. "I suppose I am," he answers after a few seconds. "I just feel like it's a pretty big part of the lifestyle; one I haven't experienced." He shrugs. "It's nothing we have to rush into, but it seems like the next step from what we just did, right?" Then he chuckles. "Or, I guess, if you think about it in terms of natural progression in childhood development, we skipped the step entirely."

I snort at that. "The age regression thing is *technically* going backwards, right? So, by that logic, it's reverse development and it would be the next step."

"Reverse development," he repeats with another laugh and a shake of his head. "That's not a thing."

"Well, I'm making it a thing."

His thick, stocky fingers tickle my sides. I'm not all that ticklish, but he knows exactly which spot to hit in order to make me flinch away with as manly a squeal as I can muster.

I love these moments with him. I can't actually recall ever being this silly or carefree with Trent, which almost makes me sad because I spent ten years with him. Ten years without this kind of freedom and joy. I can't say I regret the relationship because, without it, I doubt I would have made the choices that eventually brought me to this moment, but I do mourn for the man I might have been under different circumstances.

"Hey," London's hand is smoothing up and down my back. "Where'd you just go, sweetheart?"

I shake off the melancholy my hypothetical musings have induced and lean back against my lover's chest. "I was just thinking about how lucky I am to have you as my Daddy."

"We're both lucky," he insists, cuddling me closer. "And it doesn't matter which steps we take, or when. We're in this together for the long haul, okay?"

I nod, feeling suddenly, unexpectedly choked up. "Yes, Daddy."

God, I love this man.

Chapter Fourteen – London

We don't revisit the diaper conversation again. At least, not over the course of the next week. Instead, Stan sits me down on Wednesday to tell me that he and his business partners have gone over their options, which gives me something else to focus on.

"If you're willing to spend every second week at the new site for the next six months, the job's yours," he says with a toothy grin. "If all goes as well as I think it will, and you train your people up to be nice and autonomous, we can look at minimizing the schedule after that and have you working remotely from here with maybe a monthly visit to the new site from there on out."

Stan's leaning back in his cushy, high-backed leather office chair, his fingers interlaced behind his head. He looks like the cat who caught the damn canary.

My heart thumps in my chest. It's a better compromise than I had anticipated they'd come up with, but I'll still be away from Matt for entire weeks at a time.

But I'll also be here for entire weeks, too.

The fact that the company is willing to spend money on return airfares every two weeks is mind boggling. But…where would I stay? If I let up the lease on my apartment, I could probably afford to stay in a motel or something every other week. Something low budget. I'd only need a place to sleep and shower, really. But, if I did that, would Matt mind me moving into his place on the weeks when I'm here? I know I've basically moved in as it is, but even I know that I'm being presumptuous to think I could just spend every other week living in his house without discussing this all first.

"Can I discuss this with Matt, first?" I ask my boss. "My partner, I mean." We haven't really spoken about the potential promotion since I first brought it up. With the idea of flexibility in limbo, there was nothing to really talk about. But now there is, and I won't make this decision without his input. "I told him that you were looking into options, but we didn't really want to guess what that might mean."

Stan smiles indulgently because he can tell that I'm interested in the offer. As far as he's concerned, my talking it over with Matt is a formality at best, I'm sure. But if Matt isn't on board, I'm still turning Stan down.

* * *

"I think you have to take the job," Matt tells me over dinner. I've explained Stan's offer and, even though I tried to remain neutral, I'm pretty sure he can see straight through me. He doesn't seem upset or worried, though, and that goes a long way to settling my anxieties about accepting the promotion.

"Yeah?" I ask, wanting to be absolutely certain this won't hurt us as a couple. "You'd be okay with that? Even though it means me being gone half the time?"

With his grilled chicken breast half-eaten, Matt carefully puts his cutlery down on the table and looks me in the eye. "It's for six months, and it's better than the alternative where you could have taken the original job offer and moved across the country permanently." When I move to say something -to argue, or to reassure him, or some mixture of both- he holds up a hand to stop me. "But, more than that, we're solid. We can Facetime or whatever while you're over there, and we'll just have to make up for lost time when you're back home."

Home.

The word warms me from the inside. "We can do that," I nod, waggling my eyebrows at him suggestively.

Matt shakes his head with a soft smile. He reaches for my hand across the timber tabletop and squeezes it. "Move in with me. Make this your home for real."

Even though I'd had the same thought earlier today, it blows my mind to hear him asking me. He hasn't had to make many big decisions (or even smaller ones) since we met, since I became his Daddy…and this is *huge*.

"Are you sure?" I ask him, my eyes not leaving his. "I won't lie; I want that more than anything right now. But I don't want you to feel pressured here."

If I squint, I can see parallels to my parents' relationship and I'm still terrified of repeating my dad's mistakes.

Matt needs to know what he's getting himself into. Even though I know I'm not my father, that my situation with Matt is different to the resentful aspiring artist who knocked his girlfriend up, I still share that guy's genetic makeup.

Holding up a hand before Matt can dive all the way in, I confess, "I really need you to be sure, baby. Because I don't want either of us becoming resentful or bitter or-"

"Hey," usually it's me calming him, but right now the tables are turned. As if our roles really are reversed, Matt looks every bit his age when he gently cups my cheek and asks, "where'd that come from?"

Then I tell him everything. Obviously, he knew the basics of my baggage before now, but now I fill in the blanks. My parents were young -in their early twenties- and had a whirlwind romance which resulted in me. My dad felt pressured to stick around. To move my mother in. To play happy families when all he'd wanted to do was see the world as a free spirit. He took a job which involved a lot of traveling, and ultimately a lot of infidelity. Then, after mom found out and they had a huge fight, he walked out completely, leaving her heartbroken.

"I don't want to repeat his mistakes," I explain, sounding miserable and young to my own ears. "And I know it's not the same thing, but we've gone fast and…" I lift my palms up in a gesture that's stuck somewhere between begging and shrugging, "what if I'm like him after all?"

Matt listens through the entire confession, and it strikes me that we really have come full-circle. Only when we started this whole thing, he was the one needing the catharsis of an emotional purge. Now it's me.

"Well," Matt muses aloud, a soft, understanding smile playing on his lips, "that answers a lot of questions for me."

I feel crestfallen at those words. I've tried so hard to be open, to communicate properly, but if he still had questions…

"Stop it," Matt's firm voice interrupts my spiraling thoughts. He reaches out to hold my face between his large, warm palms and stares me in the eye. It's so rare that he takes charge, that his expression or tone match his physical appearance, that I sit in stunned silence while he says, "We're both far more mature than that, London. And, yeah, I might prefer to sink into little space and let you call the shots, but if I had any doubts at all, I'd tell you. Just like I trust that you would tell me. I mean, you just did." He leans in and kisses me. "The fact that you're trying not to repeat your parents' mistakes proves that you probably won't. I can't know the future, but I don't think we're at risk that way. So," he smiles again, "move in with me."

"You're sure?" I sound like a broken record. "It's really not too fast for you?"

It's only been three months. I love him, but I won't forgive myself for rushing him.

"I would have moved you in that first night if it wouldn't have made me seem like a clingy, crazy person," he assures me with a self-deprecating chuckle. "I'm nuts about you, London. I get that this feels like we're moving fast, but, at my age, I'm at the point where I can't let the best things in my life slip through my fingers just because I've assigned some sort of arbitrary number to how long I think society expects I should wait to have them."

Well, then. I can't argue with that, can I? Not when I feel the same way. Even if I am practically half his age, I know better than to overthink my instincts. I love him, he loves me, and we both want this.

A smile stretches across my face. "When can I move in?"

* * *

"Are you sure you want to donate all of this?" Charlie asks me on the following Saturday, standing in the middle of the living room in my apartment. He gestures at my barely used Ikea furniture. The sectional couch is as pristine as the day I bought it, and the coffee table also looks new.

"I'm keeping the bookshelves," I remind him, "but Matt's place is fully furnished, so I don't have any use for any of it."

Matt steals a kiss as he saunters past, lugging a huge box of books as though he's carrying a pile of pillows. Those muscles of his aren't just for decoration after all. "Are you sure you aren't attached to anything? What about your bed?" he asks me. "Because we can replace the one in the spare room with yours if you want."

"Nah," I wave the suggestion away. "I don't have any sentimental attachments to my furniture. I'd rather it go to someone in need." Which is why I've told Charlie to take it all and do with it what he will. Apparently, he's organized a storage unit for most of it, with plans to use it in his safe house/community center project as I'd hoped.

I bend down and heft up my own box of books, groaning a little under its weight. "As long as I've got my books and my clothes, I'm good."

It wasn't until Matt and I started to pack up my things that I realized just how minimalist my life has been until now. I don't have much in the way of knickknacks or personal effects. A fuckton of books, yeah, and a wardrobe full of clothes, but not much else. My kitchen cupboards contain the bare minimum in terms of cutlery and cookware, and all of my childhood photo albums are still at my mom's house a couple hours' drive away. So all I'm moving across to Matt's place are books, clothing, my big TV, neglected PS4 and a handful of games Matt doesn't already own.

I follow Matt to the car and load the boxes into the backseat, the trunk of my Hyundai stuffed to the brim with my clothes. The trunk of his car is packed with boxes, too. Cutting my lease short proved to be relatively easy, and all the guys volunteered to help empty out my place the second

Matt mentioned it in the group chat.

"Last chance to back out," I tease my lover, crossing my wrists behind his neck to draw him in for another kiss. It feels like I'm trying to stockpile them, knowing that spending every second week apart is going to be painful until we're used to the routine.

Matt rubs our noses together. "Not a chance, Daddy."

I dive in for another kiss, this one less innocent.

"Oh, I see how it is," Chance's voice interrupts us, and Matt sighs into my mouth before he pulls back to glare at his friend, who drops another box at our feet, unrepentant. "You've got us all doing the heavy lifting while you guys dry hump out here."

"Crude," Matt accuses the somewhat scruffy ginger-haired man.

"Says the guy playing tonsil hockey with his toyboy." Chance taunts back with a wink to let us know he's only playing.

I roll my eyes, taking the bait as is expected of me. "He's the Boy and you know it, bud." I cock my head. "Speaking of Boys, you've been very quiet in the chat lately, Chance. Any news you'd like to share with the group?"

Matt perks up at that, picking up the needling where I've left off. "Are you holding out on us? Is there a new little in your life?"

"Fuck you both," Chance laughs, shaking his head. He gestures between us. "Go back to mauling each other already."

"That's not a denial," Matt observes, grinning knowingly.

Chance rolls his eyes. "If you must know, I've been on a few dates and tried a few scenes with a guy, but we're probably not going anywhere." He shrugs when he catches the matching grimaces of commiseration on our faces. "It was worth giving it a shot, but neither one of us is devastated that it hasn't worked out."

"Still, I'm sorry," Matt apologizes, guilt painting his expression. "I shouldn't have pushed the subject." I give him a squeeze, proud of how empathetic he is.

"Nah," Chance waves him off. "No harm, no foul. Serves me right for not mentioning it in the chat. It's not a big thing."

"Still," I begin to object, but my words are cut off as Josh interrupts our impromptu pow-wow.

"What are you all standing around here for?" He asks, hefting one end of my tall, oak bookshelf. Spencer's got the other end and they're carrying it towards his truck, which is parked on the street just past the driveway to my apartment complex. Despite his leaner, more wiry frame, Spencer doesn't appear to be struggling under the weight of the timber like I might have expected. He's obviously stronger than he looks.

"Chance was just telling us to stop slacking off," I answer smoothly, and Matt hugs me tighter to his side, clearly appreciating my choice to keep Chance's woes amongst ourselves.

Oblivious, Josh grins at the bearded ginger man. "You caught them making out like teenagers, right? They've been doing it all day."

"We have not," Matt argues back with a childish lilt.

Letting out a bark of laughter, I tilt my head from side to side and smile at him. "I mean…we kinda' have, sweetheart." If I had to make an educated guess, I'd say that the anticipation and joy of officially moving in together has gotten to us both.

He takes his hand in mine and his expression turns almost goofy. "I can't help it," he declares after a few moments, "you're moving in." His words echo my thoughts as though we're in sync with each other. "I'm…well, I'm excited, I guess."

"Me too, baby." Assuring him comes as natural to me as breathing. I lean in so that my lips brush his earlobe as I whisper, "And I'll show you how much just as soon as I can get you alone and naked."

"Mmm," he murmurs back, turning his head so that his beard rubs my cheek, "do we have to get completely naked? Because I don't think I have the patience for that."

"Ugh," Josh complains good-naturedly, shooting me a wink before he starts backing towards Spencer's truck, practically dragging the other man along, "get a room."

"We're working on it," Matt sasses back.

"Yeah," Spencer finally chimes in, shifting the weight of the bookshelf in his grip, "it might even go a bit faster if you actually *worked* right now."

Stealing one last kiss in the form of a quick peck of the lips, I chuckle and take a step back from Matt with my hands held in surrender. "Alright, point taken," I acknowledge, feeling only a little guilty that these guys have been doing the bulk of the heavy lifting for the past few minutes. "I'll even throw in an extra case of beer tonight as a peace offering."

"Add extra pizza and all is forgiven," Chance throws over his shoulder on his way back into my apartment building.

I follow him and clap him on the shoulder. "You drive a hard bargain."

As a group, we continue to banter while we disassemble the apartment and take it down to the trucks outside. It takes a couple of hours, but it would have taken longer without Matt's friends, who I have also come to see as my own friends.

It strikes me, as we're all sprawled out through the living room in Matt's house (*our* house now), that I really had been living a pretty lonely existence before Matt.

Sure, I'd been busy, and I'd had surface friendships with guys from college and people I worked with, but outside of Cherie and Kate, I hadn't really connected properly with anyone. I could psychoanalyze myself for years if I wanted to, but I know that I'd been holding myself back. Until Matt.

Meeting Matt forced me to acknowledge a side of myself I'd pushed aside. He might say that he's the needy one in our relationship, but, as far as I'm concerned, that goes both ways. I think I needed someone to take care of just as badly as he needed someone to care for him. And, once I opened myself up to him, connecting with other people came easier.

"What're you thinking about?" Matt asks, nudging me with his shoulder.

Later, I'll divulge all of my revelations, but right now I just kiss him on the cheek and nuzzle his neck. "Just thinking how lucky I am to have found you, sweetheart."

"We're both lucky, Daddy."

Well, I can't argue with that.

So I don't.

Chapter Fifteen – Matteo

The first three months of London's fly-in, fly-out routine sucked hard. It took us a while to not only get used to not seeing each other every second week, but to also manage the time difference between us. I struggled badly enough during the first month that I earned myself my first genuine disciplinary spanking on London's second week back in town, because a week without my Daddy and without any intervening little time had manifested in some bratty tantrums I'm not proud of.

But, after some trial and error, we were able to make it work.

On the weeks London's been across the country, I've had little time at Ash and Charlie's place, much like I did prior to meeting my Daddy. It's not the same, but it's enough to take the edge off, and I know that Ash loves having me around for playdates. Josh even joins us occasionally, and some of the other guys are also happy to step in as caregivers when Charlie's got meetings.

On the weeks where London *is* in town, I try not to monopolize his personal time too much. We live together, so I get him all night every night, and that makes it easier to share him with Cherie and Kate, or even the guys when they drop in to hang out. I'm usually little during these catch ups, wanting to maximize my alone time with London when I'm big.

Now that we're midway through the fifth month of London's trial of his new role, things feel pretty settled. It's a Friday night and the whole gang is over at our place. We're at the tail end of a belated birthday get-together for London, who turned twenty-seven last week. We celebrated in private with some mutual masturbation via Facetime on the day, and when he flew back in I gave him his gifts (some new lingerie and a spectacular blowjob) the first night he was home. But tonight, the group convened for dinner, drinks, and playtime.

Right now, Ash, Katie and I are all little, but so is Josh, which is a surprise. More often than not, even on my playdates at Ash's place, he remains big.

I wonder if work has been stressful for him because I've never seen him sink so readily into little space. Even Charlie's keeping a cautious eye on him, which is telling. But, in little space, Josh is boisterous and happy, so I'm not too worried. I understand how freeing this aspect of the lifestyle can be and, as a cop, he probably deserves to be released from grown-up worries more than most of us.

When I get up from my spot on the rug playing with the new Duplo set Daddy bought me recently, Daddy shoots me a questioning glance. He's been sitting on the end of the couch next to Charlie, nursing a bottle of beer and chatting about adult stuff that, honestly, I'm more than happy to tune out when I'm little. But, even though he's engaged in that conversation, his focus never really leaves me. As always, I can't help but enjoy that sign that he genuinely cares about me.

"Just gotta pee," I tell him as I move to pass him and head towards the master suite.

His hand reaches out, grabbing mine to stop my movement, and he tugs me down to murmur in my ear, "You're diapered, babe."

I blink at him, a little surprised that he's bringing it up, that we're having *that* implied conversation now with all our friends around us. But his voice is pitched low, his words murmured for my privacy. Not that I really need it: this isn't my first rodeo, and the guys are in the lifestyle, too, after all. After searching his gaze for a minute, I shrug, nod, share a quick, chaste kiss on the lips with him and turn back to resume my seat on the rug.

Sinking deeply back into little space with the others comes easily as I play, forgetting all about my previous need for the bathroom until my bladder insists that it's urgent. But, little and wanting to go along with Daddy's unasked request, I continue playing through it until the resulting dampness against my skin has me squirming with discomfort.

"Come on, sweetheart," Daddy's voice is warm in my ear. He's crouching at my side and gives me a huge smile when I turn my head to face him. "Let's get you changed, okay?"

He helps me to my feet and leads me down the hallway by the hand. In our bedroom, he's got a towel spread out on the bed, with a fresh diaper, wipes and cream all set out neatly beside it. The fact that he was prepared for this both surprises me and also reassures me that he's really okay with it. I mean, he must have been, to leap on the chance like he did.

Staying in little space, I don't ask him his color. I know that if this does make him uncomfortable, he'll safe word if needed. So I lie back on the towel he's set out and suck my thumb, watching him with hooded eyes as he tugs down my play shorts and unclasps the onesie beneath. I arch off the mattress so he can push the fabric up my back, then drop back down when he requests it.

It's a practiced routine at this point, the only difference being that this time the diaper has been put to use. I can't describe why that makes it feel different, only that it seems a little more intimate somehow, but still just as *normal* as anything else we've done together.

I take a second to muse over the fact that it never felt this easy with Trent. The few times we did this had felt a little awkward, and the reason why almost eludes me. Almost.

Trust.

Some part of me never quite trusted Trent completely. Like an innate warning system, my brain had always hovered on the edge of being big in situations like this, like I knew I couldn't just let go and give him everything. It wasn't that he was a bad person, but he'd been my first Daddy and we'd had to work hard at our relationship. At communicating. At avoiding fights. At maintaining a routine. It felt formulaic with Trent, where with London it feels natural.

I really don't have to work at any of those things with London. And letting go with him is unbelievably easy. Because I trust him.

I love him and I trust him inherently.

He's rolled up the wet diaper with efficiency by the time I tune back into his actions and has wiped me clean. His large hands smooth the barrier cream over my skin almost reverently. Then he gets me to lift my hips so the clean diaper can be slid under my ass and he fastens the tabs with practiced ease, making sure it's all fitting and sitting correctly before getting me dressed again. I sit up, thumb still in my mouth, and watch as he tidies away the supplies and throws the old diaper into the little trash can in the bathroom. I hear the faucet run as he washes his hands and then he returns, coming to sit beside me on the bed, the mattress dipping with the action.

"Thank you for trusting me with that," Daddy says softly, pulling me in for a sideways hug. "I probably shouldn't have put you on the spot with everyone here…"

I shake my head, pushing out of my little space to have the necessary conversation. "It's not like it's something new or strange to any of them. I mean, Charlie and Ash disappeared for the same reason earlier." As the words leave my lips, I make the connection. I smirk a little, cocking my head as I turn to observe him. "Is that why you suggested it?"

He nods, a bit pink in the cheeks. "You know I've wanted to tick it off our list for a while. And Charlie…" he sighs and looks at the ceiling. "He and I discussed it from a Daddy perspective, y'know? And he has this whole spiel about the vulnerability and trust involved and I…" London clears his throat. "Alright, full disclosure: I got a little jealous that I hadn't experienced that, I guess." With a rueful shake of his head, he looks back at me and takes my hand. "Except, in the middle of it, I realized that I *have*. It's in *everything* we do together. We're vulnerable with each other all the time, and we're constantly proving how deeply we love and trust each other. This was just another way of sharing that, but it's not the only way. Not that it wasn't like he said it was."

Every time I think I couldn't love him more he says something like this.

Something that is far more mature and soothing than a man of twenty-seven has any right to be. I forget that he's so much younger than me when he's so perfectly authoritative on one hand and so nurturing on the other.

I don't know what else to say to him other than: "I love you."

We share those three words a lot, but it never fails to send a thrill up my spine when he returns them. Brushing his lips over my knuckles, London looks me in the eye and does just that. "I love you too, Matt."

And, in this moment, life is perfect. In a few months, I'll be forty-six. A year ago, I could never have imagined feeling this way. I can't pretend to know what the future holds for us, but I have confidence that, whatever it is, we're going to face it all together. Me and my hot young Daddy.

Epilogue – London

Matt and I survived the six-month trial of my flexible work arrangements and are celebrating my final bi-weekly return by going out for dinner. If Matt had it his way, we'd get takeout and celebrate in bed, but I want to show my boy off in public. It feels like it's been too long since I've spoiled him.

Plus, I get off on seeing him dressed up a bit. He's always hot, but in dress pants and a button down, especially paired with a tailored jacket, he never fails to get my engine running. I like to think of these outfits the same way he describes my lingerie: like wrapping paper covering a beautiful gift, and I look forward to being able to peel the clothes off him later in the evening.

Even though he's not going out in little space, I still took care of all the decisions tonight. That's my role as his Daddy, and I take a moment to consider just how much I still genuinely enjoy it. From selecting his outfit, to choosing the restaurant, to pre-perusing the menu online so I know which meal to order for him. The fact that he trusts me to make the right decisions for him even now kind of blows my mind.

"Ready to go?" I ask him once I've tied the laces of his dress shoes, grinning up from my kneeling position on the floor. He nods and smiles, handsome as ever, and we head out of the house (locking the door behind us) and to my car hand-in-hand.

We talk about Matt's work week on the drive across town, which then segues into a summary of my last trip across the country.

"Stan and I agree that they're pretty autonomous these days," I tell him as I park my trusty little Hyundai in the lot next to the cute little French bistro I decided upon. I unbuckle my belt and twist in my seat to face him, beaming because I'm so happy to report this to him. "So it looks like I'll be able to get away with visiting the office in person once a month at worst. The rest of the time, I can manage them remotely. Teams meetings, emails, that kind of thing."

Matt's expression lights up like a Christmas tree. "Really?"

I bob my head with enthusiasm.

"That's awesome!" He leans across the center console, grunting in complaint when he's stopped by his own seatbelt. His hands scrabble to unbuckle himself and I chuckle at his distracted fumbling. Then he takes a deep breath, shoots me an unimpressed glower, finally presses the button down and launches himself towards me.

His lips are on mine before I can blink, and he takes control of the kiss. It's deep, and passionate, and I lament the lack of space in my tiny little shitbox car when I can't pull him any closer against me.

"We're going to be late for our reservation," I complain lightly when we come up for air.

Matt snickers. "Does that mean we can get takeout and go home?"

I attempt to reach behind him to swat at his ass. "Be good, baby. I want to take my beautiful boy out and make everyone jealous."

Even now, after over nine months together, the compliments bring a flush of pink across the visible strips of skin above his beard. It's still adorable as fuck.

"Fine, Daddy," he moves back into his seat with a playful pout. "But you're buying me dinner *and* dessert."

"Oh, sweetheart," I take the bait, "you *are* my dessert."

* * *

Dinner goes smoothly, and I know that, for all of his complaining that he'd rather be at home, Matt enjoys the rare night out. He practically moans over every bite of the meal I selected for him, the decadence of the French cooking too delicious not to enjoy.

We play footsie beneath the table, teasing each other like we're on our first date instead of in a committed, long-term relationship. And I do order dessert, because he's been such a good boy and I'll do anything to keep that smile on his face.

But when we get home and I pull into the driveway, there's a stranger on our doorstep.

In the passenger seat, Matt tenses up, frowning as the man who had been leaning against the wall next to the front door pushes away and moves towards us.

"Trent," Matt inhales sharply, and now I'm feeling tense as well. What is he doing here? Who does he think he is that he can just turn up on his ex's doorstep unannounced?

As Trent steps into the light from the motion-sensor floodlights we installed above the front door, I can see that he's tall like Matt, and roughly around the same age at a glance, but lean and clean shaven. He has light-colored hair, something like a sandy blonde, and a long, angular face. As he gets closer and I climb out of the car having told Matt to stay put for a moment, I note that he's handsome in an ageing Hollywood star kind of way.

He stops and frowns at me. "And you are?" He asks, and his voice is higher pitched than I'd anticipated. Maybe this attitude is in compensation of not exactly having gravitas in his voice, but from the little bits and pieces Matt has let slip in our time together, I think it's more a case of Trent just being an asshole in general. Or maybe I'm projecting.

Pasting on a genial smile, I extend my hand. "London," I introduce myself. When he gives me a slow look over, starting at my feet and trawling slowly up towards my face, refusing to shake my hand or introduce himself, I ignore the distaste in his expression and cheerfully tuck my hand back in my pocket. Leaning back against my car, I cock my head to the side. "How can I help you, Trent?"

With a roll of pale blue eyes, he gestures at the car with a dismissive wave. "I'll talk to Matteo, thank you." He clears his throat when I don't budge. "Privately."

"Yeah, that's not going to happen," I bounce on my heels, remaining chirpy and overly friendly. "It's been, what, close to three years since you sent him packing without so much as a second's thought about how he was going to manage? You think he even wants to talk to you?"

Trent grits his teeth and I get the feeling he's not used to being challenged.

Well, too bad, cupcake.

"Listen, son," he patronizes me, "I've been sitting here waiting for almost an hour-"

"Well, that wouldn't be an issue if you hadn't turned up without so much as a courtesy call."

Rolling his eyes, he leans around me and loudly demands that Matt get out of the car and talk to him. Before I can insist otherwise, the passenger door opens and Matt climbs out. He's stony-faced and nothing like the sweet, jovial man I've spent the evening wooing and spoiling.

"Why are you even here, Trent?" He asks, sounding both defeated and disinterested. He walks around the car and I don't waste any time wrapping my arm around him, tucking him into my side.

Possessive? Yeah. Do I care? Nope.

"Really, Matteo?" Trent scoffs. "A boy of your own?" His tone seems to imply that he finds that concept ridiculous. Then he says, "It doesn't matter. We should talk."

It feels like I've stepped into a scene from a poorly scripted soap-opera. The inevitable 'ex-lover realizing that they've made a terrible mistake' moment. But, as amusing as that might be on paper, I can't help the stab of uncertainty I feel.

I can't help but worry that there's a possibility that Matt might prefer to go back to the man he has so much history with, after all.

Interrupting my thoughts, Matt laughs. An honest-to-God laugh of amusement. "If you think this man is my boy, you're an idiot," he says, shaking his head. "London's my Daddy, Trent. And he's a damn sight better at it than you ever were."

As he defends me, it's like I can actively see him getting closure on those painful years of his life. I can't deny the relief that sweeps through me at that. I nuzzle his neck, kissing him on the spot just behind his jaw that I know makes him all hot and bothered. "I'm so proud of you, sweetheart."

Trent just looks puzzled. "What?"

Matt shrugs. "I don't know why you're here after nearly three years of radio silence, and, honestly, I don't care." He turns his head to smile at me. "I'm in love. I have an amazing Daddy who treats me right and loves the way I look."

"Especially in a onesie," I add, and to my delight he giggles.

"Especially in a onesie," he repeats in agreement.

"But…" Trent starts, then stops. Matt and I look back at him almost in a synchronized movement. The man standing in front of us seems to slump in resignation. "So, if I told you that I made a mistake-"

"I'd agree with you." Matt's response is firm, but he still manages to surprise me with his undercurrent of kindness. I shouldn't be surprised, though. Not when I know how inherently compassionate he is. "Trent, we weren't good for each other. You were right to end things. If you hadn't…" he trails off and shakes his head. "It's been a long time. And if you're not happy, I'm sorry to hear that. I am. You're not a bad person, y'know?"

My sweet, forgiving boy.

He forges on, and it strikes me that he's probably been thinking about what he'd say to this man -his first Daddy- if ever he got the chance. "You realizing that you were wrong doesn't mean I'm going to walk away from the life I've rebuilt, but I would appreciate the apology. You did me a favor by letting me go, even if it took me a long time to see that. I'm doing you a favor now by telling you the truth."

There's an awkward silence between us all until Trent lets out a sad sigh and nods. He has the grace to appear genuinely apologetic when he looks back up from the ground. He meets Matt's gaze first, then mine. "I'm sorry for disturbing your night," he says, and it's a far cry from the bluster and pomp of his initial attitude. I still don't really have it in me to scrounge up even a lick of empathy for him, but Matt has that covered.

"It's going to get better, Trent. But whatever closure you're looking for here? You're not going to find it beyond knowing that I'm happy."

* * *

I pin Matt to the door the second we're inside and his former Daddy is gone. My lips are on his in an instant, my hands tugging off his jacket and yanking at the buttons of his shirt. I don't care if I tear the damn thing, I'll buy him a new one. I need him naked. *Now.*

He laughs when I pull away to continue fighting with the material, and the sound is lighter and more carefree than I've ever heard him. "Daddy…I'm too old to fuck against the front door."

I can't even bring myself to admonish him for the language. I wrench his shirt off, buttons pinging and clicking and clattering across the tiles at our feet, then drop to my knees to mouth at his cock through the thick, black material of his dress pants.

"You're *perfect*," I tell him, my brain scrambled with need and pride and the resurgence of all the joyful, flirtatious feelings from dinner. I rub my face into his growing hardness, lavishing him with more praise. "The best boy, partner, lover…hell, you're the best *person* I could ever imagine."

His hand threads through my hair, caressing the top of my head and I look up to see him staring back at me with amusement and adoration in equal parts. "You know, if I knew that telling Trent where to shove it would earn me this sort of reaction, I would have called him and done it ages ago."

Now it's my turn to laugh, and I shake my head. "It's not just that…but that was hot as fuck, by the way." I don't care how silly I feel making this declaration in this position. I have the fleeting, slightly feverish thought that if I had a ring, I'd probably propose, but despite the endorphins I'm feeling, I know we're not ready for that yet. But one day we will be, I'm sure of it. "These last few months have proven that we can work through challenges together, and every moment away from you has been awful.

Tonight felt like the start of something new again. Something exciting."

I allow him to pull me back to my feet and I cup his bearded jaw with my hands. "And then, whether you realize it or not, just now on the front lawn?" I jerk my chin in the vague direction of the driveway, "You chose me. You could have listened to him. You could have had the age-appropriate Daddy you have a decade of history with. But, instead, you *chose me*."

His eyes soften and glisten with tears. "London," his voice is croaky, but he's smiling at me. "I'll always choose you."

Then we're kissing again, with the same intensity as before but at a slower pace. My manic energy is building into raw need and we make out while attempting to fumble our way towards the bedroom, shedding shoes and clothes (and his underwear and my panties, which involved a lot of hopping and laughter from both of us) in our wake. Glancing behind us, it's like a miniature disaster zone, the trail of a small, if passionate, tornado.

When we finally tumble into bed, we're finally naked and I waste no time coating my fingers in lube and stretching Matt out. But, for as badly as I need to be inside him, connected with him at the most intimate level, I don't want to rush this. Instead, I plan to make love to him.

I guide him onto his side and press in behind him, lifting his thigh up and back over my hip so I can slide inside him at just the right angle. He sighs out my name, his hand reaching back to pull my face in towards him for an awkward, sloppy, utterly perfect kiss.

I set a languorous pace, rocking my hips slowly, dragging my cock out and in while I murmur everything and anything I'm thinking and feeling into the shell of his ear.

"You like that?"

He moans.

"You like it when I fuck you slowly, sweetheart?"

A needy whimper.

"You feel...*oh,*" I gasp, "so *fucking* good, baby."

I push in deeper, practically melding myself to his back, as though I'm trying to become one with him. He's panting, his cock hard in my grasp, and now I barely move, just teasing him with tiny, incremental shifts of my hips against the perfect globes of his ass. "That's it," I practically croon as he tips his head back onto my shoulder, matching my minuscule moments, drawing out our mutual pleasure, "you're my good boy." I groan as I slowly push forward again, his tight heat driving me closer to the edge. "My perfect boy."

"Oh, God…" Matt hisses as I tighten my hold on his leaking cock, twisting on every torturously slow upstroke.

Despite the languid nature of our love making, my heart is beating rapidly and I can feel my balls drawing up, can feel my body giving in to the exquisite pleasure of being wrapped in his tight heat. "I want you to come for me, Matt," I tell him, engaging my best authoritative tone, the one I know he loves. "I want to feel you spurt over my hand. I want to feel your pretty little hole clenching around my cock. I want-"

He smothers a shout, letting go and complying with my request. I groan out my own release, spilling inside him, thrusting and grinding as I ride out every last possible moment.

I pull out slowly, kissing whatever parts of his face and neck and shoulder I can reach, then gaze down to watch as my cum dribbles out with my final movements.

It's insanely hot to watch. As hot as it was that very first night we spent together. Maybe even hotter, because this time we have the intensity of our emotions behind it. We have our own history, despite it only being nine months instead of a decade.

"Stay here, sweetheart," I whisper into his ear when I catch his eyelids drooping. "I'll clean us up."

I extricate myself from the bed and, while he's still dopey and malleable, get him to move so I can pull the soiled comforter out from under him, and the blanket beneath it to cover him up with once he's clean. Then I duck into the bathroom and nab a washcloth, warming it with hot water and wringing it out lightly before returning to find Matt has fallen asleep.

I clean him up gently, not wanting to wake him, then give myself a cursory wipe before I climb back in bed behind him. I curl up at his back, the two of us still naked, mirroring our earlier position. Pulling the blanket over us, I press one last kiss to his bare shoulder and snuggle in for sleep.

Tomorrow, we will discuss tonight's events properly. I'll repeat how proud I am of him for standing up for himself and getting his well-earned closure in a healthy, mature way. I'll also reiterate how touched I am that he defended me. That he chose me. That he said he'll *always* choose me.

The night I met him, I never could have imagined that he'd turn my world around the way that he has. I'd never imagined that being a Daddy was on the cards for me, let alone to a man nineteen years my senior.

I couldn't have anticipated that going home with him would lead to anything beyond a night of fun. Perhaps even a week or two at best. I certainly wouldn't have thought it would introduce me to a supportive social network of like minded people, or that I would be comfortable enough to be myself, open about my most secret (at the time) kinks.

But here we are: a Daddy who loves lingerie and a big, buff boy, in love and ridiculously happy.

And I wouldn't change a thing.

The End

Ted's Temerity - Preface

This is Book 3 of the *Littles & Lace* series, however it can be read as a standalone.

For this novel in particular, please pay close attention to the content warnings in bold.

Please bear in mind that, while this is a low(ish)-angst (no miscommunication!), sweet & cute, instant-attraction romance, this book does contain discussion of **child loss, homophobia, parental pressure, and anxiety.**

Similarly, this book is an MM Age Play/Age Regression romance between consenting adults with **an age gap** (14 years) and includes feminization/femme play/princess play* and **spanking/impact play**. There are also very brief mentions of other characters indulging in ABDL, but there are no scenes of that type in this novel.

I am still a firm believer in not yucking someone else's yum, so if these kinks aren't for you, don't read them.

Life's too short to read something you don't enjoy.

*PS - while I don't believe that toys, clothing, and modes of play should be gendered, I'm using these terms as the generally accepted description for the kink in question

Chapter One – Ted

"...To have and to hold from this day forward until death do you part?"

The question is quite solemn, but the officiant delivering them is anything but. The short, curvaceous woman is wearing a bright pink dress and her hair, cut into a spiky pixie style, matches it. She's bubbly and bright and is grinning at my best friend, Charlie, waiting for the guy to answer.

Seeing as I'm Charlie's Best Man, I give him a little nudge. In front of us, our assembled friends chuckle while Charlie clears his throat and finally answers with the only possible words he could. "I do." From where I'm standing, I can see that the sides of his neck and the skin on his jawline and cheeks not covered by his trademark dark stubble are turning a little pink.

The officiant winks at him and teases, "Right answer!"

Everyone laughs at that. Then she turns to Charlie's fiancé and asks the whole spiel again. I can see Asher's entire face from my spot behind Charlie's turned form. The younger man is practically vibrating with joy as he stares across at the man he's marrying. His curly hair has been trimmed and artfully styled, and his hazel eyes are shining brightly under the hot summer sun.

Thank God this is a casual wedding. The grooms are dressed in matching white linen short sleeved shirts and beige khakis. Matt and I, standing for Ash and Charlie respectively, are wearing the same pants, but short sleeved shirts in a pale blue color. It's late afternoon and there's enough of a breeze that we're not sweltering, but I'll be glad when this ceremony's over and we can crack open some crisp, cold bottles of beer.

Ash gives the same answer, the officiant declares them husband and husband, they kiss and we all cheer.

"Congratulations to you both," I drag Charlie in for a hug first, then Asher right after him. "I'm so happy for you."

Charlie pats me on my shoulder blade, but Ash squeezes me tight. "Thanks, Uncle Ted." I resist the urge to ruffle his hair. I can see that effort has gone into styling it today, and probably a bit of product besides. "Next time'll be you, right?"

I snort. I've known Ash for almost as long as he's been with Charlie, which is coming up on three years now. And in that time, while I've gone on a few dates from guys I met at The Grove, the local BDSM club, I haven't found the sort of connection that Ash and Charlie share. Additionally, there's a lot about my past that not even Charlie's aware of which, after close to fifteen years of friendship, would be difficult and painful to explain now. Instead, I focus on the obvious.

"I'm almost fifty," I argue with a shake of my head.

It's a mild exaggeration. I still have a few years before I hit that milestone, but it's sneaking up fast.

At Asher's questioning glance, I sigh. "I think I'm getting too old to believe I'll find someone to settle down with now." I shrug, forcing a bright smile that I hope meets my eyes. "But this is your wedding day, kiddo. Let's not bring down the mood."

Until recently, I was also Ash's boss in addition to being his and Charlie's friend. But he graduated college, having deferred and then studied part time after he met Charlie, and is now working with his husband. Together they're building a community hub for people like us: people in the BDSM lifestyle, with additional focus to those who enjoy the age regression kink. I've been helping out with some of the legalities, but Asher's business degree has proven useful for them, as have Charlie's connections from his previous career as a cop.

I'm significantly older than both of these men, but our social circle is eclectic. That's to be expected, considering we all met through the BDSM lifestyle.

Case in point: Ash's best friend, Matt, wanders over with his Daddy's hand clutched in his. To look at them, you'd assume the roles were reversed. They're both tall, broad men, with Matt eclipsing London in height and muscle mass. Matt's arms are heavily tattooed, and his neatly trimmed beard is more salt and pepper now than the brown it once was. The shaggy hair on his head, also neatly styled back today, is turning the same. He's roughly my age, so that's hardly a surprise. But his Daddy, London, is in his late twenties with thick, black hair and the flawless skin of youth. Like Ash and Charlie, their Daddy-boy relationship has been going strong since they met.

And, alright, if Matt could still find love in his mid-forties, maybe I'll concede that hope is not lost for me after all. It just seems unlikely.

"Congrats, guys," London gives the grooms each a quick hug before drawing Matt back against his side, "that was a really nice ceremony."

"Yeah, it was," Matt agrees, snuggling against his Daddy's shoulder. His tone is wistful and dreamy. "The weather was perfect, too."

We'd all expressed our concerns that choosing to marry in the park without a backup plan for bad weather was asking for trouble, but Ash held firm. He's quite stubborn when he wants to be.

As if reading my thoughts, he casts me a smug little grin. "Told you it would be."

I shake my head. "You got lucky."

Charlie chuckles at that and tugs his new husband flush against him. "I'd say *I* got lucky," he says, aiming for schmoopy and disgustingly sweet.

Thankfully, his younger brother, Josh, has also meandered over from his spot among the guests. "Nah," he teases, "that's what your wedding night is for, isn't it?" He waggles eyebrows that match Charlie's for emphasis.

Charlie sighs with exasperation when we all snicker like teenagers. He shoots his younger brother a glare. "Fuck off, Josh."

"You wound me," Josh places a hand over his chest, then lunges for Ash.

"We're officially brothers now!"

"He gets this from Mom," Charlie tells us as an aside, as though we're not all aware of the fact.

"Speaking of," I jut my chin towards the woman in question.

She's bustling across the manicured lawn like a woman on a mission, practically dragging her husband (an older version of Charlie and Josh) along beside her. Charlie's baby brother, Axel, follows at a more sedate pace. Unlike his older brothers, Axel's short and stocky, with his mother's rounded facial features and curled hair. He graduated high school a couple of years ago, but still looks like a teenager to me. Then there's Charlie's sister, Maisy, and her husband whose name I can't remember. Charlie's family are lovely, but they're high energy and I'm already looking for my escape.

"Ted," Chance, one of the other Daddies in our little group, calls me just as Charlie's mother reaches us. I could kiss him. "Can you come help with the…uh…"

"The cooler," another younger man, one I don't recognize, steps in smoothly.

I try not to swallow my tongue as I look him up and down. I try to gauge his age and guesstimate that he's likely in his early thirties. He's immaculately dressed in a tailored suit (*in this heat? Is he crazy?*), all long limbs and big, dark eyes. He's got the prettiest smile I've ever seen, and his skin is, as Ricky Martin sang about a fictional paramour, the color of mocha. His voice is like liquid velvet, soft and sensual, and I'm too busy listening to the melodic tone to actually focus on the words.

"Sorry," I shake my head as though to clear it, belittling myself for the moment of infatuation. This man is beautiful but, even if he is kink friendly, the likelihood of him being a Little or wanting a Daddy as old as I am is slim to none. Assuming he's even single. "The cooler?"

"Yes," he looks amused, stepping in closer to me. "Can you come help with the cooler? We need to load it into the back of Chance's truck and it's just a bit too heavy for me to help properly." He bats insanely long lashes at me and I nod my agreement readily. Right now, I'd happily follow this pretty little thing anywhere.

My nameless savior apologizes to the grooms and Charlie's family for stealing me away, then leads me towards the parking lot. Finally getting my shit together, I look around for Chance, who we appear to have left behind.

Ah, well, he'll catch up. Thanks for taking one for the team, Chance.

"He said you'd need rescuing from Charlie's family," my companion tells me, interpreting my confusion correctly. "Unfortunately, it seems Chance isn't so great at improv."

"No, he's not," I agree, then stick my hand out to properly introduce myself. "Thanks for the rescue. I'm Ted."

Full, plump lips twitch upwards before he takes my hand. "Zephyr."

That…well, that was not at all the sort of name I was expecting.

Zephyr laughs. It's a surprisingly deep sound, considering the pitch of his speaking voice. "Yeah," he says, "I get that reaction a lot."

"What?" I try to recover. "I didn't say anything."

"You didn't need to. You had that 'how the hell does this guy have such a white boy hippy name?' look on your face. Don't worry; *everyone* looks at me like that." He shrugs. "My parents *are* hippies, by the way. At least at heart. I mean, Dad's an accountant and Mom's a teacher, but they're still very, uh, *creative*. So…" he gestures loosely over his lithe body, charmingly self-deprecating, "Zephyr it is."

Shoving my hands in my pockets, I rock back on my heels. "For what it's worth, I think it's a pretty cool name."

'Pretty cool'? Am I stuck in the 90s now? Why not just say 'rad' and really prove how lame I am?

Oblivious to my internal cringing, Zephyr smiles again. "Thank you."

Awkward silence begins to descend. I don't want that. "So," I start, fumbling for conversation. I'm not used to fumbling. I'm usually cool as a cucumber. Suave. Sophisticated. "How do you know Chance?"

I want to facepalm as soon as the probing question leaves my lips. I might as well have asked if they're fucking.

Well done, Theodore. Walk away now before you really put your foot in it.

Zephyr, thankfully, throws me a bone. "Actually, I met him and Asher at The Grove." His posture is deliberately relaxed, but I can see him eyeing me for my reaction.

I nod and smile. "Littles' Night? Those are Ash's favorite." And when Charlie can't make it, Spence, Chance or I usually step in as his caregiver. I cock my head, looking Zephyr up and down slowly. "I don't want to assume…"

"Oh, I'm very much a Little." Once again, he takes me out of my misery. He looks me up and down, much the same way I just did to him. It makes me feel better about the exchange, like we're on equal footing. "I'd guess Daddy, but after Chance introduced me to Matt, I also don't want to presume."

"Definitely a Daddy," I nod, trying not to let my excitement over the basic compatibility between us show. Before the silence can descend again, I ask, "Are you new to The Grove?" I haven't visited recently, but I'd definitely remember seeing him around.

"Yeah. New to town, actually. Only been here a few months, and Ash… well, you know Ash." He laughs, shaking his head. "He wouldn't hear of me not coming to the wedding when he worked out how very limited my social circle here is, so…" Zephyr extends his arms out wide, palms facing the clear, blue sky. "Here I am."

I know my expression has turned fond as I think about Ash. He's flourished from the skittish, traumatized kid he was when he first stumbled into Charlie's life. And, because he knows what it's like to be lonely and to start over somewhere new, it's not surprising that he tries to welcome every new face with open arms.

"Well, I'm glad you came today," I find myself telling Zephyr, once again wondering where all of my ability to flirt and charm disappeared to. "And not only because you rescued me from Charlie's family."

It's a clunky save, but it'll do.

"Oh, is that so?" Zephyr practically purrs, stepping in a little closer. His dark eyes practically dance with amusement. "Why else would you be glad that I, a complete stranger to you, am here, then?"

Good question.

Before I can fumble over an answer that doesn't sound creepy as fuck, Chance interrupts us, throwing his arm around my shoulder while he grins at Zephyr. Chance's enthusiasm is usually infectious, innocuous as he is with his dad bod and ginger beard, but today the interruption grates on my nerves.

"Mission accomplished," he declares, sounding proud of himself. "Now all we gotta do is try and sit at the far end of the table at the fancy-schmancy restaurant you booked for tonight, and we can avoid Mrs Walker trying to marry us all off."

Honestly, considering the casual attire of the Wedding Party, it's not like we're going anywhere that exclusive, but I don't bother arguing with my friend. Instead, I allow his comment to launch us into a debate about the merits of getting to the restaurant early vs late, and I'm thrilled beyond measure when Zephyr agrees to ride with us in Chance's truck when we finally get our shit together and leave the park.

Chapter Two – Zephyr

"So…Ted, huh?" Ash asks, dropping into the chair beside me at his very casual wedding reception.

It turned out, as his gift to his friends, one Theodore Masters hired a private room at their favorite restaurant. How do I know this? Asher and his new husband, Charlie, were sure to thank the man effusively during their impromptu speeches as we ate. Sitting beside me, the very same man tried to brush off the thanks casually, but I could tell he was genuinely happy to have been able to help his friends out.

I haven't known Ash very long, and this is only the third time I've met Charlie, but they're good people.

Well, good…if somewhat nosy.

I do my best to appear unaffected by my new friend's observational skills. "What about him?" I ask nonchalantly, reaching for the glass of sweet white wine I've been nursing for the last half hour. I'm not a big drinker, but I do have a weakness for sweet things.

The room we're in is just long enough for the extended table which seats twenty people. Ash and Charlie had taken seats next to each other in the middle, with Charlie's family down one end and his and Ash's friends clustered on the other. I found myself seated among their friends, which was nice.

It's actually a lovely space. The room is cozy and warmly lit, the walls painted cream. Fairy lights are strung above our heads. There's a small, makeshift 'dance floor' in the other half of the room, and now that dinner is over, some of the couples in attendance are swaying together to the strains of Michael Bublé's crooning.

Charlie's being begrudgingly dragged around the dance space by his mother, but when he looks over at Ash in an obvious cry for help, my new friend just giggles and blows his husband a kiss. Then he turns back to me and raises an eyebrow. "Oh, nothing," he answers my question with airy amusement, "just the fact that you've been eyeing him off all night."

I shrug. "He's an attractive man."

Ted is tall and broad shouldered, with dark brown hair and a healthy tan. He has salt and pepper streaks at his temples and artfully scattered atop his head, which seems almost artificial considering the way they perfect his silver fox vibe. A strong, clean-shaven jawline and warm light brown eyes round out the image. His voice isn't ridiculously deep, but it's smooth and measured when he speaks, likely a byproduct of his chosen career as a lawyer.

Ash's smirk turns knowing. "Uh huh. And he's an excellent Daddy."

I don't bother reacting to that, either. I'd gathered as much just from our interactions alone. When we arrived at the restaurant and took our seats, Ted slid into the one beside mine, and it seemed almost second nature for him to look after me for the course of the meal, refilling my glass, checking that things were to my liking, being sure to include me in the conversations he fell into with the people around us. I guess that, if he'd been given the chance, he would have even cut my steak for me.

After the meal, he'd been dragged into conversation with someone at the far end of the table and I'd encouraged him to go chat. I knew Chance as well, after all, and even if I do come off shy, I can socialize with strangers without any issues. But Ash was right when he said I'd been eyeing Ted all night: even with him on the far side of the room, my eyes still stray to him.

"Does your new husband know that you're trying to play matchmaker for his best friend?" I tease lightly, leaning back in my chair to stretch off the soporific effects of the decadent meal I just ate.

"Yep," Ash pops the 'p' as he speaks the word with childlike glee. "And he's all for it. Ted's been single for too long, and, honestly, we both just wanna see him happy."

"Maybe there's a reason Ted's been single," I argue, then hold up a finger to defend my point when it's clear Ash is unimpressed at the implication that his friend is somehow flawed. "And I don't mean that he's not a good guy, because it's obvious that he is. Just...maybe he *wants* to be single. Maybe he's the type that likes to hit it and quit it."

Ash scoffs. "He's a *Daddy*," he tells me in a tone that says I'm being stupid. "He has dedicated space for age regression play in his home *and* in his office." That last tidbit does surprise me, and I know it shows on my face. Ash's vehemence gentles. "Apparently, he'd just come out of a long-term relationship around the time I met Charlie. He's been on a few dates here and there, but he hasn't really clicked with anyone." Now, an almost lupine grin pulls his lips upwards. "Until now."

I roll my eyes. "And what would you know of our interactions, hmm? It's your wedding day. You've been too loved up with that handsome man of yours to be paying little ol' me any mind."

"*Please*. People watching is something Charlie and I both enjoy." There's a sharpness to Ash's grin now: a hint that he can read me better than I'd like him to be able to. "And, let me tell you, watching the man I like to think of as 'Uncle Ted' fall all over himself to keep your attention was a revelation."

I take a moment to process those words, patting the corners of my mouth delicately with my thick, white linen napkin before tossing it over the crumbed remnants of my slice of wedding cake. "Alright, so there was a *little bit* of flirting..." I hold my thumb and index finger an inch or so apart. "But it's a wedding. Don't all single people get a bit flirty with all the happily ever after vibes going on?" Not to mention the alcohol, not that I've had more than two glasses.

"You weren't flirting with Chance or Spence, though, and they're both single." Ash lets his gaze float around the room, pointing people out. "So's Max, actually." He cocks his head and muses, "I mean, I think he's straight?

I don't know. He's Charlie's former partner. Anyway, I know Tristan and Gabe are single, and they're involved in the BDSM lifestyle, too." He waves at the two men he just named when they look over. Both are, objectively speaking, handsome men. Probably too young for my taste, but with pleasant smiles and friendly eyes. "They're also new friends of ours," he adds, offhandedly. "We met them through Cherie and Kate. Tristan's a counselor and Gabe's a social worker. They're helping with the community center." He shrugs. "Not sure what their kinks are, but they're involved in the lifestyle, too."

I nod, but my disinterest in any of the men he just mentioned is almost palpable. "Okay, fine, you've made your point," I laugh, shaking my head before my gaze once again seeks out Ted. He's currently leaning against the far wall with a beer in hand, apparently engrossed in casual conversation with the woman Ash introduced earlier as Cherie, as well as his friends Matt and London. As I watch him, I can feel Ash studying me. I sigh. "What do you suggest I do about it, then?"

It's not like I'm going to actually take Ash's advice on board. I'll humor him. I'll listen and pretend to think it over, and then I'll slink out the door alone as planned.

Don't get me wrong: I like Ted. I like him a lot. And I don't doubt that he'd make a fantastic Daddy for someone. But…I'm not exactly a 'traditional' little and, as much as I can tell Ted finds me attractive, I don't know that our role-playing tastes would match. From what I've gathered just from listening to Ash talk about his circle of friends, someone like Ash himself is more Ted's type. A perfect little boy.

Not someone like me.

See, I'm little, but I like to play dress ups. Princess style.

Now, I know there's absolutely nothing wrong with that. I'm not ashamed to literally wear my kink with pride. However, I also know that finding a Daddy whose interests match mine can be difficult. Tea parties vs train sets, you know? And that's fine. I'm not desperate to find a Daddy just yet. I'm happy to have my itches scratched at The Grove for now.

Besides, I'm only slowly getting back into the lifestyle after an unscheduled break from it. Am I ready to dive in so deeply with a handsome stranger just because we've gotten along for one meal?

"Ask him to dance?" Ash suggests with a waggle of his eyebrows, bringing my thoughts back to the moment at hand. He grins. "You did tell him you're a professional dancer, didn't you?"

"Was," I correct him, doing my best not to sound bitter about it. A torn ACL ruined my dreams of continued touring. Now I teach dance to gradeschoolers.

I love my job, and I'm glad I recovered enough that I still get to dance, but the life I'm leading now has nothing on the fast pace of touring the world as a backup dancer, or the rush of performing in front of a huge audience. Hell, even being in the chorus line of a musical theater production would be awesome right now. But I had my chance, and I can't complain too much about my lot in life now. I'm not unhappy. I just miss what I once had.

"You're teaching it and that's a profession," he argues with me, oblivious to my inner turmoil, "ergo, you're a professional dancer."

"I should have guessed." Ted's sinfully smooth voice startles me and I jump in my seat, feeling heat rise to my cheeks even though the color of my skin is forgiving of my blushes. I turn to find him standing behind me and Ash, smirking. But, instead of saying something tacky about my body being 'built' like a dancer's, he says, "You're naturally graceful. Your movements are all purposeful, and your posture screams 'dancer'."

Part of me wants to slump in my seat if only out of petulance, but I remain upright with my back straight, my shoulders back and my chin high. "Is that so?"

Ted nods. "If I had to hazard a guess, I'd say you practiced as a ballerino, but..." he cocks his head, as though he's carefully deliberating his choices. He probably is. "No. Ballroom. Am I right?"

My jaw drops. "Yeah, I came up in the world of competitive ballroom dancing. What gave it away?"

"Honestly?"

I arch an eyebrow. "No. Please lie to me."

Ash snickers, then pushes out of the seat he'd commandeered, declaring that his work here is done. I wave him off, my eyes still tracking Ted as he slips into the seat, offering me a slightly bashful look. "Chance showed me your business page. It says it in your bio."

A burst of laughter escapes me. "You Googled me?"

"No," Ted's cheeks are taking on a distinctly pink flush. "Chance did."

"Uh huh."

With a put-upon groan, Ted runs his fingers through his hair. "He *did*!" he insists, then adds, "They're all trying to play matchmaker. They're worse than a bunch of meddling old women." There's a brief pause and he softens his tone. "I apologize if that makes you uncomfortable. They all mean well. But, with two of the guys paired off, Chance and Spence are trying to throw the heat off themselves and-"

"And the couples just want to see y'all as happy as they are." I finish for him, patting his thigh consolingly. "Don't worry. Weddings bring this out in people."

There's a spark of hunger in his gaze, which he directs down to my hand fleetingly. I slowly pull it back into my own bubble of personal space. Ted grins. "I can't be mad at them," he tells me. "It's not like I'm not interested in you."

Oh, but I do like how direct he is. It seems far more mature than half the guys I've dated – men closer to my own age and not involved in the BDSM lifestyle. With all the touring I was doing, I found beggars could not be choosers.

Still, even though Ted *is* a Daddy, and he knows I'm a Little, he doesn't know that I'm into princess play and that's a problem.

Instead of focusing on that, though, my traitorous mouth runs before my brain can do damage control. "Well, good. Because I'm interested in you, too."

Zephyr Cruze, I tell myself as I watch my companion's eyes light up, *quit while you're ahead.*

Chapter Three – Ted

Zephyr and I spend the rest of the party casually getting to know one another. We cover all the easy topics: nothing deep or of much consequence. I learn that he hates bananas but loves strawberries, and I share my firm belief that pineapple has no place on pizza (and he disagrees, calling me a heathen). I discover that we're both dog people, but neither of us hate cats, and it turns out that he shares my enjoyment for old Western movies. He loves musicals, which is not a surprise to me, but I am surprised when he vehemently states that he can't stand most Andrew Lloyd Webber classics.

"So, no *Phantom of the Opera* for you?" I tease.

He makes a face and shakes his head. "Ugh. No. And no *Cats*, either, thanks."

"Fair enough," I reply with a laugh. "I'm more into contemporary musical theater anyway. *Wicked. Avenue Q. The Book of Mormon.* That sort of thing."

Zephyr nods, genuinely invested in the conversation. His dark eyes sparkle under the fairy lights strung overhead and he leans in closer. "*Hamilton?*"

"Also excellent. As was the Broadway version of *In The Heights* but I can't say I loved the film adaptation as much."

He claps his hands with excitement. "Oh! I agree! I mean, the cast was fantastic, but I just couldn't get into it. I can't pinpoint why. It just didn't hit right."

When his face falls with unexpected melancholy, I lean in and reach for his hand. "What's wrong?"

Zephyr gives himself a shake and pastes on a smile that doesn't reach his eyes. "Nothing."

"No," I press, squeezing his hand, thrilled that he allows the contact to continue. "What's wrong?"

I watch him lick his lips, obviously deliberating over the concept of letting me in, even just a little bit. Not that I can blame him: I'm a veritable stranger. But my instincts have me determined to comfort and help him.

"I just…" he exhales. "I miss it. Dancing professionally, I mean." At my questioning glance, he shrugs. "I tore my ACL eighteen months ago. The surgery went well, and my recovery has been good, but my knee never fully recovered. I can dance, but not at the same level I used to, and not for as long or as intensely. It's been a bitter pill to swallow, I guess."

My heart goes out to him. After hearing him talk about his love of dance and music, I can only imagine how deeply this change of circumstances must hurt him. With his hand still in mine, I give him another reassuring squeeze. "I'm so sorry," I tell him.

Charlie went through something similar after the wound to his thigh ended his career, but I never felt like I had the right words to comfort him then, and I don't have them now for Zephyr, either.

"It could be worse," Zephyr says, and it sounds as though it's a mantra he tells himself a lot.

"It could," I find myself agreeing, "but that doesn't mean you can't mourn what you lost."

Shaking his head, he gestures around the room. Half the guests have left by now, but I've resolved to stay put until this charming man leaves first, unwilling to miss even a second of possible conversation with him. "We're at a wedding. It's like a rule to not talk about sad shit, or something."

"You can talk about whatever you want," I argue. "I won't judge."

I've got my own fair share of sad thoughts, after all, but no reason to bring them up. Not now, not ever. Is that healthy? Probably not. But there's no place for them here. Especially not in the company I'm keeping right now.

"Zero judgment, huh?" Zephyr's tone shifts into an attempt at being flirtatious. He bats long, dark lashes at me. "That's a very open promise, Mister Masters."

"I'm *very* open minded, Mister Cruze," I flirt back, deliberately dipping my voice low.

I watch as my Daddy voice registers with him, sending a visible shiver through his lithe frame. I want so badly to make this beautiful man mine. My tiny dancer, to borrow a nickname from Elton John. But I know better than to rush into things. I've made that mistake too often in my lifetime.

There's an interesting gleam in his eyes, something in his expression that hints at him wanting to test me on my playful words, but he blinks it away and says, "I do like the sound of that." Then he raises his left wrist, twisting it to check the time on his watch, and sighs heavily. "And, on that note, I should probably get going. I have early classes tomorrow."

My stomach sinks, but I don't want to come off clingy or too aggressive, so I nod and rise from my seat at the same time as him. "Do you want to share a Lyft?" When he raises his eyebrows, I realize my mistake. I want to smack myself upside the head. Sheepishly, I explain, "I meant to our respective destinations. Not…I wasn't…"

Excellent. I'm back to being a fumbling buffoon.

As frustrated as I am with myself, it's also a sign that I genuinely like this man: that I'm feeling the kind of interest that has evaded me for years now. I can't be mad about that. Even if I do wish I could prevent embarrassing myself quite as badly.

"I should hope not," Zephyr's lip curls upwards and he leans in, his breath ghosting over my ear as he murmurs, "I'd like to be taken on a real date before we start talking about going home together."

He is so close that I can feel the heat of his body next to mine, and the combination of his proximity and those words has me hardening instantly. The knowing expression on his face as he pulls back, putting space between us again, tells me that he's more than aware of the effect he has on people.

On me.

"You're a naughty little thing, aren't you?" I ask, unable to prevent the train of thought that follows my observation.

Is he a bratty boy? Is he into sexual punishments? How far does he push things? How far can I push him back?

"Hmm," he pretends to think about it, and I'm delighted that he's playing along. "Maybe you should give me your number so you can find out for yourself?"

Once again, I can't help but find his confidence insanely alluring. It's a far cry from the shy, sweet Littles I'm used to pursuing, and I'm pulling out my phone before my brain can even catch up. "Give me yours," I insist, "and I'll call you so you'll have mine." I'm not taking any chances here. I can't risk giving him my number without getting his in exchange.

Obviously, if he were to decide that he's not interested, I'd stop pursuing him (no means no, after all), but I'd like to make sure we're on equal footing to begin with. If I don't hear from him in the next few days, I'll reach out. If he turns me down after that? At least I've enjoyed his company tonight and have proven that there's still a chance for me to find someone to connect with after all, even if it doesn't turn out to be him.

As if he's reading my thoughts, he chuckles but rattles off his digits and I type them into my phone. I press the little green handset icon on my screen, and his pocket buzzes with the tell-tale vibration of a silenced phone.

"There," I say, terminating my call. "Now we've got each other's numbers." Still holding my phone, I give it a little shake. "So, want to share a Lyft?"

* * *

Three days. I wait three whole days before I give in to the urge to contact Zephyr. Sitting in my office overlooking a good part of the city, I bring up his contact and press call. It rings for a little while, and I realize that he's probably teaching, but by the time my brain kicks into gear with that thought, I'm being prompted to leave a voicemail message.

"Hi Zephyr, it's Ted. From the wedding. Uh, Ash and Charlie's wedding."

Once again, I can feel how awkward I'm being and want to strangle myself for it. I make a living by knowing exactly how best to wield and manipulate the English language. Contract law is my specialty, and I can schmooze potential clients with the best of them. But, apparently, put an attractive man whose kinks complement mine in front of me (or on the phone to me) and I lose all my carefully cultivated skills. "I'm just…touching base." *Ugh.* "And wondering if you might like to go out with me some time?" *Dear God, did my voice just go up half an octave?* I clear my throat. "Give me a call back and we'll chat." *And there I go, over-correcting. What the hell, Masters?* "Talk soon!"

I force myself to hang up before I can humiliate myself further. Staring in horror at the phone in my hand, I ask, "What the ever-loving fuck was that? *'Talk soon!'*" I mock myself in a falsetto, then rub my other palm over my face, cringing at my own behavior. "You're forty-seven. Get it together."

Am I really so out of practice when it comes to wooing a potential partner? It's not like I've been a monk these last three years, but they've been Grindr hookups or guys I've met at The Grove who were flagging for open play. I haven't exactly had to work for another man's attention recently and it shows in my lack of game.

Case in point? I just called it 'game'.

Shoot. Me. Now.

The landline phone on my desk bleats with the tone set for the firm's secretary, thankfully distracting me from my self-deprecating thoughts. I lift the receiver and say, "Yes, Sonya?"

She's a consummate professional, but her voice is always ridiculously chipper. This conversation proves to be no exception. "Your eleven o'clock candidate is here. I've taken the initiative to have him wait in the boardroom for you and Louise."

I glance at my watch, pleased to see that it's only ten to eleven. A good sign for this candidate. Early, but not stupidly so. "Fantastic, Sonya, thanks."

We're still interviewing for Asher's replacement. Technically, we'd hired someone when he first gave notice, but to say that didn't work out is an understatement. Louise (our Office Manager) and I still grumble over being so thoroughly wrong about our assessment of the guy at the time, the both of us usually priding ourselves on our abilities to read people. Now, with the two of us questioning our judgment, we're probably taking too much time interviewing for the entry-level role, but it's definitely a case of 'once bitten, twice shy'.

"Are you sure we can't just bribe Ash to come back?" Louise jokes when we meet in the hallway outside the conference room. Her long brown hair is secured in an immaculate bun at the back of her head, and her hazel eyes twinkle with mirth as she asks the question. "Aren't you BFFs with his hubby? Surely that gives you some pull."

"It's that same hubby who lured him away from us," I remind her with a put-upon sigh. "Charlie clearly has zero respect for my professional needs."

When I'd been invited to come and meet my best friend's new boy, it had come as quite the surprise to see my most recent hire of the time at Charlie's home. (And I know it had been even more shocking from Asher's perspective; something we can laugh about now.) After that, it took a little while to convince Ash that our professional relationship would be fine, and that I was, first and foremost, Charlie's friend and therefore his friend, too. The fact that he eventually came to think of me as Uncle Ted was both a relief and a privilege.

However, Louise isn't aware of the lifestyle Ash, Charlie and I are involved in. Still, she knows that our friendship is closer than most, and she's convinced that I should be able to use that to my advantage to entice her favorite employee back.

She huffs. "Well, what good is your friendship, then?"

"Aww, come on now, Lou," I cajole, laughter coloring my tone, "we might find someone just as good as Ash." I look down at the completed application and resume in my hand. "Beckett Peters," I read the candidate's name, "might be the one."

With deep resignation, Louise nods. "Fine. But if we don't find a suitable replacement soon? I'm kidnapping Ash back and you can't warn Charlie."

I reach for the door handle and wink. "Let's hope it doesn't have to come to that."

* * *

My phone rings just as I slump through the door from my garage into my empty house. The place is ridiculously big for just me, but I bought it for a song a couple of years ago and have only recently finished the restorations and renovations, bringing it into modern times while keeping its stately feel. I fish my phone out of my pocket, fully prepared to let the call go through to voicemail, when I catch the name on the screen.

Zephyr.

I can't answer it quickly enough, my thumb fumbling for the button.

Thankfully, I manage to catch it before he's redirected to my voicemail, and I know my voice is strained when I answer, "Zephyr! Hello!"

There's a moment of silence, which I interpret as hesitation. "Is this a bad time?"

"No!" I close my eyes and curse myself for the rushed, far-too-eager response. After taking a calming breath, I try again. "No. Sorry. I just got home and had to fumble for my phone."

Great. Verbal diarrhea.

What is it about this man that pulls this from me?

His delicious chuckle floats down the line. "I'm picturing it now," he teases.

Finally, something I can work with. Lowering my voice, I flirt back on my way through the large laundry, passing the equally huge kitchen and into the open plan living/dining space beyond, "Well, I do like that you're picturing me."

Zephyr snorts. "Not in the way you're hoping."

Brat. This sends a thrill up my spine. I'd love to take him over my lap and spank him for his cheek. I get the feeling he'd enjoy it. Even though I've never really been into bratty boys, I know I would as well.

"It's still a step above you *not* thinking of me, so I'll take it."

"Hmm," he makes a show of sounding thoughtful, "If your voicemail is to be taken into consideration, I'm almost certain it's *you* thinking of *me*, Mister Masters."

He's quick as a whip and I love it. Dropping down onto my white leather couch, I lean back and grin at the ceiling with my phone still pressed to my ear. "You called me back, so I can't help but think it's a two-way street, Mister Cruze." Without giving him a chance to respond, I continue, "And I'm not ashamed to admit that I haven't been able to stop thinking about you, if that helps."

"Well, now you've taken all the fun out of my teasing you." I can still hear the smile in his voice, so I know he's not offended.

I want to tell him that I can think of other ways he can tease me and that I'm happy to offer suggestions, but I stop myself. I want whatever is building between us to be more than just a quick, lusty affair. I'm a Daddy, after all. I'm driven to nurture and care for my partner, which usually involves developing an emotional attachment. Something deeper than just a handful of quick fucks. Not that there's anything inherently wrong with the casual hookups I've had over the last few years, but my heart wants more.

Still, I can't stop myself entirely from flirting back. "Tiny dancer, you can tease me however you like."

A few more beats of silence pass and I pull the phone away, glancing at the screen to make sure the call is still engaged and that I haven't muted it or something similar. When I press it against my ear again, he breathes, "Tiny dancer, huh?"

"You know…like the song?" Suddenly, I feel unsure of myself again, realizing that I've overstepped. Trying to bring back the levity, I blurt, "Or is that well and truly before your time?"

Great. Remind him that there's a massive age gap between you. Idiot.

Thankfully, Zephyr laughs and feigns affront, "I know my Elton John, thank you."

"That's a relief," I sass back, sinking back into the couch cushion now that the crisis has been averted. "Giving you a proper musical education would have become my top priority."

"As opposed to…?"

"As opposed to the date I asked you out on. Which, I might remind you, you still haven't accepted."

"Maybe I was waiting for you to ask again properly, not just via a vague voicemail message."

This beautiful creature is definitely going to keep me on my toes. Smiling, I reply, "Can I take you out to dinner and a movie, Zephyr?"

"How very traditional of you."

Oh, he's really making me work for it.

"Or, perhaps, something more casual? Like a picnic date?" There's a voice in my head telling me not to push too hard. I rack my brain for more creative ideas but, as is becoming the norm where this man is concerned, I can't think beyond just wanting to spend time with him. "Or…bowling?"

Bowling? Really? Who even am I?

"I'd love to go out with you," he finally cuts in, preventing me from spiraling into a list of random activities. But his next words cool my elation, especially with the undercurrent of uncertainty in his voice. "But you should know some things about me, first."

God, I wish that I could see his face. That I could hold his hand as I assure him: "Whatever it is, I doubt it will change my interest in you." Grinning, I try to lighten the mood again. "Even if you tell me that you secretly hate Elton John's music."

This earns me the desired reaction of snorted laughter before a light sigh comes across the line. "I'm a Little, which you know, but…" He trails off.

"But?"

"I'm a femme little. I'm into princess play and dresses and stuff." Zephyr's voice is small, as though the admission pains him. There are a thousand reasons why that might be the case, but if one of those is that he's afraid I'm not okay with it, I need to disabuse him of that notion right now.

"Is that it?" Okay, probably not the smoothest reaction I could have offered him. I rush to correct myself. "I mean, that's not a problem for me. It doesn't change my interest in you, in general or as a Daddy."

I can hear the breath he sucks in and the wonder in his voice. "Really?"

"Really." In fact, the whole concept has a feeling of excitement building beneath my skin. I haven't been with a Little who indulged in such things in over a decade, but it's not something I have zero experience with, either. Additionally, Ash has spent the last couple of years re-introducing me to the joys of teddy bear tea-parties. Besides, the whole concept suits Zephyr. The idea of pretty dresses and tea parties and makeup play just fits. I can picture it clearly in my mind's eye, and I love it.

Softening my tone, I hope to impart some of what I'm feeling, "It sounds perfect for you, tiny dancer, and I'd love to be a part of that, if you'll have me."

Chapter Four – Zephyr

I had absolutely no reason to deny Ted when he asked me out a third time. Not after he so sweetly reassured me that my additional kink wasn't an issue for him. The relief I felt in that moment surprised me; I honestly hadn't realized how attached I already was to the idea of dating him until I thought that he might actually change his mind.

So, when he followed up his declaration that he was still into me with another idea for a date, I readily agreed. Even though he changed it from going out to something that sounded far more intimate and personal: dinner at his house, with the potential for some Daddy/little play if we're both feeling it.

That was on Tuesday. Today is Saturday and the day we'd agreed for our date, and even though we've spent the rest of the week texting during the day and talking on the phone at night, the pre-date jitters are starting to kick in for me.

It's been a week since we met. Somehow, that simultaneously feels like no time at all and far too long. Our conversations have been fun and flirtatious, easy, and effortless. We've talked about everything and nothing. In the lead-up to tonight's date, we spent last night talking about our hard limits as Daddy and Little, and we went through the negotiation chat that really should happen before any BDSM interaction begins.

Considering Ted's experience in the lifestyle, I shouldn't have been surprised that his hard limits are few and far between. He's not into bondage at all but doesn't mind light impact play for fun. As for diapering, he's okay with wetting but draws the line at anything beyond that, which is beyond fine by me. Most of my little time is spent hovering at a slightly older mindset. I'm much more interested in pretending I'm a princess than being babied, and I prefer pretty panties to diapers anyway. On the off chance I wear them, I don't do wetting. Additionally, pacifiers and bottles don't do it for me at all, and Ted didn't seem upset by that, either.

So far, it sounds like we might actually be well suited to each other, at least where our kinks are concerned.

Yet, I'm nervous. I don't want to screw this up. I actually like this guy.

It's been a while since I've felt so intensely about another man. Before my injury, my affairs were casual at best. It's hard to find Daddies when you're touring, the tight quarters and constant presence of the same people day-in, day-out not helping much. Neither do the hours you have to keep, especially between rehearsals and performances and actually being on the road. Then, after my injury, I went through a dark period, where age play wasn't even on my radar. I just wanted to get off and go home, and I didn't care with whom or in what order of events that happened.

My return to the BDSM scene has been tentative and slow. The night I met Ash and Chance, I was wearing a fairly standard outfit for a little boy, not giving anyone any inkling about my desires to dress up in pretty dresses or play tea-parties, just dipping my toes back in to the world I'd left behind during the worst year and a half of my life. In fact, tonight will be the first time since my injury that I'm even considering trying.

It hits me that maybe that's a big part of why I feel so anxious.

What if I put on one of my old dresses and don't feel the same way that I used to? I used to feel pretty, and delicate, and magical. What if tonight all I feel is silly? What if that spark is gone? It's been such a big part of who I am for so long, I'm terrified of what it might mean if I've lost it. If I've changed irrevocably.

When Ted picks me up because he insisted on doing so, he gives me a hug in greeting. Then he seems to pick up on my inner turmoil immediately.

"What's wrong?" he asks, gently tilting my head to look me in the eye. "Is going to my place too much, too soon? I'm happy to change our plans if you'd rather something more public and casual."

There's something in the almost rushed way he speaks that has me blinking in surprise. With a jolt, I realize that he's nervous, too. Immediately, some of the tension I've been feeling fades away. His nerves are a sign that he's interested in me for more than just a quick fuck, right? *Right.*

I shake my head, then impulsively step forward and crane my neck to kiss him on the cheek. "You're sweet," I tell him, grinning at the way his cheeks pink from the praise, "and, no, it's not too much or too fast for me."

It's not like we're *planning* on sleeping together yet. We're just planning on testing our compatibility. But I won't complain if that happens to develop into more. Not if we're both on the same page, anyway. I know how quickly BDSM interactions can become intense. How unexpectedly relationships can turn serious simply because of how vulnerable you are being with each other.

"Then what's wrong?" He's a bit like a dog with a bone. I shouldn't be surprised, not with his chosen career. He picks up the overnight bag I packed, which is full of my little gear, and sets it on the back seat of his BMW.

Because *of course* he drives a BMW.

I sigh and come clean. "I haven't indulged in any of the femme play since before my injury." Licking my lips, I consider my explanation. "I'm just a bit anxious about it. Like...what if I don't feel the same way anymore? It's probably stupid to worry, but if I've been able to just, I don't know, shut it off for the last eighteen months, is it even still part of my identity?"

"Hey now," Ted pulls me in for a hug, carding his fingers through my hair. With my ear pressed to his chest, the steady beating of his heart calms my jangled nerves. "It sounds like you haven't really had enough time to properly explore your kinks at all, let alone since your accident. The fact that you still think about and still have the urge to do it says more about how much you enjoy it than you're aware."

I'm only half processing his words, too swept up in the feeling of being wrapped in his embrace. His chest is warm and solid, and he smells so good. His cologne is sweet and subtle, soothing in its own right. Then there's his voice, pitched low and smooth, rumbling through his chest beneath my cheek and ear. All combined, I feel overwhelmingly safe in his arms. Cared for.

He's not the first Daddy to have ever held me, but I can't recall another Daddy ever making me feel this way. At least, not without the additional post-orgasm endorphins to help.

I try to shoo away the path that thought wants to take me down, but it's too late. I'm immediately wondering how it might feel to be cradled against Ted's body in the afterglow of sex.

Thankfully, he distracts me before I can get too lost in those ponderings. Giving me a little shake, he asks, "Zephyr? Are you okay?"

He sounds genuinely concerned and I reluctantly step back so I can smile at him and nod. "I was just enjoying the hug. It's, uh, it's been a while."

Wow, that sounds pathetic.

But there's no pity in his expression. Instead, he offers me a rueful smile of his own. "I can relate to that."

Well done, Z. First rule of dating: don't bring the mood down. And what did you do? You brought the mood down.

Rallying, I try to turn it around. "Well, if all goes well, maybe we'll both be seeing more hugs in the near future."

It's an awkward attempt, but the blinding smile it earns me tells me that the sentiment is appreciated anyway.

"I hope so," Ted says, and the smile melts into something a little more sensual. "I think we'll be good for each other in a lot of ways."

I'm pretty much convinced that we will, too.

* * *

"I'm sorry, I thought you said you were taking me to your *house*," I blurt with what is probably a slack-jawed, wide-eyed look on my face as Ted pulls his car into the driveway of something I'd otherwise describe as a

McMansion. "This," I gesture towards the stately building, "is not a 'house', Ted." I use my fingers as quotation marks while I emphasize how badly his blasé description failed him. "This is a mansion."

It actually takes my breath away to look up at it as the car crawls through the gate towards it. The pretty dappled brickwork is complemented by pristine arch-shaped windows trimmed in white. It's only two stories, but the building sprawls sideways, with at least eight windows that I can count on the ground floor and six on the 'smaller' floor on top of it. Ted presses a button on the little remote attached to his sun visor and the white double garage door on the right side of the home begins to rise slowly.

Finally responding to my reaction to his not-so-humble abode, my date chuckles. "It's not a mansion. It's just a large house."

"You keep telling yourself that," I insist as he directs the car into the spare space in his garage, next to a gleaming Harley Davidson motorcycle. It looks like a cruiser? Honestly, I know nothing about the things. I eye the black and chrome beast with additional surprise before shaking my head. "I wasn't expecting that, either."

"Oh, the bike?" He shrugs. "Let's call that a midlife crisis."

"You don't ride it much?"

Shutting off the car, Ted unbuckles his belt and sighs. "Not as often as I thought I would."

I could throw statistics at him about how dangerous it is to ride them, but I save my breath. He doesn't strike me as the type to make risky decisions on the road, and there's no way to control other road users. I could just as easily be mowed down at a crosswalk as his bike could be hit by an inattentive driver. Instead, I make a vague noise of commiseration and then allow him to guide me through the internal door from the garage into a comically large laundry, with a long marble bench running the length of the space on one side, and gleaming appliances and a massive laundry tub on the other.

"Your laundry is bigger than my bathroom and kitchen combined," I mutter with only a little exaggeration.

He calls me out on it, his tone amused. "That sounds like hyperbole to me."

Before I can dig my heels in and argue that it's really not, he takes my hand and pulls me forward. We exit the laundry into a wide hallway-like space, then pass his kitchen (which, I tease, has to be at least twice the size of my bedroom) and an open plan living-dining area.

The floors throughout are gleaming dark timber, but the walls are off-white, and the counters are all topped with the same light-colored marble as those in the laundry. In the kitchen, the cupboards are the same off-white as the walls, beveled like the garage door. The furniture across all the rooms is all white as well, which contrasts spectacularly with the dark timber flooring, making the whole place feel even bigger and brighter.

Overall, it's a fabulous mix of modern and classic design, and I feel both comfortable and wholly out of place.

"There's also a formal lounge and formal dining room down here," Ted says as he continues to give me the tour, oblivious to my growing unease at the juxtaposition between his world and mine, "and a small office. Upstairs," we've stopped in the main foyer, heralded by a massive double door painted white and a grand staircase carpeted in off-white, with wrought-iron banisters curling up towards the second floor, "there are four bedrooms. Two of those are proper suites -the master and the guest- and the other two standard. Those two share a bathroom." He smiles at me. "The one closest to the master is the playroom."

"This is…" Too much. Too ostentatious. Too insane to even imagine. "*Wow.*"

I knew that, as a senior partner at law firm which, according to Google, is a pretty successful and sought-after one at that, Ted wasn't exactly lower-middle class like me, but this level of wealth makes me uncomfortable.

I mean, I'm a performer. From when I left home at eighteen and into my early twenties, I was literally a starving artist, one missed paycheck away from homelessness. Things got better when I started booking contracts to tour as a backup dancer, but I still had to watch my spending. Then, after injuring myself, even with the generous medical insurance I was thankfully covered with, I lost most of my savings and am only just now starting from scratch again.

I was exaggerating about the comparative size of my apartment to his laundry, but now as I slowly do a three-hundred and sixty degree turn to take in my surroundings, the contrast seems even more absurd.

Something of my discomfort must show on my face because Ted's expression morphs into concern. That's becoming a pattern with us already, and I can't help but feel that maybe it's a sign that pursuing a relationship with him isn't a good idea after all.

Before he can question me, I blurt, "I'm sorry. Your home is gorgeous. It's just…" I exhale. "Intimidating?"

His handsome face flickers with disappointment and something that looks almost like regret before he schools it into something more sheepish and lighthearted. He scratches the back of his neck and gestures wildly around us. "It needed a lot of work when I bought it, and I did much of that myself. It was a project. I like to keep myself busy."

The last sentence has weight behind it that I can't interpret, but I look around again, trying to gauge just what kind of manual labor he's put into it. As much as I don't try to stereotype, I highly doubt he made any structural changes himself. Or electrical or plumbing. Unless he counts hiring people to do it for him as doing it himself? But he's not like that. Or, at least, he hasn't come off that way in the week I've known him.

As if reading my mind, Ted starts pointing at the walls, "I tore off the old, peeling wallpaper and painted it all myself." He pauses, then rolls his eyes with a playful air. "Alright, sometimes the guys came over to help. Anyway," he points to the floors, "some moron had tiled over the hardwood, so pulling them up, then sanding, staining, lacquering and polishing the floors happened, too. Then there was a lot of minor stuff, just little repairs here and there, and I got contractors in to redo the kitchen, laundry and bathrooms, and the re-carpeting. It took almost a year to get it looking this way."

"Wow," this time when I say the word, it's with more awe than abject horror. "That's…intense."

"Like I said, I like to keep busy."

I want to probe into that, but there's a guardedness to him that prevents me from doing so. I figure we all have our hang-ups and baggage, and it's probably not the sort of thing to be delving into on a first date. Or would this be our second, if you count the wedding?

"So, was the intention to live here long, or are you planning on flipping it?"

Ted rubs his clean-shaven jaw with a large open palm. "Originally, I was going to flip it. It's too big a house for just me. But," he looks around again, his eyes going distant, as if he's reliving the memories of all his hard work, perhaps even memories of horsing around with that tight-knit group of friends of his as they helped, "I think I've gotten attached."

Now I feel a little bit guilty for reacting the way I did. It's obvious that he's put love, sweat and tears into this place, now that I hear him talk about it. To judge it or to judge *him* just because of its size and aesthetics was probably a dick move on my part. I don't think he'd judge me based on my crappy little apartment, after all.

"It is a beautiful home, Ted," I tell him softly, a little bit of my regret slipping into my tone. "I just wasn't expecting it. You seem so down to earth for a lawyer."

A bark of laughter escapes him. "For a lawyer, huh?" He arches an eyebrow at me, then wraps his arms around my waist, pulling me closer to him so we're practically chest to chest with only a few inches of space between us. "Was the addendum necessary?"

"Absolutely," I grin, unrepentant. I don't bother explaining my reasoning. It's much more fun to tease him.

Those amber-brown eyes of his glint down at me and he shakes his head with an almost rueful, yet entirely playful little smirk tugging at his lips. "You're going to be a handful, aren't you?"

I bat my lashes with exaggerated innocence. "Who, me?"

He practically growls a groan, his gaze dropping to my lips. My heart rate picks up, as if I'm only now noticing our physical proximity or the heat of his arms around my lower back. We've been flirting for a week now and I really want him to lower his head those couple of inches, to act on the fire burning between us. Unconsciously, my tongue darts out to wet my lips.

"Fuck, Zephyr, I'm trying to be a gentleman here," Ted complains, but he doesn't let me go or step back. If anything, his hold tightens, drawing me even closer against him.

"Gentlemen don't say *fuck*, Mister Masters."

My taunt does the trick. He chuckles, shakes his head, and then finally dips down to connect our mouths. But he's restrained, the kiss sweet and chaste, his lips warm and firm against mine. I practically melt into him anyway, parting my lips against his, inviting him to deepen the kiss. He takes the invitation, and our tongues meet and twine together slowly.

We explore each other, cataloging the best angles of our heads and movements of our mouths, setting a rhythm that has me rocking my hips into him without thought, my hands at his hips, fisting into the tight denim of his likely far-too-expensive jeans.

"Oh, tiny dancer, what am I going to do with you?" He murmurs fondly when we part for air. He drops his head lower, nuzzling at the crook of my neck before peppering little kisses up the column of my throat and to the ticklish spot just beneath my ear. I squirm and I feel his resulting laugh rumble through his chest, still pressed against mine. "You're a bad influence, little one."

I want to argue or tease back, but my brain is a puddle of goo right now. I can't recall ever feeling quite so easily attracted to someone before. I've been with handsome men before, but this is the first guy to make my heart stutter and my thoughts disappear. It's not that he's a Daddy, either. I've been with a few Daddies in my time, too. There's just something about Ted and about our connection that fries my internal systems.

Finally, after a moment or two too long to be considered normal, my brain re-engages.

"Do I get the rest of the tour?" I ask breathily, walking my fingers up the center of his short sleeved, button-down shirt. "Someone said something about a playroom?" He's still carrying my bag over his shoulder, and I tap the strap. "We can drop this off in there and then you can follow through on your promise to wine and dine me."

"You know," Ted snickers and sneaks another quick peck to my lips before he rests his forehead against mine, "for someone who said they were looking for a Daddy to take care of them, you're unexpectedly bossy."

"I'm not bossy, I just know what I want."

He pulls back and arches an eyebrow. "You're definitely a princess." Before I can defend myself against the perceived slight against my nature, his face breaks into a breathtakingly gorgeous smile. "I think I'm going to have fun with that."

* * *

The playroom, despite Ted's assurance that the room is a 'standard' sized bedroom, is at least one and a half times the size of the bedroom in my apartment. It's stunning. He has a twin sized bed tucked into the far-left corner from the door, and a white dresser on the wall parallel to it. The walls are painted with a fairy-tale mural, running around the entire room. It's a lush forest full of mythical creatures and characters poking their heads out between trees while dragons and butterflies and unicorns fly through the skyscape above the green treetops. The carpet in here is also a dark, mossy green color, completely different to the white throughout the rest of the house.

A long, low-lying set of shelves, also painted white, runs along the expanse of wall from the walk-in robe to the end of the bed. It is home to a collection of plush toys, a train set, building blocks and one hell of a dollhouse.

I cross the soft carpet to run my finger cautiously over the beautiful item. It's a four story mansion with working lights and opening doors, and I have the urge to play with it immediately.

"You like it?" Ted's gentle question startles me from my inspection of the stunning construction (so much more than a toy), and I turn to face him. He's leaning against the door of the walk-in wardrobe casually, but there's a flicker of something a bit more intense in his eyes.

Taking another glance around the room, predominantly filled with toys and items more suited to 'boyish' play (not that I truly believe that toys are necessarily geared to one gender over another), it clicks, and I feel my jaw drop.

"Please tell me," I swallow roughly, looking back down at the dollhouse, "that you had this exquisite, probably insanely expensive dollhouse *before* I told you about my preference for femme play."

"I had that exquisite, not *that* insanely expensive dollhouse before you told me about your preference for femme play," he semi-repeats dutifully.

I narrow my eyes. "You didn't really, did you?"

The material of his shirt strains across his chest as he raises his arms in surrender. "Does it really make a difference?"

"Jesus, Ted." I take a step back from the collection of toys and shake my head. "We haven't even tried a scene together yet."

"Maybe I just wanted it for my collection. Ash visits. He likes to play teddy bear tea parties. *Maybe* I thought he'd also like the dollhouse."

Well. Damn. He's got me there.

Typical weaselly lawyer. Even though the words are negative, I can't help the fondness I feel when I think them. *This man is definitely going to keep me sharp.*

With twitching lips, I concede defeat. "Alright, that's a fair argument." I look back at the dollhouse, once again overcome by the need to carefully pull it down from the shelf and open it up. It's one of those big, old-school designs with the two halves that open like a book, straight down the middle. "It really is beautiful."

"I'm glad you like it." His tone is all soft and gentle again, and my need changes from wanting to play with the grand 'toy' to wanting his lips on mine once more.

Giving myself a little shake, I look around the playroom one last time and ask to continue the tour. Ted drops my bag by the door as we walk out, and he shows me the rest of the house.

His master suite is like something out of a grand hotel. It's at least three times the size of the playroom, with an enormous bed in the middle of the wall facing the large windows overlooking the city view. Dusk is settling, the sky outside lighting up in orange, peach and pink hues as the sun slowly sets, and twinkling lights begin to speckle the cityscape in the distance. I can imagine sitting on that bed and watching the view for hours, day or night, like a fair maiden in a castle.

Like the rest of the house, the carpets are white. The walls here are more a light gray color, though, and the furniture darker and more masculine. The comforter on the bed is a darker shade of gray, matching the two armchairs nestled in the corner beneath a wrought-iron floor lamp that looks more like art than a functional item. But it's the master bathroom that takes my breath away.

The space is unsurprisingly huge, and tiled from floor to ceiling in large, dark granite tiles with gold flecks, sparkling in the sunlight streaming in from the large window overhanging a massive spa bathtub, built in and surrounded by the same granite as the walls and floor. The tub itself is clearly designed to fit two people comfortably, as is the walk-in shower on the opposite wall, designed as it is with two rainfall shower-heads and a bench seat built into the wall. A long, double vanity stretches in the space between the two decadent wash spaces, and the toilet is positioned on the remaining wall.

With all the dark tile, you would expect it to feel dated or oppressive, but it's somehow still airy and welcoming. It's certainly beyond luxury.

"Fuck me," I mutter, taking it all in, once again feeling out of my depth.

"Okay, I'll admit that I might have gone overboard here," Ted acknowledges, rubbing the back of his neck with a sheepish smile at my reaction. "But I just wanted to spoil myself, I guess. It's not like I have anything else to do with my money." There's that edge again. A hint of melancholy. Maybe regret? He shakes it off and gestures back towards the direction we came from. "The other two bathrooms and the powder room downstairs are all pretty normal in comparison. But this," he waves his arm around, "this was for me."

I finally realize that I have absolutely no right to judge him for spending the money he's worked hard for on the lifestyle he wants to live. He's earned the right to live in luxury if he so chooses. And, from all of our interactions so far, he hasn't seemed at all arrogant or dismissive of those of us (read: me) whose living situations and incomes don't exactly compare. Hell, his social circle, or at least the people I met at Ash's wedding, all seem to be in a similar socio-economic bracket to me, too.

I feel guilty that my reaction to his home has put some sort of divide between us and I make it my aim to fix that immediately. Turning sultry, I saunter over to the tub and lean against its granite frame. "Do you like to soak in this big, beautiful bath, Mister Masters?" Running my finger over the gleaming chrome faucet when he nods, I muse with faux innocence, "With or without bubbles?"

His lips curl upwards and he stalks forward, crowding me with his tall, toned frame. "I am partial to a good bubble bath," he tells me in a low, sexy drawl. "But, I'll admit, it can get a bit lonely in this big tub sometimes."

"Hmm," I make a show of thinking about how I could possibly help him with that dilemma. "Maybe, if you're lucky, we can think of a way to fix that one day."

"You're a real tease, tiny dancer," he groans, but his eyes are glinting with mirth and desire. "And, if you become mine, I will punish you for that."

A shiver of anticipation runs down my spine. *Yes, Daddy.* The words are on the tip of my tongue, but I bite them back. I'm surprised by how readily the title comes to me, but I shouldn't be. We've got real chemistry and our banter has been beyond enjoyable. Not to mention the kiss we shared in the foyer.

"Someone promised me dinner first." My own voice has gone husky, my gaze glued to his lips, wanting another taste but unwilling to make the first move. He's the Daddy here. He needs to take charge. We both know I'll stop him if I'm uncomfortable, and I trust him to respect the boundaries I set.

"Mmm," he agrees, but he closes the space between us and kisses me again, his tongue sweeping against mine, moving his mouth with a hunger that has nothing to do with dinner. It's a kiss full of longing and need and promises full of more to come, and I'm just as lost to it as I was to our first kiss.

As much as I should probably take things slowly with this man, I can feel my resistance slipping, and I'm powerless to stop it.

Chapter Five – Ted

Zephyr's presence does things to me that I just can't explain. I usually pride myself on my self-control. On my ability to remain stoic and firm and guarded when necessary. But with Zephyr I feel like the babbling, fumbling, insecure teenager I was thirty years ago. It's both exhilarating and nauseating.

Especially when I do that math. When I was younger, I was closer in age to the boys that are my 'type'. But, as I've aged, my type hasn't really changed.

There have been times I wished that my tastes were more varied. Turning down Matt's advances when we first met was difficult because he was, and still is, a very sweet man. However, I couldn't force myself to be interested, no matter how compatible our kinks are. It wouldn't have been fair on either one of us, and it would inevitably have ended poorly. Instead, we were able to build a friendship, and he found a Daddy much better suited to him.

And still my tastes haven't changed. I understand that committing to a relationship means watching your partner age alongside you, but it doesn't mean that I'm not still drawn to men of a certain build or appearance. I just can't help it.

And now? There are fourteen years between Zephyr and me. It does make me a little uncomfortable.

At least it's not seventeen years. That's my magic number. A line I can't cross.

My initial draw to the BDSM Daddy/little lifestyle is not something I like to dwell on often. My motivations were unhealthy, to say the least. I was young: barely twenty and an absolute mess, and I was looking to prove that I had paternal skills. Looking to prove that I had the ability to nurture and protect and care for a little. But I was doing it for *all* the wrong reasons. Reasons that make me feel sick to admit now.

That's not what I want to dwell on now.

Besides, through therapy, I eventually worked through all the old pain and regrets and came to love being a Daddy and being involved in the lifestyle in a healthier way. I still want to nurture and care for my boys, but not because I feel like I have anything to prove. It's for my enjoyment as much as it is for the Littles. I like to be someone's rock. I like to provide for them and make sure they're looked after and can live their lives joyfully. If anyone has the means, it's me. And it makes me feel good to make them feel good.

But it's not often that I'm taken off balance with a boy. Over the years, I've found that the interactions I have with most littles are all similar. There are the shy ones, the bratty ones, the sweet ones, the clingy ones…but Zephyr? He's unlike most boys I've spent time with in the last few years. He's an enigma to me.

He's certainly one of the most brazen littles I've had the pleasure to meet. Oozing with confidence and sensuality, he's feisty and challenging and funny. If I had to label him, I'd say he's more Middle than Little, but there are moments where the bravado melts away and I catch glimpses of his more innocent side.

In the week we've spent exchanging texts and talking on the phone, I've picked up clues which lead me to believe that, as confident as he is as a little, Zephyr hasn't had as much experience with an ongoing relationship with a Daddy. His life until recently hasn't allowed for it, so what experience he has had has been scene play at best.

I've made it clear that I'm more interested in an exclusive, long-term relationship. I know that's new to him. I don't want to rush him but, at the same time, all I want to do is wrap him in my arms and refuse to let him go. It's not normal for me to feel this way. I don't usually get so invested so soon.

It could be that I'm just rattled by other things going on in my life. It's coming up on thirty years since…

No. Nope. Not going there.

Instead, I lose myself in the kiss I've just initiated. Our second. I wanted to respect his wishes to take things slowly, but his flirting threw all my restraint right out the window.

He tastes sweet against my tongue, not a surprise given that he's confessed he has an epic sweet tooth. His body is firm, lean, and pliable under my hands as I slowly explore the plains of his hips and back and shoulders. At thirty-three, he's in the prime of his life, his body perfect for his career in dance. He's already teased me over the phone, taunting me about how *bendy* he is, and I want so badly to put the naughty thoughts that information inspired to the test.

We're flush against each other and my cock twitches when he mewls against my lips. Unconsciously, I grind against his abdomen, seeking friction.

"*Mister Masters*," he separates our mouths to breathe with exaggerated scandal, his breath ghosting over my lips as if daring me to capture his mouth all over again, "dinner first, remember?"

I want nothing more than to turn him around, bend him over the tub and plunge inside him, but the playful lilt of his voice reminds me that tonight is a test. A test for our compatibility and chemistry (which I'm certain we've passed with flying colors, if I do say so myself). But also a test of whether there is a possibility for something deeper and more real to develop between us. Making everything about sex won't help prove that we can hold more than simple conversations.

Still, I nip at his lips again before I withdraw and adjust my aching cock, much to his amusement. "I did promise dinner, yes."

His gaze lingers on the bulge in my jeans, and he makes a show of adjusting himself as well, which I shouldn't find as much of a relief as I do. I suppose it's good to know that he's just as affected as I am, that's all.

Leading him back downstairs to the kitchen, he slides onto one of the tall bar stools in front of the long kitchen counter and watches as I pull out my pre-prepared veggies and ingredients for the simple stir-fry I'm cooking tonight.

"Were you a boy scout as a kid?" he asks playfully, gesturing to the cling-film covered bowls I've set out in order next to the stove.

"Actually, I was," I laugh. "My parents were…" I search for the right word and settle on, "traditional, I guess."

They were also devout Catholics who did everything they could to try and steer their obviously gay son towards 'manly' activities, but I don't mention that. My childhood wasn't miserable, just tense at times. Then, when I left for college with a full-ride scholarship and officially came out of the closet, it became a moot point completely.

Zephyr seems to pick up on some of what I very carefully did not say, because his expression softens and he makes a movement as though he's trying to reach for me across the bench top. His hands fall back into his lap, and he rallies. "Well, mine were anything but. They put me in dance classes of all sorts and, when it looked like I enjoyed Ballroom the best, they set me on the competition circuit. And, when I wasn't doing that, I was being hauled to different sports try-outs, baking classes, 'Mommy and me' yoga sessions…" He shakes his head, his love for his parents paired with fond exasperation. "They wanted to give me a slice of everything."

They sound like everything my parents were not. But there's likely a generation between them, I'm guessing, so it's hardly astonishing that their values and experiences would be different.

"They sound like wonderful people," I tell him honestly, and start tossing ingredients into the wok I've oiled and heated. The meat and veggies sizzle enticingly. "Mine…well, they meant well. Mostly." I shrug. "It was a different time, and they were older when they had me, too."

I'd been a surprise to them, actually. After years of trying for children, they'd given up. Then, in their mid forties, along I'd come. It was a pity they felt I'd been more disappointing than miraculous in the end.

Once again, I realize that I've brought the mood down and I fight the urge to pinch the bridge of my nose.

What the hell is wrong with me?

"Are they…I mean…have they…no, that's not an appropriate date question. Forget I said anything." Zephyr winces and looks away.

If anything, the gaffe makes me chuckle. "They've both passed, yes." I answer lightly, lifting and dropping my shoulders as though it's no big deal. "We weren't close. We pretty much lost touch after I left home for college and, as callous as it sounds, it was for the best for all of us."

When they didn't even reach out during the worst year of my life, even after I told them what had happened at the time, I wrote them off completely.

"I'm still sorry for your loss, Ted."

"Thank you."

Silence descends between us, broken only by the sounds of meal cooking in front of me. This is not how I want the date to go. I want to prove that we can maintain effortless conversation, not back each other into awkward silences.

"Anyway," I forge on when the strange moment has stretched on a little too long for comfort, "the boy scout thing. I've always been a little, uh, anally retentive."

My turn of phrase has the desired effect and Zephyr snickers. "Have you now?"

"Yeah. I like things neat and tidy. I'm methodical. I don't love surprises."

With a wooden spoon in my hand, I turn to catch the widening of his eyes. "But…you're a Daddy," he argues with confusion. "Aren't littles the antithesis of neat and tidy? Or am *I* the odd one out?"

"Some activities can get messy, sure," I tilt my head in recognition of his argument, "Finger painting, blocks strewn across the room, toy cars scattered…but that's only momentary. In my house, toys are cleaned up and packed away neatly after play. It's a rule." I pin him with a pointed smirk, waggling the spoon in his direction. "The overarching arrangement of Daddy/little role play is structured. Most littles thrive on routine as much as I do. And, as Daddy, I get to set those rules and routines. I get to manage the variables as much as anyone possibly can."

"Ah," he leans across the counter now, propping his pretty face up in his palms with his elbows braced on the marble. There's an almost feline grace in the stretch of his long back. He's breathtaking. "And that's why my *bossiness*, as you so kindly put it, eats at you, huh? Don't like being challenged?"

"On the contrary," I face the stove behind me again, giving the simmering meat, veggies and sauce another stir, gauging that it'll only need another minute or two before I can toss in the noodles and then serve it up, "I'm a lawyer because I love a challenge, too."

"So...what does that mean in terms of us, then?" He's so direct and I love it.

"Well," I toss the noodles in early. Fuck it. It won't make much difference. "I'd say that you speak to both sides of me. The lawyer and the Daddy." Now I turn back and smile at him warmly. "And I like that very much."

It's gratifying to watch his own smile blossom across his features, like he feels similarly to me.

But I remind myself that I promised not to rush him, so I carefully add, "I know the concept of an exclusive, long-term thing is new to you, so I won't push. I want tonight to be about showing you how things could be. But there's no pressure, okay? We'll take this all at your pace."

Zephyr's smile morphs into one of gratitude and he nods. "I appreciate that, Ted."

Then I serve up our meal and we move to the dining table, turning the conversation to lighter, happier topics.

* * *

"That was delicious," Zephyr declares, leaning back in his chair and rubbing his belly in an adorably childish sort of way. I like to think that he's loosening up, allowing his little side to come out and play.

"I can't take all the credit," I confess, pushing back my chair and collecting our empty bowls. "This was London's recipe. Matt raves about it, and London insisted it was quick and easy to make."

"Well, then, you did a good job of following the recipe, anyway." He smiles lazily up at me, his eyes hooded with post-meal sleepiness. It's insanely adorable. I can't prevent myself from bending to kiss the tip of his ski-dip nose. "Mmm," he says, then tilts his head back and puckers his lips for a proper kiss.

Oh, this boy. This beautiful, perfect boy.

I press my lips to his chastely, savoring the brief connection before straightening up and taking our dishes into the kitchen. I pop them into the dishwasher and then pull the chocolate mousse I'd prepared earlier from the fridge.

Zephyr's eyes widen when I set his bowl in front of him. "You're trying to make me explode," he complains. "I wish I'd known there was dessert before I ate so many noodles."

Grinning, I lift a spoonful to my mouth. "I promise, if you can't finish it, you can take a doggy bag home with you."

He pokes his tongue out at me before diving in, and I love that he's starting to get comfortable enough to be cheeky in this way. It's more innocent than his earlier teasing. More childlike and pure.

The moan he releases when the chocolate hits his tongue, though, is anything but.

My cock takes interest at the sound immediately.

"*Oh*," he stretches the sound out, closing his eyes and sucking the spoon until his cheeks hollow, "Ted. This is incredible."

If I didn't know any better, I'd say he was turning dessert into sex on purpose.

He goes for another spoonful. It gets the same treatment, his pink tongue wrapping around the utensil as he makes inappropriate noises and licks it clean. Then he does it again.

I drop my spoon into my bowl with a clatter and splat.

Zephyr looks up, startled.

I can only imagine what the look on my face must be like. My pulse is racing, my cock straining in my underwear, my body rigid with need for him. With the need to hear him make those sounds in a different setting. With my cock in his mouth. In his ass.

Realization seems to dawn on him and embarrassment settles in over his pretty face. "Oh. Uh. I didn't mean…" he stammers, and I see his cheeks darken with the faintest hint of a blush on his flawless skin.

"Oh, no," I practically purr, using all my reserves to keep my hands to myself, even though I want to cup his face in my hands and kiss him stupid again. "I like that I'm able to get those beautiful sounds out of you, even if it's only my cooking that does it for now."

For now.

For all that I keep reminding myself not to push him, I can't help letting these little hopes of mine slip out. Thankfully, he just smiles bashfully and bites his plump lower lip.

"I told you I had a sweet tooth," he defends himself, drifting back into that sweet playful mood he was in.

"You did. And I couldn't help but indulge it."

It appears I can't help myself at all around him.

"Do you spoil everyone, Ted?" he asks from beneath lowered lashes, bringing another spoonful of his chocolate treat up to his lips. I can't tear my gaze from the spoon, watching as he sucks it in and swallows his treat, this time more conscious of the sounds he was making. Not quite enough to completely prevent his delight, but he no longer sounds like something I'd find on PornHub. "Or is this you wooing me?"

"I want to say it's just an attempt to woo you, but it would be a lie," I admit, content to watch him continue to eat, my own bowl forgotten on the table in front of me. "I enjoy looking after people. Making them happy."

"Then what the hell possessed you to become a lawyer?" His question seems to have bypassed his internal filter, because he looks up at me with wide, surprised eyes. "Shit. I'm sorry. That was rude."

A bark of laughter escapes me. "It was a fair question, though. But," I shoot him a firm stare, "I have a rule about watching your language, tiny dancer. My boy…my *princess*," I correct myself, "won't swear."

Cocking a perfectly manicured eyebrow at me, he smirks. "Am I your princess, Ted? Have we started to play?"

"Not yet," I concede. "But I think, if it's something you would like to do, we should go over the rules. I know we've spoken about limits, and we've got our safe words-"

"Meatloaf," he cuts me off with a laugh, then rolls his eyes at me when I don't follow his train of thought. "You know, 'cos I will 'do anything for love'-"

I groan, seeing exactly where he's taking this. "But you *won't do that*." I finish for him dryly, appalled at the joke. "That's awful."

He giggles madly in the face of my put-upon disgust. The sound is joyful and lights me up from the inside.

I push it a little further, exaggerating my reaction. "You're not actually using Meatloaf as your safe word, right?"

"I should," he continues to giggle and then scrapes at his bowl with his spoon, trying to get the last remnants of his mousse into his mouth. I half expect him to abandon the spoon and try to lick the bowl clean, considering the intent look on his face as he goes about his task. "But, no, I use the traffic light system."

It's what we had discussed on the phone and it's also my go-to. "Good." I'm back to being serious. "So. Rules?"

He pushes his empty bowl away with a mournful glance and then looks at me with bright eyes. "So far, I know about cleaning up after we play with toys and not swearing."

"Good boy," I praise, beaming when he grins back at me. "There's also being honest at all times, following instructions, asking questions if you don't understand something, and telling me if there's something new you'd like to try."

He considers these and bobs his head thoughtfully. "They're all pretty common sense."

"I'm glad you think so," I approve. Then I add, "And, as part of following instructions, there will be consequences for things like talking back and sassing me." I give him a knowing stare. He's definitely the sassing type.

His dark eyes glimmer in amusement, even though he feigns innocence. "Would I do that?"

"I think we both know you will."

It's not even a maybe. He's going to push the limits because he can and, oddly, I am looking forward to it. I've never enjoyed brattier play from my littles before, but I get the feeling Zephyr knows just how far he can take things before he crosses a line from fun to frustrating.

He runs his tongue along his front teeth. "Hmm, so what sort of consequences are we talking about here?"

I can feel my face twisting into a wicked smirk. "It depends on the severity of the infraction, of course. How many warnings I've given, that sort of thing. But I escalate from writing lines and corner time, to spankings, paddling and orgasm denial. Maybe some light humiliation play if you're okay with it." I shrug. "Sometimes the consequences are for fun and we'll both be aware that it's just a game, but other times they're serious. Obviously, we'll talk things through if it's serious."

"I…" Zephyr pauses, surprise coloring his tone. "I don't think I've ever needed a *serious* punishment. Like, it's always just been playful. Sexy. Fun."

"Well, you also said that you've only ever really done the odd scene with Daddies in clubs, right?" He nods and I continue. "It's different when you're in a full-time Daddy/little relationship. Sometimes behavior needs actual correction. Take the cussing, for instance. I'd make you write lines and neither one of us would actually enjoy that. But it would be to make a point."

He thinks this over some more, drumming his fingers on the tabletop. "But safe words still apply?"

I reach for his hand and squeeze it in reassurance. "Always, little one. You safe word at *any* time and we stop and talk about it."

"Okay," he exhales, then straightens his shoulders and smiles warmly at me. "So…are we going to play tonight?"

I push my chair back and hold my hand out to him. "There's nothing I'd prefer to do."

Chapter Six – Zephyr

"What should I call you?" I ask Ted as we make our way back upstairs to the playroom. His large hand envelops mine with warmth and I'm struck by how natural it feels to be doing any of this with him.

"What are you comfortable with?" he asks in return.

"Well, I really like the idea of going straight to 'Daddy', but if that's something you'd prefer to wait on, just in case this doesn't work out…" I trail off, saddened by the thought that there's still that possibility.

Ted stops us just outside the playroom, turning me until we're facing each other. He gently lifts my chin with his index finger, looking me in the eye. "Darling, you can call me whatever your heart desires, okay? Whatever feels right. Go with it." He drops a kiss to the tip of my nose. "And, for the record, I suspect that this is going to work out just fine."

God, I hope so.

I'm now painfully aware of the fact that I like him far too much for this to be just a one-night trial thing.

Guiding me inside the room with a hand on the small of my back, Ted starts talking again. "Now, usually I would help you get dressed, but given that tonight is about easing you into everything, I don't-"

"I want the full Daddy experience," I blurt, cutting him off. "We're doing this properly."

I know I've made the right decision when his eyes light up and his smile goes all sweet and doting. "Alright, then." He scoops my bag up from the floor and moves over to the bed, sitting on the side and rummaging through my things. With care, he pulls out the frilly purple gown I packed myself: my favorite of all my dresses. With it, he also gets out the matching panties with the lacy scalloped edges. He fingers the material of the dress lovingly. "I bet this looks absolutely gorgeous on you."

I feel my own smile turn shy and I shrug. "It's…it's been a long time since I wore any of my femme stuff," I confess quietly. "Like…before my injury."

His eyes snap up to meet mine, understanding painted on his face. "Well, that's going to make tonight even more special, then, isn't it?"

I hope so, I think again. I'm still worried that the magic is gone. That I won't feel the way I used to. That everything working up to this point will have been for naught. That I'm not the person I thought I was. That my injury took even this away from me.

"Alright, tiny dancer," Ted's voice is low and lulling, "you're thinking too hard. Time to let go and relax."

He reaches for my hands and tugs me forward so he can help me undress. I close my eyes, breathe deeply, and reach for my littler side. It's been so long since I've really gone for it that I almost feel silly. But Ted continues to murmur encouragements and soft praise, carefully pulling my shirt over my head and my jeans and underwear down my legs. By the time I'm completely naked, I'm strangely relaxed.

Ted gently taps my left thigh, silently helping me step into one leg hole of my pretty panties, then the other. He pulls them up, runs his fingers under the elastic bands until they're sitting properly, then holds up my dress. "Arms up, darling."

I comply and he steps into my space again, carefully easing the mess of satin and tulle over my head. My hands slip through the delicate cap sleeves and he helps ease the whole thing down over my body. Then he turns me and pulls the zip up at the back. When I turn back around to face him, the material of the skirt swooshing over the middle of my thighs just as I remembered it would, he steps back to get a good look at me.

"Perfect," he declares.

"Thank you," I curtsy, leaving off the title we've discussed using. I'm not quite little enough yet, still getting used to being back in my old gown. But I'm close to it, and he's not pushing me. That settles me a little bit further.

He laughs, and the sound is rich and warm and full of affection. Then he reaches for my hand, asking, "Should we break in the dollhouse, tiny dancer?"

I don't need to be asked twice. I nod excitedly and together we walk the couple of steps over to the shelves and lift the large item up, carrying it to the middle of the room. We place it on the floor carefully, and I undo the latch that keeps the two halves together. Ted helps me open the house up wide.

The inside is just as beautiful as I imagined it would be. It's decorated in creamy colored tones, with white accents and lace embellishments. There are exquisite bedroom scenes, a ballroom, a library, decadent sitting rooms, bathrooms and a large kitchen.

Shaking me from my visual exploration, Ted sets a large box in front of me. I hadn't even noticed him wandering away to get it. "Now, this is just a start," he says, gesturing for me to lift the lid.

When I comply, I find gorgeous pieces of miniature furniture, all in matching stained dark timber. There are also a couple of small dolls for me to play with as well, and I find that they are just the right size to fit on the furniture.

"They're so pretty," I tell him in awe, carefully lifting each piece out to inspect them individually. I start placing them in appropriate rooms inside the dollhouse as I do. Even though the box is large, I can see what he meant by this collection being 'just a start', because it barely fills a third of the house. But that doesn't bother me at all. I can use my imagination to fill in the rest.

I'm a little surprised when he sits beside me and picks up one of the dolls, joining me in my play. Together, we take our toys on a journey through the home. They dine in the large, formal dining room and we pretend that we're part of their very fancy dinner party, and then the dolls dance in the ballroom. Finally, they bathe in the large bathtub before we send them to bed.

As the dolls sleep, I muse on how enjoyable this has been. It's a new experience for me to spend time with a Daddy who engages in the story with me rather than sitting back to watch me entertain myself. And it didn't seem to be a half-assed attempt on his part, either. He made conversation with the dolls, he offered ideas to extend their activities within their home, and he even spoke with silly, high-pitched character voices, making me giggle raucously. It was like he actually enjoyed playing with me, and *that* thought makes my heart race.

"Can we play something different?" I ask, deciding that the dolls probably need to rest after such an eventful day. Then I remember the rules. "We can pack this up first."

"Good boy," he praises, and the words light me up from the inside. I start to carefully pack away the furniture and the dolls, and he helps me to make the task go faster. Then we put the dollhouse back up on the shelf, once again closed and latched, before he turns to me and asks, "What would you like to play next?"

I've dropped far enough into little space that I'm honestly excited at the prospect of anything. My eyes land on the tub of blocks on the bottom shelf and I know exactly what I want to do. "Can we build a castle?"

Ted smiles widely and nods, helping me pull the plastic tub out, carrying it to where we'd been playing with the dollhouse. He upends the entire thing and I gasp at the mess it makes, delighting in the familiar click-clack racket of the little wooden pieces tumbling about, muted by the carpet as they fall.

"Are we building a tall castle?" he asks, watching me with obvious amusement as I start to meticulously sort the pieces into colored piles.

"Yep." I pop the 'p'. "Super tall."

"Here," he slides the lid of the tub down between us and then settles himself into a cross-legged position. "It'll be sturdier than trying to build on the carpet."

"Clever Daddy." I tell him, barely aware that I've gotten comfortable enough to let the word slip out. It's only the hastily smothered sharp inhalation from across the small, carpeted space that has me realizing what I've done.

I look up from my stash of brightly colored blocks to catch a sweet smile on his face, but he doesn't bring it up. He just points down at the large, rectangular piece of firm plastic that separates us and asks, "So, where do we start?"

* * *

"Daddy, *stop*," I giggle, squirming away from fingers determined to tickle me into submission, "that's cheating!"

I have no idea how long we've been playing for at this stage. Tonight has well and truly surpassed how I'd hoped the evening might go. I managed to sink so deeply into little space that, once I started coming back out, I was surprised that it had happened so easily.

Right now, Ted is easing me back into my adult head space with an old-fashioned game of 'Go Fish', only we've moved onto the twin bed in the playroom because Ted's declared his back wasn't made for sitting on the floor for extended periods of time. As with all the other games we've played, he seems just as engaged and genuinely into playing this with me as I've felt all night.

Except he started blatantly cheating and, when I lunged for his cards, it earned me a tickle attack.

"Excuse me, but who tried to take all my cards away?" he argues back, all lawyerly and devastatingly handsome with those twinkling eyes and smug smile of his.

"Because I caught you picking cards out of the pile when you thought I wasn't looking."

Ted is unrepentant. "Daddy's rules say I can."

"Daddy's full of…uh…" I manage to censor myself just in time, smiling sheepishly when one of his eyebrows wings upwards. "Poop?"

Snorting, Ted waggles his index finger at me. "You can get away with that this one time, princess."

That works for me. I smile as innocently as possible and bat my lashes. "Yes, Daddy." I surprise even myself with the sexual undertone in my voice.

I'm back out of little space and the air between us suddenly feels charged.

"Should we pack the cards away?" Ted asks me after a short span of silence.

I nod.

He gathers them up silently, slipping them into the pack with practiced ease. He tosses the pack onto the little bedside table and then extends his arms. "Come cuddle and talk?"

I take in the vision of him, his shoulders loose and his back propped up with a pillow against the wall behind him. There's still no expectation in his expression or in the way he holds himself. He seems content and relaxed, and maybe a little hopeful, but I can tell that his request doesn't have any underlying agenda. He really does just want to cuddle and talk.

I crawl over the comforter and into his embrace and we maneuver until we're both comfortable, with his chest pressed against my back and his arms, toned and strong, casually draped over my shoulders and coming to rest over my abdomen, crossed lightly at his wrists.

"So, tiny dancer," he says quietly, his voice a low purr, "have you had fun tonight?"

My lips lift upwards at the memories we've just made. "I have." I sigh happily and snuggle in closer, enjoying the feeling of being held. "I didn't think it would be so easy."

I feel him press a kiss to the top of my head. "I'm glad that it was."

I hesitate only briefly before I tell him, "I think a lot of that is because you made it easy for me."

"I didn't do anything special, Zephyr."

"Bull-" I stop myself short as he clears his throat. "I mean, uh, bologna."

Ted snorts.

Smiling to myself, I try to organize my thoughts. Exploring our dynamic really did feel more natural with Ted than it has with any of the Daddies I've done scenes with before. I've never had a bad experience, but I've also never felt so *right* with another Daddy, either...not that my life to this point has really allowed me many opportunities to give it a red-hot go, to be fair.

"I'm serious, though." I eventually say, glad that Ted has allowed me a chance to try and process my thoughts properly. "I've never really had a Daddy get so into the games before. Like, sure, I've done tea parties where Daddies have joined me, but...you make it feel like you're actually enjoying what we're doing, not just the fact that we're role playing as Daddy and boy." I lean my head back on his shoulder so I can awkwardly look at his face. "Does that make sense? Like, I know they enjoyed playing the role of Daddy, but you seemed to really appreciate *what* we were doing. Ugh. I don't think this is coming out right."

A chuckle rumbles up through his chest, vibrating against my back. He kisses my forehead. "I think I'm following you. And I did have fun playing along." He pauses. "I'm sure those other Daddies do, too, in their own way. But we all get something different out of this stuff, you know?"

"Hmm," I consider, though I'm not sure I completely agree with him. "Well, is this the sort of thing you can see yourself doing more often? I know you're more used to..." I fumble over my words, gesturing vaguely with my hands, "I guess what is seen as stereotypically 'boyish' play."

I'm relieved that he doesn't just answer automatically. I want to know that he's really considering his needs, too.

After a comfortable stretch of silence, Ted finally says, "You know what? I can. Ultimately, for me, being a Daddy...or," he seems to correct himself, "in this case, being *your* Daddy is about the same thing, regardless of the scenes themselves." He shuffles our position so I lean more to the side and he can look me in the eye. "I want to look after you, Zephyr. I want to play with you, take care of the things that cause you stress, make sure you're eating well. I want to be your safe space and your rock: there for anything you need when you need me. Whether you're playing with teacups or cars makes no difference. I just want to spend time with you."

"Um, wow." I was not expecting that barrage of heartfelt information, but it gives me all the warm fuzzy feelings.

In hindsight, I can't say I'm all that surprised. Ted's a lawyer. It makes sense that he's a bit wordy. Especially when he specializes in contract law. Gotta cross all the 't's and dot all the 'i's or whatever.

I nuzzle my face into his shoulder and respond the only way I can. "I want to spend time with you, too."

Chapter Seven – Ted

Zephyr's reply to my overthought ramblings is a relief.

I can't help the silly smile that stretches my face. "You do?"

"Uh huh." He beams back. Then his expression turns exaggeratedly coquettish and he's looking up at me from beneath his long, dark eyelashes in a way that has my cock taking interest immediately. "So…" he draws the word out, sounding far too sultry for me to miss his intention, "maybe we should do something you like now, huh?"

Still, I play dumb, wanting to see where he's going with this. "Oh? What do you suggest?"

"Well, you *did* say you like to take baths, didn't you?"

Oh, God yes.

With the way we're snuggled together in a position meant to be completely innocent when I suggested that we cuddle and chat, there's no way he doesn't feel me react to the images he's just put in my head. Especially not when he moves to get more comfortable again, moving his head back to my shoulder with the length of his body practically plastered against me again. My voice is low and husky when I admit, "I did."

His perfect, plump lips draw into a self-satisfied smirk. "Do you want to share a bath in that ridiculously oversized tub of yours, Ted?"

There's no sign of his little side now, even if he is still dressed in his little princess gown. Beneath the cute veneer is a siren who knows exactly what he's doing. He's insanely sexy, all youthful, lithe and confident, and it's beginning to dawn on me that our dynamic is going to be more complex than I'd first assumed, but in all the best ways.

My previous relationships have always followed a more predictable Daddy/little pattern where I'm the dominant partner and primary caretaker. But there's nothing predictable about Zephyr. Right now, I'm getting the distinct impression that I might be Daddy, but he's going to rule the roost. Or he's going to try to.

"I would love that," I answer him, and he brings his hand behind his hip, cupping my *very* interested erection, causing me to suck in a sharp breath.

His answering chuckle is wicked. "Uh huh," he acknowledges, "so I see. Well, feel."

"*Zephyr…*" I lower my voice in warning and he laughs with delight.

"Oh, your Daddy voice is *perfect*." He wiggles his ass, teasing me further. "More of that, please."

Is this a punishable offense? 'Funishable', really. It's too damn good to actually want him to stop. My brain is slowly turning to mush as he continues to grind back on my cock.

"You're being extremely naughty, tiny dancer," I give him the exact reaction he's looking for, leaning down and moving my mouth down to the junction where his elegant neck meets his smooth shoulder. I nip at the skin I find there. "If you keep going, there *will* be consequences."

Rubbing his cheek against mine, I can feel his lips quirking. "What kind of consequences, *Daddy*?"

"Hmm," I hum, pretending to consider my options. My lips travel to the shell of his ear. He shivers as I whisper, "You seem to like teasing. Maybe edging you would be appropriate."

"*Oh…*" Zephyr mewls and rocks his hips.

It's all I can do to keep my hands relaxed over his chest instead of gripping those same hips to encourage even more delicious friction. However, I do allow myself to suck his earlobe for a moment before quietly asking, "You like that idea, kitten?"

"Mmm," he answers, rocking back against me for a few more beats, then gives himself a little shake. "So, uh, bath?"

It takes me a minute to focus and remember how we'd gotten to this point, the sensation of him rubbing against me providing a delicious distraction that I don't mind disappearing into. But then his words float through the lusty fog in my head and I realize that sharing a bath means being naked together. I can't agree fast enough.

"Come on," I give him a playful little push off my lap so we can both scoot off the bed, "let's go before I decide keeping you in this bed with me is just as enjoyable."

He laughs and climbs off, waiting patiently for me to follow. He doesn't disguise the way his heated gaze travels the length of my body, zeroing in on the bulge in my jeans.

But, even though I can see the desire on his face, I'm all about consent and communication, so I soften my gaze. "This isn't too fast for you?"

Shaking his head, he smiles back, a hint of coyness in his expression. "No. I mean, you've seen me naked already, so I'd really like to even the playing field."

"Well, I can't argue with that logic," I chuckle. "But there's no pressure for this to be anything more than just a bath, okay?"

"I appreciate that. But, trust me, I want you naked. *Now*."

* * *

The bath water is just the right side of hot when I sink into it behind Zephyr with a pleasured sigh. Even though the tub is large enough to fit us side by side, I'm sitting in the middle with him cradled in the V of my legs, his back pressed against my chest in a mirror image of the way we'd been on the bed earlier. We're immersed in bubbles, but I can feel and picture every inch of his smooth skin where it meets mine.

We took our time undressing as the bath filled, teasing each other with light touches and chaste kisses. This entire evening has been a whirlwind of exploration between us. We've been hot and heavy, innocent as Daddy and boy, flirtatious as equals, and now we're sharing this sedate, relaxed interaction. It's almost like it has been a taster event: sampling the treasures that a relationship together can provide.

"What are you thinking, tiny dancer?" I ask into the comfortable silence after a few minutes spent just enjoying the sensation of having his slippery, wet form on mine. "Are we going to give this thing between us a real shot?"

You would think that the fact that we've progressed this far so quickly would assure me that tonight has been a success, but I like having things confirmed definitively. And, even though he agreed earlier that he wants to spend time with me, I want to talk it through properly. I want to be sure we're on the same page. That 'spending time together' as a concept for him is the same as it is for me: an exclusive relationship, with me as his Daddy full-time, whether he's big or little.

"I've wanted to since you called and asked me out," he answers on a sigh, practically melting into my chest. Beneath the water, I can feel his hand running up and down my thigh soothingly. "Tonight has been everything I'd hoped it would be and more."

I can feel my heart leaping for joy. "Me too," I admit, beaming a smile before bending to kiss the top of his head. "So…dating?" It's an inadequate word for everything I want to do and everything I want to be for him. "Exclusively?"

Zephyr moves, twisting his body around until his long legs are wrapped around my waist and our cocks are brushing against each other beneath the bubbles. Water sloshes around us, slapping at the sides of the tub, but I'm focused on his face.

His expression is a sweet mixture of hopeful and bashful. "I'd like that."

"Good." The single word is all I can manage before I crash our lips together.

This kiss is much like our earlier ones, hot and demanding. Our tongues play together as though fighting for dominance. My hands scrabble for purchase on his slippery wet skin, sliding over sinewy muscle and the toning of years of dancing and aerobics. His hands are trapped between us, fingers splayed over my chest, tangling in my coarse chest hair, plastered as it is to my skin.

The sounds of the water lapping and gently splashing as our bodies rock together battle with our breathy moans and pants. When I keep one hand supporting Zephyr across his back and reach between us with the other to stroke both our dicks together, Zephyr keens into our kiss.

"*More,*" he begs, bouncing in earnest now.

Water flows over the sides of the tub, but I couldn't care less. I tighten my grip and pump us harder, chasing bliss for both of us.

"Fuck, kitten," I practically growl when he jerks away from our kiss to bite at my earlobe and breathe heavily with his building release.

"*Ted,*" he whines plaintively. "Ted, I need to come. Please, Ted. *Please.*"

I vaguely recall my threat to edge him, but denying him his orgasm right now also means denying mine, and I already feel like I've been teetering close to the precipice for hours.

"I've got you," I tell him, my own voice tight and gravelly with desperation. "Come for me, darling. Come over my cock."

He throws his head back, exposing the elegant column of his neck, droplets of water and sweat making him shimmer in the low lighting of the bathroom. "Oh, *oh,*" he cries, his face contorting into the perfect moue of mixed rapture and torture. His hips are practically rocketing into my fist now, his movements seeming to have lost their rhythm. "Shit, shit, shit…I'm…oh, *fuck.*" He draws the last word into a long, low moan and I feel his cock swell and spurt ropes of cum into the water between us.

Watching and feeling him go over the edge pushes my orgasm over, too, and I mutter something unintelligible as my release joins his. I continue to lazily pump my fist over us until he squirms and complains that it's too much.

The comedown is slow, filled with lazy kissing and nuzzling as the water around us grows tepid. Then I coerce him out of the tub and into the shower for a quick rinse off. Wrapped in big, fluffy bathrobes once I've dried us both, we move into the bedroom and flop down on top of the covers, both boneless and ridiculously happy.

Before I can ask him if he'd be comfortable staying the night, Zephyr snuggles into me and cheekily asks, "Are you cooking me breakfast in the morning?"

At this rate, I can see me offering to cook for him every morning if it means more moments like this.

Chapter Eight – Zephyr

When I wake up the next day, it takes a minute for the previous night's events to catch up with me. I'm ensconced in warmth, Ted's strong arms wrapped around me like a blanket, the heat of his skin on mine a bigger comfort than I could have imagined it would be. His morning wood is like a burning rod against the base of my spine and it's all I can do to not grind my ass back into him while he's still sleeping.

One of the things I learned about Ted during the week spent texting and talking on the phone is that he's not a morning person. He likes to sleep-in on weekends and, listening to the slow, even breathing behind me, I know that today is no exception.

I don't mind. As I might have expected, his bed is sinfully comfortable. The view through the large windows is just as breathtaking in the early morning sunlight as it is at dusk and at night. I'm content to lie here, snug in Ted's embrace, and just enjoy the peace and tranquility while my thoughts drift.

Going back to last night, I think about just how well the 'test' evening went. It felt more like an established relationship than a first date, and I wonder how much of that can be put down to the week spent getting to know each other and how much can be put down to genuine chemistry. Either way, it was good. Heck, it was better than good to be myself and let go with Ted.

It was also a relief that I was able to sink into my little head space and femme play far more easily than I thought I would. It had felt like stepping back into my skin, comfortable and homey. I hadn't had to force it, nor did I feel silly or strange. If anything, I felt whole again for the first time in a long time.

As much as Ted tried to downplay his role in that, I know that his complete acceptance and enthusiasm did more for me than I could have achieved in role playing on my own or at a club. Was that why I'd pushed the issue when it came to the bath? I hadn't felt obligated or anything. But I had really wanted to show my appreciation, riding the waves of endorphins and connection that a good scene in little space had created.

I have zero regrets there.

That bath had been perfect. When he'd added the soap for the bubbles, I'd wondered if Ted had wanted to extend the Daddy/little play, but that hadn't been the case. It had been for ambiance and the modesty that a cover of bubbles provided, not that either of us had really needed it. Still, there's always an added layer of decadence when bubbles are involved in a sexy bath.

And sexy it was.

If I close my eyes, I can recall the feel of our slick cocks sliding together, of Ted's large hand wrapping around us both, stroking us to completion in the hot water.

"Mmm," a low rumble of appreciation travels up Ted's chest and warm, wet lips find my shoulder and neck. His hand smooths down my side and over my hip, down to my cock which is hard and leaking for him already, courtesy of my trip down memory lane. "I could get used to waking up like this."

He rolls his hips forward languidly, teasing the crack of my ass with the head of his own erection. I push back instinctively. I've never slept naked with a lover before, but now I can't imagine doing anything else.

"*Fuck*, Zeph," he groans and tightens his grip on my dick.

This latest nickname (because Ted seems to be a fount of them) makes me all warm and gooey inside, despite it just being a shortening of my name. It seems more personal than any of the others and said on a whim at that. Passionate and raw.

My gut swirls with need.

"You've got lube and condoms in here somewhere?"

Instead of answering, Ted rolls away from me and I bite back my complaints when I hear the drawer of his bedside table rolling open and the tell-tale sounds of his rummaging around for the requested items.

"Thank Christ," he utters, coming back to me, victorious. "They're in date." When I crane my neck around to look at him, there's mild embarrassment on his face. "It's been a while. I probably should have thought to replace them before now, but..."

"It's been a while for me, too," I reply, too amped up to be amused by his sweet rambling.

He brings our mouths together and I'm too worked up to worry about my morning breath, and he doesn't seem to care either. We kiss languidly and Ted moves me onto my back, the *snick* of the cap from the bottle of lube the only warning I get before warm, wet fingers are probing at my hole.

"Is this okay?" he asks, teasing the rim with gentle, patient movements. "If you want me to stop-"

Consent is clearly a big deal for him. I genuinely appreciate that, but he needs to trust that I will safe word or stop him if I'm at all uncomfortable. But, before I say anything, the fleeting thought '*what kind of relationships has he had before me to inspire this behavior?*' has the words lodging in my throat.

I know I'm not the neediest little. I'm big more often than not, and I like a modicum of control over my life. I like to push boundaries and tease for pleasure, not really in a bratty way, and I like to take care of my lovers as much as they take care of me. I know that Ted is a natural caretaker and, if last night is any indication, I'm happy to roll with that. It didn't feel like I wasn't his equal at any part of the evening, even if he was Daddy and I was his boy. I was still calling the shots, just in a different way.

His previous relationships might have been more traditional, though.

His littles more submissive, maybe. Sweeter and softer and more likely to need reassurance.

But that's not me.

I'm not made of glass, and I want him to fuck me already.

"It's better than good," I tell him, grinding down onto his fingers to encourage him to pick up the pace. I meet his gaze, hoping that my need is burning into him. "I promise; if it's not, I'll tell you. Just fuck me, Ted. Please."

His eyes widen and then practically roll back in his head. "You're going to be the death of me."

"But what a way to go, right?"

"*Zeph*," he says in a tone that's an interesting mix of fondness and warning.

"*Daddy*," I chime back in the same tone, cutting myself off with a strangled groan when he plunges his thick index finger inside me. "*Yes*," the 's' in the word turns long and sibilant. "Just like that." I arch my hips up to meet his ministrations. "More."

"I knew it," he mutters, pumping his finger in and out maddeningly slowly, "I knew you'd be a bossy bottom." The words are chiding, but he sounds amused and affectionate.

Whining and wriggling, trying to encourage him to pick up the pace and stretch me further, I begin to tease, "If you think this is boss-" my words are cut off as a pleasured gasp is forced from my lips with the skilled movement of his fingers. "*Oh shit*, yes, there, Ted. *Fuck*."

"Such a naughty mouth on you, too," he laughs, but the sound is breathy and strained, belying his own arousal. "What are the rules, tiny dancer?"

"Really?" I ask, knowing I sound bewildered and incredulous. I raise my head to stare at him in disbelief. "The no swearing thing extends to sex?" For me, that's impossible. I shake my head, dropping it back onto my pillow as he crooks his finger and grazes my prostate. "*Fuck*." I breathe. "Yeah…no. That's a no. You can't enforce - oh, *God*, Ted." The second finger distracts me from my rant, stretching and burning beautifully.

"You were saying?" He sounds smug.

I writhe as he scissors and curls his fingers with practiced ease. "We're renegotiating that rule," I manage after a few moments of indulging in the pleasure. In between pants and sighs, I get out the rest of my bargaining chip. "If you ever want to see what else my mouth can do, you'll let me say whatever the hell I want during sex."

He's quiet as he contemplates my words, his fingers still working me open. "That's fair," he eventually acknowledges, then pulls his fingers out. This time I do complain when he moves aside, but the crinkling of a little foil wrapper has me hushing up. However, he takes me by surprise when he rolls the condom over *my* cock, saying, "and, as a gesture of good faith, let me show you what mine can do." Then his mouth engulfs me whole.

My brain shuts down. This fun little back-and-forth between us is impossible to maintain when my dick is surrounded by heat and suction. Then Ted's lubed fingers are back inside me and I'm officially lost to the pleasure he's giving me.

I'm a begging, thrashing mess by the time Ted pulls away from my cock and removes the condom. I want to sob at the fact that I'm so close and yet so far from coming, but he shushes me quietly and reaches across to the nightstand for another condom, this one for him. I struggle to my elbows to watch him roll it on over his thick cock, then spread my legs in invitation for him once it's situated.

He dribbles more lube over himself and lines up, his tall, broader form stretching over mine as he finally pushes in. I breathe through the intrusion, his three fingers barely having prepared me for his girth, and Ted gives me a moment to adjust. Then he takes his time, pitching his hips forward and back in tiny, teasing thrusts until he's bottomed out.

"*Ted*," my breathing hitches, "you feel…*ungh*…" The gradual, deliberate slide of his cock is indescribable. For all our playful talk about edging and orgasm denial, I get the feeling that Ted likes to draw the pleasure out. It feels amazing to have him inside me, filling me up, grazing in all the right ways as he moves with determined strokes.

"Right there with you," he agrees, breathing heavily. "You're like a vise. It's…" he moans as he pushes back in and closes his eyes, "Zeph, fuck, so tight. So perfect."

I reach up and thread my fingers into his thick hair, the flecks of silver among the brown glinting in the sunlight now streaming through the windows. Tugging his head down, I kiss him hungrily, trying to goad his tongue into a faster pace, hoping that it might then transfer to his hips.

Between us, my cock throbs, practically demanding friction. When Ted pushes in closer, his stomach rakes over the sensitive head and precum dribbles from my tip.

"Touch yourself," he demands against my lips. "Stroke in time with my thrusts."

I don't know that I have it in me to properly obey. Once I get my hand around it, I'm more likely to try and jerk myself to coming as fast as possible.

As if knowing exactly where my thoughts have gone, Ted drops his voice even deeper, adopting that dominant Daddy tone that I find so very enticing. "*Zephyr*," he warns, not losing rhythm. "Slowly."

"Yes, Daddy," I agree, only a little bit of cheek in my voice because I just can't help myself.

Then I snake my hand down between us and, using my own precum to slick the way, start sliding my fist over my neglected dick in the same leisurely pace that Ted is fucking me.

"Oh, kitten, that's so hot," he says, glancing down between our bodies to watch, mesmerized by my actions. "One day I'll get you to jerk off for me. To show me exactly how you like it."

The idea of putting on a show for him is super enticing and shoots through me like an electric shock. "Yes," I cry out, my balls tightening.

"Don't come yet," Ted demands.

Wait…*what*?

Something of my current tumultuous feelings must show on my face because his resulting chuckle is almost dark and devious. He presses another kiss to my lips, teasing them open with his tongue and slowly taunting me with it.

"We come together," he says when we part again.

"I'm so close…"

"Hold it for me, Zephyr."

Jesus Christ, he wasn't playing when he said he'd edge me, was he?

I whine.

"Zephyr." Ted's tone is all Daddy again. It sends another spark of pure arousal through me. More precum drizzles over my hand and down my shaft, an obscenely copious amount that says I'm riding a fine line right now.

My tenuous control begins to slip with every measured slide of his cock inside me. I grip my dick tighter, trying to physically hold the release back. I can feel my orgasm building, the tension inside me nearly unbearable, a tingle building in my balls.

"*Daddy*," this time I do sob the word, all trace of defiance or cheekiness gone. "I can't…I'm gonna…"

"Don't come." His order is firm.

I open my eyes, idly wondering when I clenched them shut, to meet his. They're a bright amber in the sunlight, intense with heat and desire. His jaw is also tense, his shoulders shaking as he starts to increase the strength of his thrusts. He's still moving at a languorous pace, but I can see his control weakening.

"I..I…I…"

"*Fuck*," he growls, pulling out and *slamming* his cock home. I'm pretty sure I see stars.

"Oh! Oh God, Ted…" My eyes shut of their own accord again, even though I so desperately want to watch him fall apart as he fucks into me with wild abandon. But I'm still trying to hold back, still trying to obey his order, and I'm not sure I can. Not sure I'll hold out.

"Soon, kitten." His words are separated by both heavy exhalations and rough, hard thrusts of his hips. "I'm almost there."

Hearing that confession is what breaks me. "Oh, oh no," the tell-tale tightening of my balls is almost painful now, the electric jolts of pleasure beginning to override the last vestiges of my control. "Oh shit, oh shit, *oh shit*." The first spurts are a blissful release, shooting over his stomach and chest.

He drops his lips back to mine, kissing me and riding me through my intense orgasm, then moves them to my ear, whispering a litany of praises and 'Good boy's and 'you feel fucking phenomenal's through groans as his hips jerk and he comes hard inside me.

He collapses on top of me, smearing my cum between us, and we laugh and kiss and roll about in the sheets as the adrenaline and endorphins settle. Somewhere in all that, he pulls out and ties off the condom, wrapping it in a tissue from his nightstand for disposal later.

"That was...*whoa*." I manage, breathing hard, unable to be any more descriptive than that.

"Mmhmm," he agrees, and I can hear the smile in his voice, but I can't see it because my eyes are shut, and my head is pillowed by his shoulder. The moment feels terribly domestic, but also right.

It's still early enough in the morning that I yawn and settle in for a bit of a catnap. "Can we do it again soon?"

"You're insatiable," he laughs.

I'm too tired to tease back and I allow the sound of his chuckles to lull me back into dreamland.

* * *

"You have flour on your nose," Daddy observes, his head cocked to the side and an indulgent smile pulling at his lips.

I brush my hands over the pretty, frilly pink gingham apron he gifted me earlier and then attempt to dust off my nose. The action only earns me more chuckles.

I'm making pancakes. After our early morning activities (and a super enjoyable shower once we woke up later in the morning) I craved the sweet carbs. I then set about begging for them, discovering quickly that Little Zephyr only needs to bat his eyelashes and Daddy will fold like a...like a...towel! (Okay, so metaphors aren't my strong suit when I'm little.)

I was well and truly in my little headspace when I skipped into the kitchen, and I didn't question why he already had an apron for me hanging on a hook in the butler's pantry, not even when he presented it to me with a flourish and helped me tie it around my waist.

It's probably something I'll think about later when I'm 'big' again, but for now I'm distracted by the sweet late breakfast I'm trying to make with Daddy's help.

"Come here, kitten," Daddy says when my attempts to clean off my face only serve to fuel his amusement more, "let's clean you up."

With a sigh, I push aside the large bowl of batter I've been adding ingredients to and whipping to a smooth, aerated consistency, and I turn bodily to face Daddy.

He's armed with a wet wipe and carefully, but firmly, smooths it over my nose and cheeks when I tilt my head back for him. I scrunch my nose and squirm when the cold, moist material meets my skin.

"Daddy, stop," I complain with a whine, but he only chuckles more.

"Patience, tiny dancer," he's finished with the left side of my face and moves on to my right, "almost done."

I wriggle and complain until he releases my face, then I go back to my bowl of batter. I whisk it a little longer and then, when it's the consistency I like, I turn back to Daddy. He's resting his hip against the counter, seemingly content to watch me work.

I hold the bowl out towards him. "Can you help me cook them, Daddy? I don't wanna get burned."

His eyes fill with the same warmth as when he sat on the floor and joined me as I played last night. "We can't have that," he agrees and takes the bowl from me, placing it on the counter beside the stove where a griddle pan is already waiting.

Producing a ladle, Daddy fiddles with the burners to preheat the pan and then melts some butter on its surface.

"Okay, kitten, ladle a pancake out onto the pan," he says, dutifully helping to guide my hand with the scoop of batter into the center of the heated surface. He helps me slowly tip the thick liquid into a circle, then I drop the ladle back into the bowl with a satisfying splat.

Daddy gives my butt a little tap in admonishment. "You'll be the one cleaning up the mess you make," he warns.

"Yes, Daddy."

"Good boy."

Those words thrill me more than I can properly express, and I think he knows it.

"Now, you see how the pancake is bubbling?" he directs my attention back to the pan where the slightly wobbly circle of yellow batter has puffed up and is now dotted with bubbles.

"Yeah?"

"Well, now we flip it very carefully." He hands me a spatula.

As with pouring the batter, Daddy holds my hand over the handle of the utensil. He helps me slide it under the cooked side of the pancake and, with a flick of our wrists, flips it over to reveal golden brown deliciousness.

My mouth waters almost immediately and I take in a deep breath, savoring the sweet, buttery scent.

"Can I have it now, Daddy?"

A snort is my only answer for a moment, but then he says, "We have a whole batch to cook first, darling."

I groan with impatience. I want my fluffy, soon-to-be syrupy treat immediately!

"*Zephyr...*" Daddy's tone is one of warning, but I do love it when his voice goes all low and serious like that. Still, I'm not planning on pushing my luck. I really do want to eat the pancakes.

With eyes wide with extra innocence, I bat my lashes and fiddle with one of the many hems of my frilly apron. "I'll be good, Daddy."

And I am.

It's not too long before I'm seated at the table with a stack of fluffy, perfectly cooked pancakes in front of me, a melting pat of butter seeping into the top one. Daddy pours a generous amount of syrup for me, somehow aware that I can't be trusted to do it myself (my sweet tooth would have me upending the whole carafe), and then I'm digging in with gusto.

Daddy eats his own portion with more refinement and patience, reaching for the wet wipes when he spies the mess of syrup on my cheeks and fingers.

"You're a bit of a menace, aren't you, little one?" he teases when I squeal and squirm away from the wet cloth again.

I giggle.

When I'm bigger, I'll look back on this interaction as the cherry on top of what genuinely feels like a perfect first Daddy/boy interaction. But for now I'm excited to keep exploring this whole new world of domestic scenes with this handsome man I've found.

Chapter Nine – Ted

"You look like the cat who caught the canary, the mouse, *and* the neighbor's gerbil," Charlie observes with a wide grin when we catch up for drinks on Tuesday evening. He's back from his short honeymoon, back into the daily grind of his kink-friendly community center, but married life looks good on him. "Want to share why that might be?"

He's not the first person to have noticed my good mood since the weekend. Louise has been shooting me knowing smirks since the staff meeting yesterday morning, and even my clients have said I've seemed 'chipper'.

"Yeah, well, what can I say?" I ask, unable to stifle the goofy smile stretching my lips. "Things are good right now."

"It's Zephyr, right? Ash's new friend? The one you were flirting with at the wedding?"

I can't deny it, so I don't. "Yeah."

And if I go a little doe-eyed at just the mention of his name, I'll blame the insane number of orgasms I've had since Saturday night. That boy is an aphrodisiac all on his own, and I think he's melted my brain.

Charlie raises his glass towards me and I clink mine against it. He's grinning even wider now. "It's about time you found someone who makes you happy."

"I'll drink to that." I bring my beer to my lips and take a healthy swig for emphasis.

"Ash will be over the moon, too," he continues. "Having his Uncle Ted bring another friend around for play-dates will make his year."

"Because marrying the man of his dreams hasn't?"

Charlie laughs and shakes his head. "Nah. The wedding was for my family's benefit and we both know it. We would have been happy enough just to elope to the courthouse."

"And when you say your family-"

"I mean my mother, yeah." Charlie huffs out a fond laugh, shaking his head. "I love her, but she's as crazy as ever." Setting down his beer, he sighs. "She's nagging Maze for grand-kids now. Let me tell you, Maisy is *not* happy about it."

I shift uncomfortably on my bar-stool. Talk of children always unsettles me. "I can imagine." I don't offer any more than that. I can't.

Charlie's former career as a cop is still alive and well inside him because he sits up a little straighter, arching an eyebrow at me with unveiled curiosity. He can tell he's struck a nerve of some kind, and I doubt he's going to let it go. Kids as a concept isn't something we've ever discussed. And why would we? We're BDSM Daddies, which is something *very* different.

"Did you ever want kids?" he asks me and my gut sinks.

We've known each other for a long time. I consider lying to him, because to air this dirty laundry now feels like a bad idea. Like opening Pandora's box, I don't know what's going to happen if I do.

When we first met, he was so young and new to The Grove and getting his footing as a Daddy, and our friendship developed almost accidentally as I answered his questions and took him under my wing. Now he's like a younger brother -*a pseudo son, almost, if not for the fact that he's not quite young enough*- and I know that he's probably not going to understand how I could have kept something quite so huge from him.

But I can't lie. Not to Charlie.

Knowing that I'm about to change everything between us, I take a deep breath and stare into the bubbles inside my golden brew, quietly praying for the strength to get through this conversation.

"I…had a son."

All the joy and warmth from the beginning of our conversation seems to evaporate as the silence hangs between us. Was it only a few minutes ago I was buzzing from the admission that I've got a new boyfriend? Now I'm dragging up memories that are better off buried.

"You…*what*?" Charlie's blue eyes are wide and stunned. Then the past tense in my sentence must hit him because the expression crumples into sympathy. "What…Ted, *shit*. When…" He stops asking questions (the same questions everyone stumbles over when they inevitably find out about Aiden) and just stares.

"He would've been thirty this year." I don't know where the fuck that additional information decided to come from, but I immediately regret it, watching Charlie do the mental math.

"You…you were…"

"Seventeen. Seventeen and stupid." I grab for my glass, taking another huge mouthful to try and just. stop. talking.

It's been a long time. I've been to therapy. I've worked through the trauma and the pain and…okay, so the grief hits me every so often, but I'm not a mess. I'm not. And, as always, when people hear the story and then work out that it wasn't long after his passing that I turned to BDSM as a *Daddy* no less, well…let's just say the judgment doesn't sit well with me.

"Fuck." Charlie sucks down a third of his own glass before he turns baleful eyes on me. "Why didn't you ever say anything?"

I arch an eyebrow at him. "It's not exactly the easiest thing to slip into conversation."

"Alright, yeah, I get that," he rubs his hand over his bearded jaw. "And you've just been dealing with this on your own?" I shrug, trying to ignore the narrowing of his eyes. "*Ted*."

"That tone doesn't work on me," I try to joke. "Especially because I taught it to you."

"*Ted*," he repeats.

I sigh. And then the whole story pours out. "It's a cliché, really. Or it starts with one. I was trying so hard to be straight. My parents…" I wave that mess off with a sigh. "I went to a party, got drunk off my ass, thought it would prove something if I slept with a girl-" I had to imagine the quarterback to get it up. "-and, naturally, I got her pregnant."

I close my eyes and tilt my head back, the old memories prickling under my skin unpleasantly. Jess's panic. My own. My parents' reactions. Ugh.

"I thought my life was over," I make myself continue. "Our parents forced us to be responsible. I manned up, Aiden was born just after Senior year ended. I was almost eighteen."

I know I sound detached, but I can't let myself go back to that time of my life in detail. I can't. I'll break if I do.

Still, a small smile tugs at my lips at the glimpse of memory I allow myself now. Tiny fingers and toes. Eyes like mine. Jess's button nose. The panic ceasing for the briefest moment as I held him for the first time. "He was perfect. And I was fucking terrified, but somehow we made it work. Until college. Then things got hard."

Charlie reaches across the table, gripping my forearm and squeezing it in a show of silent support. I take another mouthful of beer and steel myself for the worst part.

"I had a full-ride scholarship and had to take it. Unfortunately, it took me half-way across the country. Jess's parents wouldn't let her come with me, and I knew I'd never get custody while they were providing a roof over Jess's and Aiden's heads. So I worked my ass off at college, got a part-time job and sent them whatever cash I had, went back home for long weekends and holidays…" Away from my parents, I finally came out of the closet but didn't date. I had too much going on. "Then, one day, I get hauled out of class by a pair of cops."

I close my eyes, unwillingly picturing the moment as vividly as if it had just happened. It's seared into my brain. The sympathy and sadness on the two guys' faces as they guided me into an empty lecture hall and tore my world apart isn't something I can ever erase.

"There'd been a car accident." Despite my greatest attempts to prevent it, my throat still goes tight and tears blur my vision. "Jess and her parents died on impact. But Aiden…"

I try to clear my throat. To this day, sitting in hospitals makes me feel sick and panicky. The sterile scents, the beeping of machines, the wires and tubes, the eerie silences: I shudder at the thought.

When Charlie was shot, it was like I'd gone back in time. The worry of not knowing if the person you're waiting on is going to come out the other side of the trauma… Well, if I hadn't had Ash to look after when we'd been waiting on Charlie to recover, I honestly would have lost my mind. Of course, none of the guys know any of this.

"I got to say goodbye." This last sentence is all I can manage to force out. I refuse to relive the rest. Thankfully, Charlie doesn't push for more.

"*Jesus*," he inhales, his face pale and wan.

Almost twenty-eight years later and, when I let myself focus, the pain is as sharp as ever. I swallow it back, reminding myself that accidents happen. There was nothing anyone could have done. It wasn't my fault. Being there wouldn't have changed anything.

His fist hitting the table hard enough to make our glasses tremble and rattle has me jerking back in surprise. "I hate that you never said anything." His blue eyes are dark as he stares me down. "Not because I think I deserved to know, but because the idea of you suffering with this on your own…"

I don't argue with him because I understand. The urge to support and care for his friends is part of what underpins his natural drive to the Daddy lifestyle.

Instead, I sigh. "I've been to countless therapy sessions. I'm in support groups for grieving parents. I'm not on my own in this. I just…I don't want it spilling over into the life I built for myself *after*. My loss doesn't define me. And, Charlie," I add when it looks like he's still going to push the issue, "I'm okay. I promise."

And I am. Obviously, there will always be times that are harder than others, but I learned early on that if I didn't push forward and focus on the good things in my life, nothing was ever going to work again. And, once I changed my motivations for seeking out Daddy role play from focusing on proving that I could nurture and support someone to embracing my natural desire to do so, it made stumbling into the lifestyle as a grieving twenty-year-old a little less weird.

As if he can read my mind, my friend sighs heavily and says, "You know that, if this thing between you and Zephyr gets serious, you'll have to tell him."

I reel back a little at that. I've never told any of my partners about Aiden. It's not that I can't see how it *might* be relevant, but I keep the two parts of my life completely separate. Before and After.

Reading my reluctance on my face, Charlie pushes it further. "If only to prevent a triggering event, or-"

I hold up my hand, interrupting him. "I see where you're coming from," I answer slowly. "But I'm asking you to drop it…and to keep this just between us."

That last bit might be asking a lot, but I don't want my relationship with the rest of our friendship circle changing, either. Still, I'm the one who taught Charlie about the importance of open and honest communication being paramount in a Daddy/little relationship (or, really, any relationship). I can tell he's unimpressed at my request, but I don't back down.

His lips thin as he purses them, and I can practically see him wanting to remind me of the things I've said before. However, I've been at this for almost three decades and, as far as I'm concerned, my past has never had an impact on the success or subsequent failures of my relationships to date.

"I know what I'm doing," I insist. "I'm fine."

And I really do believe that.

Chapter Ten – Zephyr

Dating Ted is like a revelation. We spend the first month settling into routines. We both work full time, and I still enjoy a bit of time to myself in my own personal space, so we talk during the week and spend Friday nights through to Monday mornings together.

When we're apart, I don't feel the need to be little, so our calls and texts are like any standard vanilla relationship I've had before, except with a little kink thrown in for flirting. But, in person, Ted makes sure we've got a set routine in place. He's not big on surprises and likes control, which I can understand and even relate to, so it's not a big deal to know that I can expect scheduled times for being little.

That said, Ted is a bit more fluid once I've sunk into little space, not minding if we go over the few hours an evening he allocates for it. I think he just likes me to know that he's making it a priority for the both of us, considering it's something we only explore together in person.

Tonight, though, things hit a snag.

It's like a switch is flipped the second I attempt to bring his hand to my cock during bath time, with me in the tub and him on his knees beside it, bathing me while I remain little for longer than anticipated. It's a Friday evening, and I'm gearing up for a weekend spent in bed if I can get my way.

Ted goes rigid, his face turning blank, and I don't even get a chance to speak before he clearly says, "Red light."

It's been a long time since I've safe worded myself, and I've never had a Daddy safe word with me, so I freeze and come back to my adult self so suddenly that it almost feels like I've given my brain whiplash. He's pulled his arm away from the tub, sitting back on his haunches, and I fight the sudden anxiety churning in my gut for having accidentally pushed a button.

I've called him 'Daddy' during sex before, but he's been okay with that. It has to be that I'm little right now. I run back through our conversations and negotiations and realize with a sinking feeling that, somehow, the topic of sex in little space never even came up. That's on both of us.

This is why safe words exist, I remind myself, willing my heart to calm as I try to find the words to fix the strained silence that has descended.

"Hey," I reach for him, not caring about the water that drips from my bubble covered hand and onto the floor in front of his knees. "I'm sorry I…"

"No," he gives himself a visible shake, his expression turning chagrined. "I'm sorry. I should have…" He trails off and scratches the back of his neck, exhaling heavily. "That's a hard limit for me. One I should have raised earlier. It's just…most men I've been with haven't…"

"Wanted sex while little?" I prompt. It makes a little more sense now that he seems to easily ignore my arousal when he's dressing me: it's not on his radar. Little time is pure for him. I can respect that.

He nods.

"Want to talk about it?"

The vehement shake of his head in the negative begins before I can even finish asking the question. Something tells me this is a bigger deal than just disliking the concept. Ted's usually big on talking things through, with communication and honesty being at the top of our rules and all, so this flat refusal absolutely floors me.

Still, I know better than anyone not to push on uncomfortable or painful subjects. I have to trust that whatever's going on with him, Ted will talk to me when he's ready.

"Okay," I answer softly again, as though I'm trying to coax a skittish animal into trusting me. "That's fine. There are things I don't like talking about, either."

My easy acceptance seems to help, even while my mind races. What could have inspired this sort of reaction in a man who I was starting to think is always stoic and strong? Past trauma, certainly. But with what? Or whom? Another little? Even though the Daddy/boy kink is pretty pure, it is still a facet of BDSM and people have all sorts of triggers. It's possible something went terribly wrong somewhere along the lines.

I climb out of the tub and dry myself off, the mood between us awkward and strained. I don't know how to make it better, and the last thing I want is for safe wording to feel…well, unsafe, for lack of a better word.

"Ice cream?" I suggest as brightly as I can as I pull my loose pajama pants up my legs. "And a movie?" I force a grin that I know doesn't quite meet my eyes. "You can even pick the movie…but I'm vetoing anything with Kevin Costner on principal."

Finally, I watch him relax. His eyes glint with humor. "What's wrong with-"

"Dude can't act, Ted. He just can't. It's painful to watch."

"But-"

"I will give you *Robin Hood: Prince of Thieves* but only because Alan Rickman carries that whole movie."

He snorts. We've had some variation of this argument before, but I'll happily rehash it if it means watching him smile and come back to himself after whatever the fuck just happened between us. "Next you'll tell me that the first *Die Hard* movie is the best one for the same reason."

"Well, duh," I laugh at his scandalized expression. "Actually, that would probably be unfair to Jeremy Irons in the third one, but…what can I say? I'm a Rickmaniac."

"A…*what?*" Ted stops in his tracks just as we're about to descend the stairs. He looks bewildered – clearly amused and also mildly horrified. "Is that like a Cumberbitch?"

"Ooooh," I tease him back, "Look who's up with the lingo. And you try to pretend you're middle-aged." I pat his shoulder and he sets off down the stairs in front of me. "You're secretly all over the celebrity gossip and stuff, aren't you?"

"You've got me," he deadpans, "I'm totally hip."

"Hip replacement maybe."

We've reached the bottom of the stairs and I squeal as he makes a swipe for me, playfully threatening retribution for the wise crack against his age. I race for the kitchen, laughing and breathless when he catches up to me, cornering me against the kitchen bench and kissing me senseless.

"I really am sorry about earlier," he says as we pull apart, his eyes meeting mine so I can gauge his sincerity. "It's my fault for not listing it in my limits."

"Honestly, it's fine." I reach up to cup his jaw in my palm, stroking my thumb over the prickle of a day's growth. "And when *-if-* you want to talk about it, we can. But it's enough just to know that you're not into it."

This time when Ted kisses me, I can't help but feel like he's trying to apologize anyway. He's tender and sweet and appreciative, and when he rests his forehead against mine afterwards, murmuring, "How'd I get so lucky with you, tiny dancer?" my insides light up.

It's only been a month, but I can feel myself falling for this man. It's a new sensation. I've been smitten before, and I've loved before, but nothing has felt quite this intense so quickly. I don't feel like we're rushing things, but at the same time, I'm surprised by how fast my feelings have progressed.

In past relationships, my feelings have been slow to build. I had to work hard on building the foundations before I got so attached. But with Ted I think I was attached from the beginning. He draws me in like nobody I've ever met before, and the foundations (the friendship and the flirting and the things we have in common) all seem to click into place without any actual effort.

Coming back to the conversation at hand, I smile and wrap my arms around his neck. "I'd say you're not the only one who hit the jackpot, Mister Masters."

"Is that so?" With his smile turning wicked, the remnants of our earlier tension begin to melt away.

"Uh huh. See, I've got this insanely hot silver fox at my disposal…and he's going to feed me ice cream and treat me like a queen."

Even though I've said it playfully, that's exactly how the evening plays out.

* * *

By the time Wednesday rolls around, I've pretty much forgotten all about Friday's incident when I meet up with Asher for lunch. Their community center is only a fifteen-minute walk from the dance studio where I teach, so Ash and I have made this a regular event since we met, with Charlie tagging along with his husband when he's not in meetings.

I have to admit, it has been good making new friends. When I first came to the city, I was still trying to adjust to my new reality, and I'd been content with the idea of being a lone wolf. All my dance friends had moved on with their lives, keeping in touch via memes on Facebook, but never really stopping to ask how I was actually doing. It hurt too much to watch them continue with their careers, and eventually I just gave up the pretense. It was easier to be alone than to carry on with fair weather friends.

I hadn't been looking for a new social circle when I went to The Grove that first time. I really had just been looking for a bit of escapism and being little usually helped with that.

Then I'd met Ash and Chance.

Ash, for all that he tries to tell me that he's painfully shy, saw that I was alone and demanded that I play with him. He got me to open up about being new to town and somehow sensed how lonely I was, but never made me feel badly for it. He just told me that he had also started from scratch a couple of years ago and that he was always looking to make new friends. There was no sense of expectation from him, just his genuine joy at sharing his little time with a playmate.

Once they'd explained that Chance wasn't Ash's Daddy but was stepping in as Uncle Chance, he had sat back and just let us play, occasionally joining in whenever Ash prodded him. Of the two of them, he's the one that struck me as genuinely shy, though he was every bit a doting Daddy when it was required of him. Afterwards, when Ash and I had gotten changed and were 'big' again, we'd all walked together to our cars, laughing and chatting like we were old friends.

It had struck me in that moment that being a loner would never work for me, and when Ash had suggested we exchange numbers, I couldn't deny that building a new social circle sounded appealing.

Since then, I've gotten pretty close with my fellow Little. Being strong-armed into attending his wedding was a surprise, but I'm beyond glad that I went along. At the time, I suspected he was trying to set me up with Chance because we had gotten along during Littles' Night, but now I realize that he was just trying to introduce me to their entire group. The fact that I ended up hitting it off with Ted is, to Ash, the cherry on top.

When I first confirmed that we were dating, he squealed, added me to the group chat, and started planning play-dates. Today he's brought Charlie with him and I anticipate more of the same, but when Ash brings it up because we are still yet to make it happen, Charlie frowns.

That sets off a bubble of anxiety in my gut.

"What's wrong?" I prod, running a fry through a small puddle of ketchup, my appetite fading the more I look at Charlie's face.

He attempts to school his expression into something milder. "Nothing," he says, shrugging casually. "I'll run it by Ted."

I don't know Charlie as well as I know Ash, but there's something *off* about the way he says his best friend's name.

"Have you guys argued?" I hazard a guess, watching Charlie closely for his reaction.

I'll give it to him; he's pretty cool under pressure, probably because he was a cop. But his eyes are expressive and they give him away. I can tell he's uneasy, even while he blinks slowly to control his facial expressions. "Nope."

Liar. I want to call him out on it, but at the same time I don't think it's really my place to do so. Whatever's going on between him and Ted, it probably has nothing to do with me. Besides, we haven't been together long enough for me to reasonably stick my nose in where it doesn't belong.

Ash, on the other hand, has no such compulsions. He cocks his head at his husband and says, "Want to try that again?"

"Ash…" The word is essentially a plea for Asher to let it go.

Proving that we're very similar people, Ash only digs his heels in. He sets down his fork, abandoning the creamy pasta dish he'd ordered, and glares at the other man. "What happened to honesty and open communication, Daddy? Do you have a problem with Ted and Zephyr together? Because I've been begging you to invite them over for weeks now and you've made excuse after excuse."

"What? No." That, at least, is an honest reaction. Charlie shakes his head, sighing. "Look. Ted and I…things there are a little strained right now, okay? But it doesn't have anything to do with Zephyr." He shoots me an apologetic grimace. "I'm sorry if it came off that way."

"So you did fight with him?" Ash's face falls. "When? Why didn't you say anything?"

"It wasn't a fight," Charlie insists. "We just had an emotionally charged conversation and things are still a bit weird right now. I'm giving him time and space."

Hearing the confirmation doesn't really help me. If anything, it makes me more anxious because Ted never mentioned having a falling out with his friend to me, either. Ash and I exchange uneasy glances.

"Just forget I said anything, okay?" Charlie insists. "Please. He…" he sighs, then looks at his husband imploringly, "We're good, okay? Just…he asked me to back off and drop it, and I am. So…can you leave it? Please?"

Pursing his lips, Ash nods with obvious reluctance. "Fine."

In his relief, Charlie does not catch the look Ash shoots me, but I obviously do. And I nod, because there's no way we're not getting to the bottom of whatever is going on between our Daddies.

Chapter Eleven – Ted

"Oh, God, *Zeph*," his beautiful bow lips are wrapped around my cock and I'm finding it very difficult to form coherent thoughts right now.

We've disposed of condoms recently, having both tested negative for STIs, and the warm, wet suction of his mouth makes that particular decision one of my finest.

He bobs his head, swirling his tongue over my shaft and through the slit of my crown as he moves.

"You feel so good, darling," I encourage him further, trying not to tighten my fingers in his thick, dark hair.

I'm sprawled on the couch in my living room, my legs spread wide with Zephyr kneeling between them. My jeans have been thrown somewhere in the direction of the kitchen. The only reason I give two shits about that right now is the sachet of lube stashed in my wallet which is still in the hip pocket of said jeans.

Zephyr hums, sending vibrations through my cock and pushing me ever closer to orgasm.

My brain turns sluggish. "Wait, baby…I- *oh fuck,* that feels…*ungh.*"

I throw my head back against the plush couch cushion and close my eyes, reveling in the feel of him sucking me off. He smooths his hands over my thighs and then fondles my balls with one while the other dips lower, grazing my taint and teasing my hole.

My hips buck upwards of their own accord as I groan my enjoyment.

Then I remember that my intention is to not come down his throat.

"Zeph…lube. Wallet." I used to have the ability to form sentences, I swear.

"Mmm," he moans around my cock again, and it's all I can do to keep my eye on the prize. Then he pulls off and asks, "Is the lube for your ass or mine?"

Fun fact: I've never been fucked. I've had my ass played with, sure, but none of my boys have wanted to top, and I've never felt as though I've been missing out. In fact, until ten seconds ago, I would have told you I'm a strict top. But what comes out of my mouth is: "Is that something you'd want to do? Fuck me, I mean?"

Zephyr blinks at me in surprise, the blow job all but forgotten. "I've never topped."

I shrug easily. "I've never bottomed."

His eyes are wide now, his disbelief almost palpable. "But…you'd let me…?"

Reaching for him, I pull him up into my lap and kiss his swollen lips. "I trust you," I tell him simply. "My previous partners haven't been interested in topping, and I never pushed the issue. But if you want to try, I'm always up for a little experimentation." I waggle my eyebrows to keep the mood light. "It doesn't have to be today, or ever if you don't want to, but I'd be on board if you wanted it."

"Wow," he says, those dark eyes of his glazing over. "That is *hot,* Ted."

I think about it for a moment, imagining what he might feel like inside me, and my cock twitches between us at the thought. "Yeah," I agree, the heat and urgency from a few minutes ago building between us again, "it is."

He mewls and then crashes his lips against mine, kissing me with fervent need. My hands move to the fly of his jeans, popping the button and undoing the zipper with practiced ease. We fumble and shift around as he struggles his way out of them while our tongues tangle together, our breaths mingling and our mutual desire growing.

"Fuck," he hisses, breaking from the kiss when our cocks connect, both a little slick with precum, "where'd you say the lube was?"

I groan again, this time in frustration. "In my wallet. In my jeans." I gesture in the vague direction I saw them fly earlier. "Wherever they went."

"Ugh. Fine." He climbs off my lap with obvious reluctance. "Be right back."

"I'll be waiting." I fist my cock for emphasis.

I don't bother watching as he races in the direction of the kitchen, but I hear his victorious "Got it!" and the dull sound of the denim hitting the tiles before he's back in front of me again, the little square pouch of lube extended in one hand.

"For now," he says with a grin, "you're going to fuck me. But one day, we'll switch it up."

"Anything you want, Zeph." And I mean it. I want to give him the world.

But today I'll settle for a mind-blowing orgasm or two.

He straddles my lap again, kissing me as I manage to awkwardly tear open the little packet and coat my fingers. I take my time opening him up as he grinds his cock against mine, stretching him with three fingers before I deem him ready enough to ride me. I squeeze the last of the lube out into my palm and slick up my cock, then guide Zephyr until he's sinking down onto me in one smooth, swift move.

"Holy fuck," I breathe and dig my fingers into his hips. As always, the sensation of being inside him is beyond exquisite, even more so now that we've agree to go bare. "I'll never get used to how good you feel."

Using muscles toned from a lifetime of dancing, he starts to bounce in my lap, his knees on either side of my ass, sinking into the couch. "Right back at you," he says between movements, closing his eyes as my cock grazes over his prostate. "Oh, *Daddy*."

"That's it, baby. Take it. Take what you need."

I love watching him like this. Love feeling him use me for his own pleasure. It's so different to have someone else set the pace, to hand the reins over to someone else and let them control the experience, but it's also surprisingly freeing. And watching Zephyr this way, knowing that he's comfortable enough to take whatever he needs from me, fills me with pride, warmth, and affection.

"T-touch my cock," he stammers out as he finds the angle and pace guaranteed to have him hurtling over the finish line before too long. "Please."

As if I need to be begged for that. My hand closes around his length, stroking and squeezing the way he likes best, and he begins his usual litany of curses as the pleasure builds.

I focus on him. On his blissed-out expression. On the sheen of sweat on his skin. On the precum dribbling down his cock, aiding my hand's endeavors. On the panted out swear words and the sounds of him taking his pleasure from me. On the slapping sound of skin meeting skin as he rides me with wild abandon.

I'm rocking my hips up to meet him with every bounce and it's not long before the swears turn into the tell-tale train of fast cussing that precipitates his whole body tensing and ropes of cum spurting over my fist and our shirts. As always, he clenches around my cock as he comes and I'm unable to prevent myself from releasing my own load inside him.

We're a sticky, panting, practically glowing mess as we come down from the high of our mutual orgasms, but Zephyr makes no move to pull off me, not even as I start to soften. He drops his head to my shoulder and kisses my neck.

"I swear," he declares with a smile in his voice, "every time we do that, I think I'm going to black out with how hard you make me come."

"You did all the hard work this time, kitten," I remind him lazily, rubbing my clean hand over his back.

The sound he responds with is non-committal.

With reluctance, I tap his bare ass with my open palm. "Come on," I tell him, "Let's go clean up."

* * *

After an extended shower, Zephyr locates his phone and offers me a wide smile as he holds it up. "Are we going?" he asks, practically bouncing on his feet. I frown.

"Are we going where?"

"To Ash and Charlie's place," he points at the phone screen, "they've invited us all around for an impromptu cookout. It's in the group chat."

I muted the group chat weeks ago. It's not uncommon for me to need to do so occasionally. It is a large group which is becoming even larger with everyone's partners being read in, and they talk a lot of crap sometimes. The sheer number of notifications can be ridiculous and distracting when I'm at work. The guys, including Cherie and Kate, are generally accepting of the fact that I miss most of the conversations and don't participate a lot.

But I didn't mute the chat for work reasons this time.

After talking to Charlie about my past, I gave myself a time-out from the chat. I trust that he hasn't told any of the others, not even Ash. If he had, I would have been inundated with calls or messages, because our group is meddlesome like that.

Not that I don't think they'd all be supportive and kind, mind you. Because they would be. They're wonderful people. But I don't want our dynamic to change. I don't want their pity, or for things to become stilted or awkward.

Like they have with Charlie.

It hurts that my closest friend and I aren't exactly speaking right now. And, alright: I asked him to drop it and to give me space and he's done just that, so I should be grateful. Besides, it's not as though we fought. Sure, Charlie's got a right to feel a little hurt or insulted that I never confided in him, but he needs to be able to understand that I had my reasons and that it's my right to keep my personal issues…well, personal.

"Ted?" Zephyr's voice interrupts my thoughts and I look up to see his brow furrowed, his perfectly manicured eyebrows drawing down together.

While I'm tempted to tell him no, I can't come up with a valid reason to refuse Charlie and Ash's invitation. Then there's his obvious excitement at the prospect of socializing more with the whole gang. If it's a large enough gathering, I suppose it's possible that I can just avoid the awkwardness with Charlie altogether.

I twist my left wrist to check the time and smother a sigh. "What time is everyone getting there?"

Zephyr's expression morphs into surprise and then joy. "Six," he says, then his thumbs fly over the keypad on his screen, "I'm telling them we'll bring dessert."

I chuckle genuinely at that, at least. My princess and his sweet tooth. "Sure," I acknowledge. We don't really have time to bake anything, so I suggest a trip to the local bakery. I know I'm going to wind up buying far more than just sweet treats for tonight, but I can't help spoiling Zephyr and he knows it.

It's not until we're buckled into my car with a selection of pastries and cakes boxed and settled on the backseat that the anxiety I pushed aside earlier returns. Oblivious, Zephyr babbles about Ash's plan to host a play-date at the same time: the reason why Zephyr's packed himself a bag of his Little stuff for the evening.

"He said his friend Kate will be there, and so will Matt, and maybe even Josh might want to join in," he tells me, twisting in his seat to face me as he rambles with obvious excitement. "I haven't told him that I'm femme, but he'll be okay with it, right?"

I tear my eyes from the road briefly to assure him, "Of course. They all will. They're good guys."

That's not something I would ever question. My reluctance to tell them about my past and about my loss has nothing to do with a fear of judgment, at least. If anything, I don't want their sympathy. I don't want them to treat me differently. I'm still the same Ted I've always been but, if Charlie's reaction is anything to go by, they're not going to see it that way.

Zephyr nods, seemingly accepting my words at face value. But, as silence descends upon us, he places his hand on my thigh and squeezes, "Are you okay?"

Maybe he's not quite as oblivious to my anxiety as I thought.

Not wanting to lie to him, I mull over how to respond. "I'm…just thinking."

"About?"

I should have known that question was coming.

I sigh, keeping my gaze firmly on the road ahead. "The last time I spoke to Charlie, I told him something that..." I trail off.

How do I express this?

I don't want Zephyr to worry, obviously, but I also don't need him learning about the shadows in my past, either, no matter what Charlie thinks.

"That...?" he prompts.

I make a turn in the familiar direction of Charlie's place. We're still about five minutes away. Not short enough that I could feasibly brush Zephyr off. "Well," I answer, still trying to verbalize my issue with as many euphemisms as feasibly possible, "I think it changed the way he sees me."

"Oh."

Belatedly, I can see how that explanation could be interpreted in a thousand different ways – not many of them pleasant.

"I mean," I try to reassure him, "it was something from a long time ago, something I've worked through, and I don't want him pitying me or treating me with kid gloves."

While I don't love that I've had to confess that there's something pitiable in my past, I'd rather Zephyr know that than assume I'd said or done something terrible.

From the corner of my eye, I can see my boyfriend's gaze narrowing while he tries to put the vague clues together. "Do you really think he'll pity you?" he asks, and I catch the shake of his head before he answers himself, "Charlie doesn't seem the type. He's pragmatic. He might *empathize* with you, but he doesn't come off the pitying type. And as for treating you differently-"

"He already is," I huff, feeling much younger and more vulnerable than my actual age. The fact that I asked Charlie for space is something I conveniently choose to forget as I make my point. "We haven't spoken in over a month. Things are awkward now."

Instead of comforting me, Zephyr pats my thigh. "Well, the only way to fix that is to talk to him, you know."

Now it's my turn to frown. He doesn't seem at all surprised at my confession that I haven't been in touch with my best friend recently. Almost like he already...

It clicks.

"Asher," I say aloud, mildly frustrated.

Ash and Zeph have spoken about this. About me and Charlie. Hell, for all I know, today's supposedly 'impromptu' get-together is part of a plot to resolve whatever issues they think are between us.

"Don't be mad..." Zephyr has the decency to shift guiltily in his seat.

If I weren't driving, I'd close my eyes and count to ten. Instead, I flex my hold on the wheel and take a deep breath. "What did you and Ash do?"

"Nothing!" The quick, defensive reply sets off all my internal Daddy alarms.

"Zephyr..."

"I mean, we just thought that if you guys got together-"

I groan, cutting him off. I was right: this whole thing tonight has been a setup.

I've been Parent Trapped.

Unwilling to snap at him, because he really did mean well, I shake my head and indicate to turn onto Ash and Charlie's street. "You should have let it be," I manage to keep my tone level.

Zephyr remains silent.

As we approach Charlie's house and I pull up on the curb behind Chance's truck, I bite back further irritation that the guys are all here. Nothing like having an audience for tense moments. Turning in my seat to face my errant boy, I'm unsurprised to see the flat expression on his face, complete with pursed lips and folded arms.

"Zeph," I reach for him, but he leans back against the passenger window.

"Ash and I did what we thought was right," he insists, meeting my gaze unflinchingly. "You and Charlie weren't making any moves to get past whatever went down between you." His shoulders droop. "And I really wanted to have a play-date with my friend. A real one – not just at the club."

It's times like this where I'm reminded of his Little side. Zephyr acted on impulse, not even thinking about the implications of his and Asher's scheme, or how inviting the whole gang might make me feel.

Nevertheless, guilt still lances through me at his softly spoken admission. *Damn it.* It hasn't been fair of me to keep him all to myself for so long. Sure, part of that was all the shiny new relationship feelings and exploration, but I can't deny that avoiding Charlie was also a great motivator.

"You're right," I acknowledge, even though doing so is difficult. "I'm sorry, tiny dancer. I've been selfish."

Zephyr's expression softens. "I'm sorry, too. I shouldn't have just sprung this on you. I should have just spoken to you about it. And we probably shouldn't have made it a whole group thing, but we didn't want it to look like a setup…" He turns his gaze towards the house, then back to me. "If you'd rather go home, we can do that."

It's tempting, and I do appreciate the offer, but I've let this strange limbo with my closest friend go on for too long as it is. "No," I state softly, but firmly. "I need to do this."

I don't deserve the look of pride he gives me in response, but it warms me anyway.

Chapter Twelve – Zephyr

Ash and Charlie's house is lovely. From the street, it gives off a pretty cottage vibe. It's two stories, constructed out of light gray clapboard with white accents and a nice front porch complete with a flowerbed full of brightly colored flowers. It's homey and inviting and (though I hate to think it) far less intimidating than Ted's mansion.

As we walk in -with Ted just opening the front door and sauntering through without ringing the bell- the same color scheme continues inside. Ted leads me through the small foyer and past an office and staircase on my left and a carpeted lounge room on my right. When we get into an open plan kitchen/dining area which leads further on to an outdoor entertainment space, Ash notices us first. He steps away from Kate and Matt, both of whom I met at his wedding, and bounds over to greet us.

"Hey, Uncle Ted," he grins, wrapping his arms around my Daddy before turning to me, "Hey, Zephyr. I'm so happy you could come!"

I can't help smiling back in the face of his genuine enthusiasm. "Me too," I agree.

Ted, on the other hand, gives Ash a stern look.

I sigh, explaining, "We've been busted."

Ash turns back to Ted and shrugs. "We gave you and Daddy long enough to sort your shit out. You didn't do it on your own so," he spreads his arms wide, "here we are. Sorry not sorry, Ted."

"Actually," I interrupt before Ted can scold my friend. Having had the discussion with Ted and gotten a very vague idea of what happened between him and Charlie, I do feel a little guilty for just springing this intervention of sorts on him, "we're a little sorry."

Ash furrows his brow. "We are?"

"We are." I give him a meaningful look. One that says 'I'll tell you later'.

"Hmm," is all my fellow little says before he turns back in the direction of the gathering out on the deck, "*Daddy*," he calls cheerily before anyone can stop him, "Ted and Zephyr are here!"

I can feel Ted tense beside me and I reach out to rub at the underside of his arm (which is holding the large box of pastries and doughnuts) to soothe him.

"Here," chirps Ash helpfully, "I'll take those." Following through, he plucks the box of desserts out of Ted's hands and bounces into the kitchen.

Charlie makes his way inside, his hand extended to shake mine before he looks at his best friend. There's a brief, strained moment of silence between them before Charlie hauls Ted in for a manly hug, all back thumping and "I've missed you, man, how've you been?"s.

Ash and I share a relieved glance as the two men lapse into conversation from there. To be fair, it's probably not the easy and effortless conversations they usually share, and I can still see tension in the way Ted holds his shoulders. But it's a start.

"Come on," Ash grabs my hand and starts leading me towards the other Littles in the gathering, "we're thinking about getting changed and having a play-date." He juts his chin at the duffel bag slung over my shoulder. "Is that your little stuff?"

I nod. "Yeah." Now it's my turn to feel nervous. I know Ted said nobody here will judge me for being into feminization, but...*what if they do*?

We've stopped in front of Kate and Matt, and Ash is leading the discussion on whether they're interested in sneaking in some little time before dinner or not when Charlie's brother, Josh, joins the party. His entrance is boisterous, and he, too, appears to have just let himself into the house. As he enters the room, he waves at the people gathered outside before making a beeline towards his brother-in-law.

"Thanks for the invite, Ash," he says, ruffling the smaller man's hair. Then he looks over the rest of us. "So, are we doing this? Getting our little on?"

"Where's your stuff?" Ash asks him. "Or are you staying in what you're wearing?"

He glances down at the white t-shirt and jeans combination he's rocking and shrugs. "I'm easy."

"There's a joke in that," Chance teases, happening to walk past us at that moment. Josh flips him off, and the other man grabs two beers from the fridge with a laugh before returning to the group of caregivers outside.

Ash rolls his eyes at the exchange, then looks Josh over again. "Suit yourself," he says, then adds, "but I know I can't really get into the right head space if I'm wearing my 'big' clothes."

"I've got a spare set of clothes if you wanted to borrow an outfit," Matt offers him. He's a bit bulkier than Josh up top, but I'd guess they're roughly around the same size.

Josh looks at Matt for a long moment, likely considering the offer, then smiles hesitantly. I don't really know the guy, having only met him at Ash's wedding, but from everything Ash has told me about him, such an expression seems almost out of place on his handsome face. "Thanks, Matt," he says to the other buff little, "I'd like that."

And, just like that, it seems to be decided that the play-date will start as soon as we're all changed. Matt shyly seeks out London to take him to one of the guest rooms and dress him, and Katie drags her Mommy, Cherie, up the stairs after them to do the same. Charlie doesn't need prompting, he just heads towards the stairs with Ash on his heels. This leaves me to consider whether I want to ask Ted to help me, or whether I should just head into the downstairs powder room to dress myself. It's not like I need diapering or anything like the others.

Of course, I haven't warned them about my dresses, either.

"Hey," Josh's voice startles me out of my thoughts. His brown eyes are concerned. "You okay?"

It's in this moment that I realize that his brazen personality must be a façade, because, if memory serves correctly, the guy is a cop. And this serious, concerned manner he's got going on right now? It's genuine.

His voice is soft, and he reaches out a hand to squeeze my shoulder. "If you're not up for this, we can grab drinks and go join the other guys."

I've only met this guy once, but the way he so easily offers to sit out on little time to keep me company warms me unexpectedly. I smile and shake my head, even as Ted sidles up beside Josh, eyeing his hand on my shoulder with unspoken questions.

"Zeph?" Ted asks, his own concern more than obvious.

"I'm fine," I reassure both men, leaning into Ted's side when Josh releases his hold on my shoulder. Then I sigh and heft my bag up as I explain, "I didn't get a chance to tell the others."

"Tell the others what?" Josh asks, but he doesn't sound demanding. Just curious. Still gentle and supportive.

It's his tone and the open look on his face which ultimately convince me to admit, "I'm into feminization. I'm, uh, a femme little. Like, y'know, princess play and pretty dresses and…stuff." I finish lamely.

A wide, bright smile splits his face. "Katie is going to lose her shit." He claps his hands together. "*And* that means I don't have to play dress-ups with her anymore!" He lunges forward, wrapping me in a bear hug. He stops shy of spinning me around in his joy. "You're my hero!" When he sets me back down on the ground, he offers me a bashful smile. "I mean, dress-ups aren't the worst, but they're not my jam."

I can't help but think he's sweet to have still gone along with it all this time for his friend. Ted was right: these are good people. I'm safe here.

I turn back to my Daddy, my worries alleviated. "Wanna help me get dressed?"

* * *

Despite knowing that Ted's friends are good people and that I'm safe, I still clutch Ted's hand tightly as we make our way back downstairs to rejoin the group. I'm wearing a dress which Ted bought me last week. It's a very pale pink color, with a flared skirt that sits just above my knees, a fitted bodice, and spaghetti straps over my shoulders. It's perfect and summery and I feel supremely feminine wearing it. The matching ballet flats I'm wearing complete the whole picture.

"It's going to be fine, kitten," Ted assures me, bringing my hand to his mouth and brushing his lips lightly over my knuckles. "I promise."

I can't really explain why I'm so anxious about this, other than the fact that it's the first time a group of people I know will see me dressed this way. Ash and Chance have seen me in a cropped t-shirt and play shorts, but this is different. This is me laid bare. And that's what it ultimately boils down to: I really want them to like me for me.

As we cross the foyer and head towards the lounge room, finally coming into view of the others, I watch them closely for their first reactions before they have a chance to school their features.

It's only as Ash's face lights up that the tension starts to bleed from my shoulders. Matt smiles, too, but there's something softer and more understanding in his gaze. Then there's Kate, who squeals and rushes towards me, her arms extended in a bid to reach out and feel the material of my dress before she's even crossed the space.

"*Finally*," she gushes, sounding giddy. "Someone like me."

I don't know what it is about her words that do it, but I tear up at that very simple declaration. She doesn't see my gender: she just sees another little who likes to wear pretty dresses.

Before I know it, Kate and I are hugging as though we've been friends for years instead of minutes, and then there's a dog pile of people on top of us with the other Littles wanting in on the embrace. It's not until minutes later, when we're all giggling and moving off to play, that I realize Ted wandered off to join Charlie over by the couch. Cherie and London, Kate's Mommy and Matt's Daddy respectively, are back out on the deck with Spencer and Chance.

If I were in a bigger head space, I'd probably pay closer attention to the low-spoken conversation my Daddy is having with his best friend, but I'm too distracted by Kate's request to play dolls with me.

Even though I've played with dolls before (by myself, in scenes at various clubs, and more recently with Ted as my very attentive Daddy) I discover that having a little friend to play with is a whole new experience. She's every bit as enthusiastic as I am, losing herself in the imaginative play.

While Daddy joins in in a similar way, he's never quite as invested as Kate seems to be. He doesn't share the childlike glee that she and I feel, I suppose. And why should he? He's a *Daddy*, not a fellow little. His enjoyment comes from interacting with me and seeing me happy. Whereas, for Kate and I, our enjoyment as Littles comes from letting go of being adults. Of letting someone else take care of us while we give in to the urge to be completely carefree.

When we get bored of playing dolls, Kate and I move on to orchestrating a pretend tea party for them. We just dressed them up, after all. It makes sense that they should have a reason to wear their 'fancy' new outfits. Ash ambles over for this game, though, and I vaguely recall Ted telling me that Ash loves to play teddy bear tea parties.

Matt and Josh stick to racing their cars along the polished timber floorboards separating the lounge from the kitchen.

Our caregivers leave us to our own devices, though occasionally one of the caregivers will stop in to ask questions or join our play for a few minutes. I don't even realize how much time has passed when Charlie wanders back into the room having swapped out 'watching' us with Spencer to go fiddle with the grill on the deck, and he claps his hands, declaring dinner ready.

"You can stay little if you want," he says easily, as though this sort of thing happens every day, "but we should eat it before it gets cold." He chuckles and wraps an arm around Asher's waist, catching him as he tries to slip past. "But, big or little, you need to wash up first, too."

Ash grumbles, but the smile playing around the corners of his lips gives his enjoyment of this interaction with his Daddy away. Watching them like this fills me with warm, fuzzy feelings, and I fleetingly wonder if Ted and I ever look at each other the way Charlie and Ash do.

As I make my way to get changed back into my big clothes, a hopeful voice in my head says that if we don't already, I think we're on the right track.

Chapter Thirteen – Ted

I owe Zephyr an apology and gratitude for forcing me to face my issues with Charlie. The first few minutes of conversation felt a touch strained but, after sitting together and watching the littles romp around Charlie's lounge room, we're back to our usual dynamic now, or a close approximation to it. And, as I take a seat at one of the two outdoor tables which have been pushed together to create one long one, I realize just how badly I've missed this.

I'm a social creature by nature. Not having hung out with the guys in over a month was more emotionally and mentally draining than I could have anticipated. Not only that, but I can see that Zephyr needed the social time just as badly as I did. While he was quite obviously anxious at first, I couldn't deny the blatant joy and relaxation he seemed to get from playing with the others as I watched indulgently.

Guilt wells in me, churning my gut when I consider that my avoidance of my friends also prevented Zephyr from having this sort of experience.

"Whatever you're thinking, man, stop it," Spencer says lowly as he leans across me to grab for a big bowl of green salad. "You've got your 'self-flagellation' face on." He dishes himself up a healthy serving of rabbit food before handing the bowl down the line to Chance.

On my other side, Zephyr's in quiet conversation with London, their heads bowed together as they murmur softly. With him distracted, I turn back to Spencer, repeating, "My self-flagellation face?"

He nods, his mess of dark hair flopping into his eyes. "It's not a good look on you."

I want to argue, but I can't deny that he's right. Of course, I can't help snarking, "Interesting way of phrasing it. What kind of books are you narrating right now?"

He reaches for some of the chicken Charlie had cooked on the grill and smirks at me as he returns the tongs to the plate. "No changing the subject, Theodore."

I roll my eyes. "You can't use Daddy voice on another Daddy, Spencer. We've been over this."

He continues on, undeterred, "Either way, whatever's making you second guess yourself? You gotta stop that." He jerks his chin towards Zephyr. "Your boy is sweet, and you've got a good thing going. Don't get so far into your head that you let it slip away."

I don't like how accurately he was able to read me in the short time we've been seated together at the table. But I also know that he hasn't dated since his relationship with Emma ended all those months ago, and now I'm coming to see that maybe he's not so much reading me as possibly projecting his own issues onto me.

My initial reaction to bristle and snap at him softens into something a little more understanding. I even manage to sound mildly appreciative when I assure him, "Thanks, Spence. I won't let that happen."

Placing his knife down on his plate, he reaches up to squeeze my shoulder and gives me a little shake before he lets go. "I'm glad."

Even though I was irritated at first, it's just another example of how good the guys in our circle of friends really are. They look out for each other, even on this smaller level. I feel like a shitty friend for not having returned the favor lately.

"You're doing it again," Spence says, cutting off my thoughts.

I give him a one-fingered salute.

He allows me a few moments of silence before he leans in and quietly asks, "Did you want to talk about it?"

"No." My reply is quick and emphatic.

Spencer's lips quirk. "You gave that a lot of thought."

"Fuck off," I laugh. "There's nothing to talk about."

Across the table, Charlie chokes on the sip of beer he'd only just taken. I narrow my gaze in his direction. Maybe we're not exactly as back to 'normal' as I'd hoped.

"Sorry," he coughs, his cheeks a little pink, but he doesn't push the issue.

Spencer arches an eyebrow at the exchange. I ignore it.

Thankfully, Ash asks Zephyr about the dress he'd worn earlier and Kate chimes in loudly from the other end of the table, and the whole awkward moment is forgotten.

* * *

Everything goes south when Maisy, Josh and Charlie's sister, turns up unexpectedly.

Having let herself into the house, most likely realizing that Ash and Charlie were entertaining, she stomps out onto the deck and practically throws herself into her older brother's arms.

"Mom's driving me *insane*," she complains, seemingly oblivious to the way silence has fallen around the table. "I finally snapped and told her that Ed and I have zero intention to have kids and she's acting like I've told her the world is ending."

Beside me, Spencer tenses. I don't have time to think about his reaction, though, because Maisy has worked herself up into a proper rant and raises her voice, her arms flailing about wildly. Idly, I muse that while she mightn't look like her mother, their shared dramatic flair is obviously genetic.

"She even said, and I quote: 'I did too good a job when I gave you *the talk*'," she pitches her voice high in a mocking mimicry of her mother's voice. Her face contorts bitterly and she scoffs. "As if I was only careful for her benefit. Who wants to be a teen statistic? Or any kind of statistic? Unplanned kids aren't exactly-"

"*Maisy*," Charlie interrupts in his firmest voice, startling the whole table.

Ash puts a calming hand on his arm, but he continues, "Your personal opinion on that stuff is irrelevant because it never happened and Mom's just being Mom right now."

I try not to cringe at the fleeting apologetic glance he shoots my way. What happened to Subtle Cop Charlie? *Come on, man,* I try to tell him with my eyes, *be cool.*

Maisy huffs and rolls her eyes. "I'm *venting,*" she justifies emphatically, then waves her hand dismissively over the table. "It's not like any of these guys'll be offended or whatever."

"You don't know that." Charlie lectures back.

Again his eyes flicker in my direction.

Damn it, Charlie.

Maisy sighs. I can understand her likely assumptions without her needing to say anything out loud: we're a gathering of predominantly gay men, as far as she's aware. What, exactly, are the chances any of us were teen parents? However, to play devil's advocate, I would argue that we might have family or friends who were. (Unbeknownst to the guys, they've got at least one friend who was, after all.)

Still, it's obvious that she's come here directly after a volatile interaction with her mother and her words are reactionary. I don't know her well, but we've met enough times over the years to know that Maisy's not a cruel or judgmental person. I honestly wouldn't have given her words a second thought, but Charlie's making a big deal out of them and I can feel myself attempting to sink into my chair because I know why this is a trigger for him right now.

I'm the only person here who does.

And, because my seat is directly across from where Charlie is standing beside his sister, it's me she zeroes in on to try and illustrate her point. "Ted," she huffs, aiming her index finger into her older brother's chest, "tell him that you're not offended."

I breathe a little easier at the loophole. Had she asked me directly if I had a reason to be hurt by her words, that would have given me pause. But this is easy because it's not a lie. I smile softly. "I'm not offended."

Unfortunately, Charlie frowns and tilts his head sideways with mild disbelief tempering his tone, "*Ted*."

My heart begins beating rapidly in my chest because in every single imagined scenario from here, I don't know how to get out of this without having to tell the guys everything after all. Even meeting his gaze and reassuring him that I'm honestly not offended will bring more attention to the issue than should be required.

I work my jaw and eye him down, but it's too late and I know it.

Zephyr's hand lands on my tense forearm. "What's going on?" he asks softly, voicing the question I'm certain is on everyone's minds by now. But, instead of acknowledging the question, I cringe in my best friend's direction, wishing he hadn't pushed the issue.

"Damn it, Charlie," I growl the words I thought only moments ago, shaking my head, "you couldn't have left it?" I run a hand through my hair, my eyes still not leaving his. "I genuinely wasn't offended, by the way. You could have just taken my word for it."

His reply is laden with sarcasm, "I'm sorry for thinking about your feelings."

"I told you-"

His scoff cuts me off. "Yeah, well, maybe…" I watch him trail off, uneasy at the expression that crosses his face. His shoulders slump with resignation and a little embarrassment. "Maybe I was projecting." He averts his gaze, gruffly adding, "Sorry."

"A fine time to have that realization," I grumble, then sigh, silently cursing the fact that my best friend is so damn empathetic and cursing myself for avoiding properly talking the whole thing out with him when I had the chance.

"Ted…" With Charlie's own temper deflated, there's genuine remorse on his features and in his voice now.

I shake my head and say, "Don't worry about it."

What's done is done. Besides, steeling myself for the fallout is more important than listening to him apologize for…what, exactly? Caring too much? Can I honestly hold that against him?

Awkward silence descends before Maisy demands, "No, seriously, what the hell is going on with you two?" She flicks a perfectly manicured nail between me and Charlie, before her attention swings back to her older brother properly. Her long, pretty face contorts as she narrows her eyes at him. She seems concerned beneath her snark now, her worry for her older brother overriding her frustration. "Projecting what, exactly? Did you actually knock someone up in high school?"

Down the table, Josh chokes on his drink at her question, and I sigh.

"No," I answer on Charlie's behalf, rolling my eyes because even I know that he came out in his mid-teens. I don't stop to think, I don't take a breath, and I certainly don't look at anyone other than Maisy when I tell her, "*I* did."

Chapter Fourteen – Zephyr

The drive back to Ted's place is more strained than the drive to Charlie's was. I have no idea what to say after the bombs he dropped over that disastrous dinner. Guilt roils my belly, because the whole reason we even went there tonight was because Ash and I wanted to get our Daddies to clear the air.

Mission accomplished, my snarky inner voice sasses me.

Not. Helping.

I shift uncomfortably in my seat, trying to expel the memory of Ted's stony expression as he laid the whole story out for his friends and I before he carefully pushed back his chair and walked away from the table, barely sparing a glance behind him to see if I was following.

Of course I was following. I think the entire group wanted to follow him, but they seemed to know better. They stayed silent as we left the impromptu party, holding their burning questions behind eyes that burned with shock and concern. I managed to cast Ash a loaded glance, promising to talk soon without exchanging words, before chasing Ted down the front pathway towards his car, my mind reeling.

To think that Ted's been dealing with his loss and his grief alone for his entire life is heartbreaking. He did his best to assure us that he's got support. There are groups for parents who have lost their children, and he still sees a therapist on a monthly basis, but I can't stop thinking about how hard it must have been to keep such a monumental part of his life to himself. To not slip up and mention his kid once in all the years he's known the guys. *The effort of that alone...* I bite my lip at the thought.

"Did you want me to drop you off at your place?" Ted's voice startles me out of my thoughts before the question can register in my brain.

"Wait...what?" I give my head a little shake, frowning at him. He's staring resolutely at the road, his knuckles white as he grips the wheel tighter than need demands. "My place?"

It doesn't compute. It's a Saturday night. I *always* spend Saturdays at his place. We have pancakes for breakfast on Sundays and...*oh*. Is this Ted telling me that he doesn't want that now? Because Ash and I wanted to help and some comedy of errors had him spilling his tragic life story to his friends? I can't help but feel a bit of indignant rage well up within me, smothering the guilt I was feeling only minutes ago, despite some reasonable part of me knowing that he has every right to be upset with the role I played in this.

Ted's shoulders lift and drop, but he remains tight-lipped. I can see his jaw is tense, too.

"You don't want me to stay tonight?" I had hoped to keep my voice firm and strong, defiant in the face of his sour mood, but even I catch the wobble to it when the words leave my lips.

His Adam's apple bobs, but he doesn't turn his head to look at me, still feigning focus on the road. "I..." he trails off.

His reticence to answer gives me hope. If he really didn't want me to stay with him, he would have said as much.

Some of my anger fades as rapidly as it built, and I start to think rationally again, observing Ted closely.

I mightn't have known him long, but considering the nature of our relationship, I like to think I know him well now. And, on close inspection, I can see that my Daddy is tired. Stressed. Upset. But he's a proud man. An insanely independent man. And I'm his boy. Asking anything of me, especially something as huge as sticking around to support him through something tough, has got to be difficult for him.

For all his talk about open communication and honesty, this has been a blow to him. I don't feel like he's misled me in any way, but for his carefully hidden secrets (which I never assumed a right to know) to have come out the way they did will have hurt his pride and opened a wound that he was convinced was scarred over.

Then another revelation hits me.

I think back to that night not so long ago where I accidentally stumbled on his one hard limit, and it makes so much sense now. Knowing that he had a son adds an element to the Daddy/boy thing that I can't really ignore. No wonder he's got zero interest in sexual interactions when I'm little: his being a Daddy is *only* about nurture, possibly even a little unconscious guilt. How could I not have seen that before?

"I don't want to go back to my place, Ted." This time my voice is strong and definitive.

He's quiet for a stretch longer than is comfortable, but he nods. "Okay."

Tense silence falls over us again, broken only by the muted white noise of the tires against the road's surface and other traffic sounds. I rack my brain for the right words for the entire drive, still not sure what, if anything, I should say to him.

Even as we make our way from the garage, through the laundry and past the kitchen, neither one of us speaks. I can feel the intermittent vibration of my phone in my pocket that I've come to associate with the group chat, but I don't dare pull it out to read the chain of messages. I imagine that I already know what they'll say: nothing but support for Ted and assurance that they'll be there to talk to when he's ready.

I follow Ted through the house, up the stairs and to the master bedroom. He strips down to his boxer briefs with quick, jerky movements that give away his simmering frustration and slips under the covers without a glance in my direction. I can't deny that it stings.

I remove my own clothes with more care, folding them and setting them out of the way with purposeful movements, willing myself to remain calm. Ted's hurting. It's my job to take care of him right now.

I slide into bed beside him and settle in on my back, staring at the ceiling and denying the impulse to snuggle into him. It's clear that he needs space and, though my injury and the loss of my career can't possibly compare to the loss of a child, I remember being angry with the world once, too. Wanting distance and space and denying myself comfort or sympathy. Even if Ted's loss is decades old, rehashing it with his friends is almost guaranteed to have brought a lot of that pain back to the surface. I'm content to wait him out.

My patience eventually pays off, though I couldn't tell you how much time has passed when Ted's voice finally startles me out of my thoughts.

"I'm sorry, Zeph."

Frowning, I roll onto my side to face him. The room is dark, lit only by slivers of moonlight filtering in through the curtains, but my eyes adjusted to the darkness a while ago and I can make out the deep furrows in his brow and the tense set of his jaw without issue. "What for?"

I count it as a small victory when he turns his head to face me. "For being an ass tonight. I'm pissed with the situation, not with you."

"I know," I assure him, finally closing the gap between us. I slot myself against his side, nuzzling his jaw. "I get that you're strong, Ted, and that you've been dealing with your grief and loss on your own for almost as long as I've been alive, but I'm here, okay? I'm not forcing you to talk about it," I add quickly when I feel his muscles tighten, "but I'm here."

It takes him a few moments to loosen up again, and his voice is strained and gruff when he says, "Thank you."

This time, the silence between us isn't as loaded, and I shut my eyes and allow the steady rhythm of his heart beating beneath my ear to lull me to sleep.

* * *

I wake up to a cold bed, Ted's spot long empty. He's got a home gym set up in his oversized garage, and I know without having to go searching that that is where I'll find him. We have that in common: the need for physical activity to distract ourselves from our thoughts when things are too overwhelming.

I prefer to dance or to run (neither of which activity my knee will thank me for if I go too hard on it) but Ted will hit the rowing machine or attack the weights with gusto. He's even got a punching bag down there, which will also aid him to vent some of his lingering frustration.

Sure enough, when I've made my way down the stairs and back through the too-big space of his home, he's landing blow after blow on the vinyl covered surface, the heavy bag swaying with the force of each hit.

I lean against his car as I watch him, enjoying the ripple of muscle and the droplets of sweat that snake their way down his shirtless form. He's in impeccable shape for a man his age; not bulky but beautifully toned, his skin still mostly elastic and smooth, if a little weathered by time.

Ted completes his last set of swift alternating punches and breathes heavily as he holds the bag to still its movements.

"Enjoying the show?" he asks me with a hint of playfulness, wiping his dripping forehead on his forearm.

I wink at him. "You know it." I cock my head. "You done, or are you going to cool down on the bike?"

It should be strange that I know so much of his exercise routine, but we've worked out here together a few times now. He probably knows mine just as well.

"I'll skip the bike today."

Ignoring the elephant in the room is making me feel antsy, but I promised him that I wouldn't push, so I nod and wrinkle my nose when he steps towards me to press our lips together. "You need a shower," I tell him with a giggle, squirming to avoid having the fresh t-shirt I only slipped on minutes ago wind up victim to the results of his vigorous exercise.

Ted grins and lunges for me, wrapping me in his arms and smothering me while I protest loudly, the effect of my complaints ruined by my ongoing giggles.

"Oh no," he laments dramatically, smirking, "looks like you'll have to shower with me."

"I should punish you," I snark back, "and shower in the guest bathroom just to spite you."

"Now, darling, would you really do that to me?"

I laugh and shake my head at the ridiculous pout that accompanies his question. "No," I answer on a sigh. "That would be as much a punishment to me as it is to you."

"And not of the fun variety."

"Nope."

I feel a flush of relief swoop over and through me at our easy banter now – such a far cry from the tension of last night that I might almost believe I imagined it all.

Until we're back in the bedroom, pulling off our few items of clothing, and Ted suddenly tenses again. "I really am sorry," he says, down to only his underwear and looking more lost and uncertain than I've ever seen him.

"Ted…" I step towards him, reaching out, wanting nothing more than to comfort and assure him that he has *nothing* to apologize for. But he steps back, averting his gaze, as though he's determined to keep punishing himself.

A bizarre thought stirs inside my head at that. Initially, I scoff at myself, thinking it ridiculous. But, as I continue to stand there, my arm outstretched, wanting desperately to do something, literally anything, to help him, it refuses to leave me alone.

Would it even help?

He's my Daddy. I'm his boy. What I'm considering right now completely turns that dynamic on its head.

Just put it out there. You thought it yourself: he's punishing himself. Wipe the slate clean.

Before I can think better of it, I'm clearing my throat and channeling my most authoritative teacher voice, the one I use with the rowdiest of my pre-teen students. "Theodore."

That gets his attention. His head snaps up, his expression startled. "Zephyr, what-?"

"This stops now," I tell him, still firm, no hint of the boy he's used to. I stride over to the bed and sit on the edge, keeping my gaze locked on his.

"Over my lap," I demand. "Now."

He balks. "*What?*"

"You seem determined to castigate yourself," I explain, feeling more comfortable with my decision as the realization dawns in his eyes and his shoulders seem to droop, "with no end in sight. We're taking care of that here and now." I pat my thigh, covered only by my tight cotton boxer briefs. "Pants down, over my lap. Now."

His eyes are wide, but he barely hesitates before he complies, dropping his underwear and draping himself over my legs just as instructed. "Good," I praise, stopping shy of completing the phrase. *Good boy* doesn't feel right. Not given our relationship. "Well done," I add instead.

He doesn't reply, but he nods jerkily.

There's obvious tension in his back and shoulders, and I smooth my hand over the expanse of skin, trying to relax him as best I can. "You can safe word at any time," I tell him softly, "but I want you to understand that after I do this…" I pause and remind myself to be assertive and confident in what I'm doing. I can't be hesitant about it, not if I want him to take me seriously. "After I spank you, that's it. You're absolved of whatever it is you're beating yourself up about."

"It's not that simple," he finally argues, and it earns him a swift, stinging slap to one perfect, pale ass cheek. He yelps.

"I want you to imagine this as your absolution," I reiterate firmly. "Compartmentalize everything you're feeling guilty about and let go as I spank you, Ted. Am I understood?"

"Zeph…"

"*Ted.*"

It takes a moment, but he exhales slowly and then nods. "I'll try."

"That's all I ask."

Chapter Fifteen – Ted

If someone had told me even an hour ago that I'd be bent over my boy's lap for a spanking, I'd probably have laughed my ass off at them. But here I am: body tense with anticipation, expecting the first blow.

Honestly, I'm not sure how this is all going to pan out. But I trust Zephyr. Hell, at this point I might even love him. And he's right; I've been beating myself up about everything. Losing Aiden, not being there for him enough in the weeks preceding the accident, keeping the whole story to myself from my friends and every adult relationship I've had…

Well, despite therapy and support groups, it turns out I've still got some deep-seated issues about it all. Who knew?

I knew.

Of course I knew.

All these years, pretending I was fine, keeping it all bottled up… Charlie's concern was probably right on the money, to be honest.

I'm so lost in these thoughts, circling and spiraling in my head, that the first smack seems to come out of nowhere. The sound of Zephyr's palm meeting the flesh of my ass cheek rings out like an echoing *crack* in the silence of my bedroom and I yelp.

"Easy," he murmurs, rubbing the stinging spot in a gentle caress, "you took that well, Ted."

Some part of me wants to snort with amusement, glad that he's calling me by my name and not Daddy, but what actually bubbles out of me is closer to a sob.

But I don't have time to worry about how much closer I am to breaking point than I thought because Zephyr lands another stinging slap to my ass, on the other cheek this time. It forces a whoosh of breath from my lungs, but he follows it up with another smack, then another, raining them down in rapid succession until I lose count and bow my head.

I'm hardly aware of it happening, but as Zephyr doles out my spanking with confidence, my shoulders loosen and I become boneless against him. I can hear him muttering encouragement, assuring me that I'm doing so well to take the act of domestic discipline as I am, and I'm almost startled to realize that I'm crying when I register the wetness on my cheeks.

It doesn't slow him down, though. He continues on with quick, light smacks that sting almost as much as the initial harder blows did, possibly because the skin is red and sensitive to touch now.

"Come on, Ted, let it all out," his voice is warm and understanding, and that pushes me over the edge.

I bawl in a way I can't ever recall doing before (not even when I lost Aiden, or when my parents ignored their grandson's death) and, losing all sense of time passing, I accept his continued slaps as my sentence for everything I've been holding in.

And then, without warning, I'm fucking floating.

I'm hardly aware of Zephyr stopping, of him pulling me up into a hug or murmuring those same sweet words of support and encouragement into my ear. I feel high. Cocooned in a bubble of surprising bliss and relaxation.

Subspace.

The word makes its way through the haze in my brain, sobering me a little. Not enough for me to crash yet, but enough for me to understand what it is I'm feeling.

It's completely unexpected.

The extent of my kink and of my exploration into BDSM is literally limited to Daddy/boy play, with experimentation with impact play purely from a Daddy perspective. I've never even thought I personally could, or would, feel this way from being on the receiving end of a spanking.

From what I understood, there are levels of endorphin release required before a sub hits subspace. Zephyr can't have been spanking me for long enough to achieve that, could he?

Or maybe he was. I wasn't exactly paying all that much attention. I was atoning for my perceived sins, after all. Losing myself in the pain and the absolution he offered me.

As I start to come back down, I realize what comes after subspace and the thought is even more sobering: sub-drop.

I've never experienced it, but I've seen it in action. I know everyone is different, too, so there's no way to know how -or even if- it will affect me. I probably need to brace myself for the depression or the irritability, the anxiety and the fatigue that are most commonly associated with the phenomenon, but I haven't the first clue how to do that. It can hit at any time: moments after the euphoria of subspace fades, or even days.

"Hey, I've got you, Ted."

It's only now that I notice that I'm trembling in Zephyr's embrace. His arms are moving soothingly up and down my back and it is calming me now that I come down from my unexpected high.

"How are you feeling?" he asks, and I can't quite understand where this version of my lover has come from. It should feel strange having the tables turned, having my boy deliver aftercare to me, but it doesn't. "Was that okay?"

This time the snort comes out correctly as a snort and, despite feeling emotionally drained, I have to admit I do feel *lighter* somehow. "It was more than okay, kitten," I tell him, my voice sounding gravelly to my own ears. My throat is tight and scratchy; a sure sign I cried more than I originally thought I did. I try to clear it. "Thank you. I...I needed that." Another incredulous huff escapes me. "How did you know?"

His fingers card through my hair as he answers softly, "I didn't. Not really. I just...*Ugh*. The thought wouldn't go away."

"Hmm, gut instinct, then." I nuzzle into the crook of his neck, feeling vulnerable and almost lost, but also intensely grateful for this beautiful younger man. "Thank you."

Zephyr's quiet for a minute. Contemplative. Then, softly, he asks, "You're still going to be my Daddy, right? This doesn't…uh…it doesn't change everything?"

"Oh, babe, no. It doesn't change a thing."

Although, a little doubt niggles its way into the back of my brain, and I worry that maybe it *does*.

How will he ever look at me the same way again? Even ignoring the past I kept from him, *I'm* supposed to be the authoritative one. The nurturer. What we just did blows all of that to smithereens.

I swallow roughly. "Unless…I mean…" I can't even bring myself to voice those concerns, but he gets it.

"Ted, no. Whatever you're thinking, stop it." Zephyr shakes his head. "I was worried you wouldn't see *me* as your boy anymore," he confesses, as if he's somehow reading my thoughts. "It doesn't change the way I see you at all."

"Really?" I hate that my voice comes out so small and uncertain, seemingly proving to myself that my fears are valid. But Zephyr rolls his eyes and smirks at me, the hint of sassiness easing my mind more than his words can do on their own.

"Really," he insists. "You're still my Daddy, Ted. For as long as you'll have me as your boy. I…" he swallows, "I love you."

If I thought I was on a high during subspace, it's nothing compared to the electric warmth that floods me with his simple declaration. I know it's not just lip service, either. Not with what we've just done today.

Choked up, I respond, "God, Zeph, I love you, too."

Then we're kissing, and we're both crying, but they're happy tears. Tears of relief. Of mutual joy. Of love.

Then his hands slip lower down my back, brushing over the heated skin on my ass and I hiss into his mouth.

He pulls back, startled and chagrined. "Oh, shit, sorry!"

I can't help laughing, feeling lighter than I have in…Christ, lighter than I can *ever* remember feeling. I know that part of that is still the lingering endorphins from the intense scene we just took part in -from reaching fucking subspace- and the other part is the rush of affection from our mutual declarations of love, but for now that's enough.

"It's fine," I tell him, rubbing our noses together. "It's a reminder of how damn much you care about me."

"Still, we should get you some lotion." He crinkles his nose adorably. "And we still need to shower."

The thought of hot water on my stinging backside is not appealing. "Lukewarm water only."

His expression softens out into understanding and fondness. "Yes, Daddy."

As we make our way into the bathroom, I can't help but feel optimistic that, with Zephyr at my side, everything's going to be just fine.

Chapter Sixteen – Zephyr

"Wait…*what*?!" Ash asks me, his jaw dropping now that I've finished giving him the abridged version of what happened over the weekend after Ted and I left his house.

It's Wednesday again, and this time we're having lunch on our own, so we've been free to talk as one Little to another. Ted and I are solid, and we spent most of Sunday reassuring each other that we're still Daddy and boy, that nothing has to change, but I still need to talk this out with someone who will understand my perspective better.

"Uh huh," I answer, shoveling a forkful of lettuce into my mouth. I chew it and swallow as quickly as I possibly can. "I don't know what came over me. But he was *so* in his head and so determined to…to beat himself up and I just…*snapped*, I guess."

"Jesus," my friend sits back in his seat, dumbfounded. "I just can't imagine it."

"Well, I'd rather you didn't," I tease, going in for another mouthful of my salad. He scrunches up a paper napkin and tosses it at me.

"Not what I meant!"

I snicker.

"Seriously," he leans forward across the little café table, lowering his voice, "I couldn't possibly spank Charlie. I mean, he's my Daddy. It would feel weird." He cocks his head. "Did it feel weird?"

"Oddly enough, no." I've been thinking about that more than anything. I sigh. "And *that's* what freaks me out. Like, if the roles we play are Daddy and boy, why didn't it feel weird to dominate Ted? Doesn't that, like, go against the whole dynamic?"

Ash doesn't answer immediately. He takes a sip of his lemonade and seems to give my question some proper thought. "I mean," he starts, tilting his head from side to side as he continues to think out loud, "it doesn't have to be weird. It worked, right? Like, it helped him deal with…uh… everything?" Neither one of us wants to actually talk about Ted's past. It feels wrong, somehow. Disrespectful. I just nod, rolling my wrist in a gesture for him to keep talking. "And you're both adults, so…maybe look at it as you knowing what he needed? Just like he knows what you need when you're little for him."

"But you just said-"

"I know. And, because Charlie and I have never been in that sort of situation, I can only say that it would probably feel weird for us. But," he holds up a finger to stall me from saying anything, his mop of curly hair swaying as he moves, "when I really think about it, it shouldn't feel weird to do something to help him, Daddy or not."

I take a moment to process that, relaxing back into my chair and letting the general din of the café fill the silence between us. It's busy for a Wednesday lunch time, with people chatting at tables around us, the sounds of cutlery hitting plates and the muted clanging of pots and pans from the kitchen reminding me that life goes on despite my personal dramas. It's strangely comforting in its own way.

"You're right," I eventually acknowledge, pushing the remnants of my salad into the middle of the table. "It felt good to step up and do something, you know? And the fact that he trusted me…" Now I choke up a little, recalling how emotional the whole experience was.

Ash reaches across the laminate tabletop and squeezes my hand. "I'm glad you're there for him. Charlie feels awful…"

"I can imagine."

Ted and I haven't spoken about how he's going to handle his next interaction with his friends. It's not my place to push him, after all. Not about that. I wanted him to stop blaming himself. To stop hurting himself. But, beyond that, how he goes forward from here is all on him. I'll support him, but I won't force the issue. Suffice to say, I've learned my lesson about that.

"And I have no idea what to say to him, either," Ash goes on, listlessly dragging a soggy looking fry across his plate. "I mean, poor Ted."

I grimace. "Yeah, look; that's exactly what he's wanted to avoid all these years. Being treated differently once everyone knew about…*y'know*."

Across from me, Ash drops the fry and frowns. "But we love him. If we'd known-"

"It wouldn't have changed anything." I can say this with finality.

Again, though I know that the end of my dancing career can't possibly compare to the loss of a child, I understand exactly where Ted's coming from when he emphatically states that he doesn't want to be pitied.

"It wouldn't have changed his past," I add. "It wouldn't have changed the years he's spent grieving privately. It wouldn't have changed the man or even the Daddy that he is today. All it would have done is make you all treat him with kid gloves that he really doesn't want you to." I run my hand through my hair as I try to explain, "All he wants is to be treated the same way as always, and he's afraid that's not going to happen. I mean, he's built his whole life up after everything fell apart – he doesn't want that taken from him."

I can tell Ash wants to argue with me, but something I've said must have gotten through to him because all he does is bite his lip and nod. "Yeah, okay. I get that."

If only the others can be convinced.

* * *

The rest of my day after meeting Ash for lunch is uneventful. At least, until I'm locking up the studio for the night.

"Zephyr," I just about jump out of my skin at the sound of London's voice.

He and Matt approach from where they must have been waiting for me, leaning against a parked car on the street outside my workplace.

Because this isn't creepy or overstepping at all...

I frown at them both. "Uh, hi?"

They spare me the small talk and get straight to the point. "Ash called," Matt says, rubbing the back of his neck.

Of course he did.

London pulls Matt in against him in a comforting gesture. It's sweet watching them together, these two burly men whose personalities seem at odds with their aesthetic. "We're not, like, trying to get you to take us to Ted or anything."

I smile softly at London's assurances. The weekend was the first time he and I have actually spoken to each other and, after seeing me in my dress, it was surprising when he quietly started up a conversation about the best places to buy panties and other pretty things.

I'm under the impression that none of the others (bar Matt, obviously) know about London's penchant for lace, and I'm honored that he trusted me with his secret. It is that, and that alone, which has me open to hearing them out about Ted, even though I know my Daddy would be uncomfortable with the idea of this conversation taking place.

With a sigh, I adjust the strap of my duffel bag on my shoulder and ask, "So...why are you here, then?"

Matt shifts his weight on his feet awkwardly, like he's not quite sure how to explain himself. "Just...uh...we wanted to let you know that we're not gonna get all weird on him."

I blink.

Really? This is information that couldn't have been sent over text?

As if reading my thoughts, London chuckles and shrugs. "We were heading out for dinner down the block and...well, I guess you can't really get sincerity or tone out of a text message. Matt figured we'd kill two birds with one stone."

"Right." I'm not entirely sure that I believe them, but they mean well nonetheless.

"It's just, y'know, I care about Ted. A lot. I mean, our whole group does." Matt shoves his hands in his pockets. "And, if I know him, he's going to avoid us all like the plague until he's convinced this has blown over. But I thought that he might listen if it came from you." A soft smile plays across his lips as he exchanges a meaningful look with London. "If you're anything like us, anyway." He sighs heavily. "Plus, I get where he's coming from. I mean, it's not the same, but I almost walked away from the guys-"

"*What?*" I can't withhold my startled interruption. A woman walking past our assembled group jumps at my voice and I offer her an apologetic grimace before she walks on.

Matt brushes my concern off with a vague gesture of his hand. "It was ages ago. But I wasn't in the best place emotionally or mentally, and I started shutting everyone out while I tried to avoid their pity. It sucked, man. And I don't like to think of Ted being in the same boat."

Having had similar thoughts myself, I can only nod. "He'll get there," I assure Matt. "He tried really hard over the weekend to work through some of his issues, but he's going to see his therapist again this week because the whole mess has stirred up stuff he thought was buried. Just…give him some time, okay?"

I'm relieved when Matt's expression doesn't fall. He genuinely seems to understand what I'm saying and isn't going to push the issue. I shouldn't be surprised, really. I knew that Ted's friends are good guys. But seeing it in action still gives me a little jolt of convoluted emotions anyway.

Would things have been different if I'd had a support network like these guys?

I try to brush the thought away. I've moved on. Besides, through Ted, I have these guys myself now. The fact that they've sought me out and have taken me into their confidence is proof of that.

I wonder if I've given some of my thoughts away again somehow, because London claps a hand on my shoulder and squeezes, saying, "You know if you need to talk, we're here for you, too, okay?"

"Thanks," I reply, then start moving towards my car, parked a few doors up the street from the studio. "I appreciate that." I grin at them and wave them on, effectively ending the conversation. "Enjoy your dinner!"

During the short drive back to my apartment, I consider Matt's words and hope that Ted trusts his friends enough to reach out to them, too. They are good people, all of them, and Ted needs more than what I alone can offer him, even if we both wished otherwise.

Chapter Seventeen – Ted

It takes two weeks (inclusive of three sessions with my therapist) before I feel confident and comfortable to turn the notifications in the group chat back on.

Zephyr told me that the guys have been reaching out to him, asking about me, and I know I can't avoid them forever. Hell, they've given me more space and time than I've ever given them, and I'm grateful for that. But now it's time to ease back into my friendships and accept their support.

I lock myself in my office and spend my Friday morning scrolling through the thread, snorting at some of the banter between my friends.

Josh, naturally, posts inappropriate and outlandish memes and deliberately stirs the others up. The fact that Charlie takes the bait every single time is more amusing than it has any right to be and reading the way the rest of the group take turns escalating the situation has my chest tight with a mixture of emotions. Regret. Fondness. Nostalgia. Hope. They all twist together while I read the latest ridiculous interaction as it plays out in real time.

Josh: I've decided I need a harem of men.

Charlie: ...a harem?

Spencer: Don't knock it, C-man. There's a whole romance sub-genre for that kind of thing.

Chance: Read any good ones lately?

Spencer: So... @Josh, a harem?

Josh: Yeah. I'm thinking a mechanic, a hairdresser, a super hot investor, a doctor, a tattoo artist and a masseur.

Josh: It's almost like a Julie Andrews song if you pace it out right.

Ash: Boy, 'The Sound of Music' sure has changed since I last watched it.

Charlie: Baby, don't encourage him.

Spencer: These ARE a few of my favorite things...

Josh: And somehow my version is still less gay than the musical.

Charlie sends a GIF of Captain Picard facepalming.

I chuckle out loud, startling myself with the sound. And how sad is that? That I've been in such a dark place that the sound of my own laughter is foreign to my own ears... A wave of melancholy threatens to overwhelm me and I sigh.

Zephyr's been supportive, and I know he's been keeping the group posted about me, but I really do miss my friends. I miss the laughter and the ridiculous shit we talk about. I'm not in my early twenties anymore: I have a network of people who genuinely give a crap about me, and being alone just because I want to avoid the sympathy and the hard conversations is somehow more difficult now than it was in the months after the accident.

I turn my attention back to the group chat which is picking up pace again.

London: I legit ignored my phone for 10 mins & I missed the entire harem convo. Devastated.

Matt: Excuse you, but why do you need a harem anyway???

London: Like you weren't imagining your own dream team.

Chance: Come on, guys, break it up. Flirt it up in a private thread.

Chance: And don't think I didn't see you avoiding my question earlier @Spencer.

Chance follows up his second message with an 'I'm watching you' GIF of some woman gesturing at her eyes with two fingers and then pointing them at the viewer.

Spencer: No hablo ingles.

He completes the sentiment with a shrugging emoji.

Spencer: @Josh, you didn't explain what brought the whole harem idea on, anyway.

Josh: I'm checking out Grindr. So many choices, so not enough time.

Charlie: Gentlemen, I give you our city's tax dollars hard at work protecting our community. & LOL @Spencer. Smooth, my friend. Real smooth.

Josh: Fuck you, Charlie, I'm on my lunch break.

Josh adds a middle finger emoji. Spencer interjects with a GIF of a dog wearing sunglasses.

I shake my head, my spirits buoyed by the ridiculous conversation. It's good to know that they're all the same, that the world has kept turning in the two weeks I've spent feeling out of sorts. It's also a sign that I might just be able to drop back into the fold without too much drama.

God only knows the way I overreacted and overthought things was dramatic enough. I'm embarrassed by that more than I can properly explain, which also hasn't helped with my intentions to ease back into my social circle.

Before I know it, my fingers are tapping out a comment of my own and I'm pressing the little 'send' button.

Ted: I didn't realize the pickings at The Grove had gotten so slim that you needed to turn to Grindr to hook up.

It's clunky as far as playful ribbing goes, but I hope it shows them that I'm trying and that nothing has to change.

There's what equates to a stunned silence in the thread before the little notifications that people are typing pop up. I watch the screen with bated breath.

Josh's reply hits first.

Josh: Ted, man, I tell you...there's a drought of Daddies right now and it sucks.

A series of emojis follow the words. The crying face a few times, the poop emoji, and the angry face.

Josh: If you didn't have Z, I'd tell you to get your ass down there and have your choice of littles.

I glance at the clock and gauge that Zephyr is probably in the middle of teaching a hip hop class right now. I can only imagine what his reaction to that last message will be. I kind of want to see it. I like it when he gets sassy and territorial. It's hot.

Chance's is the next message to pop up, distracting me from those thoughts.

Chance: @Ted You're honestly surprised by anything Josh says these days, dude? Also @Josh maybe that's a sign you've gone through too many Daddies. Chased 'em all off.

Spencer follows almost immediately after.

Spencer: Kid's probably scared all the Daddies away with his bratty-ass ways.

Spencer: @Chance Damn it! You beat me to it!

Chance: Not my fault I'm quicker at typing.

While the note appears to say that Spencer is composing his reply, Ash's name appears on my screen.

Ash: Welcome back, Uncle Ted. I've missed you.

Before I can reply, he posts again.

Ash: Especially 'cos nobody else can keep this bunch in line as well as you.

Charlie: Hey! What am I, chopped liver?

Ash: Sorry, but you know it's the truth, Daddy. He sends a GIF of a teddy bear blowing a kiss, either to tease his husband or soften the blow of his words. Potentially both.

My lips pull into a grin and, before I can stop myself, I'm typing again.

Ted: Brains over brawn, Charlie.

Charlie sends back a line of middle finger emojis and I crack up, more of the tension in my shoulders and chest easing. It looks like things don't have to change after all, and I feel a little ashamed that I underestimated my friends so badly.

As I said before, my own reaction to having my past exposed surprised and embarrassed me. I'm the oldest of our group, and I suppose I had always thought of myself as the most stable. But panicking over the idea that they'd treat me differently says otherwise, doesn't it?

My therapist, Sandra, suggested that it's likely I haven't worked through my hang-ups about being a grieving father who turned to Daddy play as a means of escapism. That I'm still stuck on my fears that the guys might think it weird or perverted or God only knows what.

And she's probably right.

The fact that it took my boy spanking some sense into me to clear my head enough to seek help is another giveaway. On some level, I'm still feeling guilty and still feel like I'm doing something wrong, something deserving of punishment and scorn.

Sandra also suspects that I'm also more likely to be feeling raw, given that what would have been Aiden's thirtieth birthday is looming only a couple of months away now.

"There are words for spouses who lose their husbands or wives, and for children who lose their parents, but no word to describe a parent whose child has died," she said in our first session and those words come back to me now. "Because it's unthinkable, Ted. And it's understandable to continue to grieve and feel that pain, even twenty-eight years after the fact. Letting others see that you're struggling with it, especially around milestone dates, doesn't have to be a bad thing. You don't have to be strong and rational all the time. You're human."

The thing is, I know these things. I know that if my position was reversed and it was one of the other guys struggling, I'd tell him all the same stuff Sandra has said to me. But my main issue is pride and I know it. And I'm slowly working through it. The fact that the guys are letting me slip back into the chat without a fuss makes it easier.

Speaking of...

My phone's ringing brings me out of my thoughts and I'm not surprised to see Charlie's name (accompanied by a photo of him goofing around as he dressed for his wedding) flash on my screen.

What does surprise me is my lack of any inner-turmoil as I answer.

"Hi Charlie."

"Hey," he greets me, then pauses a little awkwardly. I hate that my issues have played such a large role in putting this distance between us. He clears his throat. "Brains over brawn, huh?"

I chuckle at his attempt to break the ice and lean back in my office chair, refraining from propping my feet up on my desk, though the urge to stretch out is there. "You always take the bait so well."

"Heh," he offers his own little huff of amusement and I can imagine him blushing a little, "I guess I do." There's another pause before he says, "I, uh, I wanted to apologize properly, Ted."

"I appreciate that," I respond easily, having anticipated something like this from him. I've even spoken to Sandra about it. "But you don't really have anything to apologize for. Not really."

"I was kind of a dick, man. I mean, before everything went down. I..." he clears his throat, "I told myself I was giving you the space you asked for but, honestly? I was being selfish because I had no idea what to say to you. And that was wrong of me. And then I wouldn't let it go, and everything went to hell, and-"

"Charlie, it's fine. Really."

This time it genuinely is. I admit that I was annoyed with him at first. Irritated that he had made such a big deal out of his sister's throwaway words, to the point where I'd felt backed into a corner. But distance, therapy, and time to think have helped me work through those frustrations, too. And, honestly, I can't hold it against my best friend that he was being hypersensitive on my behalf, can I? Not when I miss his company as badly as I do. He meant well. He cared. That means something to me, even if the way he showed it was frustrating.

"I'm still-"

"I swear, if you apologize again, I'm going to put you in a corner for ten minutes the next time I see you."

As expected, my threat earns me a laugh. "I'd like to see you try, old man," he taunts. "I'm not the Walker who responds to those sorts of consequences."

"Like your bratty brother really does, either." Not that I can say I've tried to school Josh. A Little though he might be, he's also not my type. He's also beyond the age limit I'm comfortable pursuing...but that's irrelevant because I'm a taken man anyway. Well, I am now. And I wouldn't trade Zephyr for anything.

"You'd still have more luck disciplining him than a fellow Daddy and you know it." Charlie's response cuts off the strange path my thoughts just went down. "But I was actually talking about Ash."

"Either way," I acknowledge, "I'm happy to leave Josh to another unsuspecting Daddy."

Charlie chuckles and, after a few more lighthearted exchanges, reluctantly says, "Alright, I'd better run, but…Ted?"

"Hmm?"

"It's good to hear your voice. I've missed you."

I nod, despite knowing that he can't see me. "I've missed you, too, bud."

After we hang up, my phone pings again, but it's a text message from Zephyr. My heart squeezes as I read it.

'Taking a 5 min break. Saw that you're back in the group chat. I'm proud of you, Daddy.'

'Are we still on for tonight?' I text him back, already thinking of all the ways I'm going to show him my appreciation for not running away at the first sign of my meltdown. I know I wouldn't have gotten through any of this if not for him.

'Sure are. I'm breaking in that pretty yellow dress you bought me.'

I grin, already imagining him wearing it and tap out my response, *'I can't wait, kitten.'*

* * *

"Another tea, Daddy?"

As promised, Zephyr and I are back in our usual routine. I helped him change into his new yellow sundress, delighting in how well the bright color suits him, and then settled in for a tea party. Even though I was a little concerned that our dynamic might be strange after he spanked me, it doesn't feel like anything between us has changed.

He's still my princess, still comfortable to indulge in his kink around me, and still happy to call me Daddy and allow me to join in his play.

The relief I feel at that is palpable.

"Yes please," I lift my delicate cup up for him to pour a measure of water for me from the functional teapot I bought when Ash first started coming around regularly. The dolls and teddy bears on either side of me aren't as lucky: their cups are full of air alone.

He chatters away as he's prone to do when he's being the host of such a gathering, and I'm once again struck dumb by how beautiful he is. I know that I've told him that I love him but, in moments like these, I don't think the words properly capture how he makes me feel.

It's like he was made for me. There's no push and pull with him, just an effortless flow to our time together. He's not demanding or needy even though he jokes that he is, and he knows exactly what to say or do even at times where I have no idea what I need from him.

I know he's put two and two together and worked out why I keep our sexual relationship separate from our Daddy/boy relationship, but he's been good about not pushing me to talk about it. Even before he learned about my past and about Aiden, he didn't demand any further information from me after I safe worded. He understood that I was uncomfortable and left it at that.

He's perfect. Utterly, completely perfect, and he's rapidly becoming the center of my universe.

"Dance with me, Daddy?"

The question takes me off guard, interrupting my saccharine thoughts and I blink at him. "What, baby?"

Zephyr pushes to his feet and extends his hand to me. "Dance with me? Like we're at a ball?"

In all the time that we've spent together, he's never made this suggestion before. I'm not sure what to expect. Does Little Zephyr dance fluidly, with grace and poise and the professionalism that comes from years of training? Or does Little Zephyr step on his Daddy's toes and stomp around a makeshift or imaginary dance floor with the enthusiasm, lack of coordination, and the blissful ignorance of youth?

Honestly, I don't know which I'd prefer. I feel like the latter option would be adorable, but the former would be beautiful. Either way, I know this is something that means a lot to him. More than the too-casual request would have me believing, in fact.

"I'd love to." I take his hand and smother a groan as he helps me back up into a standing position.

I might be healthy and fit for my age, but I'm still forty-seven. I'm just not built for sitting cross-legged on the floor for extended periods of time anymore.

Zephyr smiles a bright, childish smile at me before he prances over to the Bluetooth speaker on the bookshelf, turning it on and then reaching for his phone, fiddling until the 'boop' of a successful connection sounds out from the speaker.

Then he presses play on one of his many playlists and the sound of classical, orchestral music fills the air, violins at the fore.

"Strauss," I recognize instantly, because even someone with zero classical training knows *The Blue Danube*.

My boy's expression turns indulgent. "Clever," he says, then grabs my hand and tugs me into the open space beside the bed, away from the tea party set up on the floor. There's not a huge amount of floor space here, but we'll manage.

Manhandling me until my hands are positioned the way he wants them, Zephyr steps in close, pressing against me as he leads us in a limited waltz to the music. I'm not at all disappointed to find that he's dancing gracefully and not clumsily like one might expect from a child. This is ingrained into him, after all. And he began learning ballroom dance at an early age besides.

Step back, step to the side, slide feet together. Step back, step to the side, slide feet together. The motion is easy to follow, aided by the music. We glide across the carpet in our little contained square of space, and after a little while, Zephyr rests his head on my shoulder and turns us around, changing his movement, allowing me to suddenly lead the dance. *Forward, side, come together. Forward, side, come together.*

"You're good at this, Daddy," he murmurs against my chest.

I smile and kiss the top of his head. "It's not my first dance, darling…but I am a bit rusty."

His giggle is light and tinkling. "I wasn't gonna say anything."

I lower the hand on his waist and pinch his ass, making him squeal. "Cheeky."

We waltz together for a little while longer, until the song fades out and a new one begins. Zephyr pulls away and curtsies, pulling the hem of his skirt out widely on either side of him. "Thank you for the dance, good sir."

Chuckling, I bow. "And thank you, tiny dancer."

He claps his hands together. "Okay, tidy up time!"

I love that he still follows the rules and routine that we discussed that very first night together. In hindsight, I can't believe that I suspected he'd be bratty and naughty. Yes, he's sassy and cheeky, but my boy has a praise kink a mile wide: being a good boy is far more enjoyable for him.

Together we pack up the dolls, teddies and the tea set, setting aside the two cups we drank from, as well as the teapot itself, to be washed downstairs. Then, once the space is orderly again, Zephyr tugs his dress over his head. He carefully puts it on a hanger and ducks into the walk-in robe to hang it with care. This leaves him in the lacy white thong he arrived in (which he'd been wearing beneath his jeans until playtime: a very welcome surprise for me) and nothing else.

I swallow reflexively as he saunters back out of the walk-in, swinging his hips and stalking towards me like I'm his prey.

"We should go dancing for real sometime," he tells me, his dark eyes smoldering, no hint of his Little persona to be found.

At this point, I'd agree to almost anything he says. "Sounds good," I tell him, my voice having taken on a husky bite.

Zephyr's lips quirk upwards, like he knows exactly what he's doing to me. And, hell, he probably does.

Chapter Eighteen – Zephyr

Ted laughs as we tumble into his bed, and the sound is music to my ears. I haven't seen or heard him feel so free in weeks. I'm not deluded enough to think that his issues have all been resolved, because mental health does *not* work that way, but between talking things out at his own pace and seeing his therapist, he seems genuinely happier again. Closer to the man I met at Asher's wedding.

I can't properly express just how excited I was to see that he had commented playfully in the group chat earlier today. If nothing else, that was the biggest sign that he's starting to heal again. And I was immensely grateful to the rest of the guys for playing it cool and treating him the same way they always have. Even though both Matt and Ash told me they would, seeing it in action was far more reassuring.

"You're thinking too hard," Ted complains lightly, nipping at my bottom lip, "which means I'm not doing my job right."

"Speaking of too hard…" Snickering, I arch my body into his, rubbing our lengths together. He's still way overdressed in comparison to me, seeing as I'm only wearing a lacy thong and he's in his jeans. We discarded his shirt somewhere on the way to the bedroom.

Ted groans against my mouth. "God, I feel like a fucking teenager when I'm with you."

"I mean, I'm in my thirties, so *that's* disturbing."

"Brat."

"You love it."

His gaze softens and he ghosts his lips over mine, whispering, "I love *you*."

Every time he says those words, I feel like I could just float away. "I love you, too."

When we kiss again, it's slow and sweet. Our tongues intertwine almost lazily while Ted's hands traverse my body, igniting fire beneath my skin. Our hips rock together and I sigh into his mouth.

"Your jeans have to come off," I tell him, keeping my voice low and gentle, not wanting to break the mood.

"Mmm," he agrees, but makes no move to put the acknowledgment into action.

I giggle and attempt to undo his fly, distracted by the way he's now nuzzling at the crook of my neck, licking and sucking the path his hands only just traveled.

"Oh, fuck, Ted," I gasp when he gets to my nipple, arching my back when he rolls the little nub of flesh between his teeth. It's almost like there's a direct line between my nipples and my cock, because jolts of pleasure seem to shoot straight down to my already hard and aching length. "Yes," I breathe, the 's' sibilant as I draw the word out, "more."

He shuffles us around until I'm flat on my back and he's replaced his teeth with his thumb and index finger, moving his mouth to my other nipple.

"Jesus…fuck…" It's like my pleasure receptors have all lit up, synapses firing through all my nerve endings.

His resulting chuckle is deep and rich. I think I'd like to record the sound and keep it on repeat. Maybe make it my ringtone or text alert tone or something.

"Pants," I remind him before I lose all control of my thoughts. "Pants off now. *Please*." I bite back the instinct to add 'Daddy' to my plaintive whine.

I haven't called him Daddy in bed since before everything went down at Ash and Charlie's place. While he didn't seem to have an issue with it before, I'm not sure I'm comfortable pushing that boundary right now. And I really don't want to stop what we're doing to have a heart-to-heart about it. That can happen later.

Thankfully, Ted takes pity on me and pulls away to struggle out of his jeans and boxer briefs. I lick my lips as his beautiful cock springs free of its confines, hard and glistening invitingly at the tip. But, before I can beg him to fuck my face, he's crawled back over to me and has hooked his fingers into the delicate band of my thong.

Ted is ever so gentle as he eases the material over the slight curve of my hips and down my long legs, careful not to stretch or tear the lace. He tosses it over his shoulder once it's free of my ankles and licks a stripe over my balls and shaft, making me whimper.

But instead of sucking me down, he settles his body over mine, sliding our cocks together. I moan at the feeling of skin meeting skin, the glide aided by our combined pre-cum. It gets even better when Ted adds lube to the equation, but he doesn't jerk us off together. He just slicks us both up, then settles back over me again, bracing his forearms on either side of my head before he starts rocking his hips in earnest.

I can't remember the last time I got off like this with another man. Blow jobs and hand jobs and occasional anal, sure, but frottage? As my eyes roll back in my head, I question why I haven't done this more often.

"You feel amazing, kitten," Ted murmurs, nibbling at my earlobe while he continues to drag his cock alongside mine. His hips are pressed close to mine, the friction and pressure of his body providing the perfect amount of stimulation right where I need it most. With every thrust, the pleasure mounts.

"Oh…*God*…" I can feel my brain turning to mush as the sensation escalates. He starts to swivel his hips a little and I can feel my cock dripping as I get closer to the edge, a ball of delicious tension tightening somewhere in my gut as my balls draw upwards.

Ted keeps talking, his voice husky as he whispers, "You…" he exhales roughly, "you fit against me so perfectly, Zeph…"

I wonder if he can feel just how rapidly my heart is beating. Even though we've made love slowly before, this feels different somehow. More intense, even though he's not even inside me.

I have the strangest urge to hold him tight, tears -of love, of happiness, of empathy for the pain of his past- burning my eyes and threatening to spill down my cheeks. I want to meld into him, to somehow extend this experience forever.

"Feels…so…good." These words that I offer him in return are nowhere near enough to properly express any of what I'm feeling, but they'll have to do, even if my voice is curiously tight even to my own ears.

Ted's mouth descends over mine again in yet another gentle kiss and now my tears do spill over, because I'm convinced that I can feel all the same things in this kiss that I couldn't quite put into words. I close my eyes as they trickle out of the corners and down the sides of my face.

He shifts his weight so he can bring one of his hands up to cup my cheek, smoothing his thumb over the tracks my tears are making. "Baby…"

"I'm good," I assure him, forcing my eyes back open. My smile feels tremulous, but it's genuine. "I just…this is…" I gasp on another thrust, the movement causing his belly to brush over my sensitive cock head, "I love you."

Dipping his head down, he brings our lips back together and this time the kiss is harder and more desperate. As though we've given ourselves a green light, our hips pick up pace and our breathing intensifies.

Ted pulls away from the kiss and rests his forehead on mine. "Oh, fuck, Zeph, I'm gonna…" his deep warning is cut off by his blissed-out groan and I feel his cock pulse next to mine, then the heat and wetness of his release between our bodies.

With his cum coating my cock, I cry out after a few more shaky thrusts, adding my own mess to his.

"Wow…" I utter, catching my breath in the afterglow. "That was…" Intense. Emotional. Beautiful. Special. Unexpected. None of the words that spring to mind completely cover the way I'm feeling.

Ted's fingers card through my hair. "Yeah," he agrees quietly, even though I haven't finished my assessment out loud. "It was."

I snuggle into his side, heedless of the discomfort of our fluids drying on my skin. There's time for a shower or a bath later. Right now, I want to soak in how right this moment feels. How right it feels to be held in his arms right here in his home: the same place that so intimidated me the first time I visited.

I relish in the comfort I feel here now. I'm able to see this place, Ted's home, the way I should have to begin with. It's grand, yes, but it's also an extension of him. His warmth and vibrancy are imbued in it.

It's in the artwork he chose for the walls. It's in the few photographs on the mantle over the fireplace, including one of Aiden, which I watched him place there with shaking hands just last week. It's in the meticulously planned details of his renovations, and in the careful drape of his jacket over the back of the chair by the bay window on the other sided of this very bedroom. The whole place *screams* 'Ted', and I can't imagine him living anywhere else now.

In addition to that, I soak in the feelings of utter relief washing over me.

The relief of our relationship seeming stronger than ever, of Ted working towards a healthier way of living with his grief and trauma, and of knowing that he's ready to let me and the guys in. It all settles in my bones, filling me with warmth and contentment.

From my own experience, I know that it's going to be a roller-coaster from here. Ted's bound to have downs as well as ups. I mean, I still do and I always will. But, together with the tight knit circle of friends he and Ash have introduced me to, we're going to support each other at our own pace, and it's going to be okay.

Epilogue – Ted

"Are you sure you want me to come with you?" Zephyr chews his bottom lip, his dark eyes searching mine from the passenger seat of my car. "I can wait here if you're more comfortable with that."

I reach across the center console and squeeze his hand. I appreciate that he's so concerned for me. God only knows that I've given him and the guys plenty of reasons to feel that way over the last few months. Nevertheless, I'm confident in my decision today. "I want you with me," I tell him firmly. "I *need* you with me."

Six months ago, I would have been too proud to admit that. I was, as Ash likes to tease me, the Daddy of our whole group. Daddy of Daddies. Strong. Stalwart. Stable. I wasn't supposed to show weakness or need help. Yeah, I'm aware of the hypocrisy there, the advice I've given Charlie (or, to a lesser degree, Spence and Chance) over the years somehow never applicable to me personally.

But now? With therapy and multiple deep and meaningful discussions with my friends (which turned out to be far easier to face than I'd imagined they would be), I can admit when I'm struggling.

I still find it difficult to do; don't get me wrong. But I *can* do it, and the end result of asking for help is usually worth having to bite back my pride and ignore my hang-ups.

Case in point: Zephyr offers me a smile full of empathy and understanding as he nods and opens his car door. I meet him on the grassy verge next to the curb where I parked, and he holds out his hand for me to take. My grip tightens almost imperceptibly as we walk across the immaculate lawn to our destination.

It's been years since I've been here. Too long, really.

In my other hand, I clutch a small bouquet of flowers and my chest aches when I finally place them down on the smooth marble headstone engraved with my son's name and dates of birth and death.

In my head, I make my apologies: for never visiting his resting place, for having missed his thirtieth birthday, for essentially having kept him a secret for my entire adult life. But I don't say anything aloud. Big, impassioned speeches to invisible audiences have never really been my style, and I'm not deluded enough to think that, even if he could hear me, this would be my only chance to tell him any of this.

Zephyr doesn't push me, either. He just holds my hand and lets me breathe and think whatever I need to.

Some part of me was afraid that I wouldn't be able to handle this moment. That facing Aiden's headstone would trigger another meltdown or something similar. But, though I feel the pang of loss again, and my chest aches, I don't feel any worse for having finally visited for the first time in years.

If anything, guilt begins to lift from my shoulders.

When all is said and done, this is just another location. Visiting (or not visiting) doesn't change my past or absolve me of my perceived sins or shortcomings. The only person judging me for how and when I choose to remember my son is me, and I've been too hard on myself for too long.

It's funny that doing the one thing I told myself I never would turned out to be the thing I needed to do in order to truly start to process and heal. Well, as much as anyone who has lost a loved one can.

(I still refuse to tell Charlie he was right, even if we both know that he was.)

"Thank you for coming with me," I say later, when Zephyr and I are on the drive back to our hotel. It's the first I've spoken since we approached

Aiden's grave, and I'm beyond grateful that Zephyr understood what I needed.

He always seems to just know.

In fact, the evening proves to be another example of just that. When we're safely ensconced in the lavish suite I insisted on paying for, Zephyr sits on the edge of the bed and pats his lap.

"I think you need this," he says softly when my heart leaps into my throat and tears of gratitude prick at my eyes.

I swallow roughly and nod.

Neither one of us question how or why this works for us anymore. Perhaps it's something I've always needed and never knew it? Or maybe it's just Zephyr's attention and love that makes it feel so right. Either way, I trust him in a way I've never trusted anyone, and it allows me to let go completely.

In turn, the next night we're back to being Daddy and Little Zeph, and I watch how free he is with me.

I marvel over how much he has grown as a person since we met, too. He was anxious when I first met him, though he had been doing his best to hide it. He'd been learning to re-embrace his kinks and his identity in little space, and his bravery to try it all with a complete stranger *-with me-* was astounding even then. Now he is brazen and dominating when he's big, and bright, bubbly and confident when he's little. It's an intoxicating mix, but not one I'd ever have labeled my 'type' before now.

Honestly, Zephyr is everything I never knew I needed.

"Whatcha thinking about, Daddy?" he asks, having just spent the last ten minutes dancing across the large, open space of the hotel room. His cheeks are flushed, and his eyes are shining, and I am struck yet again by how insanely beautiful he is.

I stand up from my seat in the 'audience' (on the bed) and walk towards him. He squeaks when I pull him in for a hug.

"Just thinking about how lucky I am to have found you when I did, tiny dancer."

"Hmm," he murmurs against my chest, sounding less childlike now as he comes back out of his little head space. "I'm lucky too."

I pull backwards and tilt his head up to meet mine, bringing our lips together in a gentle kiss that says more than I can properly put into words. I love him. I'm grateful for him. I'm amazed by him. I trust him.

I need him.

Even though the kiss was sweet, we're both breathing heavily as we part. "Zeph," I whisper his name into the small pocket of air between us, my voice thin with a desperation that seems to have sneaked up on me, "Baby, I want you to fuck me."

We talked about it once months ago, and then in the ensuing drama of my meltdown, we never brought it up again. It wasn't until this moment that I realized how badly I want to do this: to share something with him that I've never had with anyone else. It seems only fitting that we do this here, on neutral ground, taking advantage of a moment already so fully imbued with emotion.

He inhales sharply and his dark eyes are intense and focused as he looks into mine. Little Zephyr is gone and he's most certainly back in his adult head space. "Are you sure?"

I cup his clean shaven jaw with my palm, smoothing my thumb over the subtle prickle of today's growth as I nod. "I want everything with you, Mister Cruze."

The sharpness in his gaze softens into understanding and love, but there's a hint of flirtatious teasing in his reply. "And I want everything with you, Mister Masters."

Zephyr punctuates the sentiment by gripping my ass firmly and pulling me tightly against his body, where I can feel his growing arousal against mine.

He backs me up until I feel the mattress of the bed against the backs of my knees, and then, with a smirk, he shoves me backwards and I land with an amused '*oomph*'.

"I'm gonna take good care of you, Ted," he declares, prowling over my prone form with the grace of a mountain lion (or the professional dancer that he is). His hands work quickly to divest me of my clothes and he sucks and licks wet kisses over every inch of skin that he reveals as he goes.

I've never done this before. Not just bottoming, but letting my lover take complete control of the situation. But with Zephyr it's okay. It's right. This is the man who still takes me over his lap and metes out spankings that I never before knew I needed. This is the man who showed me that it's okay not to be okay. This is the man who never once pushed me beyond my limits, but wouldn't let me hide behind a false façade, either. The man who watched me fall apart and, instead of running away, stood by my side and helped me as I worked to put myself back together - properly this time.

As he brings lubed fingers to my hole and massages my rim slowly and patiently, murmuring praise and reassurances when he finally works one of his long, slender digits inside me, I'm once again reminded that he's not like any other Little I've been with before.

In fact, right now, there's no sign of that part of him at all. Even though he's never topped before, he's all confidence and self-assurance. He's the embodiment of strength and passion. He's the caregiver right now, and I'm his to take care of. And fuck but it feels good to let go and let him do this.

At his urging, I spread my legs wider and I can't describe the sound I make when one finger becomes two and then three. I get even louder and more insistent when he curls them and, after a few moments of searching, finds that spot inside me which makes me see stars.

Yes, the stretch and the burn is uncomfortable, but it gives way to pleasure the more Zephyr grazes over my prostate again...and again...*and again*. My cock is aching and leaking pre-cum, but neither one of us reaches for it. I don't want to risk coming until he's inside me. I want him to feel me squeezing around him when I finally go over the edge.

I'm babbling incoherently by the time he finally deems me ready for his cock. I can't even tell you when he undressed, but when I open my eyes to complain that he's removed his fingers, he's naked and stroking himself with lube, his gorgeous dark skin glinting gold under the hotel room's warm lighting.

He's an absolute vision.

And he's mine.

"*Zeph*," his name falls from my lips on a moan, "kitten, you're so fucking hot..."

"I can't promise I'll last long," he says apologetically, sliding his hands under my thighs to manhandle me into position.

With the leaking head of his cock nudging my hole, I shake my head emphatically. "I don't care. I almost came from your fingering. I-*unnnngh...*" The wanton sound is forced from me as he slides inside me with one long, slow push of his hips.

The burn is greater than his fingers had been, and he makes shushing sounds, sliding his palms over my sweat-slicked thighs which tremble around his hips. He doesn't move, waiting for me to acclimate. My beautiful, perfect, considerate boy.

"*Ted*," he groans, "you're...this is...you feel...I...thank you. Jesus, fuck," he gasps. "*Fuck*, I love you."

His rambled words help me to relax against the intrusion of his cock inside me, and I can briefly imagine how overwhelmed he probably feels right now, too. The tight, slick heat that surrounds him. The emotional connection between us. The insane amount of trust we've given each other over the past few months. I feel that way every time I sink inside his young, lithe body, too. But the first time? That's intense all on its own.

"I love you too, kitten," I pant through the last twinges of pain, experimentally rocking my hips and feeling the sparks of pleasure flaring in its place, "now, baby, move. Please."

He doesn't need to be asked twice. As if by some unspoken agreement, we're both content to take it slowly. Zephyr is gentle but purposeful with every roll of his hips, and the praises and commentary he's murmuring are equal parts arousing and endearing.

"Oh, shit, fuck...Ted...*Daddy*...I'm so close," he eventually declares, stretching out over me to bring our mouths together in a sloppy, strung-out, desperate kiss. His hand finds my cock and starts to fist it with his thrusts. "You...you feel..."

He swivels his hips and I cry out, my hands scrabbling for purchase in the sheets beneath me as he finds my prostate again.

"There?" he asks, repeating the motion without waiting for my answer.

Between his hand milking me and his dick suddenly moving with precision, I'm a whimpering, blathering mess when I erupt between us, seeing stars. I barely register Zephyr's hips stilling or his babbled stream of "Daddy, *Daddy*, oh, oh fuck, I'm co… *Daddy*, oh fuck, *fuuuuuck*" as his cock pulses jet after jet of his passion inside me.

My heart is still pounding as my boy carefully pulls out and then collapses on top of me, smearing my cum over both our bodies.

I'm sated and boneless and feel lighter than air. My thoughts are a jumble of happiness and hopes for a future that suddenly looks even brighter than before. It's funny how an orgasm can do that.

Closing my eyes and catching my breath, I rest my chin on top of Zephyr's head where it's pillowed on my chest. I'm still amazed at how much has changed in such a short time. When we met, I couldn't have predicted the path our relationship would take.

If anything, I thought we'd have a little bit of fun and part ways as friends. Now, I can't imagine not having him in my life at all. I feel complete. Whole again, after a lifetime of living in barely fused together pieces.

And all of that can be attributed to the man in my arms now.

I never thought I'd find a life partner or a Forever Little, especially not at my best friend's wedding, but if I had the chance to do it all over again…even all the hard stuff?

I wouldn't change a thing.

The End

Thank you so much for reading *Littles & Lace: The Complete Collection, Vol. 1.* The Littles & Lace gang mean a lot to me, so I genuinely hope that you enjoyed the first three books.

Anyway, I'd love it if you could leave a review on your retailer of purchase or on Goodreads.

Reviews not only tell the algorithms that our books deserve attention, but honest feedback also encourages and inspires me to keep writing. Even a star rating helps, and I greatly appreciate you making time to do so.

Speaking of my writing, I don't have a sneak peek for you with this one, but the 'Also By The Author' section has information about all of my other books currently available (at time of publishing). Additionally, *Littles & Lace: The Complete Collection, Vol.2* continues on to close the series with Books 4 – 6.

And, if you'd like a free ebook copy of *Charlie's Contentment* (a 10,000 word zero-angst, low-plot, high-fluff novella which functions as an extended epilogue for *Asher's Answer,* but can also be read as a super sweet stand-alone) subscribe to my newsletter here:

https://annasparrows.com/newsletter-subscription/

For updates, release dates, competitions and more, follow me on Facebook. The link is in the 'About The Author' page.

About the Author

I've been writing* for as long as I can remember. I started with silly short stories as a kid, moved on to fanfiction in my teens (and still write it now), and am also a published MF romance author under a second pen name.

I have been an avid reader of MM romance my whole life. (Ask me about my beginnings with *Buffy* fanfic, haha.) I wrote a sweet and kinky MM romance novel in 2022 and the reader response changed my life. From there, I knew I had found my niche.

And thus Anna Sparrows was born.

*All of my writing is 100% my own. No part of it is generated by Artificial Intelligence (AI) software of any kind. Yes, that means that it's sometimes flawed, but I'm okay with that.

You can connect with me on:

- https://annasparrows.com
- https://www.facebook.com/AnnaSparrowsAuthor
- https://www.instagram.com/annasparrows

Subscribe to my newsletter:

- https://annasparrows.com/newsletter-subscription

Also by Anna Sparrows

www.ingramcontent.com/pod-product-compliance
Lightning Source LLC
Chambersburg PA
CBHW030350310726
48979CB00001B/245

* 9 7 8 0 6 4 5 8 7 6 2 3 9 *